NOBLEMAN OR ROGUE,
HER HEART WOULD OBEY!

His eyes glimmered with humor. "Don't you want to know if you're giving your maidénhood to a French nobleman or an English spy?"

She felt his hands on her body, moving slowly, lightly over her skin. His fingertips caressed her, the sensation subtly enticing. A sweet, warm sensation flowed through her, and she felt as if she had become no more than a fluid held in shape by her skin. She opened her eyes to stare up at him.

"Tell me that you don't want love," he said softly. He watched her, knowing the answer.

She remained stubbornly silent while his fingers traveled up her body to tease her languidly. Then she closed her eyes, knowing that finally she must surrender . . .

Sweet
Wild Wind

Joyce Verrette

A DELL BOOK

Published by
Dell Publishing Co., Inc.
1 Dag Hammarskjold Plaza
New York, New York 10017

Dell ® TM 681510, Dell Publishing Co., Inc.

ISBN: 0-440-17634-4

Printed in the United States of America

First printing—August 1982

Chapter 1

Although Vale Kendall had been educated by one of the finest tutors in the colonies and had lived in Boston for fifteen years, the first twelve winters of his life had been spent among the Abnakis. His adopted Indian father, Walking-in-Honor, had so thoroughly taught him the tribe's ways that he yet moved through the forest with the alert, soundless steps natural to a hunter. Vale still felt more comfortable in the garments of the Indians than in the clothes of his white ancestors; so whenever he left the city for the wilderness, he put on a doeskin shirt and breeches and the soft, silent moccasins of his childhood.

Vale's skin retained its tan from the preceding summer, when he had supervised his Boston employer's shipyard, and the spring sun had already darkened him further; but his resemblance to the Abnakis ended there. His brown hair appeared dark in the shadows under the trees, yet the sunlight falling in shafts through the leaves struck golden lights on its strands. His eyes, as he shifted them over his surroundings, were a mixture of gray tints. It was the peculiarly dappled surface of his eyes that had inspired the Abnakis to name him Lightning-of-the-Winter-Moon.

Walking-in-Honor's previous teachings had risen one by one to Vale's consciousness until he felt as if the Indian's spirit walked beside him, reminding him to step over a dry branch that might crack under his weight and thus reveal his presence, and to scan the surrounding bushes with eyes that penetrated their shadows. And Vale was grateful for what the Indian had taught him, particularly now while he was in the area of Montreal.

Vale was wary not so much of the threat of wild ani-

mals but of Indians. Montreal was a French territory; and
the Algonquins who lived in the region decidedly favored
that nation, whose colonists had so long ago befriended
them and even sometimes married their daughters. Vale's
English background automatically branded him an ally of
the Iroquois and an enemy of the Algonquins. Even
though Vale spoke French fluently—as any well-educated
man would, despite the war between England and
France—he knew his accent was less than perfect, his
pronunciation a bit too careful. The Indians, alert to the
nuances of a language not their own, would be even more
likely than the French colonists to detect the slight difference in his speech and conclude he was an English spy. If
he spoke to the Algonquins, in Abnaki, he theorized, they
would perhaps regard him in a friendlier light, given their
bitter feelings for the British, who had forced them to flee
their Massachusetts homeland some four or five years earlier. Vale decided he'd rather not have to test his theory
on Algonquin or Iroquois alike.

Nearing a large meadow, Vale cautiously paused to
study the sunlit clearing. Then, choosing a fat pine tree
growing on the edge of the glade, he crawled under its
earth-sweeping boughs. Sitting cross-legged in the conical
opening that the branches formed near the trunk, he
silently watched the clearing.

Vale's ability to move through the forest like an Indian
explained only in part why Andrew Carleton, his employer, had sent him to inspect the forested land near
Montreal. Vale's features hardened with tension as he reflected on the many reasons why he had been given this
assignment.

Although the war between France and England had
spread from Europe to North America, where it had raged
for nearly six years, drawing even the Indians into the violence, merchants and manufacturers continued at their in-
dustries. Government officials struck bargains that had
little to do with their public political declarations. The
government of Montreal was riddled with such officials.
One of them, thinking to accumulate as much wealth as
possible in the event that Montreal fell to the British, had

sent Andrew Carleton a secret offer to purchase a parcel of land rich in virgin forest that could produce the huge, heavy timbers necessary to shipbuilding.

Carleton, his oldest son, Paul, and Vale had been discussing whom to send to Montreal as an agent the afternoon that Timothy, the youngest Carleton, had burst into Andrew's office exclaiming that Vale's mother had had an accident and was at the Carleton house.

Snatching Timothy's arm, Vale had rushed out of the office while Timothy gasped out the details: Bess Kendall had driven her carriage too quickly around a curve in the road, and the still icy ruts had sent the carriage careening into a tree. The vehicle then toppled over her. Vale remembered how he had driven recklessly through the early spring afternoon, arriving at the Carleton home even before Benjamin, the third Carleton son, had returned with the physician. Julia Carleton had stepped away from the bed where they'd laid Bess. The somber look in her normally merry blue eyes had confirmed Vale's worst fears. Then she had firmly escorted Timothy from the room to leave Vale and Bess alone.

Never would Vale forget Bess's appearance when he'd approached that bed. Blood seeped through the thick coverlet. Her face was pale and rigid as she hurriedly told him about the past she'd kept hidden from him for so long.

"I know I'm dying, Vale," Bess had said breathlessly, trying to ignore the torment of her broken body. "Now I must tell you things I perhaps should have said long ago." Tears had flooded her eyes as she'd defended her previous silence—as if he would have blamed her for anything. "But I loved you like my own son from the beginning. I never had the courage to tell you I'm not your mother."

Even now, a month after Bess's coffin had been laid in earth still spongy from frost, Vale's heart constricted as he remembered her words. Even now he was newly shocked each time he recalled the story she'd told him. He was not Vale Kendall. He was in reality Valjean Étienne d'Auvergne, the illegitimate son of a Frenchwoman, Simone d'Auvergne, and a British spy. Simone had been betrothed to a nobleman in Paris but had fallen in love with the Englishman whose name she'd never disclosed despite her parents' threats and pleading. Her family had hurried her away from Paris for an extended "holiday" in the southwest of France so that she could give birth in secret. Then as soon as Valjean was able to travel, the d'Auvergnes had sent the infant and his nurse, Bess, to the colonies, thus concealing the entire affair so that Simone could marry the nobleman as they'd arranged.

Vale's forehead knotted in a frown as he recalled the rest of his past, piecing together her final story with what Bess had previously told him. The ship the d'Auvergnes had put Bess and Valjean on had been engulfed by a storm as it had neared the Massachusetts coast; and the crew, sure that the badly listing vessel would be driven onto the rocks and ground to splinters, had decided to abandon it. The captain had put Bess and what he'd assumed was her son on a dinghy with one of his sailors. That dinghy had been the only boat to reach shore safely.

The Abnakis had found them and treated them kindly; and while they were recovering from their ordeal, winter had set in, making travel of any kind impossible; so they'd had to stay with the Indians until spring. By then Bess and the sailor had decided not to try to find a white settlement. They would remain with the tribe because both had found Abnaki lovers.

Walking-in-Honor had not only loved Bess and Vale but married her and adopted him. Vale often thought affectionately of Walking-in-Honor and the Abnakis. He remembered clearly the sense of loss, the grief he'd suffered when Walking-in-Honor, the only father he'd known, had been killed in one of the many skirmishes the Indians had fought with the encroaching whites. Vale had just approached the age when boys in the tribe began earnestly to train to become warriors; and Bess had decided he must not learn to kill the people who were actually his own. She'd taken him from the tribe to the nearest white settlement, which was Boston.

Bess had shortened and anglicized Valjean to Vale and had given the boy her own name, Kendall, to conceal his half-French ancestry from the British colonists. Anyone with a French background would be unwelcome not only because of the frequent wars between Britain and France but mostly because of attacks on the western British colonies by the French and their Indian compatriots. Finally Bess had gotten a job as a maid with the Carleton family.

The Carletons, he mused, had always been his friends. He'd been a part of their family, growing up with their sons and even taking his lessons with Paul and Benjamin's tutor. Bess had become housekeeper by the time Vale was old enough to think of employment. Andrew had hired him first as an apprentice in the shipyard and later, as Vale had learned the business, promoted him to a position second only to Paul's. Andrew, Vale had quickly observed, firmly believed in a man's earning his place whether he was a son or not. There was no rivalry between Vale and Paul, in any case. They were too good friends. Benjamin had always wanted a career in law, and Timothy seemed inclined toward medicine.

Although Vale's thoughts were turned inward, his eyes and ears were not. When he heard a brief rhythmic rustling nearby, all thoughts of his past temporarily vanished, his attention focused on the direction of the sound as he calculated what might have made it. If it was an Indian, he was being careless and must have companions to be so confident. Or perhaps it was a white man—Vale wasn't that far away from one of the fortresslike villages that had sprung from Montreal's outskirts like watchtowers on the walls of a medieval castle.

Vale's tension faded when his sharp eyes perceived the shadowy forms of several deer through the trees, though he continued watching for a moment more to make sure they weren't being guided in his direction by a stalking hunter who wanted them to move into the clearing so he could get a better shot. Finally satisfied that the deer were idly foraging, Vale again settled his back against the pine trunk and continued his reflections.

When the physician had arrived at the Carleton house and tapped on the door, Vale had lifted his head from Bess's no longer stirring breast. Heartsick with grief, he'd wiped his eyes and gotten to his feet. He'd said nothing to

Julia and the physician had passed him. He had left the room and gone immediately to the parlor, where Andrew and his sons were anxiously waiting for news of Bess's condition. After Vale had told them of her death in a voice shaking with emotion, Andrew had entreated him to sit down while Paul had poured them each a dose of brandy. Only after he'd taken several sips of the liquor did Vale realize how what Bess had told him could affect his life and his relationship with the Carletons.

He was *not* Vale Kendall but Valjean d'Auvergne—not British but only half-British and half-French—not Bess's son but a bastard. He'd briefly considered continuing the masquerade Bess had begun for him. Then he'd decided it would be dishonorable to mislead them now that he knew what he was. He'd never regretted telling the Carletons the truth. They'd been shocked by his story, but they'd accepted it with a grace that really shouldn't have surprised him. They'd been more concerned with the grief they all shared over Bess's death, and had brushed aside the news of his strange heritage—that could be thought over more clearly at a later time. All that he was that they cared about they'd learned long ago, whether his name was Vale Kendall or Valjean d'Auvergne.

The days leading to Bess's funeral had been a blur of aching sorrow and confusion for Vale. He'd felt as if a terrible wind had torn through his life, ripping up his roots, sweeping him into a land that appeared the same but where he was an alien. Julia, perceiving his conflicting emotions, had wisely suggested that Andrew send Vale as his agent to inspect the timberland near Montreal. As Andrew had immediately realized, the change of location might help dull Vale's sharpest grief; and the assignment would certainly turn at least some of his thoughts from worries about his lineage. Besides, more than anyone in Andrew's employ, Vale was capable of moving through the forest safely and inconspicuously and mingling with the people of Montreal without attracting attention.

Vale's lips curled sardonically when he remembered that he had felt he had lied when he'd signed the register at the Hôtel Dieu with his real name; bitterly he'd had to remind himself that he *was* Valjean d'Auvergne and not an impostor named Vale Kendall. Still, whenever the desk clerk or the waiter in the dining room or the maid addressed him as *Monsieur* d'Auvergne, he felt like a fraud.

The sound of a horse's low nicker drifting across the meadow made Vale stiffen with tension. His head automatically followed the course of the sound, and his eyes turned to the far side of the clearing. A brilliant afternoon sun hung low over the treetops. His eyes, turned silvery from the brightness, narrowed to penetrate the glare but saw nothing. The horse was still in the forest, he surmised. It never occurred to Vale that a human being might not accompany the animal. There were no wild horses in the region. A horse was so valuable an animal that few Indians could possess one, and even many whites in Montreal couldn't afford a horse but instead used dogs to haul their carts. Recalling the tone of the horse's nicker, Vale realized the animal had been speaking softly, even affectionately to its owner. The tension began to leave him, but he still intently watched the far end of the meadow until a dark shape emerged from the deeper forest and moved toward the clearing. When it paused at the edge of the meadow, he caught his breath in surprise.

The horse was tall, slender, and long-legged, a breed brought from Europe where such animals were used as racing horses and occasionally as saddle horses. It appeared to be black as it stood in the shade of the trees ringing the clearing. It held its head high as it surveyed the area with a haughty air. The Carletons owned several such horses, and Vale knew the animal he was looking at was a fine example of his breed. Then, emerging from the shadows at the thoroughbred's side, a slight figure swung easily up into the saddle.

Vale couldn't see from his distance if the rider had given the horse a signal, but he sensed the animal's attitude change. The haughtiness was replaced by a distinctly mischievous air. The pair seemed to poise like a bird who, before it made any outward move to indicate flight, first caught its breath. Then horse and rider leaped forward into the meadow.

The Thoroughbred's coat changed from black to deep reddish-bronze in the light. The rider's hat bounced to the ground behind the flying hooves. Long, curling auburn hair streamed free, like a flame writhing in the sun. Vale's lips parted in surprise. The slender figure that wore boys' breeches and rode astride like a boy, was unquestionably female!

Vale felt as if time had suddenly slowed its march, as if the moment were magically lengthened, while he breathlessly watched the fiery girl and her horse move like one creature, bounding wildly, joyously across the meadow. Forgetting that he might be discovered by Algonquins or Iroquois—forgetting even whether he was Vale or Valjean—he slithered out from under the pine tree, leaped to his feet, and in the full glare of the sunlight, stood staring at the beautiful girl as her horse moved with reckless abandon.

The horse galloped directly toward a partially fallen tree that, caught by one end on a stump, formed a slanted barrier. The horse's sleek body gathered itself, uncoiled; and the horse and girl leaped gracefully over the tree trunk. As they neared the bounds of the clearing they gradually slowed to a canter and turned. At the moment the girl noticed Vale her horse abruptly stumbled in a hole. The horse quickly recovered its balance, but the girl, distracted by Vale's sudden appearance, slid over the animal's shoulder and struck the ground with a sickening thump. Pulses pounding in his temples, Vale raced toward her.

Aimée had not lost consciousness. She lay still, merely disgusted at her error. Remembering her horse, afraid he might have been injured even though he'd stayed on his feet, Aimée closed her eyes tightly for a moment, delaying the sight that might fill them. So lightly did Vale run, Aimée didn't hear his footsteps. Suddenly she felt a strong arm very gently sliding under her shoulders, and her eyes flew open in surprise.

"Monsieur . . ." she began, then stopped. The eyes looking intently into hers seemed to be composed of flecks in varying shades of gray, all glowing with points of light as if lit by the fires behind them, as if his will were lighting the shadows of his thoughts.

The bronzed face holding those eyes frowned. His lips moved, and the sound of his voice startled her as he asked softly, "Mademoiselle, are you injured?"

"I think not, monsieur," she answered automatically, still staring up at him, wondering about his garments. Was he an Indian? Those eyes didn't resemble those of any Indian she'd ever seen. His high cheekbones and very masculine features, which gave him a look of reserved inner strength, were too refined for an Indian, she thought. Yet the Algonquins were a fine-featured tribe, many of them handsome even by European standards. His hair was loose, not tied in the neat queue of a white man; but though it was straight and dark, the sunlight turned its edges to gold.

"May I help you up?" Vale offered.

Aimée nodded and extended her gloved hand. Suddenly remembering her horse, she leaped to her feet without his help, exclaiming, "Oh! My poor Brandy!"

She ran to the horse's side, took his bridle, and walked him forward a few steps, all the while murmuring comfortingly to him. Her fears were realized; he was limping. She tore off her riding gloves, dropped to stoop beside him, and ran her hands slowly and carefully over his leg. Another hand—sun-bronzed, strong—reached past her. When Vale's fingers brushed Aimée's, an airy little tingle thrilled through her despite her concern for the horse; and she withdrew her hand, turning to look over her shoulder at Vale.

His eyes, studying the horse's leg, held an expression as benign as the sky; and his voice, when he spoke, was as gentle as the sunlight: "I believe he might have pulled a muscle, mademoiselle. He will recover, I'm sure; but you shouldn't ride him in the meanwhile."

Aimée sighed with relief and straightened to put her cheek against the horse's shoulder. Her arms slid around the animal's neck as if they were used to the gesture. *"Mon Dieu, merci,"* she whispered fervently.

Vale too had risen to stand close behind her, but he didn't move a more proper distance away. A lock of her disarranged hair seemed to reach out toward him, and he stared at it a moment. His eyes passed from the long tumble of blazing curls to the trim lines of her wool jacket. Although it was a boy's jacket, as were her breeches, the dark green accented the sunfire of her hair; and its lines clung to her curving waist as she embraced the horse. Her stance pulled the hem of her jacket up, revealing the gentle roundness of her hips in the tight fawn breeches and the unusual length of her well-shaped legs.

Her delicately oval face turned to look up at him with eyes that, in the sun, matched her horse's name—Brandy. Her small, full mouth was slightly open, as if she were surprised to see him standing so near. The creamy skin of her throat turned faintly pink, reminding him of the tints of a tea rose. Still he didn't move back.

Standing so close to him, she felt as agitated as a cat before a lightning storm. Wondering at the feeling, she managed to smile up at him, though she involuntarily stepped back. "I'm grateful for your help, monsieur," she said quickly.

"It's my pleasure to be of service. I'm Valjean d'Auvergne," he replied politely. He said nothing more for a long moment as he continued to gaze at her.

Why did she feel so strangely, she mused; but she nevertheless looked at him steadily. He was tall and slim as a rapier; and it occurred to her that he might be as dangerous. At the same time her good sense reminded her that he'd immediately come to her aid and had been nothing but courteous. She was making up fantasies. A thrill of anticipation ran through her. His steady eyes seemed to pierce her mind, even her soul; but she recovered her wits enough to say, "I'm Aimée Dessaline."

"Do you live in Montreal? If so, it will be a long walk back," Vale commented.

"Not actually Montreal itself, but on the edge of the city in the settlement you may have seen a little south of here," she replied.

"That's too far for you to go alone," Vale observed, adding firmly, "I'd best walk with you." He turned to her horse's side and unbuckled the saddle's girth.

She watched him silently, wondering if she should protest. His tone told her he'd ignore any argument she might present. He patted Brandy's neck and picked up the reins. Brandy surprised Aimée by following Valjean obligingly. Ordinarily no one except Aimée herself could lead him without a struggle. When Valjean started walking in the direction she'd indicated, she fell into step beside him, wondering at her own willingness to follow this stranger.

As if aware of her thoughts and inner misgivings, Vale said, "It wouldn't do for a band of Iroquois or even a British spy to come upon you alone and with a lame horse."

For the first time she noticed a slightly different inflection to his words; and she looked at him from the corner of her eye, wondering if this stranger might indeed be a British spy himself. Trying to sound casual, she inquired, "You said your name was Valjean, monsieur?"

He remained silent a moment, remembering with surprise how easily the name had come from his lips when he'd introduced himself. Perhaps blood was, after all, influential enough to overcome a lifetime of experience. "*Oui*, Mademoiselle Dessaline," he finally answered. "Valjean d'Auvergne."

He wondered if she'd noticed his accent, faint as it was, wondered if he should say that he was newly arrived from France or that he'd spent his early years with the Indians. He decided that unasked-for explanations might make her more suspicious. He couldn't let her guess he'd come from the British colonies; he could *not* let her know he'd come to buy land from a Montreal official.

"I'm surprised your family allows you to ride alone in the forest in such unsettled times," he said.

"They don't like it. I have to slip away dressed in Marcel's old clothes," she replied. Aware of his sideways glance, she added, "Marcel is my brother."

"Do you have many brothers?" Valjean asked to make conversation.

"Only Marcel." Needing to say something, and thinking Valjean might conclude Marcel was merely a boy, she added, "When I said 'old clothes,' I meant it. I got these out of a trunk. Actually, Marcel is seven years older than I, twenty-four."

As Valjean absorbed this information he reflected briefly on the luxury of knowing for a certainty that who you were never would change—of not having a father whose name you would never learn, a mother across the ocean whom you had never met, and a loving imposter of a mother who was forever out of reach.

Feeling the tension in Valjean's silence, Aimée finally said, "I have a sister too—Mignon. She's sixteen."

Sensing Aimée's uneasiness, he replied, "I have no family other than a mother in France."

Aimée grew thoughtful. *That* was what she'd noticed in him—loneliness. Perhaps he came from a province in France different from that of anyone she'd met lately; that could explain his slight accent. Wanting to believe this—and not that he was a spy or anything wicked—she asked, "Are you here on business, monsieur?"

He thought of his assignment and answered cautiously, "Yes, mademoiselle. My employer is a shipbuilder. He's considering opening a shipyard in Montreal."

"New France is a long way to come to open a shipyard," Aimée commented.

"My employer thinks the colonies have a promising future, despite the political situation now," he replied carefully, then again fell silent.

Glancing at him from the corner of her eye, Aimée noticed the relaxed way he moved in his doeskin garments, the sureness of his moccasined feet that, as if by long habit, stepped carefully over the dry twigs, displacing nothing—not even a leaf—in passing that would reveal his presence. She wondered how a man newly arrived from France would be so at ease in a forest near Montreal.

She took a deep breath, then ventured, "Have you ever spent any time with the Indians, monsieur?" At his sudden surprised look she quickly explained, "You move through the wilderness as if you're accustomed to it."

"There are forests everywhere, even in France," he replied obliquely. Noting that her eyes were on his doeskin shirt, he added, "I bought these clothes at the trading post in Tadoussac. They're more comfortable in the forest."

"I suppose they are," Aimée conceded.

If he'd been at Tadoussac, his employer must also be considering building his shipyard near Quebec, a very practical location, she surmised. There were so many questions she would have liked to ask; but she had been taught that curiosity was impolite prying, and so it never seriously occurred to her to inquire further. What did occur to her was that he might very well return to Quebec before they would have a chance to get better acquainted. She wondered why the girls at Quebec always seemed to have good fortune on their side. Most of the eligible young officers coming over from France married in Quebec before even visiting Montreal. The girls of Montreal had to contend with a scarcity of local men as it was, she thought resentfully.

As if she had uttered her thoughts aloud, she turned her head to glance guiltily at Valjean, whose eyes were on the trail ahead. She quickly faced forward but continued to watch him from the corner of her eye and wonder if he possibly found her attractive. His forehead was clear of the frown he'd momentarily worn, and his face revealed nothing of his thoughts. She looked at him appraisingly. In profile his nose was straight and high bridged, and his chin firm and strong. His lips were slightly pursed. Perhaps he was a little perplexed by something. No, she decided, he was not perplexed; his lips were rounded in repose. Her thoughts rested on the possible softness of such a mouth, how it might be to kiss him. Astonished at the direction her mind was taking, she moved her gaze to his eyes. The shadow of his dark lashes made them as deep a gray as a stormy night sky, their odd inner glow like lightning flashes behind the clouds.

Although Valjean would have liked to turn and study Aimée as minutely as he knew she was scrutinizing him, he realized this would alarm her. Instead he contented himself with memories of how she'd looked riding in the sun, and the wildness of spirit that her decorous conduct now concealed. He couldn't help speculating how she would behave if she'd been raised by an Abnaki-family—naturally, without inhibitions. His fancies sent a warmth running through him; he recognized his desire. At that moment his eyes lit with a silvery fire that caused Aimée to catch her breath and turn her gaze from him.

He was aware of her reaction without looking at her. It confirmed his suspicion that her decorous attitude was a veneer others had taught her. She was a high-spirited girl with deep wells of passion she was mostly unaware of, and those she knew existed she looked not too closely into. Instead, he was certain, her instincts occasionally startled her—as they had a moment ago.

Even though Valjean's senses were constantly alert for any danger the wilderness might present, superimposed on them was an awareness of Aimée's being that he couldn't ignore. His nose perceived each scent of the forest while at the same time the fragrance of Aimée's freshly washed hair made him want to bury his face in its fiery curls; and the sweet scent of her sun-warmed skin gave him visions of the creamy flesh he'd glimpsed through the momentarily gaping neckline of her blouse. His eyes noticed every leaf that fluttered in the light breeze as he recalled the burnished arch of her delicate brows, the warmth of her long-lashed eyes, like brandy in a crystal goblet drunk before a fire on a chill evening. His ears faithfully registered the rustle of a squirrel bounding up a tree, but lilting through his memory was Aimée's voice.

Although Valjean and Aimée moved along the path without speaking, their similar thoughts reached out to touch, then grasp, while their bodies carefully never even brushed each other.

They were walking through a grove of pine trees that murmured in the gentle wind. It was then that Aimée said, "We are nearing the settlement, monsieur."

The words were so softly uttered. Valjean paused in his steps hoping that he'd heard only the sighing of the trees, that they wouldn't have to part so soon. When he looked down into her eyes, he saw the regret in their depths and knew she felt as he did.

"Which way must we go?" he asked.

Lifting a hand to gesture the direction, she answered, "Just ahead is a meadow. Across the meadow is the settlement—and my father's house."

Valjean turned to resume walking. A dozen paces away he saw the meadow she'd described through the thinning trees. Again he stopped. Aimée looked up at him questioningly, but he said nothing. He turned away to caress Brandy's neck, then dropped the reins he'd held so they trailed on the ground and the horse wouldn't wander. Valjean continued standing with his back toward Aimée, and she wondered at his purpose.

After a long, silent moment she asked, "Is there some reason to remain here, Monsieur d'Auvergne?"

"Yes, mademoiselle, there is," he replied. Still, he waited a moment longer before slowly turning to face her. He made no effort to explain their pause on the trail, gazing at her with a softness she didn't understand. She looked at him steadily, trying to understand.

A breeze from the meadow enveloped the couple in a warm rush of spicy-sweet fragrance that mixed with the crisp, cool scent of the pines.

"Mayflowers," she whispered, and lamely fell silent.

"I know," he replied, laying his hands lightly on her shoulders. He bent to brush his lips against hers. His kiss was infinitely gentle, as warm and sweet as the wandering spring breeze, and asked nothing more from her than the breeze did. Because his caressing lips made no demands, she responded with an ease that delighted him. His mouth moved pliantly, tenderly, melting any fears before they had a chance to form in her mind. His hands slipped from her shoulders to the curve of her back. Then he paused, his lips but a breath from hers.

She opened her eyes to look into his. Their lights had softened, blending into a steady glow the color of cats' eyes. The breeze freshened into a light wind, and the scent of mayflowers surrounded them anew. His mouth again reached for hers, and her lips sought him with an eager naïveté that stirred a poignant tenderness in him, softening, yet adding to, his desire. His hands moved over her back, his arm's now encircling her until her body leaned lightly against his.

It seemed to Aimée that the wind's sweet warmth rushed through her senses, yielding her up to him like an offering. His mouth caressed hers sensually, coaxing her lips to become supple, willing to learn. Her body, barely resting on his, eased closer to discover that the lean length of this man was firm and lithe. A fire seemed to pierce her heart and run through her body, stirring every nerve to new life. Although his kiss yet demanded nothing but the sensation of her lips, her instincts compelled her to press closer to him.

As lost as he'd become in the kiss, when he heard her soft gasp he moved away to look down into her unfocused eyes. Amber fires were rising from their depths. He sighed, gently kissed her forehead, and stepped away.

Aimée gazed at Valjean wordlessly, still too overcome by the sensations he'd aroused in her. She watched as he picked up Brandy's reins. Then he took her hand and started walking rapidly toward the meadow.

Recovering herself, Aimée wondered at his silence. Finally she burst out, "Will you say nothing, monsieur?"

He turned to look at her but didn't slow his steps as he answered, "I'd thought that kiss we shared said everything I felt far better than any words I might choose."

Aimée thought about this for a few paces, then asked, "And will you now travel back to Quebec, from there to France? Will I never see you again, monsieur?"

Valjean smiled at her innocent candor. Then, as he remembered his assignment, the smile faded. "I wish I could promise that I'll arrange for a mutual friend to properly introduce me, that I could ask your father if I might call on you at home. But I cannot. I must leave Montreal too soon to encourage these feelings I already have for you. It would be too painful for me; it would be unfair to you."

Aimée was silent as she stepped into the sunlit meadow. Twin streaks of separate fears tore through her, and she was so shaken by their pain she stopped walking to face him.

"Monsieur, are you already wed to someone? Or is it only that you don't care to become better acquainted and wish not to tell me?" she demanded.

Valjean's hands lifted to her temples. "I think, after such a kiss, you should call me Valjean," he said softly, then added, "I am not, nor have I ever been, wed. This I swear, Aimée." He bent to brush his lips to her cheek; the perfume of the mayflowers swirled around them again. "*Ma petite amie,* you fear that I don't like you enough to stay; but it's *my* misfortune—a cruel twist of fate, I think, for my part—that I must leave Montreal and you." He moved away; then taking her hand, he led her into the meadow.

They walked swiftly through the ankle-deep flowers—those flowers had added magic to the enchantment of their kiss. Aimée's emotions were a whirl of confusion as his words echoed again and again in her ears. How could he say their parting was his misfortune, a cruel twist of fate, even call her his sweetheart, while he planned to leave? Wasn't this man even a little in control of his life so that he could delay his departure, she thought bitterly, even though she knew he was right. Seeing each other again, becoming better acquainted, would only make him dearer to her—and maybe her to him, as he implied—so his later exit from her life would be that much more difficult. The white masses of flowers at her feet blurred as tears filled her eyes.

She didn't notice when they left the meadow, when they passed the walls protecting the settlement from the Iroquois and the British; she didn't know that they approached the gate to her house until her feet automatically stopped before it.

"Look up at me, Aimée," Valjean said quietly. She blinked away her tears and obeyed. "I regret my leaving as I have regretted little else. I vow, *chérie,* never will I forget you. I will never again smell mayflowers and pine without remembering you and that moment in the forest." He took her hand, lifted it to his lips, and kissed it lingeringly. "Yes, Aimée, you're like that wind to me, spicy and sweet, appearing placid and docile when inside you're wild and free. You're a sweet wild wind that blew for a moment through my life and gave me dreams I shall never forget." He put Brandy's reins into her hand, closed her fingers around them, then turned and walked away.

Aimée stood at the gate, silently watching until Valjean disappeared through the opening in the settlement's protective walls. She felt as if her palm had been seared by his kiss, leaving a scar to mark her forever.

Chapter 2

While Philippe attended to Brandy's leg Aimée rubbed the marks of her saddle from the horse's shining coat. Although she spared no efforts on Brandy, her mind was focused on Valjean's kiss and what he'd said to her. Constantly winding through her thoughts was the scent of mayflowers. Finally she gave Brandy his good-bye pat and left the stable.

Aimée used the servant's door to enter the house, not wanting to meet either Mignon, who would distract her thoughts, or her mother, who would surely scold her for riding alone, as well as for dressing in Marcel's old clothes. Creeping up the back stairway, Aimée recalled how silently Valjean walked, the lithe power of all his movements. Once inside her room, as she changed into a dressing gown, she wondered if indeed she and Valjean would ever meet again.

She pulled open the window facing the meadow, then sat on the cushioned seat that formed the window's wide sill. Inhaling the scent of the blossoms, watching their masses move in the wind, she wondered if Valjean would change his mind about not visiting her again before he left the area. Such thoughts lured her mind into a pretty little dream where Valjean, dressed like a gentleman from Paris, drove up to the gate in a fine carriage to court her properly. But she found she couldn't visualize Valjean wearing an afternoon coat or lace-edged sleeves. She couldn't imagine Valjean with his hair drawn back and dressed with powder.

Her mind rejected that scene and switched to the more comfortable image of a midnight meeting in the garden,

with Valjean clad in his doeskins and the two of them
stealing hand in hand into the meadow. Her instincts began to seduce her mind into imagining what would follow
after they were out of the view of the sentries. When her
thoughts approached that forbidden realm, she stopped
them. Instead she relived Valjean's sun-warm kiss, the feel
of his arms around her and the lean strength of his body
touching hers. Finding that memories of these sensations
invoked their return, she couldn't resist them.

Her fantasies abruptly ended when the door to her
room opened. She turned quickly to look guiltily over her
shoulder and saw only Mignon standing on the threshold.
"It would be more thoughtful, Mignon, if you knocked
first," she reminded her sister.

Mignon's golden curls drooped over her shoulder a moment as she contritely gazed at her feet. "I'm sorry,
Aimée. I just wanted to . . ." She paused to glance warily
into the hall behind her, then stepped inside the room and
closed the door. She continued in a whisper, "I just
wanted to know who you were standing with at the gate."

Aimée stared at her sister in surprise. "You saw us? We
were there only a moment!"

"Oh, he was handsome," Mignon breathed.

"Do you really think so?" Aimeé asked curiously, adding quickly, "I hope Maman didn't see us too. She'll
describe the many reasons why I shouldn't be seen with so
unpolished a man, in addition to how improper it was for
me to dress in Marcel's breeches, *et cetera, et cetera, et
cetera.*"

Mignon came a little nearer. "Will you tell me about
him?" she asked hopefully. "You know I won't tell Maman—I promise I won't."

Aimée softened and held out her hands. Mignon took
them and, still holding them, sat at the other end of the
window seat.

"Will he return to visit?" Mignon asked anxiously.
When Aimée slowly shook her head, Mignon exclaimed,
"*Non!* I was sure he was enamored of you—"

"Enamored? Mignon!" Aimée protested, blushing in
guilty remembrance of her fantasies.

Mignon lowered her eyes. "Well, he liked you very much at the least," she amended, then raised her eyes to her sister and insisted, "The way he looked at you! Oh, I thought he would do more than kiss your hand—even in front of the house!"

"We did kiss in the forest," Aimée admitted, her flush growing deeper.

"How did it feel? How did it happen?" Mignon asked conspiratorially, her blue eyes pleading to experience, even vicariously, a moment her strict upbringing had so far not allowed her.

"It was enchanting, wonderful," Aimée whispered. Her eyes softened as she focused on a memory Mignon could only envy as she went on to describe the afternoon, reliving it as she spoke.

After Aimée had finished, Mignon's mouth formed a small pink circle of wonder. Finally recovering herself, Mignon said softly, "Perhaps he will return."

Aimée's eyes glimmered with tears as she answered sadly, "That's what I thought, at first. Then I realized I was fooling myself. It will be difficult, but I must accept that I'll never see him again."

Mignon reached out to lay her hand sympathetically on Aimée's shoulder and said, "I think you will see him again." Seeing Aimée's hopeful expression, she added firmly, "I shall light a candle for you, offer mass for your intention. I'll say a rosary every night before I fall asleep."

Aimée was touched by her sister's promise. "In return, I'll pray that you meet someone just like him—someone you will love," she vowed.

"It will take no less than a miracle for us to find *two* such men in Montreal," Mignon said so solemnly that Aimée laughed.

Still laughing—though close to tears—Aimée put her arms around Mignon; and the two girls hugged each other comfortingly until there was a tap on the door. Before Aimée could answer, their mother stepped into the room to regard them curiously.

"What a delightful picture you make on the window seat, embracing so affectionately," Jeannette Dessaline commented. "Your father will have a surprise to tell you when he comes home this evening. You'd best begin dressing for dinner so you can greet him prettily."

Aimée and Mignon quickly hopped off the seat. When their mother announced a surprise in that tone, they knew she expected them to be very pleased with it. They also knew it would serve no purpose to try to persuade Jeannette to tell them what it was; so they remained silent, trying to imagine what their mother had in mind.

Jeannette's blue eyes were warm with pleasure as she said, "You'd best choose your dresses. Mignon, why not wear your blue velvet? Aimée, what about your cream? You know how your father enjoys seeing you in those gowns."

"Maman . . ." Mignon began.

"Non, non, non." Jeannette shook her head to Mignon's unasked question. "I'll give you no hints. I'll save the pleasure of the telling for your father. Now, *mes petites filles,* I'll send Josette to arrange your hair and make sure you're ready on time." She turned toward the door and opened it; but before stepping outside, she turned to give Aimée a long appraising look. Then she nodded and left.

"Did you see how Maman looked at me?" Aimée whispered. "Do you think she saw Valjean?"

"Non, Aimée. If she had, she would, as you said before, have had a great many things to say about it," Mignon answered, then dismissed the question of Aimée's possible discovery and said thoughtfully, "I wonder what Papa's surprise is. If Maman wants us to put on his favorite dresses, if she even sends Josette to attend us—"

"It must be a very impressive surprise," Aimée finished.

When Hilaire Dessaline came home, he greeted his daughters with his usual affection. Even if Jeannette hadn't already told the girls, Aimée would have known from the sparkle in his hazel eyes he had a secret. But he told them nothing before dinner.

All through the meal Aimée watched silently as her parents and brother discussed the family business. Hilaire bought pelts from the trappers of the region, and his employees prepared and preserved them; and he shipped the treated furs to Europe. New France had a wealth of wild animal life, most of them fur-bearing. Hilaire was a connoisseur of fur quality and made his purchases wisely. His employees were handpicked experts, and the furs he exported were exquisite. The pelts that had been collected during the last winter were some of the finest Hilaire had ever seen. Hilaire and Marcel were jubilant at the prospect of high profits.

As Aimée listened to her father and brother she began to wonder if the promised surprise was a special gift to celebrate their success—or perhaps a party. Marcel knew what the secret was, Aimée guessed. Usually poised and quiet, Marcel resembled both Aimée and their father physically; and his temperament was much the same as theirs. He could keep a secret from his lips but not from his maple-colored eyes.

Unlike Aimée, Mignon didn't remain silent. She asked questions and made comments that would flatter her father. Aimée saw Jeannette in Mignon as her sister tried to coax Hilaire into revealing the surprise. She was amused by Mignon's methods, which were charming and harmless. Mignon not only behaved much like her mother, but she resembled Jeannette. The same delicate features framed by blond curls, the hyacinth-blue eyes and long, golden lashes, and fair pink complexion made them both seem as fragile as porcelain figurines. Although Aimée had always considered her features to be presentable enough, she thought her rebellious auburn hair, like her spirit, was sometimes too conspicuous, each needing their own kind of discipline.

It wasn't until dessert had been served that Hilaire finally said, "Today I received a letter from your uncle Antoine in Paris." He paused to glance at each member of his family before continuing, "He, your aunt Victoire, and your cousin Claude are well and send us their affectionate regards. You can read the letter later to learn the details, but there is one bit of news I want to discuss with all of you together. Antoine has written that a lady of the court, a Madame de Pompadour, noticed his fur designs and was

so impressed with them that she brought them to the attention of King Louis, who ordered several items for Queen
Marie. Antoine's furs have become so popular with the
royal family his majesty plans to appoint Antoine *fourreur
du roi* this autumn. Antoine invites us all to come to Paris
and be guests at his home so we can attend the appointment."

"There is no mention of any honor or appointment to
be given you, Papa?" Aimée inquired, miffed that her
uncle should become royal furrier and her father would
get no credit, when it was he who supplied his brother
with the furs.

Hilaire shook his head and answered gently, "*Non,*
there was no mention. To the king and his court, I am
merely in the *pelleterie.*"

Hiding the flash in her eyes by staring at her dessert
dish, Aimée wasn't fully able to conceal the anger in her
voice as she muttered, "It isn't fair."

"That sometimes is the way of life." Hilaire shrugged,
then fell silent.

Wanting to lighten the conversation, Jeannette quickly
said, "Your father is considering accepting Antoine's invitation."

Mignon's face lit at the thought of visiting France, and
she asked excitedly, "Papa, do you think we could?"

"I wanted to learn what everyone else thinks of the
idea," Hilaire replied. He smiled and commented, "I can
see from Mignon's expression what she thinks, but how
about Aimée?"

When Hilaire had first announced Antoine's invitation,
Aimée's mind had been riveted by one thought: Valjean's
mother lived in France; he must live there too. Was it possible that destiny was already arranging for her to meet
him again? "I would love to go to France!" she breathed.

"Having a relative appointed to the royal court certainly
isn't an everyday occurrence. Witnessing the event, attending royal court, is an opportunity given very few, one I
doubt we'll be offered again," Jeannette pointed out. "It
would benefit our children to be introduced to the culture
and the society of our former homeland; and I'm sure, if

we refused, Antoine and his family would be much disappointed."

"It's a long and sometimes dangerous voyage," Hilaire warned.

"Sailing in the summer shouldn't be too dangerous," Jeannette said quickly. It had always been her wish that her children, especially her daughters, marry well. Ever since the girls' femininity had become more than a promise, she had worried that a lack of proper suitors would force them to accept lesser husbands. Remembering Aimée at the front gate with that handsome, unrefined-looking young man, Jeannette shuddered anew. Her daughters wouldn't marry trappers or mere adventurers if she could prevent it. Turning to her husband, she said, "Hilaire, Aimée and Mignon are no longer children. You know there's a scarcity of attractive eligible young men in Montreal. Beautiful as our girls are, they'll have a difficult task finding worthwhile husbands here."

Hilaire knew Jeannette had gotten the girls to wear these particular gowns for dinner to underline the fact that they were no longer children. While agreeing with Jeannette's reasoning, he found it hard to accept that they might marry in Paris and remain there. "These days Montreal is filled with handsome young officers from France, Jeannette. There are also a great many men of wealth in Montreal whose sons are unmarried. I don't think we must search for husbands in France to prevent our girls from becoming spinsters," he replied.

"Those young officers marry in Quebec before they even see Montreal," Jeannette promptly reminded him. "You know that most of the men of means in Montreal are political officials and—"

Hilaire gave his wife a warning glance. He didn't want her to speak of political corruption before their daughters.

But Jeannette was determined. "You don't really wish to see our daughters become the wives of such officials, do you?" she asked.

"I want our daughters—and Marcel too—to be happy," Hilaire said, glancing at his son. "It would make *me* happy if they could live within a distance manageable for visiting. Do you want to have grandchildren you'll see once every few years? We wouldn't even learn of the birth of our grandchildren until they were at least two months old!"

The idea of seeing her children so seldom was something Jeannette had considered before. The anticipated loneliness was an ache in her heart she tried to ignore. "Of course, Hilaire, I do wish to see my children more often. As for babies, you know I'd like to be within a carriage ride's distance." Jeannette sighed. "I suppose God will decide our futures in any case."

Hilaire was reminded of yet another reason for making a voyage to France, one more compelling than arranging good marriages for his daughters. He didn't want to discuss it in front of his wife and daughters; he didn't want to frighten them. "I must consider all these matters before making my decision. Jeannette, you should think about the preparations you'd have to make, the closing of the house for the time we'd be away. I have to consider the business and its operation if we left—also the expenses such a voyage would involve."

"But, Papa, weren't you and Marcel just discussing the high profits you expect from this winter's pelts?" Mignon asked.

"What we expect isn't always what we get," Hilaire advised. "I'll think about all these things and will give you my decision tomorrow." He looked at Marcel. "Shall we have a glass of brandy in the study? I would like to talk with you about some things."

"Of course, *mon père*," Marcel replied.

Aimée followed Jeannette and Mignon into the parlor. As she worked on her embroidery, she wondered if her father might decide not to accept Uncle Antoine's invitation. She prayed he wouldn't. She thought about Valjean and France for the rest of the evening.

Aimée was so withdrawn and quiet in contrast to Mignon, who chattered about France all evening, that Jeannette began to worry if the surprise had been so intoxicating to Aimée that she was feeling weak from overexcitement. After the girls had wished their mother pleasant dreams and had gone upstairs to prepare for bed, Jeannette sent Josette with a warming pan to Aimée's room to make sure she wouldn't take ill. Jeannette only hoped Aimée wasn't so well acquainted with the young man she'd seen at the gate that she was secretly saddened to think of leaving him behind. Jeannette thought, If the voyage did nothing more than distract Aimée from such men, it would be worth the trouble and cost.

Hilaire handed Marcel the snifter of brandy he'd just poured, then motioned for his son to sit. Hilaire himself didn't sit down but stared at the liquor in his glass while he thought about what he wanted to discuss with Marcel.

"If you're worried about who will run the business should you accept Uncle Antoine's invitation, you worry needlessly. I will," Marcel finally said.

Hilaire glanced up in surprise. "You're very generous to offer to sacrifice going on such a trip, Marcel," he said.

"It's not generous at all," Marcel declared. His maple-colored eyes lit with a warmth that was no mere reflection of the fire before him. "I don't intend to go to France and allow François to gain favor with Lisolette while I'm absent."

"I didn't realize you were so interested in Mademoiselle Marais," Hilaire commented thoughtfully. "I'd thought you were merely friends."

"That was how it began. I believe it's developing into more. If so, you might have a wedding to attend when you return from Paris," Marcel advised.

Hilaire was silent a long moment while he absorbed this information. His growing pleasure with his son's future plans suddenly faded at the thought of another problem that had been worrying him. "What if the violence comes to Montreal?" he forced himself to ask.

"Montreal won't be attacked by the British just because you've gone on a voyage, *mon père*," Marcel chided.

"Your mother and sisters are enthusiastic about going to Paris for the obvious reasons. I've been wondering if it would be safer for them to be out of the colonies for a while," Hilaire said slowly.

"We've recently made some advances against the British," Marcel reminded. "General Montcalm's arrival has turned the tide, I think."

"I pray it is so," Hilaire said fervently. "Although the winter was profitable for us, it's too easy for us to overlook the starvation in Montreal last winter. Living outside the city, we had a garden and grew much of our own food; and what we needed we had the money to buy. Those in the city, who aren't so fortunate as we and couldn't pay the outrageous prices for the little food there was, had a hard winter. I'm afraid of what next winter will bring. We would be in France throughout the winter, you realize."

"I know, *mon père*," Marcel replied. "If I remained here, I would be sure our garden was tended and the crops were harvested, even if I had to do the work myself. I wouldn't starve. Have no fear about that."

"What of the Indians?" Hilaire asked. "They may be our allies, but they know we need them to fight the British and they take advantage of it. I was in Montreal, don't forget, after they massacred the British at Fort William last August. A more terrifying night I have never spent. The Indians roamed the streets of Montreal harassing anyone unfortunate enough to pass them. The next day was no better. They threatened the women when they went to do the morning marketing. They frightened the children and tried to tempt the men into fighting with them."

"I don't think General Montcalm will allow that to happen again," Marcel reassured him. "I think our leaders learned then not to reward each of the Indians with two kegs of brandy after a battle, if only because several members of important families were accosted by drunken Indians then. Anyway, I don't think the Indians will bother us here, just as they didn't bother us then. We aren't in Montreal."

"Perhaps, perhaps," Hilaire said worriedly. "But what if the British do attack? Our troops are much disheartened. There have been many desertions. The Indians won't fight the British alone."

"If the British seem ready to attack, I'm sure the deserters will return to the battle," Marcel said calmly. "However disheartened they may be, they have families and homes to protect. Besides, most of the deserters only went back to their farms to tend their crops. They didn't go to the British."

Hilaire knew the truth of this, but it was comforting to hear it spoken aloud. He took a sip of his brandy and let its warmth ease the pain he felt at the thought of his son's being harmed by either the British or the Indians. "What if the worst does happen?" he forced himself to ask. "What if Montreal falls?"

Marcel raised his head to regard his father. "I think it would be better if Maman and the girls weren't here to see it," he said quietly.

Hilaire looked at his son in wonder and pride. Though Marcel argued against the probability of the dangers he'd mentioned, he knew his son had also thought they were possible, and wanted his family out of the country. "Marcel . . ." Hilaire began, then stopped. He didn't know what to say to this young man who was willing to face the dangers alone.

"Tell me what to do, Father, just on the possibility that such a thing might happen," Marcel said calmly.

Hilaire shook his head, tears in his eyes. He could not speak.

"I would, of course, do my best to save the house and business," Marcel said too matter-of-factly. "It might be a good idea if we decided on some safe place to hide whatever money I could rescue."

"I'll have to think about that," Hilaire managed.

"It would be a good idea to have some hiding place in mind, whether you decide to go to France or not—just as a precaution," Marcel commented.

"*Oui,* I suppose that's true," Hilaire conceded. He blinked away his tears and faced Marcel. "Whatever happens, save yourself before you worry about the house, the business, or the money," he said firmly.

Marcel got to his feet. "Does that mean you'll accept Uncle Antoine's invitation?"

Hilaire was silent a moment. He knew the danger was

nearer than either of them wished to admit. That Marcel spoke in this fashion only confirmed his own fears. Finally he nodded and said, "I'll tell your mother and the girls in the morning."

"I'll get a list of the ships that will be in the harbor a couple of months from now so we can have some idea which one you'll want to buy passage on," Marcel offered.

Hilaire nodded solemnly and put down his brandy glass. As they walked toward the door, he paused and whispered, "Don't tell your mother or sisters what we've been talking about. They have no idea how serious the situation has become, and there's no point in worrying them."

"I'll say nothing about any of this. Let them think only about which bonnets and gowns to pack for the voyage," Marcel answered. Then, seeing how concerned his father was, he smiled and put his arm around Hilaire's shoulder, adding, "We're worrying for nothing, I'm certain. I will probably spend the most boring winter of my life here in Montreal while you'll be enjoying yourself."

"You'll be bored keeping company with Mademoiselle Lisolette, even though your mother and I won't be present to keep our eyes on you?" Hilaire inquired. "If that's the case, I think you should forget about marrying her."

Marcel glanced at his father in surprise, then, realizing that he too was trying to lighten the mood, squeezed Hilaire's shoulder and said, "I can't admit to my own father what my private plans for the *mademoiselle* are, can I?"

Hilaire put down the chuckle that was rising within him, but it remained in his eyes as he said sternly, "You will remember the family honor while your mother and I are gone."

Marcel smiled sweetly and replied, *"Certainement, mon père. Je suis toujours honorable."*

Chapter 3

Aimée paused in the hotel lobby while her father made arrangements with the porter to send back to their ship the few pieces of baggage the family had used during its overnight stay in Boston. She stepped away from the group to make a path for a boy carrying a large bundle. Finding that she had a clear view of the windows, she remained where she'd moved to, and gazed idly out at the passing carriages while she waited.

Boston, she decided, seemed as populous as Montreal and certainly as industrious. Thinking of Montreal reminded her of her brother, and she wished Marcel were coming to France with the rest of the family. It seemed unfair that he would miss the voyage and the adventure of visiting Paris, yet she could understand why he would want to remain in Montreal close to Lisolette. A good part of France's attraction for her was the irrational, yet persistent conviction that the trip would somehow bring her again into contact with Valjean d'Auvergne.

She wondered, as she had several times, why Marcel had bought passage for the family on the Spanish ship *Santa Luisa* rather than a French vessel. It was irksome, she thought, to have to stop in Boston for a day and a night to pick up additional cargo and passengers before going on to France—and to delay the meeting with Valjean that she was so anxious for.

Aimée and Mignon had no way of knowing how badly the war with the British was going. Even Jeannette wasn't fully aware of the gravity of the situation. Niagara had already surrendered to the British. Quebec was under siege, and supplies had to be smuggled into the stricken city. Hilaire and Marcel had so carefully shielded the women from news of the defeats the French had so far suffered during the summer that they couldn't know how many British warships were waiting at the mouth of the Saint Lawrence to capture any vessels flying a French flag—civilian and military alike—in an effort to cut off the supplies the French colonists so badly needed.

The *Santa Luisa* was neutral, free to sail where it would. Only the owner-captain's family knew that although his father had given him his Spanish name and citizenship, he had been born in New Orleans of a French mother and so secretly favored France in her struggle with Britain.

Hilaire, having to conduct business with many nationalities, spoke several languages fluently, English being one of them; and he had taught the language to Marcel, who in turn had tutored Aimée. Aimée spoke English haltingly and understood it if it was spoken slowly and clearly. Catching the last few words of a comment a woman made as she passed through the hotel lobby, Aimée glanced self-consciously down at her dress, wondering why the woman had spoken critically about her. The gown she'd chosen to wear that morning in Boston was a town dress she'd thought suitable for travel. It was as fashionable as any in either the French or British colonies—they were all a year behind the styles in Europe. The dress was cut simply, and its unobtrusive delicate gray tint complemented her coloring without over-accenting her hair. Her curls were neatly tucked under her hat, and only a few locks rested lightly on her shoulders. She wondered if the woman's criticism had to do with her unpowdered hair—it was impossible to keep so formally dressed a *coiffure* during a voyage, she reasoned. Aimée didn't realize that it was her sister's and mother's conversation in French that had caught the woman's attention, and that her remark had been meant for the entire family.

Because Hilaire was so protective of his daughters, they thought of the war as a distant series of frontier skirmishes having little to do with them personally. Aimée didn't understand that the Dessalines were regarded by the Britishdescended Bostonians as at best a curiosity and at the worst part of an enemy people.

Hilaire, having overheard the Englishwoman's remark, noticed Aimée's perplexed, self-conscious expression. He turned to the girls to suggest in a voice rather more cheerful than he actually felt, "Shall we go into the tearoom and have breakfast before we return to the ship?" Ignoring the surprised glance of the desk clerk, who had not heard him speak French before this, Hilaire took his wife's arm and led his family toward the restaurant.

After they had ordered hot chocolate and muffins with strawberry preserves and little tubs of pale freshly churned butter, Hilaire immediately began to speak about Paris, describing the city he'd last seen when he himself was but a youth recently married and preparing to emigrate to the colonies. Soon Jeannette joined in, reminiscing about how they'd first met at a party, describing their courtship and the social life they'd led before boarding the ship to the New World. Hilaire kept only half his attention on Jeannette's conversation. The other half of his mind was on Marcel and the possible dangers he faced by staying in Montreal to manage the family business.

Aimée was fascinated by her parents' description of a country that she'd never known, though it was part of her heritage. She wondered if she would discover Valjean at a party, the way her mother and father had met. She remembered how she'd looked when he'd last seen her, wearing Marcel's old breeches and jacket, her hair a flaming tangle; then she dreamed of what he would think of her dressed in a party gown, her hair elegantly curled and powdered and glowing with silver in the candlelight. He would dance with her, walk with her in the garden in the moonlight, then possibly—no, surely kiss her again.

"Andrew, please do let us avoid passing Faneuil Hall. It's such a clamor at this time of day," Julia Carleton reminded her husband.

"We would if we could, my dear; but this is the most direct route to the wharf; and Vale will have no time to spare before his ship sails," Andrew Carleton answered as he noted that the driver was guiding the horses pulling their carriage in precisely that direction. He added, "You will want to allow a moment to say our good-byes to Vale."

Julia nodded, her eyes beginning to blur with tears at the thought of the long voyage Vale was about to begin. She blinked quickly several times, silently scolding herself for such sentimentality and, at the same time, knowing that she would weep for Vale as surely as she would do for one of her own sons.

"It doesn't matter what time of day it is," Vale observed. "The entire market district is congested from dawn to dusk."

"It wouldn't do at all to reach the wharf only to find that the *Santa Luisa* had just sailed away," Paul Carleton remarked.

"Oh, my, no!" Julia agreed. "But why did you buy passage for Vale on a Spanish ship rather than one of our own English vessels?"

"Because the owner, Captain Mareto, is agreeable about the special requirements we have for delivering the shipment Vale will bring back with him," Andrew explained.

"Also because Captain Mareto's ship can sail into a French port without being captured," Paul added.

"If Vale were to wait for another ship to arrive, make repairs, reload, then depart, he might very well not leave Boston Harbor before autumn. There could be some ugly storms to weather that late. His voyage could turn out to be extremely uncomfortable, as well as hazardous," Andrew pointed out.

"It will be hazardous enough as it is," Julia said worriedly. "When I think of that great ocean and all the perils it holds, I know I won't rest until Vale has returned safely."

"Please don't distress yourself so, my dear," Andrew said soothingly. "He will be quite safe at this time of year."

Julia was silent for a moment, then turned to address Vale. "How do you plan to go about locating your real mother? Truly, I have no idea how one might even begin such a task."

Privately Vale himself wasn't sure how he would accomplish this, but he replied, "I don't know whom she married, so I'll have to use her family name—d'Auvergne—in my inquiries. If her husband is a nobleman as Mother—I mean, Bess told me, possibly I'll be able to trace her."

"Perhaps you can ask Mr. Bossuet to help," Andrew suggested. "He might, at least, give you a clue as to how to begin."

"I dislike imposing on your business associates for a personal matter," Vale objected. "It's been good of you to allow me to combine your business with my own errand—"

"Vale, we've known you almost all your life," Andrew interrupted. "We've looked after you like one of our own sons. It's unthinkable not to help in any way we can to clear your mind about your heritage in France."

"We've seen that faraway look in your eyes while you've wondered about your real mother," Julia said. "My heart has ached for you, wishing I could tell you what you need to know. If this is the only way for you to find the answers to your questions, then, as much as I'll worry while you're away, I know this is what you must do to find peace."

"Tell Mr. Bossuet you're trying to locate a relative in Paris," Andrew suggested. "I'm sure he'll be willing to help you. After all, he is eager to secure future contracts with us."

"It does seem odd to do business with a man from a nation that's supposed to be our enemy," Julia mused.

"Both Britain and France are a great distance away," Andrew reminded her.

"If King George would lower some of the tariffs we have to pay to keep in business, we wouldn't have to buy fittings for our ships from a French manufacturer," Paul put in. "We have to pay a tax to get our cargo loaded in England, then we have to pay another tariff to get it unloaded in Boston. Bribing the officials on both sides of the

Atlantic, as we've been doing, is becoming too expensive."

"But how will you avoid the tax collectors when you return to Boston?" Julia asked anxiously.

"The ship won't draw into Boston Harbor proper," Andrew replied. "It will stand outside Massachusetts Bay until nightfall, then sail into one of the inlets south of the bay. We'll have wagons waiting to carry the supplies to our shipyard."

"The entire procedure does seem dangerous—and somewhat disloyal to the Crown," Julia commented.

"It won't be dangerous if it's done properly, and Captain Mareto is the man to manage it," Paul assured her. "As far as being disloyal to the Crown is concerned, it's ridiculous for the king to expect us to pay so many taxes. Then too, the royal treasury has gotten none of the bribe money we've already paid."

"It's just that it seems as if we're smugglers or pirates or some other sort of disreputable people," Julia murmured.

"I'd say it's more humiliating than disreputable," Paul remarked, a tint of bitterness in his tone.

"Quite humiliating," his father agreed, then added, "Ah, we have arrived—and with little extra time, as I'd predicted."

Julia was happy to change the subject. Paul was so angry about the matter of tariffs that she feared his volatile temper would one day flare up before someone who would think him one of the group of men rumored to be meeting nights to discuss their complaints about the Crown. She extended her hand so her husband could help her out of the carriage, and found herself instead being aided by Vale. Once again her eyes began to blur.

"You *will* be careful," she whispered. He nodded, and she added, "Having only sons will be the death of me yet—and you, another boy, must be added to my worries. I wish you'd been a girl who could forget chasing across the world and concentrate on establishing her own family right here in Boston," she scolded affectionately.

"I doubt even if I were a girl, I'd be able to forget I'd been born on the wrong side of the blankets," Vale said quietly.

* * *

While the Dessalines stood among the crowd waiting for the passageway to be secured in place so that they could enter the *Santa Luisa*, Aimée lifted her head to gaze at the masts and the rigging so delicately outlined against the backdrop of the sky. She thought of the powerful air currents that would drive the ship across the ocean, and wondered how those slender spires could hold the sails straining in such winds. The ship itself, which had seemed to loom so high above her when she'd first approached it in Montreal, now appeared humbler, more fragile; and she couldn't help questioning its ability to contain the weight of its cargo and passengers and yet remain afloat. As she reflected on the mighty depths they were about to travel, a shiver of apprehension ran coldly along her nerves.

"Mr. Kendall, do you have any more baggage?" a man's voice called.

"No, Charles. That's all of it," a nearby voice replied in clear, crisp English.

Aimée felt as if a blow had struck the breath from her. Telling herself the answering voice was merely similar to the one she'd longed so much to hear again, she slowly turned. Aimée stared incredulously at the man standing less than thirty feet away, somewhat removed from the fringes of the crowd.

Although the man's back was turned toward her, she recognized the set of his shoulders, even if they were covered by a smartly tailored black coat instead of buttery doeskin. She knew the length of his legs, though they wore pale gray breeches, and the golden glimmer of the sun on his dark hair now drawn into a neat queue instead of blowing loose in the breeze. Her heart resumed its beating, then began to pound as if it would burst from her breast when he turned and she saw his face. *It was Valjean!*

Aimée lowered her parasol, by habit snapping it shut; as she lifted one foot, ready to hurry toward him, a hand firmly gripped her arm to restrain her.

"It is your young man at the gate," Jeannette said softly.

Aimée nodded.

"Vale, you must promise to be careful." An elegantly groomed woman of about Jeannette's age approached him.

Aimée watched as Valjean opened his arms to embrace the woman and murmur reassuring promises. Was this his mother? Aimèe wondered. Wasn't his mother in France?

"That is his name, then, Vale Kendall?" Jeannette quietly asked.

Aimée's heartbeat was suspended. Baffled by the situation, she whispered, *"Non,* Maman. His name is Valjean d'Auvergne."

"It is very odd to meet a Frenchman in Montreal, then to find him in Boston answering to a British name and speaking English," Jeannette gently pointed out.

Aimée watched the man those others called Vale warmly clasp the hands of the two well-dressed men standing with him beside the carriage. "Maman, what does it mean?" she breathed.

"What would an Englishman be doing in a Montreal forest, speaking French, and using a French name except spying on us?" Jeannette replied softly. Aimée moved as if she yet would approach and speak to him, but Jeannette tightened her grasp on Aimée's wrist. *"Mais non, mon innocente.* You cannot go to him . . ."

Aimée remembered the slight oddity she'd noticed in Valjean's accent; she recalled having briefly wondered if he could be a spy. How could she have so lightly thrown aside her caution with a stranger? How could she have so readily assumed he'd spoken the truth? Tears filled her eyes, and her throat closed.

Jeannette's fingers slid down to grasp Aimée's as she whispered, "Come with me, *ma petite.* At least, keep your dignity. Don't let him know how you care." Then, squeezing Aimée's fingers comfortingly, she added, "In Paris you will have fifty suitors at your feet—and none of them will be spies."

He must not know how I've dreamed of him, Aimée was thinking. I must not humiliate myself even more by showing I recognize him. I must make him believe I've forgotten all about him. Aloud, she remarked, "Fifty suitors, Maman?"

"And every one of them a nobleman," Jeannette assured her. "Come, *ma chérie*. We can board the ship now."

Unable to speak another word, Aimée nodded. She realized she would have to pass close by Valjean. She wondered how she would manage it. What if he spoke to her? She thought of the kiss they'd shared. Had he supposed she was an innocent little country girl who would believe his lies, who would be so thrilled by his kiss that she would always remember it and the mayflowers? Thinking bitterly that it was probably true, she grew angry. She raised her head and straightened her shoulders defiantly.

Jeannette noted the flash of her daughter's eyes and approved. It would be easier for Aimée to forget this roué if she was angry. She loosened her grip on Aimée's fingers and released them.

The Dessalines began to move forward with the other passengers, and Aimée determinedly kept her eyes straight ahead. The group paused in its steps, and she realized she was momentarily standing almost beside Valjean. Yet she resisted the impulse to glance at him. Even once. She was aware of his stare. She ignored him—or seemed to.

"Aimée," he whispered before she moved away and stepped onto the passageway.

Valjean heard Julia call his name, turned, nodded tolerantly at one more reminder to take care of himself and smiled affectionately at the Carletons. When he entered the passageway, he discovered that Aimée was far ahead of him. Hurriedly stepping on deck, he turned to follow her; but a man whose thinning auburn hair and angry hazel eyes matched Aimée's stood solidly in his path.

"Sir, I don't know what you said or did to so upset my daughter; but I advise you not to follow her," Hilaire said coldly.

"I did nothing . . . We didn't speak . . ." Valjean began.

"Please don't attempt to speak to her later," Hilaire warned, then turned and marched after his family.

Valjean watched Hilaire disappear into the crowd. With

a sigh he turned to stand at the ship's rail. Catching sight of Julia's lace handkerchief waving at him, he lifted his hand to return the gesture; but he waved automatically. Instead of seeing the Carletons, he was again seeing Aimée's expression as she'd passed him on the wharf—angry, hurt, trying not to show it. The memory contrasted sharply with how she'd looked the day she'd ridden out of the forest—carefree, intoxicated with life, her hair like a flame in the wind. It was the way he'd wish her always to be. What had he done to upset her? he wondered, for a moment completely baffled. Suddenly the realization of what she'd concluded struck him; and he was shocked. He vowed that, despite her father, he would find a way to approach her, to make her understand that he, of all people, couldn't spy for the English or French.

Whether Aimée believed his explanation or not, and even if she never spoke to him again, he knew he would never forget that meeting in Montreal's spring forest, the sweetness of her inexperienced kiss, the spirit as bright as her hair that he'd glimpsed for a moment in her eyes.

As during the voyage from Montreal to Boston, the ship operated on a strictly maintained schedule; and there were certain areas on deck where passengers could stroll only at designated times, and other places where passengers were never allowed. Although Hilaire, Jeannette, and Mignon promenaded daily, Aimée remained in the family's compartment except for mealtimes, when she accompanied them to the dining room. She didn't want to be alone on deck and by chance meet Valjean.

Despite her conviction that he'd lied to her, despite her certainty that he was a spy, she was unable to dismiss the memory of the feelings he had evoked in her in the forest near Montreal. She was not at all sure that she would be able to turn him away if he spoke to her again. She was, however, quite sure that she would want to throw herself into his arms if he touched her.

Having heard Jeannette's sparse explanation about Aimée's reaction to Valjean's presence on the wharf, Hilaire was alert for any sign of his appearance on deck so he might prevent Valjean's approaching Aimée. Although Hilaire never spoke to his daughter about the incident, she was always aware of his protection. Jeannette too didn't question Aimée about Valjean. She understood the pain she saw in Aimée's eyes. Mignon regarded her sister's first romantic disappointment with the awe of one who has never experienced even her first kiss, but she also didn't mention it. In the face of her family's discreet support Aimée was comforted; and eventually she felt secure enough to join them on their daily strolls.

One morning, as the Dessalines were on their way to breakfast, Jeannette noticed a small opening in the seam of Hilaire's coat and hurried him back to the cabin so that she could mend it. Aimée and Mignon moved to the rail where they stood, awaiting their parents' return.

"Bonjour, monsieur. Bonjour, madame," Mignon said politely to a passing couple.

The man touched his hat; the woman nodded; they murmured their greetings in English and moved on past the girls without pausing.

"It *is* tiresome to take so long a voyage on a ship where so few people can understand more than a couple of words of our language." Mignon sighed.

"Some of them understand us well enough, but this wretched war makes them feel awkward about talking to us," Aimée remarked.

"But *we* aren't anyone's enemy! I don't understand politics anyway," Mignon protested.

"I think Papa hasn't told us all there is to tell about this war. I think it's a much more serious matter than he's led us to believe," Aimée said.

"But why wouldn't he let us know?" Mignon questioned, becoming alarmed.

"To avoid upsetting us as you're now becoming upset," Aimée replied.

"Dear Papa," Mignon whispered. She fell silent, considering the war in new terms, thinking of their odd position in relation to their fellow passengers. Finally she said wistfully, "Yet, it would be pleasant to pass some conversation with the others, perhaps make some friends."

"There are a few French passengers," Aimée reminded.

"*Oui,* but the ones you've seen—do you want to engage them in conversation?" Mignon returned. Aimée sighed and shook her head. Mignon added, "I do believe that every unpleasant person in Montreal has joined us for this voyage. It's no wonder the British passengers avoid us. They're being cautious lest we too should be some of these riffraff."

Wanting to change the subject, which depressed her, Aimée turned to look at the ocean and commented, "Sailing on the Atlantic certainly is different from sailing on the Saint Lawrence, isn't it? The ocean seems endless, the ship so far away from everything."

"I feel lonely out here and helpless. I've often wondered how the captain can know where we—" Mignon did not complete her statement.

"He uses a sextant and a compass and has charts to guide him, mesdemoiselles," someone behind them said in French.

Immediately recognizing Valjean's voice, Aimée stiffened with tension. Should she ask him to explain why he, an Englishman, had been in Montreal? Should she demand an explanation for his seeming to have two names? Sensing that he stood directly behind her, she wanted only to turn into his arms. How should she behave toward him? she wondered, feeling panicky. Then remembering her mother's admonition to at least maintain her dignity, she was comforted. If her mother could make the same assumption, it must be true that he was a spy for the British. Arranging pride like an armor around her, Aimée regathered her badly shaken composure before she slowly turned to face Valjean.

"We are confident, monsieur, that Captain Mareto will manage to keep us on course," she said coolly.

Valjean silently gazed down at Aimée as he gauged her reaction to him. Her eyes—like sun-warmed brandy in Montreal—now seemed chiseled from amber.

He began cautiously, "I was very surprised to see you on the dock in Boston, Aimée. Are you going to visit relatives in France? Perhaps friends?"

Aimée's chin lifted in an unconscious gesture of defiance. "I don't doubt you were surprised, monsieur. And are you traveling to visit friends in London? Perhaps at Buckingham Palace?"

Hoping to distract Aimée somewhat from her suspicions of him, he quietly reminded her of the day they had met: "Surely it hasn't been so long since we've spoken that you've forgotten my name. Will you call me Valjean as you did in Montreal?"

"I'm not sure that is your name, monsieur. I heard you called by another name in Boston," she replied shortly.

"I am, as I told you, Valjean d'Auvergne," he answered patiently. "Will you allow me to explain? I'm not what you're thinking, though you have a right to assume what you have."

"Monsieur d'Auvergne or Mr. Kendall—whoever you are—I do not associate with imposters any more than I associate with spies."

"I'm neither, Aimée," he denied. He looked at Mignon, who was staring at him as if enthralled by the situation. "Mademoiselle, will you excuse us for a few moments so that we can discuss a private matter?" he asked.

Mignon's blue eyes looked helplessly from Valjean to her sister. She thought Aimée should hear him out, but Aimée didn't seem to want her advice, nor did she even glance at Mignon to signal her to leave them. Mignon couldn't remember when she'd last seen Aimée so disconcerted yet anxious not to show it.

"Monsieur, an honest man doesn't need two names, using one or another at his convenience," Aimée said coldly.

Valjean's hand touched hers, and she quickly stepped back, feeling as if a lightning bolt had shot through her. But his hand had just as quickly grasped hers. She lowered her eyes to gaze at the tanned fingers covering hers, unable for a moment to think of anything but his touch—and not daring to lift her gaze for fear that she would burst into tears from the turmoil of her emotions.

"If you don't want to hear the truth, Aimée, I can't force you to listen." His voice, coming closer, was soft.

Upon realizing he'd bent toward her, she discovered she could hardly breathe. She wondered how she could stand on such shaking legs.

"I won't disturb you again during this voyage, Aimée," Valjean said quietly. "I hope we'll meet in the future on a day when you're willing to listen." He lifted her hand to his lips, and her eyes helplessly followed the gesture to look up into his face as he added, "But if we never meet again, *ma petite amie,* I know I shall never forget you." He brushed his lips to her fingers, then released her hand, turned, and walked quickly away, leaving the girls staring after him.

Valjean kept his word. There were several times when Aimée saw him standing on deck; but although he was always alone, he never approached her. Twice he noticed her staring at him across the distance. He looked at her for a long moment, his eyes initially dark as storm clouds, gradually relighting with their peculiar silvery gleam until they regained the smoky, dappled look she remembered from Montreal. But each time, he merely nodded politely, then glanced away; and each time, her heart leaped in her breast, making her wonder if it had beaten even once since the time she'd last seen him.

Aimée refused to answer Mignon's gentle, though persistent questions; but she couldn't deafen her ears to her sister's observations about how fascinating Valjean's eyes were, how tall and attractive he was, how politely he spoke, and how well he dressed. Although Aimée's replies were designed to dampen Mignon's enthusiasm, every night she dreamed about a shaded path perfumed by mayflowers and pine where moccasined feet moved lightly and surely beside hers; about a lean, hard body clad in buttery, sun-warmed doeskin pressed against hers during a kiss that made her feel as if the crystal lightning behind his eyes had reached out to fill her being and bind her to him.

Weeks later the ship docked at Le Havre on France's craggy west coast. As the Dessalines disembarked, Aimée couldn't restrain herself from glancing furtively at the other passengers in the hope of having one last glimpse of

Valjean; but he was nowhere in sight. Hilaire and Jeannette pretended not to notice Aimée's distraction as the family boarded the coach Hilaire's brother had sent to await their arrival at Le Havre and carry them to Paris.

As the coach passed through the French countryside, Aimée stared out at the forests, rich with the tints of autumn, but saw none of their beauty. She was blind to the farmlands harvested of wheat and prepared for winter. Even the scent of the orchards, sweet with ripe apples, was lost to her. The coach stopped at intervals to rest the horses and give a few minutes of leisure to the passengers. At such times Aimée would step out, drawing her shawl closer in the crisp autumn air; she would tell herself again and again that Valjean d'Auvergne was Vale Kendall, a spy who had amused himself with her naïveté that afternoon in Montreal, deceiving her with romantic pledges. At the inns where the Dessalines spent two nights, she would fall asleep silently repeating her litany of denial, though her stubborn heart refused to accept it.

Memories of their encounter on the deck of the *Santa Luisa* plagued her. He had denied that he was a spy; he had insisted that he could explain why he had two names; and this worried her. Perhaps she'd been unjust and, in refusing to listen to him, had lost a love as precious as the dreams that had shaped her idea of love. Frightened now by the pain rising inside her—would she be able to bear it—she tried again to think of him as a spy. Her confusion made her angry, and she transferred her anger to him. *Why* did he have to be so mysterious? Why did he have to be so complicated? The mixture of grief and anger made Aimée grimly silent during the days.

On the last evening of their overland journey, as the coach crossed a series of rocky ridges that formed the lip of the basin Paris had sprung from, Aimée stared at the rain streaming down the window. Whatever Valjean was, she told herself, he'd passed out of her life—she must be sensible and forget him. A flash of lightning momentarily lit the Seine, which flowed darkly beside the road; and she shivered from the damp that invaded her bones. Murmuring gratefully as her mother tucked the lap robe more closely around her ankles, Aimée closed her eyes and leaned back against the seat. She remembered Jeannette's reassuring words: In Paris she would have fifty suitors—all handsome, all wealthy, all noble. But, she wondered wearily, could even such a crowd of suitors make her forget one British spy? She reminded herself that Valjean—Vale Kendall, as she would prefer to think of him—was having a pleasant voyage to England. Did he have friends in London who would greet him—perhaps a girl?

Aimée had no way of knowing Valjean had boarded one of the smaller boats that traversed the Seine between Le Havre and Paris, and was at that moment settling himself at a table in a restaurant in the heart of the city.

Chapter 4

"*Charmantes! Quelles jolies filles! Je suis enchanté, enchanté.*" Victoire Dessaline exclaimed as Aimée and Mignon followed their parents into the foyer.

Aimée handed her mist-dampened cape to a waiting servant and smiled at her aunt's immediate warm embrace. "Thank you, Aunt Victoire," she murmured against a cluster of golden curls on a perfumed shoulder.

Victoire drew away, and Aimée found herself looking into a pair of blue-green eyes that sparkled like the ocean on a sunny day. "Hilaire, no one would mistake this young lady's parentage," Victoire flung over her shoulder as she continued to gaze at Aimée. "No one could deny that that auburn hair or these eyes are those of a Dessaline."

While Victoire inspected Aimée with a curious, but kindly air, Aimée made her own appraisal of this aunt she had not met until now. Victoire was a small woman whose dainty features were animated with a vivacity that seemed to center in eyes as shrewdly intelligent as they were caring.

When Victoire moved away to greet Mignon and comment on her charm, Antoine took Aimée's shoulders gently in his hands, bent, and kissed her cheeks, murmuring his welcome. Hilaire's brother also had the Dessalines' maple-colored eyes, now glazed with tears; but his hair was brown and liberally streaked with gray.

Claude, their son, was probably Marcel's age, Aimée guessed. Although he approached slowly, he took her hand with a practiced grace that told Aimée he wasn't at all shy. Tall and slender, casually, but elegantly dressed, he was, Aimée guessed, the perfect example of a wealthy

Parisian, though his auburn hair was unpowdered. His blue-green eyes were warm with compliments as he kissed Aimée's hand and murmured, "It's a pity you and I are of such close blood, *chérie*."

Aimée smiled in answer, pleased to be found attractive by someone she guessed to be successful with women far more fashionable than her. Aimée's first glance at her aunt had made her feel uncomfortably outmoded.

"But all of you must be hungry and weary." Victoire suddenly remembered. "I have so many questions to ask, so many plans to tell you about, I've been thoughtless." She turned to Jeannette. "Would you like to have a little supper while we talk and the maids put away your baggage? Afterwards, you can all go up to your rooms for an uninterrupted night's rest. *Oui?* What would you wish?" she asked solicitously.

"I think your suggestion is best," Jeannette agreed. "But perhaps we could rinse our hands?"

"Oh, *mais oui!*" Victoire exclaimed. Turning to a maid, she directed, "Show the ladies to my sitting room." Then she took Jeannette's hand and explained, "I keep a basin and towels for my own use there so I needn't climb the stairs so often. Germaine will bring all you need to make yourselves more comfortable while I see what the cook can arrange for your supper."

Jeannette thanked her sister-in-law for her trouble. Then she and her daughters followed the maid down a carpeted hall to a room cozily lit by a fire glimmering on the hearth. While the maid lit several candles, Aimée looked over the damask-covered walls and the Aubusson carpet, wondering at her uncle's wealth. The basin she rinsed her hands in was of the finest gold-edged porcelain, so thin she feared the smallest splash would crack it. The towel the stern-faced Germaine handed her was of the softest linen edged with creamy lace. A standing mirror only confirmed her previous decision that her gown, which she'd worn for today's arrival because it was one of her favorites, was out of fashion. She felt very humble indeed, standing before the reflected backdrop of fragile white and gold furniture and graceful brocade drapes.

Although the maid, Germaine, wore a dour expression, her attitude was very solicitous and her hands efficient. She had helped the three women tidy their hair, and so, when Aimée entered the salon, she felt a bit more comfortable. Victoire again greeted them warmly, inviting them to seat themselves at the small table she'd had arranged.

"We couldn't know quite which day you'd arrive, and it was difficult to plan a meal to greet you. The cook could only offer some soup, cold sliced meat, and fruit," Victoire apologized.

"Such light fare will be best at this late hour, Victoire," Jeannette answered agreeably. "Our evening meal at home always is simple anyway."

Although Aimée's appetite had diminished to nearly nothing ever since she'd seen Valjean on the wharf in Boston, she found the hot soup very welcome. She nibbled at a slice of chicken, ate a few grapes, then gratefully turned to her steaming cup of tea.

Victoir and Antoine asked about Marcel and had a thousand questions about life in Montreal. Their comments about the war with England confirmed Aimée's suspicions that Hilaire had kept most of the bad news from his daughters. That Marcel knew the truth was unquestionably tied in with his decision to stay in Montreal. Aimée wondered if her brother was, after all, enamored of Lisolette or if he'd only claimed to be to give him an excuse to stay home and manage the business.

When Hilaire congratulated his brother on his imminent appointment to court as *fourreur du roi*, Aimée once again felt a pang that her own father wasn't to be similarly honored—a sentiment Antoine himself echoed, acknowledging that the garments his business produced wouldn't be so successful but for Hilaire's exquisite furs.

Finally Victoire controlled her enthusiasm for conversation and reminded them that they all must go to bed so they could be fresh for the activities she had planned for the next day. The clothes Victoire had ordered at Hilaire and Jeannette's written direction had been ready to be fitted for a week; and because the royal appointment was scheduled in just another week, if any alterations were to be made, they must be done immediately.

Aimée followed another maid, Danielle, to the room adjoining Mignon's, which had been prepared for her. Head spinning with excitement and weariness, she dismissed Danielle and undressed herself. After she'd let down her hair, she sat silently for a moment at her dressing table dreaming about her new wardrobe. A soft tapping at the door aroused her; and putting on a dressing gown, she then went to open it.

Anticipating Mignon, she was surprised to see Claude standing in the hall.

"I know this isn't the hour a gentleman calls on a lady," he whispered apologetically, "but I brought you a cup of hot chocolate."

Aimée stepped back to allow him entrance, though she wondered at the propriety of a midnight visit to her room, even by her cousin.

Claude glanced appreciatively, though not lingeringly, at the fit of her dressing gown, crossed the room, and went directly to the small table beside the bed. He turned to see Aimée's uneasy expression, smiled, and put the steaming cup on the table.

"I thought you might find it difficult to sleep after all the excitement, and hot chocolate might soothe you," he explained. "I'm putting it here; so after I've left, you can drink it while you're in bed."

"That's very thoughtful of you, Claude," she managed to say, though her blush at his presence had not faded.

"It's no trouble, *chérie*," he answered lightly as he approached the door. "I've had an arrangement with the cook since I was a little boy. He preferred to teach me how to make a decent cup of chocolate rather than be roused in the middle of the night to make it for me."

Claude opened the door, glanced carefully into the corridor, then moved closer to brush her cheek with his lips. "Do stop being so wary of me, Cousin Aimée. Although I admit I regret our close blood ties, I'm resigned to them. I just will enjoy watching what you'll do with the crowd of admirers who will shortly pursue you." He squeezed her hand. "If my lovely little cousin ever needs advice about any of them or their intentions, I hope she'll feel she can ask me." He closed the door softly behind him.

Aimée turned to go thoughtfully to her bed. As she sipped her chocolate she began for the first time seriously to hope that Paris would distract her from Valjean and that she would eventually forget him. But after she'd blown out her candle, she closed her eyes only to see Valjean's face etched on the inside of their lids.

Opening her eyes again, she remembered how he had watched her through the distance on the deck of the *Santa Luisa,* the ocean wind ruffling his hair which shone with gold in the sun; his eyes, narrowed and thoughtful, had seemed to penetrate her aloofness and perceive the emotion inflaming her.

An *amourette,* a romantic girl's first encounter, she knew older and more sophisticated women would call it. Yet, she felt it must be more than that. She couldn't believe a mere infatuation would so devastate a person.

Angry that Valjean could affect her so strongly even in his absence, she rearranged her pillows and, drawing the coverlet up to her chin, hissed into the darkness, "You won't haunt me forever, you rogue. Soon I'll have so many beaux your memory will mean nothing. Maman, Aunt Victoire, and even Claude have predicted that my admirers will be legion!"

Then she determinedly shut her eyes and concentrated on the sound of the rain that was again pattering on the windows.

The rain stopped before dawn; and by the time Josette came to awaken Aimée the windows were bright with sun, giving the elegant white and gold room a coziness that cheered her while she dressed.

After a breakfast of *croissants* still warm and fragrant from the oven, Victoire tactfully hurried her guests into their cloaks so they could get to the *couturière*'s without delay.

Aimée listened to her aunt and mother's conversation with half an ear as she absorbed the sights of the Paris streets. The rain had cleansed the city, and the crisp autumn air was clear and bright. As the carriage passed a small park Aimée smiled to see children playing with a ball near their *gardiennes*. People were sitting in the sun conversing and tossing bits of old bread to the pigeons. A few russet leaves floated to the yellowing lawn. Chrysanthemums and asters were bright splashes of yellow and orange against the weathered wood of a flower stall. Strolling ladies in fashionable dome-shaped skirts and capes of soft cashmere were followed by servants whose baskets were filling with purchases. A few early customers sat sipping steaming coffee or chocolate in the cafés.

When the carriage came to a halt, Aimée looked at the *couturière*'s shop with the chagrin of a woman who knows in advance she's dressed like a bumpkin. Her opinion was confirmed when the proprietress appeared from between the draperies separating the dressing rooms from the front portion of the store. The appearance of this woman, Madame Perrault, was a perfect contrast to her own. But Madame Perrault, after one glance at her customers' apparel, made no disparaging remarks, nor did she even indicate with a look her disapproval of their clothes. As soon as she learned they were the women her seamstresses had been working so industriously for, she sent an assistant scurrying to brew tea and ushered them into the fitting rooms.

Aimée forgot her troubles as soon as she saw the gowns Victoire had chosen with no more to guide her than a list of measurements and descriptions of their complexions.

Cognac satin embroidered with burgundy flower motifs, deep blue velvet trimmed with black lace, creamy silk with pale pink ruffles, peach brocade, rose taffeta, ivory batiste, fawn cashmere, deep gold serge, and emerald worsted wool. Artificial flowers, ribbons, bows, feathers, tassels, and braids. Ecru ruched lace. Reembroidered fichus. Petticoats, chemises, and *paniers*. Dainty high-heeled silk shoes, parasols, hats, and fans to match each gown.

Scarcely able to breathe in the tightly laced corset Madame Perrault had insisted she wear as she tried on the gowns, Aimée spoke very little, only nodding happily each time Victoire asked her opinion.

When the assistant brought out the formal gown Aimée would wear to the royal court and the ball that was to follow, she could say nothing. She was stunned by the vision of herself in the mirror as Madame Perrault personally fastened the last of the gown's hooks. It was pale ice-green brocade embroidered with ivory and soft cocoa, its overskirt split to reveal a cascade of ivory lace ruffles that echoed the lace trimming the décolletage and dripping from the elbow-length sleeves.

She was distracted only by Mignon's delighted exclamations from the next room. Then her sister burst in, too excited about her own ball gown to tap on the door or call out. Aimée stared at Mignon's light blue silk embroidered with pale yellow and pink. The hem, picked up with yellow ribbons at intervals, revealed pink lace flounces like those at her neck and sleeves.

"*Mes belles,* no longer my babies," Jeannette whispered, blinking away tears.

"Do you approve of the gowns?" Victoire asked anxiously.

"*Oui, oui,* your choices are superb," Jeannette quickly answered, then inquired, "But, girls, do *you* like them?"

"Maman, Aunt Victoire, they're more beautiful than I could have dreamed!" Mignon cried, turning so quickly from Aimée that her wide skirt swept the pins from the fitter's hands.

Aimée, unable to take her eyes from the image in her mirror, answered that the gown was exquisite. She was wondering what Valjean would have thought to see her in this gown.

"Imagine how beautiful they'll look after their hair is formally arranged and powdered. Perhaps some small flowers or even a string of pearls could be twined in their hair," Victoire was saying behind Aimée.

"Yes, they'll be beautiful," Jeannette answered softly, still amazed to see the lovely young women her children had become.

Aimée tried to imagine her hair dressed with powder

and pearls and again wished Valjean could see her dressed
for a court ball. Then, remembering her resolution to put
all thoughts of him from her mind, she was annoyed at
herself. She tried to imagine how she'd behave at court, at
the ball afterwards. She found that the prospect of
mingling with noblemen and ministers intimidated her,
while competing with court beauties frightened her. In
such a polished, witty company she was sure she could
only hope to be ignored. As humiliating as that would be,
it was preferable to being noticed for a faux pas and la-
beled a colonial bumpkin.

Madame Perrault unhooked the gown and, with the
help of two assistants, lifted it from Aimée's shoulders.
Aimée managed to smile at her mother and aunt, though
she now was sure their compliments were heavily influ-
enced by love—not a realistic view of how unpolished in
manner, how provincial, a girl from Montreal really was.

She was still thinking such thoughts when, dressed in an
exquisitely fashioned lavender gown with a matching cashmere cape, she silently took Mignon's hand and followed
Jeannette and Victoire out of the shop. Madame Perrault's
enthusiastic promises to have the still-unfinished gowns
ready within the next few days seemed to Aimée like the
fading echoes of a crumbling dream.

Aimée was so immersed in her private thoughts as the
carriage passed through the streets that she didn't notice
that male eyes, attracted by the bright flare of her unpowdered *coiffure*, lingered; and turning heads followed the
progress of the carriage. That she was untalkative aroused
neither her mother's nor her sister's concern. Her habit of
lapsing into silence while she daydreamed was well known
to them, and the lavish new wardrobe was enough to be-
muse any girl.

Later, at lunch, affected by both the restaurant's gay at-
mosphere and the large glass of wine she had been served,
Aimée felt her moodiness dissolve. She forgot her previous
misgivings as she listened to the plans Victoire had made
for them. Suddenly she became aware of someone standing beside her chair.

A voice above her said, "Madame Dessaline, how generous it was of you to delight the eyes of every gentleman in this room by bringing so many lovely companions."

Aimée looked up to see a man standing at her side. Although he'd spoken to Victoire, his brown eyes were fixed on Aimée for the moment, then discreetly moved to the others, including them in the compliment.

"Ah, it's the duc de Mirabeau. Your Grace, it's always such a pleasure to meet you," Victoire replied. "Please allow me to introduce my sister-in-law, Madame Dessaline, and her daughters, Aimée and Mignon. They arrived only last night from Montreal."

"Enchanté, enchanté," de Mirabeau said as his dark eyes traveled to each face, again lingering on Aimée. "I've been told and so, of course, having never been to the colonies, believed that they were populated mostly by savages and wild beasts, that the land is cold and harsh; but I see now I must revise my opinion. Such exquisite blossoms could not possibly survive in so hostile a climate." He bent toward Aimée, taking her hand in his, and inquired, "And you, mademoiselle, are Aimée or Mignon?"

"I'm Aimée, Your Grace," she replied, then added, "Montreal is far from uncivilized. Even roses bloom in our garden." She fell silent, wondering if she'd spoken too boldly, realizing that the wine had dissipated her normal reserve.

The corners of the duke's eyes crinkled with amusement. "I suspect you, mademoiselle, are not a rose but perhaps a tiger lily," he returned. As he lifted her hand to brush his lips to her fingers, he murmured, "But then I have a preference for wild flowers." He straightened, relinquished Aimée's hand, and turned to Mignon. Raising his voice so the others could again hear him, he smiled and lifted her fingers to his lips. "And you're Mignon, surely a rose as delicate as your name." He kissed Jeannette's and Victoire's hands in turn, complimenting them as well.

"Tell me, Your Grace, will you be attending the ballet tonight?" Victoire inquired. To his negative reply she asked, "Then what of the premiere of Monsieur Molière's play tomorrow evening?"

Again he shook his head. "Non, Madame Dessaline, I

regret . . ." He glanced at Aimée and amended, "I especially now regret I must spend the next few days at my *château* near Fontainebleau. A small problem, but one which I must personally look into," he apologized.

"Will we not have your company at my husband's appointment and the ball to follow?" Victoire inquired anxiously.

"But of course. I would—be disappointed indeed if I missed such an occasion," he assured her. He took a step backward. "And now, beautiful ladies, I must take my leave if I'm to attend to Fontainebleau's problem and return without delay." Again he looked directly at Aimée as he added, "It has been my very great pleasure to meet your enchanting sister-in-law and her daughters. *Au revoir, mesdames et mesdemoiselles.*"

After he'd turned away, Mignon breathed, "How exciting to meet a real duke!"

"He's a very charming man and quite attractive," Jeannette observed. Having noticed the duke's interest in Aimée, she cautiously added, "The duchesse de Mirabeau must be in a quandary preparing for a royal ball while having to manage two estates."

"He has more than two estates, but there is no duchesse de Mirabeau. The housekeepers the duke employs remain at each of his estates, so they always are very well managed," Victoire quickly answered. She knew what Jeannette was thinking. "It's a pity, is it not, that so handsome a man remains unwed even though he's nearly thirty years old?"

"A man like that sometimes doesn't marry out of choice," Jeannette answered dryly.

"Oh, it's true enough that he's very successful with the ladies of the court; but I don't think he's an incorrigible carouser," Victoire said.

Aimée, who faced the direction the duke had taken, watched him pause for a moment at another table to greet a distinguished-looking man. The duke turned as he conversed so he could look at Aimée. Her heart pattered faster at his attention, though she managed to return his gaze without blushing. He wasn't as tall as Valjean, she noticed;

but he moved with the grace of a man who was skillful at fencing and who, perhaps, rode daily. His abundant hair had been drawn back in a queue and powdered, but she could see from his brows and lashes that he was brunette. His features were strong and even; and his manners, though charming, weren't foppish. She appraised his figure, clad in a coat of dark green serge and clinging buff breeches, as he resumed moving toward the door. He seemed to lack none of the attributes she found attractive in men, she decided. The duke would be a very appealing companion. Perhaps he could even distract her from Valjean. Was he, she wondered, the sort of man who, by the time he returned to Paris, would have forgotten a girl like her? She hoped not.

Victoire, watching Aimée's eyes with interest, finally said, "If you've all finished your lunch, we should be on our way. Before we return home, I must visit Versailles to receive some final instructions for Antoine's appointment ceremony."

Their attention was immediately captured.

"Versailles?" Aimée breathed.

"The palace?" echoed Mignon.

"Yes, my dears, the palace," Victoire replied with a smile.

The carriage traveled up the avenue de Paris, past even the place d'Armes. Aimée stared at the lawns, green as if it were midsummer, the precisely shaped shrubbery and trees, and the graceful fountains. She was breathless when the carriage finally stopped just before the marble courtyard. How could she possibly associate with the kind of people who walked this way freely and without awe—she who was so intimidated by its grandeur? Staring up at the palace, she could almost feel the presence of the king's power. How could *she* attend a ball where King Louis XV might watch her dance?

"You may step out and enjoy the view of the gardens while I'm gone," Victoire advised as she alighted from the carriage.

"Step down? Truly?" Aimée breathed.

"His Majesty is pleased when his subjects appreciate the beauty here," Victoire answered. "I won't be long, so you'd best not dally if you wish to walk around a bit."

"Maman, may I?" Aimée begged. When Jeannette nodded, Aimée turned to her sister. "Will you come with me?" she invited.

Mignon shook her head. *"Non,* Aimèe. I think I would faint," she whispered in awe.

"I too am a bit light-headed," Aimée admitted, "but I'll go anyway. It's an opportunity I would never forgive myself for missing."

After the footman had helped Aimée alight, she turned to gaze at the expanse of rolling lawns separated into patterns by precisely clipped hedges. Suddenly she was hesitant; but she had already told Mignon she would explore, and she didn't intend to get back into the carriage immediately like a coward. Taking a deep breath, she began purposefully forward. Her resolve carried her only beyond the first row of bushes. All of the paths were bordered by tall, carefully clipped hedges that were identical. Twenty paces and she was sure she'd get lost. She sought out a bench where she could sit and gaze at the lawns without venturing farther, and where her mother and sister wouldn't see her lack of progress. She sat down to gaze at the formal gardens and dream of what it would be like to attend a ball at Versailles. Again, she was intimidated and wondered how she would manage it.

Aimée fervently wished that, like Marcel, she had elected to remain in Montreal. War or no, she wanted desperately to be at that moment riding Brandy through a sunlit meadow or walking along a shaded avenue beneath her familiar, beloved pines, listening to the music of the boughs in the wind.

"Bonjour, mademoiselle."

Rigid with fear that she'd encroached on some area forbidden to commoners, Aimée turned and saw not a guard ready to warn her away but a man dressed in hunting clothes, dusty from his ride, his unpowdered hair falling loose, its golden strands tangled. She breathed a sigh of relief and replied, *"Bonjour,* monsieur."

King Louis's dark eyes flickered with surprise. Almost immediately he realized she was a stranger to Versailles and hadn't recognized him. His surprise was replaced by humor. "Are you awaiting the arrival of a friend, or perhaps you have an appointment with someone?" he inquired, then added impulsively, "Or would you like to be directed to Parc aux Cerfs?"

Aimée's face registered her shock. She'd heard of the Château of Deer where the king amused himself with paramours. "Monsieur, are you poking fun at me?" she demanded.

"The ladies who visit Parc aux Cerfs don't usually consider the experience a joke, nor have I heard they feel insulted," Louis answered coolly, then asked, "May I share this bench with you, mademoiselle? I've been hunting and am weary."

Aimée nodded and gathered together the folds of her wide skirt to make a place for him to sit. She regarded him curiously for a moment before saying, "I am Mademoiselle Aimée Dessaline, monsieur."

"Enchanté," the hunter replied.

She waited for him to introduce himself; but when he remained silent, she inquired, "May I ask your name, monsieur?"

Instead of answering her question, he smiled engagingly and said, "Forgive my previous remark, Mademoiselle Dessaline. Let us resume our conversation." Noting the wariness that entered her eyes, he added, "Let us not speak of the king and all the gossip one hears about him, however." He continued amiably, "What are you doing here, mademoiselle? Are you simply enjoying the view? Do you find pleasure in the garden?"

"The garden, the palace, is grander than I'd imagined, monsieur," she replied, wondering why he seemed to fear identifying himself. "I'm overwhelmed by its beauty. It's glorious."

The hunter seemed pleased by her praise. "You're just here to admire the accomplishments of the royal gardeners?" he asked.

Aimée, who had decided the man might be afraid she would report his dawdling in the garden, turned to address the hunter. "I'm waiting for my aunt Victoire to return to our carriage, which is just beyond this hedge."

His eyes warmed with understanding. "You wanted to see the garden but feared losing your way if you went farther?"

Aimée blushed with embarrassment and nodded. "I didn't want to return to the carriage too soon and let my sister know I was as great a coward as she after I'd bragged I wasn't afraid."

The hunter glanced at the hedge, as though his eyes could pierce the branches and see the waiting carriage. He lowered his voice conspiratorially, "Your aunt Victoire's business in the palace—what is it?"

"Uncle Antoine is to be appointed *fourreur du roi* next week. Aunt Victoire needed to know some details about the ceremony," she explained. "You see, then, I'm not here because I'm significant in any way."

The hunter's eyes lowered thoughtfully, his long lashes catching gold lights from the sun. "Your own significance, I would think, is considerable," he commented.

Thinking he'd misunderstood her meaning and wanting to reassure him that she would carry no tales to cause him trouble, Aimée shook her head. "My family is from Montreal; and my father, who supplies the furs Uncle Antoine uses in his creations, isn't even of enough importance for the king to honor like Uncle Antoine; so I suspect I'm of even less significance, monsieur."

"You feel that your father is being slighted, then?" he asked curiously.

Aimée felt her old pang of anger that her father wouldn't be honored like Antoine and answered sharply, "*Oui.* If it were not for my father's exquisite furs, my uncle's designs would be less noted." She quickly added, "It isn't that my uncle isn't talented. It's the two of them together, do you see?"

"*Oui.* I do understand," the hunter said thoughtfully,

then suggested, "Perhaps the king isn't aware of this, mademoiselle."

"Although I'm sure he has many matters on his mind more important to the realm than this, yet it is a matter of justice," she replied adamantly.

"You seem to have a low opinion of the king, mademoiselle," the hunter observed. "Perhaps, if this oversight was corrected, your opinion would be improved?"

"Infinitely improved," she answered confidently. "But how could that happen? *Non*, it will not. I won't even hope for it." Her head drooped as she thought again of her father. Without realizing it, she sighed audibly.

"Come, now. Don't be so sad. It isn't suitable for such a charming girl to be so unhappily disposed," Louis said. His fingers under her chin coaxed her to look up at him. He was silent a moment, observing her features carefully, as if memorizing them. Noticing her growing self-consciousness, he smiled and removed his hand. "I must take note of your face, mademoiselle, if I would recognize you later. When you return to the palace for the ceremonies and the ball, you will undoubtedly have that firebrand of hair powdered like all the rest of the court. I won't be able to pick you out easily from the others."

Aimée was perplexed. How could a simple huntsman expect to attend such an elite function? Before she could question him, he got to his feet.

"I must leave you now, mademoiselle. I have something I must attend to," he said abruptly, as if he'd just remembered a task and it was overdue. *"Au revoir."* He turned on his heel and quickly walked down the path.

She watched him recede in the distance, still puzzling at his strange remarks. Realizing he had never told her his name, she wondered if he might be a poacher. She saw him turn onto an intersecting lane, amazed at his obvious familiarity with the maze of paths concealed by the tall hedges.

Aimée returned to the carriage just as Victoire was approaching; and Mignon had so many questions to ask her aunt about the inside of Versailles and the upcoming ceremony that everyone momentarily forgot that Aimée had strolled in the garden. Aimée never mentioned the huntsman. She had found him and their conversation more than a little mystifying; but she didn't want to discuss the incident.

When they arrived home, Victoire found a small stack of calling cards left for both Aimée and Mignon by various gentlemen who had seen the girls traveling about town that day. The girls were thrilled to learn they'd been noticed and admired by so many men, and Aimée, no longer preoccupied with the huntsman, was particularly excited to find the duc de Mirabeau's name engraved on one of her cards. Even Germaine's habitually stern expression didn't dampen Aimée's happiness when the maid gave her the little bunch of forget-me-nots that had been delivered with the card.

Chapter 5

Entering the ballroom at Versailles was a dazzling experience—like stepping into the shimmering heart of a yellow diamond set in gold filigree—Aimée thought as she gazed at the splendor of the room.

The vaulted ceiling, divided into sections by gilt bands, was adorned with richly burnished paintings. The molding under the ceiling was a wide festoon of delicate designs embellished at each corner by an enlarged reproduction of the king's crest, gold fleurs-de-lis on deep blue, the whole intricately framed. At intervals the white marble walls held great ovals carved with scenes of France's glory, the ovals wreathed by ornate gold frames topped by hovering gilded angels. Each of the immense gold-encrusted chandeliers held perhaps twenty to thirty large tapers, ornamented with innumerable crystal prisms, which multiplied the light until even the marble surface of the ballroom floor blazed with the reflections of countless shimmering flames. Aimée could well understand how the title "Sun King," had been coined.

Aimée assumed that she and her family had been ushered to the front of the ballroom, near where the royal chairs had been placed, because Hilaire was so closely related to Antoine. She often glanced self-consciously at the lords and ladies of the court who stood farther from the king's seat than they. At the same time she surreptitiously searched the crowd for the duc de Mirabeau.

Aimée had thought that her pale green gown was fabulously extravagant with its delicate embroidery and yards of fragile lace; but as she compared it to the gowns of the ladies of the court, she could see that her own dress was average. She wondered how the slender bodies of those women could bear the weight of such ostentatious gowns. Her dress was so heavy that she wasn't sure she could manage to lift a foot to dance. Her waist was so pinched by her corset that she'd already decided she couldn't possibly taste a morsel of the lavish buffet she'd heard was served at such occasions.

The entire volume of Aimée's waist-length hair had been piled in coils atop her head, with only three locks gracefully descending to her shoulder and a few wisps turned into curls falling over her ears. Pale green silk leaves had been twined at the base of her locks. She'd thought the arrangement of her powdered hair elaborate in the extreme—she and Mignon had teased each other about all their coiffures after the hairdresser had left; but the towering arrangements worn by the other women made their own hairdos seem conservative. Mignon had already tugged at Aimée's fingers a dozen times to draw her sister's attention to fantastic coiffures that held jewels, ribbons, feathers, stuffed birds, and more flowers than their garden in Montreal. The only woman who wore as relatively simple a coiffure as the Dessalines' was the notorious Madame de Pompadour.

In the roomful of elegantly powdered heads the former Jeanne Antoinette Poisson's dark blond hair was conspicuous. King Louis's favorite mistress was pretty, though not beautiful, Aimée thought. There was an air of confidence about her, which seemed to bear out the rumors that her scepterless hand held more power than Queen Marie's. La Pompadour wore a pale blue-gray gown of heavy satin and cascading white lace embellished with rose ribbons. Her complexion was exquisite but, to Aimée's mind, so translucent as to make her wonder if Madame de Pompadour had some lingering weakness.

Aimée couldn't help but speculate what the king looked like; as the Dessalines had been escorted through the palace to the ballroom, she'd seen a number of paintings of the various Bourbons but none of Louis XV.

Aimée was aroused from her thoughts by the signal that the royal couple were ready to enter the room; and like the other women, she sank into so deep a curtsey that her wide skirt became a pool of shimmering silk on the floor. Although her head was lowered, her upraised eyes swept the crowd of nobles once again. Nowhere among the deeply bowing men did she see the duc de Mirabeau.

The Dessalines were so near to where the king and queen passed that Aimée, having to keep her head lowered, could only raise her eyes high enough to see the skirt of the monarch's velvet robe, which was embroidered with fleurs-de-lis and bordered with ermine. After he'd seated himself and taken his gold staff in hand, the company straightened from their bows and rose from their curtseys with a rush of whispering satin and brocade.

Queen Marie's hair was simply arranged to allow for her coronet; and her dark purple gown was richly sewn with great teardrop pearls and other jewels. Her magnificent royal robe, which, like the king's, was velvet and trimmed with ermine, had an elaborate train that swirled around the hem of her gown to trail down the dais step.

Aimée turned her attention to the king. Louis's velvet robe consisted of an independent front panel, then became a sort of cape in the back, ending in a long elaborate train. A wide ermine collar covered his shoulders and fell midway down his chest. Through the slits in the velvet robe she glimpsed a slender body clad in gold-embroidered satin. His coat sleeves were widened like bells at his forearms to make room for the tiers of white lace ruffles that poured out of them. His hair, like the queen's, was carefully coiffed and powdered. Aimée's own neck ached as she thought of the weight of the jewel-encrusted crown his head bore.

While Queen Marie might once have been pretty, now Her Majesty's countenance reminded Aimée of an old painting; it lacked warmth, as if she were not used to smiling. The king, on the other hand, seemed as if he might smile at any moment. His eyes were brown, set well apart; and his mouth was excellently proportioned, though it gave warning of his sensuality. Aimée decided that while the queen's features held the expression of an experienced chaperone, the king's face seemed more inclined to tolerance. He did appear familiar in some way, and she wondered whom he resembled. Her thoughts were interrupted by a page's call for Antoine Dessaline to approach the thrones.

As Aimée watched her uncle step forward her heart warmed with sympathy. How nervous he was—the stiffness of his steps and the faint shine of his forehead told her that. When the page called for Hilaire Dessaline to approach the royal couple, Aimée's eyes widened, and her lips parted in shock. She turned slowly to look at her parents.

Jeannette was as pale as a person about to faint. Aimée was grateful to see that Claude, standing between Victoire and Jeannette, had quickly slid an arm around each woman's waist. Although Jeannette remained pale, Aimée saw her mother's brilliant smile break through her shock; and she heard Jeannette whisper hastily to her husband that he must not keep the king waiting on her account. Only then did Hilaire leave his wife's side; and Aimée's heart swelled with pride as she watched him approach the thrones. Unlike his brother, he seemed completely at ease. His manner was dignified, though his face was lit with pleasure. His bow was faultless.

King Louis gestured for the two men to approach more closely; and while Aimée admired her father's quiet poise as he faced the king, she felt Mignon's hand slip into hers. Giving her sister a sideways glance, Aimée smiled happily. So excited as she watched her father receive his appointment of *pelletier du roi,* she heard neither what the king said nor Hilaire's reply.

Aimée wondered at her father's seemingly impromptu appointment. Who could have told King Louis about her father's part in supplying the royal furs? Had Aunt Victoire mentioned it to someone in the palace when she'd gone there for final instructions about the ceremony? *Non,* Aimée decided. Uncle Antoine was wealthy; but neither he nor Aunt Victoire had the blood, or the position in court, to broach that subject. It would have seemed as much like a complaint as a suggestion. Suddenly she remembered her conversation with the huntsman. Was it possible, she wondered, that the man was a nobleman close to the king? And she'd assumed he was a poacher, she reminded herself, chagrined. If he was attending the ball, she hoped she might speak to him sometime during the evening and thank him for his help—as well as apologize if she'd behaved impudently toward him.

Aimée saw the king turn to one of his courtiers and whisper in his ear. The courtier promptly left the king's side and approached the combined Dessaline families to speak softly to Jeannette and Victoire. Mignon, who was standing close enough to hear his words, flashed Aimée a surprised look. Aimée was mystified at the courtier's purpose when she saw him turn from the women. Her mother and aunt began to follow him. Claude made a barely perceptible gesture with his head, and Aimée realized then that the entire family was to be presented to the royal couple. Awed and excited, almost unable to breathe, Aimée remembered how poised her father had been as he'd approached the king. Keeping his example firmly in mind, she followed Mignon.

Victoire, Claude, Jeannette, and then Mignon met Queen Marie before moving on to the king. Aimée was the last in line. She was so dazed she heard nothing the queen and king said to the others or their responses. Only one thing was clear to her. It was a moment she would never forget.

Aimée's body managed a graceful enough curtsey before the queen, though when she looked into Queen Marie's eyes, she didn't know what to say—she hadn't understood the queen's murmur. Blushing furiously, Aimée whispered, "I'm honored to meet Your Majesty." When the queen's eyes glanced away, Aimée knew it was her dismissal, rose, and moved aside to drop again in a deep curtsey before the king.

"Please do rise, mademoiselle," King Louis said immediately. When she had obeyed and her eyes met his, he commented, *"Enchanté,* mademoiselle. How lovely you are."

"Your Majesty, I'm honored," Aimée whispered, not knowing what else to answer.

"Your eyes are very unusual," Louis observed. Then

turning to his wife, he commented, "They're the same color of our own Victoire's—amber, wouldn't you say?" Queen Marie peered at Aimée and nodded. King Louis again addressed Aimée. "Our daughter has black hair, but I suspect yours is auburn. Am I correct?"

Looking into the king's face, hearing his voice, Aimée felt as if a wheel were turning in her mind. "Yes, Your Majesty," she replied.

"Your eyes remind me of those of a deer I once caught in a hunt," he observed.

So, King Louis was the huntsman she'd spoken to in the garden. The sudden realization was like cold water being dashed in her face. Her blush vanished. She opened her mouth, wondering how she could apologize; but the king smiled warmly.

"I think, mademoiselle, this occasion has made you overwrought. You seem pale. I think you should have a sip of wine," Louis suggested.

"*Oui,* Your Majesty. I feel quite weak. I'll do as you say."

"Your family awaits you," he said, taking her hand and turning her slightly. When he saw that she was ready to curtsey again, he shook his head.

"I'm grateful, Your Majesty—honored," she began.

Still smiling, he waved her dismissal.

"*Ma petite,* what did he say to you?" Jeannette whispered anxiously after they had returned to their places.

"You were so long," Hilaire added in concern.

Aimée smiled weakly. "Congratulations, *Monsieur le Pelletier du Roi,*" she said happily, then answered their questions: "His Majesty only compared my eyes to Princesse Victoire's, then observed that I was pale and suggested I have some wine."

"You *are* pale," Jeannette agreed.

"I'll get wine," Hilaire said, signaling to a servant.

"It's the excitement," Aimée protested.

"Tell me about him," Mignon urged.

"But you met him too, *mon poussin,*" Jeannette scolded her affectionately.

"But he didn't engage me in conversation!" Mignon returned.

The servant handed Aimée her wine; at the same moment the musicians began to play. Mignon was silenced as everyone turned to watch the king and queen step down from the dais to lead the first dance. Someone had removed their court robes and cumbersome trains. A smaller coronet replaced Louis's unwieldy crown, and he no longer held his golden staff.

"We must all join in the dance," Victoire warned, reaching for Antoine's hand.

"I'm sure Their Majesties will excuse Aimée from this first dance," Hilaire said firmly, and took Jeannette's arm.

"Drink your wine slowly," Mignon advised as Claude led her onto the ballroom floor.

Aimée nodded and lifted her goblet to take a small sip. Then she turned her attention to the dancing couples. She was privately relieved that she didn't have to be on the dance floor with the king and queen, feeling again as if everyone's eyes were on her.

King Louis and Queen Marie danced only a short time before they separated and he led her back to her chair. This wasn't unexpected; it was well known that though the queen liked music, she wasn't fond of dancing. Other couples began to move out onto the ballroom floor. With the dancers' numbers rapidly increasing, it was anticipated that Louis would dance with Madame de Pompadour. Aimée could see the expectant look on his mistress's face; but Louis instead turned to one of his courtiers and spoke softly. Wondering at the king's purpose, Aimée was surprised when the courtier approached her.

"Mademoiselle Dessaline, if you have recovered, His Majesty wishes you to join him for this dance," the courtier said, then asked, "Are you recovered?"

"I think so, monsieur," Aimée answered automatically. Without waiting for her to say more, assuming that the king's wishes were to be obeyed as usual, the courtier took the wine goblet from Aimée, tucked her arm under his, and led her to the king, who had again stepped down from the dais.

Louis allowed Aimée to make the customary curtsey a lady gives her partner, though he immediately took her hands to prevent her from sinking into a deep curtsey, such as one made to royalty. He merely inclined his head slightly rather than bowed as another man would.

He was silent for the first few moments they danced, and Aimée had no idea what to say to him. Finally he commented, "You didn't recognize me until you were presented to us."

"No, Your Majesty," Aimée admitted. "Please forgive me."

"You probably thought me a poacher or some other ne'er-do-well," he remarked, a glint of humor in his eyes. Noting Aimée's renewed blush, he knew he was right. He added, "I would prefer you to be less friendly with suspected poachers on the palace grounds."

Realizing he was teasing, Aimée managed to smile as her flush began to subside.

"*Bon*, Aimée," the king approved. "I like you better as the girl I met in the park who didn't know who I am. I meet too many people who behave so formally with me that I have to guess what they're really thinking."

Aimée looked up at him in surprise. Did His Highness actually sometimes regret his elevated status?

As if he'd read her mind, he nodded and said, "*Oui*, Aimée. Being king can become wearisome at times. It's pleasant, I've found, to speak with someone who doesn't know who I am. Thank you for that happy moment."

"Majesty," she began.

"*Non, non, non*," he said softly. "Just be my friend as you were that day. Let me pretend for a moment that I am just a man."

Wondering how she could possibly manage that, Aimée nodded. "I'll try," she promised.

"I was right that day. I do prefer your hair unpowdered," he said. After Aimée had thanked him, he commented, "No doubt you have gathered a great many admirers since you've arrived in Paris."

"If so, they do little more than admire from afar.

Though they leave their calling cards, I see few of them personally," she replied.

"After having seen me dance with you, I expect their timidity will be overcome," Louis advised.

"If you'll forgive my saying so, Your Highness, I would hope any admirers would approach because of me—not because I danced with you," Aimée said.

Louis was surprised at her remark. He was used to both men and women courting his favor just because they wanted to draw attention to themselves. "You're wise to want to be valued for yourself," he commented. He was thoughtfully silent for a moment before saying, "Then you'll have to become acquainted with that most rare of men, those who honor me while remaining themselves."

"If such a man is so rare, I'll have difficulty finding one," Aimée replied.

Louis's face lit with a smile. "That's true," he said, glad that Aimée wasn't likely to pay much attention to trifling men and so wasn't about to become easily enamored. He had decided he would have to think of a way to keep her nearby so he would have the opportunity to win her for himself. It wouldn't be easy, he realized, to persuade so intelligent a lady to become his mistress; and he'd never been interested in ordering or forcing girls into his bed. After the music stopped, he handed her over to a waiting courtier with a simple comment that he'd enjoyed the dance, leaving her wondering at his suddenly changing moods.

Aimée quickly discovered that Louis had been right. She'd hardly returned to her family when she, like Mignon, was surrounded by men begging to dance with her. In a few minutes both girls had filled their dance cards, though Aimée reserved the last dance for her father, and Claude had begged two.

While she was dancing with her cousin, he commented on her sudden popularity.

"I know it's because of the king's attention," she admitted. "He warned me this would happen."

"Did he." Claude's remark was a comment rather than a question. He was thoughtfully silent a moment before saying, "After you've gotten counsel from the king, I suppose you won't need any from me."

"Don't say that," Aimée protested. "When you brought me that chocolate the night I arrived in Paris, and offered to give me advice about any men I should meet, I was grateful—and happy that you cared. I'll probably never speak to His Majesty again. How would I, after all?"

"I always will stand ready to help if you need it, Aimée," Claude said warmly. Then glancing beyond her shoulder, he added, "I have a feeling you *will* speak to the king again—and soon."

Claude had noted the approaching courtier—the same one who had announced Louis's wish to dance with Aimée. They stopped dancing. "Mademoiselle, monsieur, His Majesty requests the lady's company for a moment in his salon," the courtier said.

Aimée looked at Claude in surprise. She didn't know what to think of Louis's attention.

"You *must* go, Aimée," Claude said, looking a little annoyed. "You can't keep His Majesty waiting overlong."

"But . . ." Aimée began, then stopped. She was baffled.

"Don't worry, Aimée. I'm sure His Majesty has some more excellent advice to give you," Claude said coolly. "Save that other dance for me."

"Yes, of course," she replied in confusion, then turned to follow the courtier.

As the courtier stood aside so Aimée could enter the salon, she discovered the king wasn't alone. Another man, elegantly dressed in a brocade suit the color of champagne, stood with his back to her.

Louis immediately gestured a servant to pour a small glass of sherry for her and nodded that she come forward. The man turned. It was the duc de Mirabeau.

"I have been considering your dilemma, Mademoiselle Dessaline," Louis said after she'd risen from her curtsey. Noting her questioning expression, he explained, "You said you'd prefer to meet men who aren't overly impressed by the attention I've shown you?"

Aimée nodded, glanced at the duke, and felt a blush again rising in her. "Your Majesty, I—"

"Personally, I have no objection to my king's introducing me to so lovely a young lady," the duke quickly said.

Aimée realized he didn't want her to annoy the king by telling him they'd already met; and wondering again at Louis's interest in her affairs, she said slowly, "I'm grateful for your concern, Your Majesty."

Louis knew that almost any other woman would have been openly delighted to have him introduce her to a handsome duke, and he judged Aimée's hesitance as further evidence of her lack of sophistication, which gratified him. Because he had once contracted a venereal disease, he had since insisted on his paramours being virgin when they came to him. He desired Aimée as he had desired few other women; but his instincts told him she was a girl even a king could not approach directly. He planned that Mirabeau would escort her to social functions at the palace and thus bring her into contact with him—he was sure he could eventually seduce her; at the same time Mirabeau would seem to monopolize her time, and no other man would have the opportunity to attract her interest. Although Mirabeau was a womanizer *par excellence*, he was above all else pleased to remain high in his king's favor. Louis knew that however much Mirabeau might want Aimée for himself, he would be cautious in his behavior toward her, since the king seemed to have appointed himself as her protector.

After Louis had introduced the couple, the duc de Mirabeau immediately took Aimée's hand and lifted it to his lips. *"Enchanté,* Aimée—if I may call you that," he said.

Although Aimée was happy to meet the duke again, she didn't want him to think she'd been anxious. She allowed herself only a polite smile as she replied, "But of course."

Louis perceived Aimée's continuing wariness and assumed he'd been correct in his guess that she was inexperienced with men. Pleased that events seemed to be moving in the direction he had chosen, he cheerfully lied, "I must assure you, Mademoiselle Dessaline, His Grace is the least likely of my noblemen to pursue a lady merely because I've shown an interest in her well-being."

"*Merci,* Your Majesty," Aimée replied. "You're much too kind."

"Some others I know think their king can never be kind enough," Louis commented dryly as he lifted his glass of brandy. "May you find whatever you're searching for in life," he said.

Aimée lifted her sherry, murmuring her thanks, hoping that forgetfulness was what she'd find—forgetting Valjean at last.

When Aimée stepped out of the royal salon, she was aware of the sudden hush in the ballroom. Conversations were almost instantly resumed, although everyone's eyes had glanced her way. She was grateful that it was the duke who held her arm and that King Louis had not accompanied them back into the ballroom, for she realized that being seen too often with the king, in so short a space of time, would foment gossip.

"Will you dance with me now, Aimée?" Mirabeau asked quietly. He too was aware of the danger of wagging tongues.

"I'm afraid my dance card has already been filled, Your Grace," she replied regretfully.

"Let me see whose name is on it," he said. She produced the card; he glanced at it and smiled. "That gentleman won't be likely to interfere if it is I who enjoy this dance with you instead of him," he remarked. Not explaining further, he took her arm and led her confidently onto the ballroom floor.

The duke, Aimée noted, was an expert dancer. After a long silence, she asked, "Do you practice with the rapier, Your Grace?"

"Please call me Alain," he urged, before answering. "Yes. That was why the gentleman this dance belongs to won't approach us. He made the mistake of challenging me once." At her look of alarm he added, "Drawing a bit of his blood was sufficient to settle the matter. Why do you ask?"

"Your dancing has the grace of a fencing master," she replied.

"I'm not exactly a master."

She knew that he was being modest. He spoke little more during the remainder of the dance, but the warm glint in the dark eyes that gazed into hers told her he was pleased that the king had reintroduced them.

After the dance he suggested they have something to eat. Again she answered that the dance just beginning had already been filled in on her card. Again he asked to look at the name.

"Neither will he bother us." Alain dismissed the possibility at a glance.

"Have you also drawn a bit of his blood?" Aimée inquired.

Alain smiled. "He owes me money and has lately been avoiding my company. Have a seat, Aimée," he urged. "If you don't mind, I'll have a servant fetch our supper from the buffet."

After they had seated themselves at a small gilt table, Alain said, "I thought of you often while I was at Fontainebleau. I regret my business there kept me longer than I'd anticipated, as I'd planned on asking you to the theater or for supper before this occasion. I only returned to Paris late this afternoon with just enough time to dress for this ball—and then I was late."

"I'm glad you remembered me," she replied, then impulsively added, "I thought of you from time to time since we met at that restaurant."

"You should never tell a man such things," Alain said, smiling at her honesty. "You should keep him in suspense, make him think he has many rivals, so he'll feel he must win you."

Aimée looked up at him. "But you *haven't* won me," she exclaimed in surprise, then added, "And neither of us can be sure yet how many rivals you may have."

Alain laughed softly. "You're delightful, Aimée," he remarked. "Continue being as you are—so innocent and candid one moment, a bit tart the next—and all men will ever be in suspense with you."

"I'm not sure I have the patience to play this cat-and-mouse game you seem to think must go on between a man and a woman," Aimée said. Realizing how her comment might sound, she quickly added, "I mean only that I'm sure I'll be very ineffective at flirtation."

"You have a more effective style than any woman of the court I've met," he assured her.

For the remainder of the evening the men who had so eagerly put their names on Aimée's dance card found themselves abandoned. Except for Hilaire's and Claude's promised dances, Aimée spent the entire evening with Alain. Jeannette, observing her daughters' popularity, was becoming more and more agitated, especially over the duke's constant attentiveness to Aimée. Her plans for finding handsome, wealthy husbands for her daughters were, she feared, working only too well. Given the real possibility that the girls would marry in France and remain there, anticipated loneliness gnawed at her.

In the weeks following the ball Alain was a frequent visitor at the Dessaline house; and among the many calling cards left in the silver dish in the foyer, the ones engraved with the name of the duc de Mirabeau were many.

Aimée enjoyed Alain's company. She had never met a man like him—refined, elegant, able to enjoy her wit instead of being intimidated by it as a number of other admirers were. She was dazzled by the many entertainments she attended with him—the glittering parties, the salons abuzz with sophisticated conversations, the theater, opera, and ballet, and the shimmering balls at Versailles. At first awed by the people she met, she soon learned to enjoy their company. Noblemen and ladies, ministers and diplomats, as well as artists, composers, and even the writers of the day whose shocking ideas, though publicly frowned upon, were privately read—all accepted her as Alain's regular companion.

Presents from Aimée's and Mignon's admirers began to trickle into the Dessaline house—floral offerings, amusing trinkets. But among the gifts sent to Aimée were items far more valuable than trinkets; these were costly presents delivered by unidentified messengers and left without cards to reveal the sender. The first was a scallop shell which, when opened, was found to contain a watch on a silver chain, its case solidly set with seed pearls. Then came an intricately carved powder box made from pink jade; the shell of a nautilus engraved with elaborate designs and edged with gold, attached to an alabaster base shaped like a mermaid; a silver cup, daintily carved and set with amethysts.

Having no idea who had sent the gifts, Aimée couldn't return them, although she was alarmed at the possible reasons the sender didn't reveal himself. Jeannette suspected a wealthy married man; but Victoire denied that, pointing out that such a man would know Aimée wasn't likely to begin, much less carry on, an *affaire d'amour* with him. The puzzle continued.

Early one evening, just as Aimée had finished dressing to attend a presentation at the Louvre and a dinner at the palace afterwards, another unsigned gift was delivered; and she had only partly unwrapped it when Alain arrived. He urged her to continue, his tone more casual than he felt. As she drew from the package a costly amber ring encrusted with gold, he was stunned.

"Who sent you such a gift?" he asked, trying to sound calm.

"I wish I knew," she answered, looking baffled. "There's never a card."

"What else have you received?" he asked, becoming suspicious. After Aimée had told him, he said angrily, "They're the gifts of a man who wishes to buy you!"

"That's what Maman thinks," Aimée admitted. She shrugged. "He's a foolish man wasting his money, because I'm not for sale. Yet I can do nothing to stop him if I don't know who he is."

Recalling the gifts he'd sent her—which, though more proper than those of that other, unknown man, paled in comparison—Alain grew more suspicious. "Are you certain you have no idea who sent them?"

"*Mais non*, of course not," she answered, surprised at his tone.

"It must be more than one man. Only a king could afford so many costly gifts," he said sharply.

"You'll have me wondering if I'm being pursued by every man in Paris," she replied sarcastically.

Realizing he'd annoyed her when she was after all innocent in the matter, Alain was penitent. "Forgive me, Aimée. I know you've done nothing to encourage all this. It's only that it's an insult to you if the man is already wed. My anger at such an insult overcomes my reason."

"I forgive you, Alain," she said soothingly. "I'm distressed by all of this too."

"I want you to promise me that when this man does reveal himself, you'll tell me who he is," Alain said impulsively.

"So you can challenge him?" Aimée asked in alarm.

"So I can denounce him," Alain replied. "Promise you'll tell me."

Looking at the fires that burned in Alain's dark eyes, Aimée doubted he'd merely denounce her mysterious admirer; but she also knew that Alain wouldn't relent until she agreed. Finally she sighed and said, "I promise, Alain."

During the evening, although Alain was as attentive as usual toward Aimée, he was distracted by jealousy. He knew personally every man of any appreciable wealth in Paris; and after he'd considered each married man, he'd come to realize that there was only one who would dare to so court Aimée. This particular man Alain could neither challenge nor denounce. About this man he could do nothing—it was none other than the king himself.

Madame de Pompadour was ill and for some years had been dosing herself with potions and following special diets in an effort to regain the strength necessary to keep King Louis contented in her boudoir. She had failed, and the string of royal mistresses passing through Parc aux Cerfs had become legend. Because Pompadour's illness was known to very few, even in the royal court, the king's always immoderate sexual appetite had been greatly exaggerated to the point that most considered his passion prodigious. Among the more sophisticated people at court, his *affaires d'amour* had been accepted and now were mostly ignored. But so many rumors about Louis's exploits were floating about the streets of Paris, there was an occasional public outcry about his excesses. Alain considered this to be beneath notice, as the opinions of the peasants always were beneath notice—even though many of the girls Louis coupled with were the daughters of peasants and merchants. When Louis grew tired of a girl, he sent her away with financial benefits sufficiently generous to silence her parents. Many of the girls subsequently married better than they could have hoped before they'd become the king's mistress.

Alain was stunned to realize that if Louis was the man sending Aimée such gifts, he was giving her more attention than he'd shown any other woman except Madame de Pompadour, before she'd become his mistress. Alain began to wonder how he might keep Aimée away from the palace and out of the king's sight. This he knew would be very difficult. Most of his social obligations originated at the palace, or involved people of such high status that he must of necessity mingle with the court. To continue to enjoy Aimée's company, he would have to take her with him.

He was well aware of her parents' plan to return to Montreal in the spring, when the weather became safe for traveling; but his time limit was also the king's—and that realization brought another matter to mind, which convinced him it was indeed Louis who had sent Aimée those gifts. He'd recently learned that Quebec had fallen to the British in September just after the Dessalines had sailed for France, and Montreal would be threatened after the spring thaw. He'd carefully not mentioned it to Aimée out of fear that the Dessalines would immediately leave Paris for home. He realized, now that he was thinking of it, that very few in the royal court knew about the colony's plight. The news had been withheld. No one could smother such important news except the king. Had Louis decided to conceal the gravity of the situation for the same reason he himself had not mentioned it to Aimée? It seemed so. This revelation only confirmed Alain's suspicions that it was Louis who had sent Aimée those gifts and had an interest that went far beyond concern for her well-being.

It wasn't going to be easy to compete with the king, Alain acknowledged. Although he'd been too long unmarried to propose readily to any girl, he realized that this was his one great weapon: He could eventually offer Aimée marriage, the king only an affair.

After Alain had taken Aimée home, she prepared for bed in silence, arousing the maid Josette's curiosity; for Aimée ordinarily chatted about her evenings while she undressed. Aimée was thinking about Alain's annoyance, his jealousy when he'd learned about the mysterious gifts. She hadn't realized before that Alain would be jealous. She was afraid that if the man who had sent the presents to her revealed himself, Alain would challenge him. She wanted no blood to be shed on her account, even if the man's attention was insulting to her.

As Aimée stared into the darkness, thinking about her problems, Alain's remark suddenly arose in her mind: "Only a king," he had said, "could afford to send so many costly gifts." She remembered too King Louis's remark that evening about her beautiful amber ring. Fear abruptly streaked through her. Was it possible the ring had been a royal gift? She remembered each of the other items she'd received. Louis had commented on having a liking for shells and jade. She sat up in bed with a start. Louis had also admired the watch when she'd worn it for the first time in his presence.

"Mon Dieu!" she whispered. Was her mysterious admirer King Louis? How did one refuse a king? To what ends would he go to effect her surrender? Being from the colonies, she didn't know that Louis's mistresses were volunteers later well rewarded. She only thought of the king's awesome power.

She lay back again, pulling the blankets over her shoulders; but their warmth didn't stop the shivering that emanated from within her. She turned her face into her pillow and began to weep. She wished she'd never come to Paris at all. She wished with all her heart that she'd remained with Marcel in Montreal.

Later, exhausted from weeping, she fell asleep thinking

longingly of familiar forest paths, of riding Brandy through a meadow.

In the morning Aimée awakened from a dream in which she was kissing Valjean. As aroused as she was by the dream, she knew her excitement, when she'd kissed Valjean in reality, had been no less. Alain had kissed her several times during recent weeks. The first kiss had been gentle, hesitant—questioning if she would allow it, and when she had, his kisses became more sensual, more demanding. Comparing even his later kisses with Valjean's first, she had to admit that Alain—charming, handsome, witty, and a duke besides—didn't make her feel as Valjean had made her feel.

Chapter 6

Simone, the Comtesse de la Tour, paused at the gilt-framed mirror outside her drawing room to give her appearance one last inspection. She looked much too pale in the deep rose of her morning dress, she decided. Valjean—if indeed her visitor really was Valjean—would know at a glance how ill she was. She wished Valjean to judge her for herself, not out of sympathy. If her visitor wasn't Valjean—or if her son turned out to be no more than a fortune hunter—he would find her spirit not nearly as weak as her body was becoming.

"Ariel, please get my pink fichu," Simone directed. The maid had anticipated this decision and had discreetly carried the shawllike garment concealed behind her skirt. As Ariel arranged the ruffles of the fichu at her neckline, Simone sighed. "What would I do without your help, Ariel?"

"It's just that I'm used to you, madame," the maid replied.

Simone patted her arm affectionately and commented, "My wing feathers would be unpreened and my robe disarranged without you—that is, if I go to heaven."

"You will, madame, but maybe not as soon as the doctors claim," Ariel said firmly. She stepped away so her mistress could view herself. "It gives a nice glow to your complexion," she remarked.

"I remember a time my complexion wore its own glow, not a reflected one." Simone sighed, then added more cheerfully, "This fichu will do very well. Thank you, Ariel."

The maid inclined her head. She was relieved at Simone's changed tone. She often worried that Simone might be hastening death with her dejected attitude. "Will you serve Monsieur d'Auvergne tea or perhaps brandy?" she asked.

"I'm sure brandy would be more to a man's taste than tea," Simone replied.

"And yourself, madame?"

"A bit of claret may help to warm my flesh," Simone replied, adding, "You needn't wait with me."

"I'd thought, at least, to see you comfortably seated."

Simone took the maid's arm. "*Merci*, Ariel. You're so thoughtful. I believe I'll recline on the divan." Simone walked slowly across the room, then sat on the divan. The maid immediately stooped to lift her mistress's legs so that they rested on the cushions; then she arranged the folds of her skirt so that they fell gracefully to the floor revealing only the very tips of her satin slippers. "I'm sure that will do very well," Simone said.

"Is there anything else you wish, madame? I could bring a book for you to read while you wait," Ariel suggested.

"Get Monsieur d'Auvergne's letter. I would like to read it again. It's on the desk," Simone instructed.

After the maid had obeyed, Simone dismissed her. She wanted to be alone to think about the letter, to look out the window beside the divan and observe him before he knew her eyes were on him. Once again, as she had done so many times since the letter had arrived a few days before, she unfolded the cream-colored page and studied his handwriting.

It was open and well spaced, the writing of a well-tutored man. She'd been relieved to know that her son, after all, had been properly educated. His manner seemed neither arrogant nor sly. He appeared to take nothing for granted. The letter was discreet, not referring to their possible relationship—saying only that she'd seen him once when he was an infant, that he'd understood from Bess Kendall that they were closely related; asking if the countess would answer a few questions about a family matter. He'd signed his full name—Valjean Étienne d'Auvergne. Valjean—an unusual name traditionally used by her male ancestors. D'Auvergne was her family name—she'd dared not tell her parents the name of her lover, but she hadn't known at the time that he'd already been killed. It was the name Étienne that made her sick heart beat a little stronger; for that was the French version of her lover's name, Steven. It was the only part of his father that Valjean could possess, the only part that he'd ever know, and no one but Bess had known why she'd chosen this second name for her son. It was possibly another thread of truth in the tapestry she hoped she was weaving: that it was really her son coming to visit her after all these years, the son she'd thought she would never see again.

"Steven, help me to be wise in the way I behave toward our child, in the decisions I make about him now that he's a man," she prayed. "Help me during the short time I still have left here before I join you, my darling."

She wondered again what Valjean thought about what she'd done, how much Bess had told him. Did he hate her for seemingly giving him away and now merely wanted to tell her so? Might he only be seeking the inheritance he'd been cheated of by fate? Or was he, as the letter implied, simply interested in knowing about his background?

Remembering the infant she'd held for so short a time before he'd been taken from her, she reflected that her husband had never given her a child. The comte de la Tour had berated her often, claiming it was she who was at fault; and she'd had to remain silent, unable to deny her barrenness by telling him she'd already borne a healthy son. Arousing herself for a moment, she noted that several tears had fallen on the ink. She took the letter, hoping to flick off the moisture without causing the ink to run; but the writing, when she looked at it again, was smeared.

She laid her head wearily back on the cushions. "Perhaps I should have denied him the appointment, Steven," she whispered. "Maybe I'm only going to cause myself more heartbreak with this interview. I have no idea what he's become. No, my dearest, I can't fool myself after all. I couldn't refuse to see him just as you couldn't resist coming that one last time to say good-bye to me before you sailed, even though it was that short delay that caused your death. I *must* meet our son just once before I leave this world to find you again. I have to try to make peace with him."

As she spoke she lifted her head to stare again at the street below. She was concentrating so intently on her dead lover, on the past that was involved so intimately with her present, that at first she didn't realize the cab coming down the street might contain Valjean. She was even a little surprised when the driver drew up his horse before her house—so few visitors came to her. Suddenly she realized whom the cab probably held; and she sat up straight, tense as she watched, her heart pounding in a way that wasn't good for her.

She saw a hatless man get out of the cab. He wore a black coat trimmed simply with light brown braid, and matching brown breeches. He stood as if uncertain before the tall iron gates that marked the entrance.

"He's so slender, Steven, so plainly dressed. Can it be that his profession, whatever it is, has given him no rewards?" she whispered. "His hair is the same color as yours was; and whether or not he has prospered, he holds his head the way you always did—with pride." She smiled, adding, "Whatever fortune has done to him, it hasn't humbled him or made him slovenly." She bit her lip anxiously. "I do wish he'd look up, just once, so I could see if he wears your features or mine, or possibly a stranger's." She saw Valjean open the gates and proceed up the walkway to the house. "He moves just like you did, Steven. How I teased you about your walking so silently, gracefully," she added, smiling faintly at her memories. She seemed younger and healthier, as she thought about her lover. Then she remembered that in a few short minutes Valjean would be entering the room. Her smile faded as she again leaned back against the cushions to wait.

During the cab ride to Simone's house Valjean's apprehension at meeting his mother grew to such proportions that he wondered if he should have the driver turn around, and later send Simone some sort of excuse for not keeping his appointment. He rejected this idea, feeling foolish. He had come to France to locate her. He had persistently traced his family name to a mountainous district in south-central France bearing that name, only to visit the estate of the d'Auvergnes and discover that it was occupied by servants. The comtesse de la Tour, last living member of the d'Auvergne family, was staying at her house in Paris for the city's social season, the housekeeper had informed him. Valjean had doggedly made his way back to Paris carrying with him the memory of the sumptuous estate and creating unflattering mental pictures of a wealthy widow who had inherited her husband's and her own family's obvious fortunes.

She would be suspicious of his motives for locating her after all these years, he was convinced. By the time he stepped out of the cab, he had decided that he'd embarked on an errand doomed from the start. He should have taken Julia Carleton's advice and let the past remain dead.

He paused before opening the gates; and in that moment his Abnaki stepfather seemed to whisper in his ear. He was aware that someone in the house was watching him—as surely as he'd known when a lynx had been studying him in the New England forest. The dappled shading of his gray eyes shifted its tints to a lighter hue, and he unlatched the gate.

The butler answered Valjean's rapping almost immediately. With an attitude that could not have been more respectful, he addressed him as Monsieur d'Auvergne and informed him that the countess was waiting in the drawing room. Without further delay he led Valjean down a hall carpeted with precious oriental rugs. Light streamed in through a row of windows that looked out on a formal garden, which he decided must be located in the shelter of a wing of the house.

The butler ushered him into a room where the walls were lined with pale green silk. Golden oriental carpets covered the floor, and dark green velvet with heavy gold fringe draped the windows. He saw immediately that a woman reclined on a divan at the far end of the room, but the light coming from the window behind her made it impossible to discern her features at a distance. She was not at all like any of the images he'd conjured up in his mind.

Her hair had once been blond, he surmised; the sunlight cast lights on a few strands mixed with the gray. Her eyes had once been extraordinarily beautiful, he knew. Now their dark brown depths were lackluster and surrounded by shadows. He recognized that her thinness had nothing to do with how tightly she'd laced her corset. She was gravely ill, he decided, and was saddened. But as he approached, a smile crept slowly over her lips, lighting her eyes with new life and putting a flush of color back into her pale cheeks. She held out her hands in welcome.

"Valjean," she whispered, sounding as if she could not quite believe it truly was he. She swallowed once, caught her breath, then said brokenly, "Please take my hands, Valjean. You need give no proof of your identity. I can see you are Steven's son."

Valjean felt his own throat catch, and he reached out to grasp her fingers. They were cool and thin, and he wished he could lend them some of his own warmth and strength.

"Madame, you must have some of your medicine," said the maid who had somehow appeared beside him. She held out a goblet with a pool of dark liquid at its bottom. When the countess refused the goblet, she begged, "Please, madame, do take it. You know you're more excited than is good for you."

"Yes, Ariel, thank you," Simone said, and, accepting the goblet, swallowed the liquid quickly. "Now, Ariel, please get some brandy for Monsieur d'Auvergne and a claret for me to wash this dreadful taste from my mouth." The maid took the goblet and hurried away. Simone looked again at Valjean. "Please sit down. *Non,* not a chair so far away— sit beside me. There's enough room," she urged.

Valjean, holding her hands in his, obeyed. "Forgive me if I must accustom myself to the idea of addressing you as Mother," he said softly. The pain in her eyes caused him to add quickly, "It's only that I'm unused to it, not that I particularly object."

"You aren't angry with me? You don't bear me a grudge for giving you away?" she asked incredulously.

"If I'd been told when I'd been a child, I might have borne a grudge; but Bess didn't tell me until this spring. I was disturbed, of course. I'd grown up believing she was my mother. I admit I was angry for a time, but I don't believe that bearing grudges really accomplishes anything," he replied.

The pain in Simone's eyes faded, and they turned to shine with pride on him. "Dear Bess," she murmured. "Dear Valjean." She touched his cheek, blinked away her tears, then asked hesitantly, "If Bess had let you think she was your mother all that time, why did she decide to finally tell you the truth?"

"She was in a carriage accident and was dying. She thought I should know the truth," he answered simply.

Simone flinched as if he'd struck her. "Bess was my friend. I loved her so much," she whispered. She sat, silent for a moment, her eyes lowered as she remembered handing Bess—then only a girl herself—the blanket-wrapped infant she had thought she was parting with forever. The scene was blurred in her memory, for she'd seen it through weeping eyes so many years ago. She took a deep breath, gathered her composure, and lifted her head. "Were you a happy child, Valjean? Did you love her?"

Valjean nodded. "I was very happy, and Bess and I loved each other very much." He looked at Simone steadily for a long moment before asking the question that had been burning in his mind since Bess had told him the truth. "And my father—what was he like?"

Remembering the only man she'd ever loved renewed Simone's smile and brightened her eyes as she said, "I recognized you by your eyes and by your hair, Valjean. They're the same as his. You have that much of him—and your height, your nose. I wasn't able to give you his family name; but I did manage his Christian name, Steven, as a middle name for you. No one but Bess knew his name."

"She never told me she knew. She said he was dead. What was his family name?"

Simone shook her head. "It truly no longer matters, Valjean. He was killed by soldiers before he got back to his ship. His family never even knew I existed, so they wouldn't acknowledge you now." She paused, seeing the conflict in his face, then continued, "My family name, d'Auvergne, is an honorable one. My father, your grandfather, in his heart never stopped regretting having to send you away. My husband never gave me a son, and I was my parents' only child. Your grandfather—his name was Valjean too—would have liked to know our family's name didn't die with him, that one day you might have a son to keep the name alive."

"You won't tell me my father's family name?" Valjean spoke the words slowly.

"After I know you well enough to be sure you won't try to disturb his family, I'll tell you. I only mean to spare you humiliation, Valjean. They're a powerful family, and no one would believe you. If you persisted in asking questions, or tried to convince them of your kinship, they might bring charges—and what could I, a citizen of an enemy country, do to help you?" Simone reasoned.

"There have been from time to time illegitimate members of even the British royal family," Valjean reminded her dryly. "But I do understand your reasoning and have no desire to be insulted or humiliated."

"I can show you a picture of him later, Valjean," she offered. "I still have the locket he gave me with a miniature of me in it. After he died, I had an artist paint a miniature of him according to my description. The artist was quite good, and the painting beside mine in the locket is a true portrait of him."

"I'd like very much to see it," Valjean replied.

Simone took another sip of her claret, began to put the glass down, then changed her mind and finished the wine as she braced herself for the difficult task ahead. "Valjean, I want to tell you about what happened between your father and me, and I have a thousand questions about your life while you were away from me, but . . ." She paused, again took his hands in hers, and finally continued: "But I have something more I must tell you. I think I have to tell you now while I have the courage. Afterward I have to ask something of you, something very important to me."

"What is it, *ma mère?*"

Simone's eyes filled with tears, and she said brokenly,

"All those years I dreamed of you and couldn't see you. So long a time I've had a child and never been called that—'my mother.' Oh, how sweet it is to hear it at last." She began to cough, a dry but persistent cough. Valjean offered her his brandy. After she'd taken a few sips, her cough relented. She gave him the brandy and leaned back against the cushions. "*That* is what I must tell you about, Valjean," she said softly.

"You have a disease of the lungs? Why don't you move to the estate in the south? It's warmer there. The air is cleaner and drier. It would be better for you."

"I stay in Paris to be near my physician. It isn't my lungs but my heart that makes me cough," she said. She paused a moment, trying to control the emotions that were rising in her, trying to conceal from him her fear and sorrow. "Valjean, the doctor has told me I have no more than four or five months to live."

Valjean felt a cold streak run down his back. "Four or five months! Maman, surely something could be done—medicine—*something!*" She shook her head. "What was it your maid gave you? It was medicine of some kind, wasn't it?"

"Only a temporary measure. I've been to a dozen doctors. The one I have now is the best in Paris—in all France—and he agrees with the others. We must face reality, Valjean. My heart is weak and becoming weaker. One day not too far in the future it will stop."

Valjean was silent. He stared down at his knees. He could not look up at her for a long moment. Why, he was thinking, why, why, why? Just when he'd found her at last, before they were even acquainted, he must learn that he would lose her. Lose her as he'd lost his father before he'd even been born, as he'd lost his adopted father, Walking-in-Honor, as he'd lost Bess. As he appeared to have lost even Aimée. His own heart seemed to stop beating.

Simone looked at her son wonderingly. Only moments before he'd entered the room she'd questioned his reason for coming to see her; she'd been haunted by the possibility that he might only want to tell her how he hated her.

But he received this news of her imminent death with the emotion of a son who had been with her always.

When he finally looked up, she said quietly, "When I learned that my illness would have no cure, I felt cheated, sad, even angry; but now, for the first time, I feel such profound regret, such grief, I can't bear it. *Mon fils*, it's *your* sorrow I cannot bear. Yet, there's so much we don't know about each other that I must explain my purpose."

Valjean continued looking at her steadily, but he was distracted.

"The question which is so important to me, Valjean, is this: Now that we've found each other, can you stay with me until it's over? *Will* you stay with me until then?" she asked softly. When he said nothing, she added, "I would like to have someone besides my lawyer and the priest, and perhaps an official or two, attend my funeral. I need to know that someone I love will be with me at the end."

The pain in Valjean's eyes—Steven's eyes—turned Simone's faltering heart over. "By the time you'd been born, I knew your father was dead; and though I loved you that much more because you were all I could have of him, I was too young, too frightened, to make so scandalous a decision as to keep you. My parents thought they were doing what was best for me. Even though the choice to give you up wasn't mine, as it turned out, I've done nothing for you all these years," Simone said. She reached out to put her hand on his. "Valjean, you're my only child, all the family I have left. You're truly the heir to both the d'Auvergne and the de la Tour fortunes. Couldn't you stay to learn about your own heritage? After I'm gone, you'll be part of the aristocracy . . . *After* I'm gone? No, *now*! I'll send for my attorney tomorrow and have him make whatever legal arrangements are necessary to legitimize your birth. As the last member of my family, though I'm a woman, I *can* pass on the d'Auvergne name to you legally. I'm sure of it," she said determinedly.

"Don't think you have to repay me for the past, *ma mère*. I understand what your position then was. The money means nothing to me." Valjean waved his free hand in a gesture of denial. He stood up and gazed thoughtfully out the window for a moment. "Even that I would no longer be a bastard means little to me at this moment," he said softly as if he were thinking aloud. Finally he looked down at her. "I'll stay as long as you do, *ma mère*," he said quietly. "I'm sorry but I can't promise that afterwards I'll remain in France. I grew up in New England. I'm at home in Boston, while I feel like a stranger here. There are people I love in Boston, people who care for me and cared for Bess. My employer and his family are like my own family. It's only because of their generosity that I was able to come to France."

"And now as my son and heir you'll be able to repay their generosity, their faith in you," Simone reminded.

"I suppose you're right," Valjean conceded. Again he fell silent for a long moment as he considered his odd position as the child of two countries, two enemy countries. Then he said, "I just can't promise you that I'll want to stay in France."

"Whether or not you stay is your choice to make, Valjean," Simone replied. "If you decide to return to Boston, you'll be able to establish yourself in a new position that will be more to your advantage. That in itself relieves me of worry about your future." She caught his sleeve and urged, "But will you give the country where you were born a chance? Will you let me teach you about France?"

Valjean nodded. "My first personal reason for coming here was to find you; the second was to learn about my heritage."

Simone's anxious expression vanished and was replaced by a brilliant smile. She took a deep breath, then began to talk rapidly: "Maurice, my butler, will arrange for your things to be brought from the hotel this afternoon. Tomorrow I'll send a message to my attorney. Perhaps I can arrange for a tailor, maybe even the hairdresser, to come. In the evening, if you wish, we could attend the ballet—"

"Maman, you're chattering so fast I can hardly understand you," Valjean interrupted. When she raised her face to look up at him, he said, "Remember, I wasn't born speaking French. I learned it from a tutor—after I'd learned English."

Simone smiled at his reminder. "It doesn't matter, *mon fils*. You'll soon speak French as if you were born in Versailles. Ah, Valjean, you've given my heart new life, new strength." Catching his hand in hers, she said fervently, "I'm so glad you're here at last. I'm so proud of the kind of man you've become. I'll pray every night for Bess out of gratitude for all she's helped you to be."

"She was very good to me," he said simply.

"I can see that," Simone agreed. "Maurice will help you pack, Valjean; but is there anyone, perhaps business acquaintances, who must know your new address? If so, you should tell them immediately."

"Yes, there are a couple of people," Valjean admitted. "And I'll have to write to the Carletons to tell them I've found you and to let them know I may not be back as soon as I'd planned." He paused, then explained, "You can imagine how long it takes for the mail to get to Boston. I have to allow Andrew—that's my employer—enough time to make an alternate plan, if he wishes, to receive the cargo I'm contracting for him." As he remembered the forbidden cargo and the plans they'd had for smuggling the goods into Boston, he smiled. "Later, Maman, I'll have to tell you something about my work."

"I want you to tell me all about your work, yourself, *everything*," Simone replied. "But attend to your other errands now so they'll be finished that much sooner."

Valjean smiled, bent to kiss her cheek, then left her.

When Ariel returned to Simone, she found that her mistress had swung her feet to the floor without assistance. Alarmed that Simone might have strained herself, Ariel let the gentle scolding die on her lips. Simone wore the expression of a girl who was anticipating having to run off and dress for a party. Ariel's heart melted, and she couldn't resist asking, "Monsieur d'Auvergne was what you'd hoped he would be?"

"Even more, Ariel, even more," Simone answered happily.

That evening Simone and Valjean exchanged experiences over dinner and continued to talk so late into the

night that Ariel finally came to beg her mistress to go up
to bed before she exhausted herself and found herself unable to do all she wished the next day.

In bed, Simone said a rosary for Bess; and Valjean, in
his own room, lay staring at the faint reflection the street
lamps made on the ceiling. He was thinking about Simone's melancholy past, wondering why, now that a happier future lay before her, her life must be ending.

The next morning Simone's attorney was the first to arrive. He was followed by a steady stream of visitors: a
barber to dress Valjean's hair; a tailor with two assistants
burdened with samples of cloth; Simone's social secretary;
her physician who promptly sent for a nurse to supervise
Simone's activities that day; representatives of the court of
Louis XV and officials of the church, who would begin the
necessary steps to legitimize Valjean. After the last of the
visitors left late in the afternoon, an alarmed Ariel and
Valjean finally persuaded Simone to take a nap. Simone
had been planning to attend the theater that evening with
Valjean, but now she was too weary, and they remained
home, talking quietly about the day.

In the weeks that followed, Simone insisted on taking
Valjean to the opera and to the Louvre, where he saw the
art that France had produced; and on a day that the
palace was usually quiet, she took him to see Versailles.
King Louis was away at Rambouillet, so Valjean never
glimpsed him, though Simone submitted her petition that
Valjean be accepted by the court as the future comte de la
Tour and marquis d'Auvergne.

One afternoon, before the weather became too cold, Simone took Valjean to the de la Tour estate, which was
only a few miles outside Paris. As Valjean inspected the
sumptuous house, which Simone had deserted after its
master had died, he could visualize her loveless existence
there. The furniture and chandeliers were draped with
dustcovers, giving the effect of myriad silent ghosts; yet he
could appreciate the elegance of the house, and, as well,
be chilled by its formal loneliness—it had nothing of the
friendly warmth of the d'Auvergne estate in the south.

One evening at the theater both Valjean and Aimée were in the audience, and had he known, he would have been stunned and overjoyed. If they had come even within proximity of each other, he would have had to study Aimée to recognize her. The auburn-haired girl, who had worn her brother's breeches as she rode in the meadow near Montreal, had been transformed by Paris into an elegantly dressed lady; and her modishly coiffed hair was powdered, its natural fire cooled to a moonlight glow. She also would have had difficulty picking him out in the crowd. His hair too was powdered and dressed; and his brocade suit, lace-ruffled shirt, and fur-trimmed cloak had nothing in common with the doeskins he'd worn in the forest, or even the simple suit he'd worn on the wharf in Boston.

The night that Valjean and Simone attended the ballet they emerged from the theater to discover that the first snow was falling. Although they laughed as they compared the beauty of the lacy flakes that they each caught on their sleeves, Valjean was aware that Simone's weakness was progressing; and she was trying to hide it. After that, he insisted on spending more time at home with her, using the excuse that they must give thought to preparing the house for Christmas and that the servants had to be supervised in the decorating of it. Simone knew his purpose, but she was too weary to argue or protest.

She sent Maurice to the various places where books forbidden by the Ministry of Censorship could be bought, and presented Valjean with reading material expressing ideas that were revolutionary and scandalous in that era: Helvétius's newly published *On the Mind,* Montesquieu's *Spirit of the Laws,* Voltaire's *Candide,* Turgot's *Discourses on Universal History,* Quesnay's *Tableau Économique* (which even the king had read), Rousseau's *Discourse on the Origins of Inequality,* and of course Diderot's *Encyclopédie.*

She had chosen those particular books purposefully. Long absent from Versailles and no longer associated with the royal court, she'd gotten a new perspective on the movement of the times and foresaw trouble in France's future. Her opinions were confirmed by the occasional riots that were beginning to plague Paris—riots of angry peasants pressed by landlords heavily taxed by a government headed by a pleasure-loving, wildly extravagant monarch. If Valjean should decide to remain in France, she would advise him to sell the town house and the de la Tour property, which was so close to Paris, and live on the d'Auvergne estate in the country, where he would be safe from revolutionaries in a future that she knew would be turbulent.

On the day before Christmas Simone's lawyer came to the house and presented them with the fully executed legal papers that made Valjean legitimate. Simone, it seemed, handed Valjean his new status as a gift. As Simone signed her new will she warned Valjean not to expect a great stir in the court over this event; and it wouldn't necessarily speed his presentation to the king either. The lawyer, who had become Simone's friend and so was casual in his conversations, confided that copies of the documents would be put into storage somewhere in the ministry, the event recorded in the church's dusty books and likely forgotten. The court was at the moment more interested in the gaiety of the Christmas season.

Nothing could dissuade Simone from going to the cathedral to attend Christmas mass; and Valjean, though unfamiliar with the Roman Catholic faith, found that he did not feel alien in the church; the teachings of the Episcopal church, which he was familiar with, were too similar, and many of the prayers the same as those he heard now. The ceremony gave him a certain inner peace, and he knew that Simone too drew strength from her visit to the cathedral.

Simone and Valjean spent Christmas alone except for the servants, whom Simone encouraged to forget their status and enjoy their day. Though quieter than the celebration in other houses, theirs was warm with the glow of the emotions that gave Christmas its meaning. When Simone and Valjean exchanged gifts, they laughed over the many amusing trinkets they unwrapped. Then in a moment of great solemnity Valjean presented Simone with the little gold cross Bess had kept for him since his infancy. Simone immediately recognized the cross: Steven had given it to her, and she'd put it on the infant Valjean before handing him to Bess. She had wanted him to have something of his father, even if he was too small to know it. Eyes filled with tears, she put her arms around Valjean and, weeping, clung to his strength.

In turn she finally produced the locket that held the miniatures. Valjean looked at the paintings of Simone and his father. They were young and happy then. His throat closed with emotion. She'd been, as he'd guessed, a beauty; and there was a kindness, a tenderness, about his father's strong features that proclaimed to the viewer that he was deeply in love.

Late that night Valjean and Simone sat listening to carols sung by a group that had stopped before the windows. She decided then to ask a question she'd long wondered about.

"Valjean, have you a fiancée in Boston I'm keeping you from?"

Valjean, still looking at the carolers, said that he did not. Something in that quick response made Simone suspicious.

Sliding her arm under his, she said, "Do not lie to your *maman*, Valjean. I *am* keeping you from a girl you care about, and you don't want me to worry that I'm disrupting your life. Tell me the truth, *mon fils*. There is a girl on your mind."

Valjean sighed. "You're right, Maman; but she isn't waiting for me. If I met her by accident—and that's the only way I'll ever find her again, I suspect—she probably wouldn't speak to me. She thinks I'm an English spy."

Simone caught her breath in surprise. "An English spy! How can this be? She's French, then? You must tell me about this girl and this misunderstanding."

"Aimée is from Montreal," Valjean said; then meaning to give her a brief account of how he had met Aimée, Valjean found himself telling his mother everything he knew about her, each detail of her appearance and their two meetings.

After Valjean had no more to say and Simone's questions had all been answered, she shook her head and commented, "And she thinks you're an enemy spy. You, of all the unlikely people. How ironic."

Quiet for a time, she gazed into the flames crackling cheerfully in the fireplace and thought about the perplexing situation. Finally she looked at Valjean, who was staring into his brandy, remembering the color of Aimée's eyes.

"*Mon fils,* will you sit beside me?" Simone asked.

Valjean obeyed without speaking. He knew from her solemn expression that she had something of great moment to tell him.

"I know you dislike my referring to the time when I'll no longer be with you, but please hear me out, Valjean," she began. He nodded, and she continued, "I have no idea what actually happens after death, but I do have a firm faith in our immortality. If, after I've gone, it is possible for me to be . . ." She hesitated, as if suddenly shy about what she had to say. She took a breath and warned, "You must not laugh at what I'm about to say, Valjean."

"I would never laugh at what you say unless it was something humorous," he quietly assured her.

"I want you to know that, if it's possible, I would like to watch out for you, to be a kind of guardian angel to you," she said awkwardly. His smoky eyes told her how touched he was by her proposal, and she smiled tenderly, adding, "I think you love this girl, Aimée; and I see little chance of your finding each other by accident." She reached out to caress his cheek with her thin fingers. "I suppose that as an angel one has some abilities one doesn't have as a mortal. Perhaps then I could help you and Aimée find each other—if indeed I have the grace to achieve angelhood."

Valjean turned his head to kiss her fingers. "You have the grace, Maman," he whispered.

Chapter 7

Aimée had begun the day with an aching head, a reaction to the early February chill, punctuated by a drizzle that was half snow. An afternoon of preparing herself for King Louis's birthday celebration had done nothing to ease her pain; and then the operatic performance preceding the royal ball had been unusually long and tumultuous. Her pain had intensified with every lusty peal and piercing aria until her hammering pulses seemed ready to burst from her temples. Finally she'd whispered excuses to Alain and left the royal theater.

Finding a small salon near the music hall, Aimée sighed with relief as she sank into a rose velvet settee. She was profoundly grateful that her only company was the porcelain figurines cavorting in the glass insert of an elaborate ormolu clock that made no sound other than its dignified ticking and an occasional whir.

Focusing her eyes on her reflection in the mirrored wall opposite the settee, she gloomily wondered how she would manage even one dance during the ball following the entertainment. As she thought about the ball, she automatically began to arrange the folds of her gown. The pale peach satin embroidered with gold fleurs-de-lis in honor of the royal birthday and the amber lace ruching, complemented her natural hair color so well that she'd forbidden the hairdresser to powder her coiffure. But now the rich flame of her auburn hair seemed only to mock her pale complexion; and she wished for some rouge to give color to her cheeks and lips.

Staring unhappily at her reflected image, she raised a hand to better secure the gold bodkin she wore in her

curls, and was reminded of the set of amber hair ornaments she'd recently received from her unknown admirer.
Those ornaments would have been perfect with this gown,
as would the matching jewelry, each piece of which had
been delivered on its own: the bracelet, the necklace with
fragile amber pendants, and the ring, which had come the
evening Alain learned about her mysterious and generous
admirer.

Alain hadn't mentioned the anonymous gifts since that
night, and Aimée sometimes wondered if he even remembered the incident. He had exacted her promise to tell him
who the gift sender was if she could ever learn his identity, and Aimée feared that Alain might challenge or publicly denounce the man. She wanted no blood shed on her
account, nor did she want the embarrassment of such a
scandal. And now she was even more fearful, because she
had reason to suspect that the king himself was her anonymous admirer. On Christmas Day she'd received a cape
made of silk velvet the color of her eyes and lined with
sable so sumptuous that her parents' gift, an exquisite
dove-gray cashmere cloak trimmed with silver fox, paled
in comparison. That her parents' beautiful gift of love
should be diminished in any way by a present that was in
actuality a bribe from a wealthy and, no doubt, married
man had so piqued Aimée that she'd thrust the cape into
her wardrobe. Slamming the door, she vowed never to
look at it again. The person who had sent it to her would
never see her wear it; nor would she wear or use any of the
other anonymous gifts. She'd promptly packed them all in
a trunk and latched it.

She observed, with some satisfaction, that her renewed
anger had at least brought fresh color to her face. But her
satisfaction suddenly vanished at the sound of a voice in
the adjoining room.

"Lebel!" King Louis hailed his valet in an ominous
tone.

Aimée heard the scrape of Lebel's feet as he made a
sudden turn, then the cracking of knees as he knelt before
his king.

"I didn't realize Your Majesty had already returned from *Parc aux Cerfs*," the valet apologized.

"Returned? I never went! Would you expect me to take even one step into that miserable rain?" Louis inquired sarcastically. "La Charonne was sent to me."

"Of course, Your Majesty," Lebel agreed. "Would Your Highness now wish to be dressed for the ball?"

"In a moment, in a moment," Louis said impatiently, then added sharply, "Did I give you permission to rise?"

"No, Highness," the servant returned in a pained tone.

Aimée knew Lebel had an arthritic condition that must be pure torment on such an evening, and she wondered at Louis's deliberate punishment of the man by making him continue to kneel.

"Didn't I tell you long ago I wanted nothing other than virgins?" Louis demanded.

"Yes, Majesty," Lebel replied warily.

"When Madame de Pompadour saw the abbess bringing La Charonne to me, she warned that the girl was no longer a maid. The abbess immediately questioned the girl and obtained the truth—she was not a virgin," Louis said sternly.

"Highness, I didn't know!" Lebel exclaimed in alarm. "Monsieur Meusnier assured me Mademoiselle Charonne would meet all your requirements!"

Aimée caught her breath in shock. Meusnier, she knew, was a high police official. Inspector Meusnier procured girls for the king's amusement? Wishing fervently that she could leave the salon, she realized she dared not try because she'd have to pass the open doorway to the next room and might be seen.

"Obviously Meusnier was wrong," Louis was saying. "Obviously you also didn't check into La Charonne's past as carefully as you should have."

"Majesty, I believed Monsieur Meusnier," Lebel said, his voice breaking as if he were near tears. Aimée heard a shuffling sound. The servant, still on his knees, was struggling closer to the king. "I beg your pardon, Highness," Lebel pleaded. "It will never happen again. I swear it!"

Louis was silent a long moment, and Aimée knew he

was deliberately withholding his pardon to further terrorize the valet. Finally he said in a cold tone, "I will forgive you this one time."

"Thank you, Majesty, thank you," the servant whispered.

"Get up and go to my suite to ready my garments for the ball," Louis commanded. "I'll be with you shortly."

"Yes, Highness," the servant said.

There was a scraping and shuffling noise, and Aimée knew Lebel was painfully struggling to his feet. She heard the limping footsteps recede and then the sound of a door closing.

Afraid to move lest Louis glimpse her, she slouched down in the settee, hoping the king wouldn't see her head over the settee's back, which would face him if he exited through the salon. Not having heard Louis's footsteps on the thick Aubusson rug, she was stunned when he stepped around the settee and sat beside her.

"Your Majesty!" she gasped, and began to rise to make her curtsey. This time Louis didn't stop her; and when she'd sunk into her gesture of obeisance, his hand on her shoulder pressed her into so deep a curtsey that she slipped to her knees. His hand under her chin encouraged her to look up, but he still didn't give her permission to rise from the floor. When her eyes met his, she knew he wanted her to remain humbly at his feet, as Lebel had.

"Aren't you going to wish me well on my birthday?" Louis asked quietly.

"Your Majesty, I congratulate you on this occasion; but I wish you a healthy, joyous life and a long, glorious reign always," she carefully replied.

"Gracefully said," he commented. He was silent a moment, then observed, "You aren't wearing that pretty amber ring I saw some months ago. What a pity. It would complement that gown, as would the other amber jewelry and the hair ornaments."

Aimée caught her breath. She'd never worn the hair ornaments in his presence. How could he know she had them unless he'd been the sender? Her suspicions about him confirmed, she didn't know how to reply. She dared not say what was on her mind.

Louis leaned forward until his face was so close to hers that she could feel his breath on her lips. "Why aren't you wearing that jewelry?" he asked softly.

"I didn't know it was you who'd sent it," she finally whispered.

"I should think the succession of so many costly gifts would have given you an idea," Louis murmured.

"Majesty, I couldn't imagine why I deserved such attention from you," she managed.

"I'll show you why," he returned.

Aimée wanted to move away, but his fingers under her chin tightened as his face came closer and his lips met hers. His mouth was warm as he kissed her lingeringly. She could see that his reputation with women wasn't exaggerated. Under other circumstances she would have found his caresses exciting; but Queen Marie stood like a stern ghost between them, and Aimée's fear of his power momentarily stopped any response he might have aroused in her. When he drew away, she stared up at him with eyes like a startled fawn's.

"Mirabeau, I understand, has managed nothing more intimate with you than such kisses," Louis said thoughtfully.

Too terrified to say a word, Aimée nodded, feeling as if her heart were pounding so hard the king must see it against the lace trimming her low neckline. She wondered how the king could know what she and Alain had done together, but she dared not speak.

Louis's dark eyes seemed to draw her thoughts from her brain. He smiled coldly. "My power is absolute, Aimée. I can learn whatever I wish about anybody."

Did Louis mean Alain himself had reported his progress with her? Aimée wondered, stunned at the idea.

"Unlike La Charonne, you are innocent. I already know," Louis commented.

"I'm afraid I don't understand your meaning, Your Majesty," Aimée managed to lie.

"Having learned that La Charonne was sadly misrepresented, I'd anticipated my evening ruined; but perhaps it is not," Louis said pointedly.

"Majesty, I . . ." Aimée began hesitantly.

"If you have it in mind to refuse me, you'd best think again," Louis interrupted.

Horrified to realize that the king could order her dragged to his chamber and rape her, Aimée's lips parted to speak; but she couldn't think of what she might say. His fingers left her chin, and his hands now gripped her shoulders, lifting her with surprising strength, forcing her to sit beside him. His fingertips caressed her skin; his hands slowly slipped to the base of her throat, then cupped her temples, again drawing her face to his. His mouth explored her yet parted lips, caressing her with an expertise designed to arouse any woman despite her hesitance, his tongue following the contours of her mouth; so for a moment she forgot who was kissing her, and responded. When he felt her resistance melting, his hands left her temples, sliding down her throat to the décolletage of her gown, his fingertips moving sensually over the warm mounds of her bosom, slipping beneath the lace and satin to close around her breasts, insistently caressing until an exquisite flame flared in her.

Surprised by the sudden surge of sensation, Aimée gasped and pulled away to stare wordlessly into the king's darkly glittering eyes.

"I knew from the first moment I saw you in the garden that you would be the most passionate of women," Louis said, a hard edge to his voice, which Aimée recognized as desire.

"Majesty, I . . ." she began, then stopped. What could she say? How could she refuse *him*?

"You realize, Aimée, a man of my position could have effected your surrender long ago by one means or another," he said bluntly. "But a king discovers that it's a rare woman who will challenge him, and I find your resistance most intriguing. I think my winning you will be that much more exciting in the end." Noting the expression on her face, he laughed softly. "Did you think I would ravish you, my dear?"

Aimée gathered up her courage, took a deep breath, and blurted, "If I'm to be allowed a choice, Your Majesty, my answer is no."

Louis's smile faded. All warmth left his eyes, and his features grew taut with irritation. "You should give some serious thought, Aimée, to how advantageous an alliance with me could be for you—how uncomfortable it might become if you were to arouse my disfavor."

"You *do* intend to force me into becoming one of your paramours," Aimée observed.

"Behave like a woman, not a child!" Louis snapped. Then his voice lowered as he continued more calmly: "You really have no idea how much power I hold. 'Absolute' is only a word you think you know the meaning of. You will learn, Aimée, that sometimes even the word 'choice' means little more than an inevitable conclusion." He stood up to look down at her. "You're one of my subjects, and I'm about to leave your presence."

Hating now to make any gesture of homage, Aimée forced herself to sink into a curtsey. She knew he wouldn't permit her to rise: he wanted her to remain at his feet.

"Look up at me, Aimée."

She raised her eyes only as far as his chest, refusing to look at his face, and wondering what more he would say.

"I won't trouble you again this evening, mademoiselle," he said tightly. He reached out to stroke her curls, then closed his hand tightly on her hair, forcing her to look at his face. In the same softly menacing tone he'd used with Lebel, he finished, "Sometimes it isn't a question of what a choice will be, but *when* you'll make it." Releasing his hold on her, he turned and walked out of the room.

Only after Aimée was certain that Louis wouldn't return did she get to her feet; and with her heart still pounding in fear, she turned to the mirror to try to repair the damage he'd done to her coiffure. Fearful but angry eyes dominated her face, which held a pallor that was almost translucent.

"Aimée, do you . . . ?"

She whirled to face Alain who had entered the salon

and stood staring at her, an alarmed expression on his face.

"Aimée, you look ill," he said concernedly.

"I must go home, Alain. Now. Will you take me?" she asked tersely.

"Of course," he replied, "but we must take a moment to give our excuses—at least to extend our good wishes to the king—"

"I've already given him as many good wishes as I can," she interrupted. She crossed the room to face Alain as she finished in a chill tone: "His Majesty will know why we're leaving."

During the long drive from Versailles to Paris Aimée offered Alain no explanation of her strange behavior. After she'd stepped from the carriage, she merely thanked him for taking her to the ball, then turned to enter the house without inviting Alain inside; nor did she say good night to send him off. Consumed with curiosity about her peculiar attitude, he followed her into the house.

In the foyer, he asked impatiently, "Aimée, what are you thinking of? Aren't you going to tell me what's wrong?"

"Come with me into the parlor and I'll tell you," she answered tensely, then turned to lead him into the adjoining room. Once inside she began to pull the double doors that opened onto the hall, then, distracted by her troubles, turned to Alain, forgetting to shut the doors completely.

"I must ask you one question before I say more," she said. At his nod she inquired, "Have you been reporting all along to the king each time you've kissed me? Have you been describing every detail of our embraces?"

Alain looked shocked. "Certainly not," he answered.

"How does he know?" she demanded.

"What are you talking about, Aimée?" he exclaimed.

Aimée turned away. She couldn't face him while she described what had happened in the salon before he'd arrived; she felt ashamed, cheapened. When she'd finished, she felt Alain's hands on her arms and glanced at him over her shoulder as she added sarcastically, "Now that you know who my mysterious admirer is, will you denounce him, Alain? Or perhaps you'll challenge him to a duel to defend my honor?"

"I can do neither, Aimée. You know that," he said softly. Grasping her shoulders, he firmly turned her to face him. "You're overwrought, worrying needlessly."

"How can you say that? He all but threatened me!" she cried.

"*Non, non,* Aimée. He didn't mean it, I'm sure. He won't force you to do anything. He has never forced himself on any of his mistresses," Alain soothed.

"Can you take what he said so lightly?" she asked incredulously.

"I take nothing the king says lightly, but I know him better than you," Alain replied. "Come, Aimée. Sit down with me and I'll tell you why you shouldn't be so worried."

Aimée let Alain steer her to a couch and sat down. Alain seated himself beside her.

Taking her hand comfortingly, he explained, "His Majesty's marriage was arranged when he was only fifteen. I've heard that at first he seemed enchanted by Queen Marie; but fifteen is a very impressionable age. Ten years, ten children later, he found her less enchanting; but you can imagine that between fifteen and twenty-five a man changes his mind a great many times. The ladies of the court always were accessible to him, and he has a very ardent nature. Doesn't it seem natural for him to enjoy these noblewomen?"

"Does Inspector Meusnier arrange liaisons with noblewomen? Does Lebel? Was this Mademoiselle Charonne from some illustrious family?" Aimée asked sarcastically.

"Aimée, put aside your provincial attitudes. This isn't Montreal," Alain reminded. "Madame de Pompadour held his undivided attention for some time, but . . . You must promise, Aimée, not to speak of this to anyone," he warned. Intrigued, she gave her promise, and he continued: "Madame de Pompadour is ill. She hasn't the strength to keep him happy in her boudoir, but they remain in love in their way. I heard her comment once that these other women only temporarily have his body and she has his heart. Yes, Pompadour knows and even encourages him to have other women to keep him happy. Because he always returns to her. Lebel finds him women—police lieutenants, even Inspector Meusnier, find him women. He insists on virgins so he won't contract a disease. The woman he called the abbess is Madame Bertrand, the wife of a high-ranking military officer; and she supervises Parc aux Cerfs."

"Everyone seems to applaud this, this *licence*," Aimée remarked disgustedly.

"The women he keeps in Parc aux Cerfs come of their own choosing. When he tires of them, they and their families are handsomely rewarded. Many of the girls marry better than they could otherwise have dreamed," Alain replied.

"They're satisfied as long as they're paid enough," she commented, thinking of how her parents would react to payment for her loss of virtue. "Well, Alain, even King Louis doesn't have enough money to buy me."

"But you do understand now, Aimée, that he won't force you, that you don't have to fear him in this?" Alain asked.

"Perhaps not," she said slowly; but remembering the hard glitter in Louis's eyes as he'd stood above her, the coolly threatening tone in his voice when he'd told her she might have only one choice, she wasn't reassured. She said firmly, "Whatever his intentions, Alain, I can't face him again. I can't return to Versailles."

"Perhaps it would be best if you avoided the palace for a time—until he notices someone else and forgets you," Alain conceded. "I'll take you to entertainments outside Versailles for a while."

"But you have to attend some of the functions at the palace, don't you?" Aimée asked.

"It's almost Lent. There are no important social occasions at Versailles during that season. The few dinner parties I might be invited to I can attend alone," Alain promised.

Aimée accepted this proposal without further questions;

but later, as she prepared for bed, she doubted that Alain would attend any palace function alone. There were too many women who found him attractive. She hadn't been blind to the many flirtatious glances thrown his way whenever she was with him; she wasn't deaf to the subtle suggestions that women move into their conversations when he was present. She knew, from the occasional cautious remarks he'd been making lately, that he was considering proposing marriage to her. She wondered if he would be faithful to a wife, and realized she doubted it. Alain spoke so casually about the king and his paramours; his attitude toward love seemed to her as amoral as that of most of the other aristocrats. The pleasure-loving court appeared to ally themselves at their whims, married or not.

Aimée sighed inwardly as she began to brush her hair. The king had told her she was behaving like a child. Alain had advised her to forget what he called her "provincial attitudes"; Paris wasn't Montreal. That was true enough, she admitted. Paris certainly wasn't at all like Montreal. Neither was its genteel society what she'd anticipated—not under its gracefully mannered surface. The entire court seemed to have substituted the word "love" for "sex" and forgotten the meanings of both. Even Alain seemed to think loyalty was negotiable.

As often happened, her thoughts drifted to Valjean; and she wondered what his attitudes were in these matters. She wished she hadn't been so impulsive when he'd approached her on the ship, condemning him instead of hearing him out. He'd said then that he wasn't a spy, but she'd brushed aside her opportunity to learn what his purpose in Montreal had been. She bitterly regretted that she could now never learn anything more about him.

Placing the hairbrush on her dressing table, she stared into the wavering candle flame that lit her mirror—thinking about Valjean, remembering his quick smile, his dappled eyes, the way he moved—the way he kissed.

"Not even the king, however practiced he may be in love, can kiss like you, Valjean," she whispered into the flame. "How can I forget you? I feel your body against mine at all times, your lips kissing me. The sensation of you is engraved on me, as if you always were touching me, though you're miles and miles away."

Earlier that evening Mignon too had returned from a dinner party with Roget, the baron du Dieudonné. The baron had become so insistent in his courtship that she was no longer certain how she'd be able to hold his attentions at a manageable level while she made a decision about him. As much as she liked him personally, she wasn't sure she loved him; and his greatest flaw, habitual gambling, was something she couldn't ignore. Unable to sleep for worrying, she'd gotten out of bed, put on a dressing gown, and made her way down to the kitchen to brew a cup of soothing chocolate. There she'd found Cousin Claude; welcoming her company, he merely added more ingredients to the drink he was brewing for himself.

As they tiptoed back upstairs carrying their steaming cups, voices came through the partially opened doors to the parlor; and recognizing Alain's exclamation of shock, Claude and Mignon exchanged looks of surprise.

Instinctively wanting to protect Aimée, Claude was prepared to march into the parlor, but Mignon gripped his sleeve, signaling him to wait and listen a little longer to learn if Aimée really did need his help. The conversation they heard alarmed them both, but Mignon tugged Claude up the stairs, pleading with him not to interfere. Having seen him enter his own room, Mignon crept down the hall to her parents' bedchamber.

"Maman, Papa, I must speak to you," Mignon whispered, gently shaking them in turn.

"What are you talking about, *ma petite?*" Jeannette immediately asked.

"What is wrong at this hour, Mignon?" Hilaire responded, his voice muffled by sleepiness.

"I think Aimée has a problem she won't want to tell you about, but you should know," Mignon whispered. "I just overheard her talking to Alain about it."

Hilaire swung his legs from the bed, his long nightshirt tangling around his knees. He hastily put on his robe, then got up and lit a candle. He faced his daughter. "What did you hear, *ma petite fille*?" he asked trying to keep the alarm from his tone. "Sit down and tell me what's troubling you so."

Mignon repeated what she'd heard on the steps. Hilaire and Jeannette soothed her, telling her to go to her room and not to worry. They would decide what must be done.

Hilaire watched the door close behind Mignon, then turned to his wife. "Perhaps Alain is sure King Louis will do nothing more about Aimée, but I've heard stories about him that make me less confident," he said softly.

"I too, *mon amour*," Jeannette replied worriedly, then sighed. "I'd thought our daughters might marry well and be happy here. *Mon Dieu,* I never forsaw such problems! Our little Aimée being pursued by the king himself. Mignon pressured by the baron, who gambles his fortune away . . ."

"Don't overlook the baron du Dieudonné's penchant for chasing other women—or Alain's either, for that matter," Hilaire grumbled. "I have no intention of leaving our daughters in France with husbands who will make them unhappy. They haven't been raised to think that a wife must overlook her husband's indiscretions, as many wives here seem able to do."

"They've had their father's example of fidelity to grow up with," Jeannette reminded him.

Always warmed by Jeannette's praise, Hilaire smiled and patted her arm. "Their mother has been a constant source of inspiration to them, *ma chérie*." He was silent a moment, thinking about Aimée's dilemma. Finally he said, "Alain's suggestion that Aimée stay out of the king's sight makes sense. Perhaps His Majesty will forget her."

"Forget that little *sorcière*? *Mon amour,* have you looked at the girl lately?" Jeannette asked pointedly. "Aimée is not, I think, so easily forgotten—nor is Mignon. Our daughters have bloomed into real beauties." Seeing Hilaire nod in silent agreement, she added worriedly, "Maybe we were wrong in so protecting them all their lives; but, *mon amour,* it saddens me to see their innocence eroded by their having to deal with such base problems. Before we left Montreal, neither of them could have dreamed of such matters as paramours, unfaithful husbands, and compulsive gamblers."

"I know, *ma chérie,* I know," Hilaire agreed. "In Montreal Aimée would have been too shy to have such a discussion as the one Mignon told us she'd heard coming from the parlor." Hilaire sighed heavily. "I expect the first passenger ships to begin arriving from the colonies around Easter. I'll inquire with each captain about the condition of the ice in the Saint Lawrence. As soon as one of them can be sure the river is navigable, I'll arrange for our passage back to Montreal," he promised.

"What about the British? Won't their blockade stop a French ship?" Jeannette questioned.

"I intend to arrange our voyage on a ship flying another flag," Hilaire assured. "That, *ma chérie,* would only be a precaution, I think. We've not heard of further British advances in the colonies. Perhaps King George is more concerned about King Frederick's advances than about the French colonies in North America."

Although Hilaire spoke confidently, he privately wondered why he'd heard no news of any kind about the colonies in New France for so long a time. He suspected that Montreal and Quebec were suffering through so severe a winter that not even cargo ships could approach the ports, and thus they couldn't bring back news. Grateful that Marcel had the produce of their own estate to feed the household, that his son had a competent mind and a sensible disposition, he didn't want to worry Jeannette unduly with discussions of Montreal's problems.

"Our daughters' romantic troubles aren't all that worries me, *mon amour,*" Jeannette was saying. "The French peasants are becoming very short-tempered, and who can blame them? When a man sees his family shivering because they have only rags to wear in the winter, how could he not resent the extravagant entertainments at the palace? When a peasant's landlord is applying every pressure he can for his tenant to produce more because he's being so heavily taxed, and the peasant in turn can hardly afford to feed his own family, it's natural for people to be angry. There have been demonstrations about the gambling and corruption, the pleasure-seeking aristocrats—even about Parc aux Cerfs. There occasionally have been riots— quickly put down, *oui;* the news withheld, *oui*—but riots! I'm growing afraid to remain here."

"How did you learn of these things, *chérie?*" Hilaire asked cautiously.

"I know you try to protect the girls and me from such news; but, *mon amour,* I hear the rumors. Even Victoire, as much as Antoine tries to conceal the situation from her, knows what it is. We've talked about it. Do you know what the king has said? 'After me the deluge.' As if he can do nothing about the extravagance. Can't? *Won't!* He and that Pompadour are ruining France. Carrying on wars they can't win while they carouse! Running through the treasury until the country is almost bankrupt. Pouring the young men of France into a bloodbath—it's no surprise so many of our soldiers desert. I tell you, *mon amour,* there will come a day when there will be a revolt. Have you seen any of those censored books? People are thinking for themselves now. They aren't accepting the king's decisions as if they came from the mouth of God."

"*Mon Dieu, chérie,* don't speak so loudly of such things. It's like applauding treason," Hilaire said in alarm.

"Who will betray me? Antoine? Victoire? Perhaps Claude? I think not. They're as concerned as we," Jeannette replied firmly. "We can return to Montreal in the spring, but what of the meantime? Aimée and Mignon might be caught in a riot while coming home from a party. Victoire and I could be attacked by a mob when we're shopping."

"Antoine and his family won't betray you—but they have servants we don't know," Hilaire reminded her. He put his face in his hands. He couldn't deny the truth of Jeannette's conclusions. He took a deep breath and lowered his hands. "*Ma chérie,* the corruption you speak of is a fact. Antoine and I have also discussed it. He, too, has been thinking about emigrating to Montreal; but he has a wonderful future here if all these problems can be resolved peacefully, so he hesitates. It grieves me to admit I see no likelihood of King Louis changing his habits or the government being put in order. Perhaps Louis is right in thinking that after him the monarchy will fall, but it could happen before that. He is a relatively young man, and I wonder if France can survive for so long a time in its present situation."

Jeannette took Hilaire's hands in hers. *"Mon amour,* France itself isn't my immediate worry. I'm concerned first for us and our daughters. I have a plan—see what you think of it: Aimée and Mignon should not go out separately with their escorts; they are to attend parties together. Then they won't have to worry about Alain's or Roget's attentions becoming too intimate, because they'll be chaperoning each other. Also, with both Alain and Roget and their combined footmen and servants always following them about, the girls will be protected if they should ever find themselves approached by angry peasants."

Hilaire sighed heavily. *"Chérie,* you are, as usual, both practical and a genius. Your suggestion is perfect. Will you talk to the girls about it so they can arrange their social comings and goings together?"

"Mais oui," Jeannette answered eagerly. "I know both of them will respond well to this idea. Victoire and I can make sure always to take extra servants when we go out too."

"Meanwhile I'll try to persuade Antoine to move to Montreal. No matter what happens in Europe, I believe the colonies have a promising future."

"I'm sure you're right about that, *mon amour,"* Jeannette agreed. She squeezed Hilaire's hands affectionately and added, "You always have been so wise about the future. You have imagination and the courage to look ahead—you have vision."

Hilaire smiled, kissed his wife's cheek, then blew out the candle and prepared to go back to sleep; but he lay awake for a long time thinking about the troubles they'd discussed, hoping the solutions they'd planned for their own problems would be enough.

Aimée and Mignon said nothing to Alain and Roget

about their reasons for maneuvering the men into always going to the same entertainments together. Roget, however, assumed Mignon found this a convenient way to delay for a while her decision about marriage. He resolved to be the epitome of good manners and character, thinking that after he'd gained her complete confidence, he could resume his previous course and eventually win her surrender.

Alain quickly decided that the new arrangement was designed to cool Roget's ardor; and he didn't mind this turn of events, as it suited his own plans very well. For one thing it would neutralize any speculation about his visiting the palace a bit less frequently, when he was seen at the ballet, plays, and receptions given by hostesses whose ties to the court were intimate. When Alain did have to attend some function at Versailles, it was easy enough for him to find a female partner, and that would put to rest any questions arising in King Louis's mind about why Aimée didn't come to the palace.

It was too droll, Alain thought; while Aimée assumed he was protecting her he would have the opportunity to resume his love affairs with the various noblewomen he'd known before, as well as begin affairs with a few others who had recently caught his attention—a pastime he'd sorely missed while he was occupied solely with Aimée.

He troubled himself not at all about the increasing reports of the Parisians' discontent with their government. As his carriage rolled through the slushy streets, he was confident that his footmen and various escorts could defend his property in the unlikely event that the lower classes should actually dare to approach and try to detain him.

Chapter 8

Valjean stood before the window absently holding his coffee cup midway to his lips while he stared at the mist visible in the light of the street lamp. Finally he roused himself to take a sip, then glanced over his shoulder at the clock on the mantle. It was nearly dawn. He was only mildly surprised. The almost continuous early spring rain had cast a pall of fog and gloom over the days, merging them with the nights, displacing time; but the weather was only part of the reason he had lost count of the hours.

Although Simone had been bedridden several times since Christmas, she'd always managed to regain enough strength to recover. No matter how brightly she'd behaved after these periods of weakness, each of those sieges had left her weaker; and he sensed this latest battle was likely to be her last.

They'd had so little time to get to know each other—merely a winter, he reflected; but she'd tried to condense all the years they'd been separated by using the months as fully as possible. He realized now that from the moment he'd walked into the house, she'd fooled him into thinking she was stronger than she really was, and had gallantly disguised her weakness to take him—while she yet was able—to places that hadn't been available to him before, to introduce him to experiences and ideas that would enrich him, as well as help him decide whether to make his life in France or return to Boston. Not accidentally, she also was preparing him for his place as comte de la Tour, marquis d'Auvergne, if he remained in France. All the while she'd predicted a bright future for him, whichever way of life he was to choose.

"Monsieur le Marquis?" Ariel inquired, using his lesser title, though it was the one he preferred because it was truly his family's—not Simone's by marriage.

Valjean turned to face Ariel, dreading the possible announcement that Simone's strength was fading even more.

"Madame has awakened," Ariel said.

Valjean let out the breath he hadn't realized he'd been holding. "I'll go to her," he replied, and put down the empty cup to follow the maid.

Simone had been very slender when Valjean had first arrived at the house, but now she was skeletal. Each time he walked into the room, even if he'd been away for only a few minutes, her appearance shook him anew. She seemed so fragile, as if her life were slipping irrevocably away; and he so fiercely wanted her to grasp and hold on to it. Although her dark eyes were clear and focused on him, they held an expression he could only define as seeming as if something behind them were withdrawing. He could have wept, but he fixed a smile on his lips and approached her.

"Do you feel strong enough after your rest to have a little broth?" he asked, sitting in the chair at her bedside.

"Maybe later," she replied as usual, not wanting to eat anything, but also not wanting to worry him with her complete refusal.

He knew her purpose and didn't press her. He reached out to take her hand. "Maman . . ." he began.

Perceiving that he really didn't know what to say, but was searching for some words to cheer her, she forced herself to smile. "*Mon fils,* will you tuck the blanket around my feet? They feel cold."

"Of course," Valjean replied as he rose to obey, trying not to notice the purple tint of her feet.

Simone knew that he had not really accepted her imminent death, that he fought the idea and his battle was tearing him apart. She wished to convince him—to make him face the truth, to save him from some of this pain. She gathered together the last shreds of her resolve and commented, "Ariel has told me it's Easter morning. What a pity that beautiful hat you bought for me to wear to the cathedral will go unused."

As she'd anticipated, he quickly replied, "The priest will come this afternoon to give you communion; and another Sunday, a week or two from now, you can wear your hat to mass." He continued arranging the blanket at her feet, though it needed no further tending; he dared not look up at her.

"*Non, mon fils,* the priest will give me communion and the last sacrament as well. Do not deceive yourself. The time has come and you know it as well as I."

"Don't speak that way. One must have hope. There have been other times you took to this bed only to—"

"Not this time, Valjean," she said quietly. "One does not hold on to one's soul by will alone. There is a higher Will that one cannot argue with."

Valjean brushed away his tears—there was no way to hide them now. He felt so helpless. He couldn't speak. He looked up at Simone and was surprised that she could smile at him now—not a smile she forced, but an easy smile, genuine.

"I feel that I might fall asleep again, Valjean. Each time I close my eyes I'm not sure if they'll reopen to see you or your father, so come closer. Let me hold you a moment before I fall asleep, will you?" she asked.

He sat on the edge of the bed and wordlessly put his arms around her fragile shoulders.

"You're so like your father," she whispered. "Did I tell you before his name was Steven? It was why I made your second name Étienne?" He nodded against her shoulder. She felt one of his tears slide down her neck. "*Mon fils,* don't feel so bad," she soothed. "When the moment arrives, think of your father coming for me, and think of me as the girl I was when I last saw him, running into his arms."

"I'll try," he whispered, but continued to cling to her.

"Remember, Valjean, what I said Christmas night?" When he didn't reply, she put her hands on his temples, pushing him slightly away to look into his tear-filled eyes. She shook her head sadly—much as she would have gently chided a child—as if his grief disappointed her. "That girl—that little red-haired minx Aimée—that you've been dreaming about. She is somewhere in this world, *mon fils*. If I can, I will help you find her. Steven will help too. I'm sure of it. I think he helped bring you to me after all." She sighed. "My eyelids, I'm sorry to say, are growing heavy again. Let me sleep for a while—perhaps you should lie down too—you look tired," she murmured, her eyes closing in spite of her efforts to stay awake.

He felt her body relaxing, her hands slipping from his temples; and taking her fingers in his, he tucked her arms under the blankets. Then, still bending over her, he listened, as he had so many times, to make sure she was still breathing.

"Monsieur le Marquis?" Ariel said from the corner where she'd sat ready to help her mistress if needed, to get her new master anything he might request.

"Yes, Ariel," Valjean replied without turning.

"Forgive me if I seem impudent; but you should do as she suggested and get some rest yourself," Ariel said concernedly, rising and coming nearer. "Let me have the cook make you some chocolate laced with brandy while you bathe. Then perhaps you can sleep too. I'll awaken you if there's any need," she promised. As he shook his head she added hurriedly, "You've had so little rest all this week—only short naps. Your eyes are sunken and shadowed. It will alarm madame to see you so when she awakens. She worries about you—she's told me."

Valjean rose from the bed. "I'll bathe and shave, but have the cook make a pot of coffee for me. No brandy in it. Just coffee—and tell her I want it strong."

"*Oui*, Your Grace." Ariel sighed as she dipped her head. She turned to leave the room, her posture betraying disapproval for his decision to force himself to remain awake.

Valjean followed Ariel out the door and went to his own room. A while later he returned to Simone's bed-chamber clad in a dressing gown. Ariel reentered moments afterwards with a coffee urn, her mouth set in a disapproving line as she set the tray on a table next to a comfortable chair. She poured the steaming liquid into a cup, then straightened and turned to face him.

"Will you at least sit down, Your Grace?" she asked.

Valjean nodded, did as she requested, and lifted the cup to his lips. Taking a sip, he said over his shoulder, "I'll call if I need you, Ariel. Thank you."

He heard the sound of the softly closing door. Ariel had said nothing in reply, which indicated that she was disgusted with his decision to remain awake. He smiled wryly as he thought of the devotion she'd transferred from Simone to him, knowing she was as attached to his mother as Bess had been to the Carletons.

Remembering Bess and the Carletons, the life that he'd led so short a time ago—and that would be undeniably changed when he returned to Boston—he drained the coffee from his cup and leaned his head against the chair's high back. Despite his resolve, his eyes closed, and he dreamed of Aimée walking hand in hand with him on a hillside near Boston, the soothing murmur of the nearby Atlantic, the fragrance of mayflowers floating on the breeze.

Ariel returned after a time to find Valjean asleep. Glad that he was at last getting some respite from his worries, she brought her embroidery into the room, seated herself nearby, and watched over her charges as the morning became afternoon. She forbade the other servants to enter lest they disturb the room's peace with even the smallest sound as she waited for the priest to arrive.

The day's gloom clung until almost sunset, suddenly lifting to reveal a sky blazing with orange-gold fire. Even though all plans to wear spring finery to the cathedral on Easter morning had to be reconsidered, the elite of Paris were not disheartened; for neither rain-soaked slippers nor sodden hems could dampen the ball at Versailles that night.

When the combined Dessaline families arrived at the palace, Aimée was quickly joined by Alain, who had been at Versailles all afternoon, on court business, Aimée had supposed. An hour later Roget, who had spent the day gambling in a fashionable salon, arrived to take Mignon's arm, making charming excuses she sensed were lies.

The week-long drizzle had altered the royal plan for an outdoor party, and for several days now the staff of palace gardeners had been scurrying in and out of the ballroom bringing part of the famed royal gardens inside.

Trees just going into bloom had been hastily potted and now lined the walls of the ballroom to form an orchard surrounding a central meadow where guests strolled on paths bordered by flower containers so closely placed that they appeared to be entire beds. As passing couples brushed the low-hanging limbs of the potted trees, apple and cherry blossoms showered over their shoulders. A fountain had, by some miracle of engineering skill, been transported indoors, and even a pavilion had been erected in the ballroom. Covered with budding roses, it would later form a fragrant arbor for the dancers beneath. Nature, at King Louis's orders, had obediently hurried summer's arrival.

Dinner was served from buffets scattered with flower petals. Ice sculptures of swans and deer banked with spring blossoms sat at intervals among the dishes. Guests seated themselves where they would, as if it were a sumptuous picnic.

Aimée strolled at Alain's side, enjoying the fantastic scene and the music of the violins that formed a background for the conversation and laughter; she wondered at the cost of such a dazzling *fête*.

Spring, represented by a boy and a girl swathed in robes so diaphanous Aimée could see the shadow of rosy nipples through her garments, rode into the center of the room on a white pony whose mane and tail had been braided with flowers. Aimée began to wonder if this party celebrated Easter as a religious holiday ushering spring into the world or as a Roman bacchanal. When a dwarf, naked but for the leaf clusters around his hips and genitals, came skipping into the room playing a flute, Aimée was too shocked to make even the gesture of applauding the tableau's cleverness. The dwarf approached the two youths, who had dismounted, to skip in circles around them while they

danced gracefully to his piping notes. The dwarf represented Pan, Aimée concluded, and he was encouraging the
boy and girl to become lovers. The couple, she estimated,
were no older than ten or eleven. How could their parents
have allowed them to participate in such a scene?

"Charming, aren't they?" Alain remarked.

Aimée nodded, unable to tell him her real opinion,
which would surely again brand her as provincial in his
eyes.

As the couple led their pony out of the room, merrily
preceded by the dwarf, the girl took off the garland of
flowers she wore in her hair and tossed it to Aimée as she
passed her. Surprised, Aimée still managed to catch it; and
the applause was now aimed at her. Blushing self-consciously, she smiled and nodded, not noticing until after
the violins had resumed playing that hidden among the
blossoms and leaves of the garland was a note attached to
the bouquet's foundation wires.

Curious about what the tightly rolled cylinder contained, wondering why the girl would write a note to her,
Aimée turned to Alain. "I can feel one of my hair ornaments coming loose," she said. "Will you excuse me,
Alain, while I go to fix it more securely?"

Alain nodded, then watched Aimée thread her way
through the crowd, her free hand holding one of the
pearl-studded bodkins whose ribbons matched the sea-
foam lace of her gown.

Once inside the lounge, Aimée waved aside a maid who
offered assistance with her coiffure, found a solitary chair,
and sat down. Now able to inspect the garland more
closely, Aimée discovered there was more than a note attached to its wires. Tied to a flower stem by a narrow ribbon, which had seemed only to decorate the fragile
headpiece, was a ring.

Aimée untied the ribbon with trembling fingers to reveal
a circlet of gold set with a large blue sapphire surrounded
by dainty pink diamonds. Wondering if it was Alain who
had thought of this romantic way of offering her a be-
trothal ring—if this was why he'd come to the palace earlier that afternoon—she unrolled the cylinder of paper.

She read its single line of writing in a glance. She could not believe its meaning and read it again, slowly, pronouncing each word in her mind to convince herself of its purpose.

It was not Alain's proposal of marriage but a summons for her to go to Parc aux Cerfs after the ball. Though it was unsigned, she presumed it was in the king's own handwriting.

Aimée's lifeless fingers allowed the note to reroll itself in her lap as she stared at the ring, whose sparkle now seemed to her more like the glitter of a serpent's eyes.

"*Sacrée mère de Dieu!*" she breathed. "What can I do now?"

In the evening a paroxysm of coughing roused Valjean as quickly as it did Ariel, who had fallen asleep over her embroidery. He leaped from his chair, almost upsetting a coffee urn as he wheeled around to hurry to the bed.

Simone's dark eyes, enormous in her emaciated face, were rimmed with tears from her coughing; but as Valjean lifted her shoulders from the pillows, supporting her while he held a handkerchief to her lips, her glance seemed disoriented. Assuming it was the continued coughing that made her eyes appear unfocused, he held her closer, whispering soothing words in her ear. As her attack seemed to subside he nodded to Ariel, who stood ready with a spoonful of the medicine the physician had prescribed.

Valjean leaned a little away from Simone, coaxing, "Take this medicine, Maman. It will ease your cough and soothe your throat."

Simone's eyes moved to look into his face; and though they still were tear-filled, she smiled and managed to whisper, "Whatever you say, Steven, *mon amour*."

Valjean exchanged looks of alarm with Ariel. "This is Valjean, Maman," he said gently.

For a moment she looked confused. Then a new smile broke over her face. "You look so like him, Valjean," she replied. "But he *is* here, you know."

Valjean swallowed, recovered himself, then said brokenly, "*Non*, I didn't know."

"Let me lie down again, *mon fils*," Simone whispered. "I'm so weary."

"Of course, Maman," he said, carefully settling her back on the pillows. He watched her eyes close; perfectly silent, he listened for the sound of her breath. Relief rushed through him as he perceived she was breathing deeply, as if now in comfortable slumber. He stood up and turned to face Ariel, who was regarding her mistress with worried eyes.

"She must have been dreaming of my father and awakened coughing to think I was he," Valjean said hurriedly.

"*Oui*, I'm sure that was it," Ariel agreed, her eyes still clouded by shadows.

"It's late, Ariel, well past suppertime. Why don't you go downstairs to eat?" Valjean suggested.

"Will you have something if I bring it, Your Grace?" she asked. When he shook his head in the expected no, she didn't scold or even try to persuade him to change his mind. She sighed in resignation and left the room, knowing she too couldn't eat.

After Ariel had gone, Valjean turned to pour himself another cup of coffee and found it had cooled. Although he was sure Ariel would shortly remember to bring in another urn, he drank this cup cold. He was determined not to fall asleep again. He would keep watch. He would listen.

Aimée remained sitting in the lounge for a long time, wondering how she could refuse Louis, how she might return the ring, as well as all the other gifts he'd sent, without too much angering him. One could refuse an ordinary man and he would have to go away, however disappointed he might be; but rejecting a king, who was used to obedience in all things, was sure to arouse his ire. That she might accept his summons and become one of his paramours never occurred to her.

Finally, deciding that Alain knew more about the court than she, that his personal acquaintance with King Louis might give him some insight on how she could deal with this dreadful situation, she got to her feet and set off to seek him out.

Aimée stepped into the ballroom and glanced self-consciously at the chair Louis had been occupying when she'd left. She was relieved that, although he'd risen and moved but a few steps away, he was engaged in a conversation with Madame de Pompadour. Recognizing Alain's valet among the servants standing on the far side of the room, she began to make her way through the crowd in the hope the valet would know where his master had gone.

"Mademoiselle Dessaline, it has been so long a time since I've had the pleasure of dancing with you!"

A hand on Aimée's arm stopped her progress, and she turned to see it was no less than the duc de Brienne who had spoken. "Bonsoir, Your Grace," she replied, carefully adding, "The evening is enchanting, don't you think?"

"It would be perfect if you would accept my invitation to dance," he replied. He knew she was putting him off. He'd been sending her his calling card daily for months, but she never accepted his offers to take her to one or another event, always on the excuse that Mirabeau had already asked her to the same amusement.

"I'm sorry, Your Grace, but—" she began.

"Surely if Alain already had his name on your card for this dance, he would be here dancing with you," the duke interrupted.

"I was detained by something else," Aimée said quickly. "I've been searching for him."

Brienne's eyes narrowed thoughtfully. If the foolish little innocent *must* pursue that fox Mirabeau even now, he decided, he would point her directly to Mirabeau's lair. Then, perhaps, Aimée would look at other men than Mirabeau, he hoped. "Maybe I can help you find him," he offered slyly.

"Do you know where he went?" Aimée asked. "If so, merely tell me; and I'll be in your debt."

Indeed you will, Brienne decided. "If you'll go into that corridor, you will find a small salon on the left side. Are you familiar with it?" After she'd nodded, he continued, "Behind the tapestry in the salon there is a door that

opens onto a stairway. Go upstairs and you'll find Mirabeau in the third room on the right."

"Are you sure that's where I'll find him, Your Grace?"
Aimée wondered why Alain would be in so obscure a
place.

"I'm very sure," the duke replied. "You should go
directly into the room, mademoiselle. I know the conversation will fascinate you."

Brienne's remarks perplexed Aimée, but she thanked
him for his help and turned away. He watched her with a
satisfied expression which, as she disappeared into the corridor he'd indicated, broke into a wide smile.

Too concerned with her own immediate problem to give
further thought to Brienne's obscure comments, Aimée
concentrated on following his directions. Still a little
breathless from her rush up the narrow stairway, she
counted the doors and stopped at the third. She automatically raised her hand to knock, then remembered Brienne's
instructions to walk into the room unannounced. She
opened the door.

The room's interior confused Aimée's perception for the
moment it took her to realize that all four walls were mirrored—even the ceiling was mirrored. The scene reflected
above made her catch her breath in surprise.

A man was reclining facedown on the enormous couch
that was the room's only furnishing. His pale skin was a
vivid contrast to the deep rose satin throw that irregularly
covered the couch. She could see the back of his head
with its tangled dark hair, the broad shoulders, the long
curve of his back disappearing under a fold of the
rumpled satin, then his legs emerging farther down, his
ankles tangled in another ripple of satin. He was propped
up on his elbows, she finally realized; and as he leaned a
bit to one side, she saw his profile. It was Alain. Then
Aimée saw the breast he was caressing, the long golden
hair that was spread over the satin. Alain was with a
woman!

Another head of light brown curls suddenly emerged
from beneath the satin, and Aimée was stunned anew. A
second woman?

When the blonde's eyes fell on Aimée standing in the doorway, they momentarily widened in surprise before she turned her head to whisper in Alain's ear.

Aimée was still too astounded to speak or even blush as Alain turned over to look at her, muttering in annoyance, "*Le diable . . .*" Then he exclaimed, "Aimée!"

For a long moment Aimée remained silent. Finally, surprising herself with the sound of her voice, she said coolly, "Although your name is on my card for this dance, monsieur, I can see you're much too occupied." She turned and left the room, Alain staring incredulously after her.

Aimée was halfway down the stairs before her full reaction exploded through her shock. Anger scorched her brain, and she stopped in her descent. How dare Alain hold her hand so tenderly less than an hour ago and describe his devotion to her! She turned, very tempted to go back upstairs and smash every mirror in that room, including the one on the ceiling.

"*Vous êtes un aristocrate? Vous êtes un cochon!*" she muttered. She clenched her hands into fists at her side, and the gems in Louis's ring cut her palm, the sudden pain jolting her memory to the reason she'd sought Alain. "*Le roi aussi—non, un pire cochon,*" she declared, and ran down the stairs.

When Aimée reentered the ballroom, her head was as high as if she were Queen Marie, her face frozen in a mask that hid her anger, like a core of white heat searing her.

"The worst pig," she muttered again as she threaded her way through the crowd; a woman gave her a startled look as she passed.

Approaching the king, who turned to regard her with a triumphant expression, Aimée sank into a deep curtsey. After he'd given her permission to rise, she straightened as gracefully as if she were dancing.

Louis anticipated that Aimée would make a complimentary remark about the ball and refer to the ring in some disguised way to acknowledge its receipt and his proposal—as any other woman of the court would have done; but Louis had forgotten that part of what he liked about

Aimée was that she behaved like no other woman he
knew. He said cheerfully, "What does the charming Mademoiselle Dessaline think about my indoor garden party?"

"The setting is clever and very beautiful, Your
Majesty," she replied. Then extending her open hand to
reveal the ring, she inquired, "Is this item yours, Your
Highness?"

Stunned that she would ask him directly, wondering
what exactly she intended, he said cautiously, "I believe
my valet was going to give it to someone."

"Then would Your Majesty agree it must be Lebel who
wishes me to meet him later tonight?" she asked coolly,
giving Lebel, who stood nearby, a sideways glance.

Now becoming embarrassed that Queen Marie was at
his side listening to the conversation, Louis answered,
"Perhaps so."

"I beg Your Majesty's pardon for my interruption,"
Aimée said dryly, then sank into another deep curtsey
and, without waiting for her dismissal, marched toward
the valet to confront him.

Amazed at the incident, Lebel stared at Aimée as she
took his hand and pressed the ring into his palm, closing
his fingers around it.

"Monsieur, thank you for your invitation; but I will not
meet you at Parc aux Cerfs later," she said clearly enough
for the king to overhear. "I have gathered together the
other items you anonymously sent me, and will engage a
messenger to return them." She dropped a small curtsey to
the stunned valet and turned away.

The line of people standing nearest Aimée separated, receding as if loath even to be brushed by her skirts as
she passed. The cold smile still fixed on her lips, Aimée
nodded to them and walked straight across the center of
the room, threading her way between the lines of dancers.

When she reached Hilaire and Jeannette, she caught
their hands and began to draw them away from the couple
they were standing near. Although they hadn't seen
through the crowd what Aimée had done, they recognized
the anger in her eyes. They made hurried excuses and followed her into an alcove.

"*Ma mère, mon père,* I think I must leave the ball now," Aimée said under her breath.

Jeannette was too dismayed to speak, but Hilaire asked in a low tone, "What are you talking about, Aimée?"

"The king arranged for a note to be given me asking that I go to Parc aux Cerfs tonight. With the note was a costly ring. I just now asked if the ring was his. He said Lebel's. I went to Lebel, gave him the ring and refused the assignation, saying I would return his other gifts as well."

"His Majesty realized what you were saying to Lebel was meant for him?" Hilaire asked softly.

"He, as well as a few others standing nearby, surely did," Aimée whispered, the magnitude of what she'd done beginning to penetrate her anger.

Jeannette stared at her. "You've embarrassed His Majesty?"

Aimée's fear began to wind into her being like a serpent's cold coils. "I'm afraid so, Maman," she whispered.

Jeannette turned to Hilaire. "What shall we do? *Mon Dieu,* what shall we do now?"

"Aimée's right about leaving the palace at once," Hilaire said, his tone low and calm as if he were discussing a business problem. "Where is Mignon? Does Alain know what happened?"

"Alain is upstairs with two women," Aimée whispered.

"Shouldn't we ask his advice?" Jeannette inquired.

Aimée caught her mother's hands and hissed, "You don't understand, Maman. They were naked."

Jeannette's eyes widened in a fresh assault of shock. "Upstairs? Two women?" she echoed.

"*Oui. À la trois,* in a mirrored room," Aimée replied under her breath.

Jeannette grasped Hilaire's hand, but her eyes hurriedly scanned the crowded room. "Where is Mignon?" she demanded.

"I don't know, *chérie,*" Hilaire replied, his eyes searching for their daughter among the dancing couples.

"I'm sorry. I'm so sorry I've caused this trouble," Aimée apologized.

"Although I wish you had refused the king more

discreetly, don't apologize for refusing to go to Parc aux Cerfs," Hilaire said angrily.

"What's wrong?" asked Mignon, who had approached from another direction. Her eyes were filled with concern. "I saw the way you looked, Aimée, as you crossed the room. What happened?"

"We're leaving the ball, Mignon," Jeannette said, grasping her daughter's hand.

"But why?" Mignon asked again.

"We'll explain after we're in the carriage," Hilaire advised. "Let us get our cloaks now."

Although Simone's breathing had made only the slightest of sounds, when it stopped, Valjean leaped up as if a thunderclap had exploded in his ear. He leaned over her, intending to shake her, to do *anything* to make the breathing start again; but before he could even touch her, he heard the long sigh of her lungs emptying and knew for a certainty there was nothing to be done. Bending over her for a long moment, he stared at her body in disbelief. Finally he straightened, stepped back, and sank into the chair where Ariel usually sat.

He wondered why he had no impulse to weep, why he was numb; his thoughts leaped from one subject to another, focusing on nothing at all—as if his mind were fleeing from the one bit of dread news before him. He'd thought that he'd finally accepted the idea of her dying. But he hadn't. He realized he didn't believe it even now. He glanced at the clock on Simone's dressing table. Not quite midnight. He shook his head in wonder. It didn't matter what time it was. Why was he thinking of that? He decided he wasn't rational. He was in some sort of shock. He needed fresh air. He *had* to leave this room.

Compelled by the idea of escape, Valjean got to his feet and walked swiftly to the door. He glanced back once, briefly, at Simone's slight, blanket-covered form, shivered, and stepped into the corridor, shutting the door behind him.

In his own room again, as he changed into riding

clothes his mind was devoid of all thoughts but one: He had to leave the house.

In the hall again, Valjean noticed Simone's door was open; and he paused to see who was inside. Ariel was standing beside the bed. She turned, her eyes filled with tears, and saw him standing in the doorway.

"She is gone, Your Grace," the maid said slowly.

"I know, Ariel. I was with her at the end," he replied.

"I've sent Henri for the doctor and . . . Are you leaving, Your Grace?" she asked, noticing then how he was dressed. "Where are you going at this hour? Henri can do what's needed."

"I have to get out of the house for a while," Valjean replied, stepping to one side of the doorway to let the butler pass.

"But there are thieves and murderers afoot at night," Ariel protested. Now very familiar with his expression of determination after her efforts this past week to persuade him to eat a meal or get some sleep, she knew it would be a waste of time to argue with him about staying home. Instead she said, "In the desk downstairs there is a set of dueling pistols. Madame's husband bought it long ago. Take one of them with you."

Valjean nodded and turned away. As he stalked down the hall, he heard Ariel's clear voice floating from Simone's doorway.

"*Oui*, Maurice. He *is* very upset, but he's been in the house all week. He'll be all right."

Valjean wanted a horse large enough to intimidate any robbers who might approach him on foot, a horse that would outrun any mounted thief's; so he saddled the big black bay Simone had bought for him late that fall, then led the horse out of the stable to the street. He stood for a moment beneath the lamp in front of Simone's house. The road to Versailles would have been kept clear despite the rain; there would be no potholes for his mount to trip over in the dark, he reasoned. He gathered up the reins and swung into the saddle, then turned the horse toward the road to Versailles.

Chapter 9

"Alain *avec deux*?" Mignon repeated, not sure if she'd heard Aimée correctly over the rattling of the coach's wheels.

"Alain *à la trois, oui*," Aimée confirmed.

Mignon's eyes narrowed, and she frowned as she tried to imagine the scene. "But—" she began.

"Please, let us not dwell on *that*," Hilaire said firmly.

"What has the company of aristocrats done to our daughters? Before we left Montreal, they didn't know what such things meant. Now they speak openly of it." Jeannette moaned. "To think of my Aimée being escorted by such a man, pursued by a lecherous king as well! It seems to be a blessing that Roget merely gambles away his fortune."

"I suspect Roget does a few other things besides gamble," Aimée commented. "Almost everyone gambles."

When Jeannette grew even more pale, Mignon quickly assured, "Maman, neither of us would marry such as they."

"And I certainly wouldn't submit to Louis, king or not," Aimée vowed. "To think he would buy me, add me to his house of paramours as other men add a new riding horse to their stable!"

"There must be children born of his affairs," Jeannette said. "I wonder what happens to them—poor things."

"I understand he has given the mothers large sums so they could support their babies," Hilaire replied. "Madame de Pompadour herself has presided over several births."

"Madness, all madness," Jeannette whispered.

"I think they're revolting," Aimée declared. "I can only

hope Louis will forget me. After all, a king should have more important things on his mind than one stubborn girl."

"A girl who has the courage to refuse a king will stand out too much from all those others who do anything he asks. No, he won't forget you," Hilaire said thoughtfully. "The best we can hope for is that he'll forgive you."

"By pretending to accuse Lebel, I'd hoped to preserve His Majesty's dubious honor. I couldn't think of another way of tactfully refusing him. Do you suppose he might see it that way?" Aimée asked.

No one had a chance to answer, because Gaston, the coachman, rolled back the communicating panel and called, "Monsieur Dessaline, there are lights ahead. I can't see how many, but it looks like quite a few people standing in the road. What do you wish me to do?"

"Footpads!" Jeannette exclaimed. "Let him lash the horses and rush through!"

"Nonsense. It isn't likely there are thieves on the road to Versailles itself. Too many soldiers travel this way," Hilaire said. "I'm sure all that rain has eroded the soil from around the roots of a dead tree and it has toppled—or possibly part of the road has collapsed. Maybe those people have already had an accident. Gaston! Slow down or we may find ourselves in need of help!"

"*Oui*, monsieur," Gaston replied, and reclosed the communicating panel.

The coach slowed, then, after a few minutes, stopped. Aimée opened the curtains covering the window at her side and looked out.

"There are a lot of them," Hilaire observed, peering through his own window. "They look like peasants. There must be an emergency of some kind in the neighborhood." He slid forward on his seat to open the door. He put one foot out on the carriage step and stood half bowed in the doorway as he called, "What's wrong, messieurs? Can we help in some way?"

"He's one of those aristocrats," a man said.

"Just what we're looking for," growled another.

Aimée watched her father's profile in the wavering

torchlight, then turned again to pull aside the curtain over her window. "What do they mean?" she whispered, baffled by the rough comments of the men outside.

"Messieurs, has there been an accident?" Hilaire inquired more hesitantly.

"It's no accident we had to eat our horses this last winter!"

"While our children cry themselves to sleep with hunger, such as you have filled your bellies at the king's table!"

"You've been dancing at a ball while we haven't the money to buy boots, much less silk slippers, for our wives!"

"They sound drunk," Aimée said softly.

"They sound dangerous," Jeannette concluded. She reached out to tug at Hilaire's coat. "Let us go from here," she urged.

Aimée looked more closely at the angry faces beside the coach. "Papa, it appears to be some sort of demonstration. Perhaps they intend to present their grievances at Versailles."

"If so, they don't need our help," Mignon said, feeling very uneasy.

"*Mon amour,* close the door and let us be on our way. I'm getting frightened," Jeannette declared, tugging more sharply at Hilaire's coat.

"They're a ragged-looking bunch. I can't blame them for being angry," Hilaire said over his shoulder.

"They had enough money to buy liquor," Jeannette remarked nervously. "Please, *mon amour,* let us go!"

Aimée saw two of the men reach toward her father. Fear streaked through her like cold fire, and she opened her mouth to warn him. She was too late. Hilaire tumbled off the carriage step into the muddy road.

"Papa!" she cried, and leaped from her seat.
Jeannette, too, had gotten up; but the hoops of her wide dome-shaped skirt caught with her daughter's, jamming them in the doorway.

"What folly is this, messieurs?" she demanded. "Hilaire, get into the coach and let us be on our way. These men are—oh!" She stopped when she saw Hilaire, who had risen to one knee, being dragged to his feet. "*Mon amour,* get into the coach," she pleaded. She didn't realize that Hilaire could do nothing of the sort. The two men grasping his arms held him back. But Aimée saw.

Jerking her skirt loose from around her mother's, she leaned out the doorway. "Let him go, you blackguards! He isn't the cause of your troubles. We aren't even from Paris—but from Montreal in New France. Find someone else to tell your grievances to! Go to Versailles. That's where they all are," she called.

"Look at the pretty little lady," the nearest man said drunkenly. "I'll wager some equally pretty little duke or marquis has his seal on you. Why don't you come with me and I'll teach you what a man can do better than those little fops?"

"Monsieur, I have no 'pretty' anybodies," Aimée snapped. "Your business is at Versailles, not here. I'll thank you to get out of our way so we can be about ours."

The man reached out to grasp her elbow, pulling until she lost her footing on the step and fell against him. "You have so many petticoats on, I wonder how those dandies in the palace can even see you're a woman," he said, his speech slurred.

"Let's take off all those petticoats and see if an aristocrat is anything like one of our own women!" another man exclaimed, reaching out to grasp Aimée's shoulder with a grimy hand.

"Let us see what all of them look like under these fancy clothes!" someone else called.

Several hands groped for Jeannette who, still standing in the doorway, slapped them. Her gestures seemed to encourage the men, who laughed and reached for her almost halfheartedly, as if her blows were too puny to take seriously.

Horrified, Hilaire snapped, "Stop that, you fools! The soldiers patrol this road regularly. You're wasting your time with us. Go on your way before the king's men come and capture you."

"Your concern for our welfare is touching," said the

drunk, still holding Aimée. He looked down at her. "I wouldn't mind risking a patrol's coming to get better acquainted with this little *mademoiselle*." As he spoke he reached around her back and, with one effortless stroke, tore open the hooks that held her gown. The front sagged, revealing the top of her chemise. He smiled at the sight of the satiny skin under the gauzy cloth and announced to the others, "A noble lady isn't much different except she smells better."

When Aimée cried out in protest, Hilaire, until then too shocked to struggle, suddenly twisted free of his captors and leaped at the man who held her, battering the peasant's face with his fists. Another man stepped quickly behind him, caught one of his arms, and tried to drag him away. A third man rushed forward with a snarl, then appeared to punch Hilaire in the stomach. Hilaire sank to his knees, blood spreading over his coat front.

Aimée saw the knife in the man's hand. Gasping in horror, she knelt beside her father in the muddy road. "Papa, Papa!" she screamed.

Hilaire's eyes were open. With gasps interrupting his words, he whispered, "Aimée—get back in—the coach. Get away. Leave me."

"*Non*, Papa, *non!*" she cried. She leaped to her feet and faced the men. "Filth! Cowards!" she screamed.

The men stared at her for a moment, aghast at what had happened. Then their eyes lit with new violence, stirred by the helpless girl's defiance and the sight of her loosened hair and the gown hanging crookedly to reveal her seductive flesh.

Although Aimée's attention seemed fixed on her father's attackers, she was sharply aware of her mother's weeping as the men who stood at the coach's open door took Jeannette from the step; she offered no resistance. Aimée knew too that Gaston was being threatened with a pitchfork held to his chest; and he dared not move from his box.

The man who had torn Aimée's gown stepped forward; and before she could do anything, he grasped her wrist and yanked her closer. A second man caught her free arm;

and they began to pull her in opposite directions, each wanting her for himself.

"Would you tear me in half?" she cried.

"Later, *petite aristocrate,* perhaps you'll feel that way," the first man said harshly. A fresh wave of terror coursed through her. He jerked her arm free of the other man's grip, and she fell against him. His liquor-soaked breath nauseated her.

"*Non!*" Aimée cried, managing to pull herself only an arm's length away from him. His hold on her was unbreakable. She knew it was hopeless; she couldn't get free. He, and as many of the others who wished it, would do what they pleased with her. Aimée looked down at her father who stared up at her, helpless. She finally began to weep.

A sound like the explosion of a thunderclap shocked Aimée's ears. Her attacker seemed to leap backward, then fell to the road. A sudden silence fell over the mob, and they stood as still as if they'd been frozen in mid-gesture. Aimée lifted her tear-streaming eyes. A man on a great black horse was silhouetted against the torches as he paused for a moment at the far edge of the mob.

"Get back, you swine," he snarled, and started his horse forward through the crowd.

A man who refused to move was brushed aside by the horse's shoulder as easily as if he were a weed. Another man cried out as the horse's hoof smashed his foot; and the other peasants, now frightened, moved aside to let him pass. Aimée could sense the fierce anger, the barely controlled violence emanating from the dark figure bearing down on them; but when he stopped before her, he said quietly, "Madame, mesdemoiselles, will you help your driver put the gentleman into the coach? I regret I cannot."

The stranger's cloak hid his clothes, and Aimée wondered if he was a soldier off duty, or even a highwayman. He seemed threatening enough for either profession. The torches, now behind him, hid his features from her; and all she could see was the shadow of his hair outlined with gold from the firelight.

As the intruder was speaking to the women, several of
the nearest men ventured a step or two closer; but, aware
of their move, he warned, "I have a second pistol."

The men retreated to where they'd stood before.

Maneuvering his horse around so the animal's sleek
body shielded the Dessalines, Valjean faced the crowd,
leveling the second pistol at them while the driver, assisted
by the women, struggled with Hilaire's weight. Valjean appeared to take no notice of the Dessalines and their driver.
His attention seemed concentrated solely on the grumbling
crowd. The wavering torches made silvery lights in his
dappled eyes.

The driver announced that they were finished, and the
coach door was closed. Valjean glanced back over his
shoulder to see Gaston climbing up to his seat. In that moment one of the rebellious peasants leaped forward to
catch the bridle of Valjean's horse. Valjean fired the pistol;
and the man flew backwards, landing against the others,
blood gushing from a gaping hole in his chest.

"He has to reload now!" someone shouted.

"Kill him before he has the chance!" another cried.

At a word from Valjean the horse scrambled backward
until he was even with the coach driver's seat. Before Gaston could move, Valjean tore the carriage whip from his
hand, and the long coil snaked out to lash the nearest of
the mob. The sound of the whip frightened the already
nervous coach horses, and the pair leaped forward so
quickly that Gaston almost lost the reins.

Again and again in lightning succession the whip
cracked through the air, tearing open foreheads and ripping through shoulders; so the crowd momentarily retreated. Valjean took advantage of their confusion to turn
the big horse and race into the darkness after the coach.

Inside the vehicle Aimée was shredding her petticoat
hem for a bandage her mother could use to slow Hilaire's
bleeding. Glancing out the window, she saw in the moonlight the dark figure that yet was galloping beside the
coach; and she wondered at the identity of the man who
had rescued them. The horse and its rider were little more
than shadowy figures; but the dark cloak flowing in the

wind, the thundering hooves, the whip still in his hand streaming behind, added an eerie effect to the violence of the night. Aimée remembered how the torches had cast golden lights in his hair, and she wondered if their escort was a devil or the archangel himself.

The coach now rattled noisily through Paris's empty streets. The cloaked figure remained at its side. Finally Gaston drew the horses to a stop before the Dessaline house; and Aimée took one relieved breath before she threw open the coach door, preparing to thank the stranger who had unquestionably saved all their lives. She heard him call out to arouse the servants in the house; but in the few seconds she took to dash around the coach, the rider had turned his horse. She watched as the shadowy figure vanished into the darkness.

Antoine's butler, Hilaire's valet, and two maids hurried from the house to the gate. Seeing Aimée's torn gown, her muddied face, they raced to the coach.

"Mademoiselle, what hap—?" The butler stopped mid word as his eyes fell on the coach's open doorway: Hilaire lay on the floor; Jeannette knelt beside him, holding a bloody wad of rags to his abdomen.

"Get blankets, something to carry him in!" Jeannette cried.

"*Oui*, madame," the butler said as he spun around to race back up the walkway.

Mignon, kneeling on the seat, holding her skirts out of her parents' way, began trembling uncontrollably. She pressed her face into the bunched-up brocade and wept.

The sudden commotion of horses galloping down the street startled Aimée, and she whirled around to see another coach grind to a stop behind theirs. The door flew open, and Roget leaped out to dash to her side.

Glancing at Hilaire through the open doorway, Roget turned to Aimée and shouted, "What happened to you?"

The servants, now returned, were eyeing the wounded man, trying to decide the best way to attend him. The butler then gave one end of the blanket to Jeannette so that she and Mignon could aid in wrapping Hilaire.

Her eyes remaining on her father, Aimée quickly

described to Roget how they'd been accosted by the mob and ultimately rescued. He listened in silence, then said hurriedly, "I left the palace not only out of concern for Mignon but because I heard about what you'd said to Lebel. An order has been given to get a squad of soldiers ready. I think it's possible they're being sent in pursuit of you, Aimée. I had my driver take all the shortcuts he knows to get here first. Even if, like you, the soldiers meet that mob on the road and are delayed, they'll surely be here before dawn."

Aimée tore her gaze from her father to face Roget. "A squad of soldiers to get me?"

"I can't know for certain; but if they do come, it will be too late to do anything about it," Roget warned.

"What could I do anyway?" she cried.

"Have you spoken to Alain about this incident?" Roget inquired.

"He and I had a disagreement earlier this evening, so I can't go to him for anything," Aimée answered angrily.

"Your disagreement with Alain stirred you up enough to throw away your caution and approach Lebel? Alain might be especially glad, in that case, to plead your cause with His Majesty to regain your affections. He's very talented at negotiating with the king, very persuasive," Roget suggested.

"To convince His Majesty to forgive me for not wanting to be one of his mistresses? Maybe later, after the scandal has cooled, His Majesty would only have me kidnapped anyway," she declared.

"I've heard rumors that he's occasionally had a girl abducted, but I don't believe them," Roget said. "There are too many girls who are not only willing but eager."

"And if he regards my reluctance as a challenge that only fires him with more passion? From what I've heard about his earlier pursuit of Madame de Pompadour, I'd judge his methods then were similar to those he's using on me now," Aimée said. At Roget's doubtful glance she added, "You haven't seen the trunkful of presents he's sent me—costly gifts, jewels, furs."

"I did glimpse that ring you gave Lebel. It was beautiful—and very expensive," Roget conceded.

"If Louis is sending soldiers for me now, at least I would be spared the suspense of wondering each night whether some agent of his will pluck me from my bed," Aimée said bitterly.

"If you could hide somewhere, he might lose interest in you," Roget suggested.

"Long before the time I could be sure of that, my family would have sailed for Montreal and I with them," Aimée said. "My father was planning to make arrangements—only now, I don't know." Thinking about Hilaire's condition aroused such grief in her that for a moment she couldn't speak. She looked up at Roget, eyes filled with tears, and finally managed to whisper, "What a dreadful night this is! Father perhaps is dying; I'm about to be imprisoned; and Alain . . ." She stopped to think about the scene in the mirrored room, then sighed, "Alain is a roué and always will be, I'm sure."

Assuming that Alain's many love affairs had been the subject of Alain and Aimée disagreement, Roget nodded. After a moment of silence he said slowly, "I know your parents don't approve of my interest in Mignon, and I also know why; but despite my shortcomings, my feelings for her are genuine. I had intended to promise her tonight that I would stop my gambling and any other activities she finds unattractive. As a token of my sincerity, would your mother agree to all of you coming to stay in my house until your father recovers and the king forgets about you?"

Startled by Roget's offer and his impulsive confession, Aimée studied his face. She saw that he was serious. "I'll ask my mother," she said, breathless with sudden hope.

"Don't be too long deciding. We can't know how soon the soldiers will break up that mob and be on their way here if they're coming," Roget reminded her.

Aimée promptly brushed aside the servants, who were about to lift Hilaire out of the coach, and whispered hurriedly to her mother and sister.

Jeannette waved Roget to come closer. "Wouldn't the

king realize you'd offer to shelter Mignon?" she asked worriedly.

"Everyone thinks I'm a useless rogue, not exactly the sort of man who would hide criminals and chance angering the king," Roget said bluntly. "I would send you to my house outside Paris, which I've had closed for the last several years. I would remain in my house in the city as usual. I think, as long as the house outside town continues to appear empty except for a few servants, anyone who even remembers I own it won't investigate," he reasoned. He reached out to touch Jeannette's shoulder and said softly, "There's a physician I know well who will remain silent if I ask him. I'll send him to help with your husband. I have no servants at that house; but if you've brought any with you from Montreal—or maybe Antoine and Victoire will loan you some of theirs—your family shouldn't be too uncomfortable."

"Baron, I think we all have underestimated you. I apologize," Jeannette said feelingly. "I will gladly accept your offer of shelter and am more grateful than I can say."

"You're welcome to any help I can give you, Madame Dessaline," Roget said quickly. "I don't know how much time we have, so I must remind you to hurry. Have your servants gather up only what you and your family will need for the night. I can bring the rest of your baggage to you later. I'll give your driver directions and then leave right away to get my friend. He can meet you there."

Jeannette reached out to give his hand a squeeze. "Again, Baron, thank you."

Roget gave her a brief smile before turning to Mignon. He reached past the doorway to touch her fingers. "Be brave, *ma belle fleur*."

"Roget . . ." Mignon began, then stopped. She didn't know what to say.

"I'll meet you at the house," he promised, then turned away.

Aimée gave Roget a grateful glance as he passed, but she hadn't the time to speak because she was instructing the servants about what to pack.

Inside the coach, Jeannette looked at her husband and

wondered how she could bear it if he died. How would she manage anything without him? He'd been her strength all through the years. Now lying there so pale, so helpless, he seemed like a stone statue that had toppled. She bent closer and, whispering encouragement in his ear, put her arms loosely around his shoulders, as if her own body could shield him from the danger that hovered over them all.

Chapter 10

When Valjean had glimpsed the injured man and the muddied, disheveled girl, helpless as the two grimy peasants
pulled her back and forth—like a pair of dogs worrying
over a rabbit—he'd been fired with anger. Although he'd
never before pointed a pistol at a human being, his fury
had blotted out his normal scruples. He had even felt a
certain satisfaction at seeing one of the girl's attackers go
down with his first shot. When the girl had lifted her tear-
stained face to gaze at him from eyes suddenly relit with
hope, his outrage at her plight had become overwhelming.
The impulse to do violence had charged him and taken
control, driving him to send his horse into the crowd of
men; and he'd felt no qualms, no hesitance, about shooting
the second man and flaying the mob.

During the race back to Paris Valjean's temper had
cooled enough for him to realize the shooting was sure to
raise a hue and cry, especially if the men died—and he
was certain their wounds had been fatal; so he'd decided
to ride away without identifying himself in the event the
people he'd rescued were questioned and would give his
name to an investigating soldier.

Later, as he lay sleepless, Valjean knew it wasn't the
prickling of his conscience, or worrying about the possibility of his identity being discovered, or even Simone's death
that kept him awake. It was the girl.

In the wavering torchlight her eyes had flickered with
amber streaks, exactly as he'd always imagined Aimée's
eyes would do in firelight. The girl he'd rescued even had
lips shaped like those he'd kissed in the forest near Montreal. Recalling both memories and comparing them,

Valjean realized the girl in the coach bore a startling resemblance to Aimée.

He tried to recall the family name Aimée had said when she'd introduced herself in the forest, but it eluded him. Did the people who lived in the house where he'd left the coach have the same name? It was odd, he mused, that he could remember the name of Aimée's horse—Brandy—yet could not recall her family name. But then brandy was the color of Aimée's eyes.

Valjean had no doubt that the girl in the coach was a noblewoman. Although her dress had been soiled and torn, the sea-green lace was of the most fragile, costly kind; and the elegant gown was of the latest mode. He wished her coiffure hadn't been fashionably powdered so he might have seen its color; he knew he'd never mistake the rich flame of Aimée's hair. Because there was so great a difference in the style of the two women, he tried to imagine how Aimée would look with her hair formally arranged and powdered, dressed in an elaborately hooped ball gown. The first time he'd seen her she'd been wearing her brother's breeches. On the few occasions he'd seen her on the ship, she'd worn simple dresses suitable for traveling.

Aimée and her family had left the ship at Le Havre, and he realized with a start that they too could have traveled to Paris. Why hadn't he thought before that she might have come to Paris? He'd probably been too distracted by his search for Simone and, once he'd found her, too absorbed with her company and worried about her illness. He realized, though, that Aimée was never far from his thoughts. The kisses they'd shared, the few brief meetings, had awakened a passion in him no other woman had ever aroused. Aimée's aloofness on the ship, he admitted, had only added to her fascination, making her a challenge in his mind—like a glove slapping him lightly, but persistently, on the cheek.

Valjean swung his legs off the bed and, while the glow in the fireplace slowly dimmed, sat on the edge of the bed, resting his chin in his hands as he thought about Aimée. It occurred to him that he'd never learned why she and her family had come to France; and speculating on the possible reasons, he suddenly remembered it was not at all unusual for a girl of a good family, though born in the colonies, to be promised to a man in Europe after she'd grown into a woman. His heart seemed to stop beating as he realized the lady in the coach might well have been Aimée who, now wed to a nobleman, had assumed her new role in life. He wondered if the wounded man was her husband.

By the time Ariel tapped on his door to arouse him for breakfast, he'd decided to revisit the house where he'd left the coach and inquire how the injured man had fared. He was certain, if he waited until late in the afternoon, any questions to be asked by the king's investigators would already have been answered.

Although Valjean's day was filled with a succession of visitors as he made arrangements for Simone's funeral, he continued to think of Aimée and the possibility that she might have married. His head reverberated with the pain that had begun that morning at sunrise. The clergymen, attorneys, and officials had now left, and as Valjean dressed to go out he wondered if his mind, shocked by grief for Simone, had merely made the lady he'd rescued seem to resemble Aimée in the darkness and excitement.

Hilaire finally stopped hemorrhaging. The doctor, shaking his head, said he couldn't repair the inner damage done by the peasant's knife, then proceeded to take out his leeches, preparing to bleed Hilaire. Aimée gasped in shock; but Jeannette, shrieking that her husband had already bled too much, drove the doctor away with a string of venomous phrases in the argot of trappers in the Montreal backwoods.

Jeannette had often enough nursed injured trappers, so now she seated herself on the edge of Hilaire's bed to attend him herself. She painstakingly stitched her unconscious husband's wound. Aimée sat beside her, holding a basin of water in her lap while she handed Jeannette the various items she needed. It was too bad the doctor hadn't understood the finer points of Jeannette's colonial French, Aimée thought angrily each time the needle pierced her father's flesh: Jeannette had cursed him fully and in detail. Mignon held the lamp steadily enough for Jeannette to see her work; but the girl's tears ran down her cheeks, dripping off her chin to spot the blankets.

Aimée was exhausted as she later lay in her own room across the hall. She couldn't erase from her thoughts the image of her father's pale, drawn face and the sudden fragility of his body. Weariness finally began to win over her worry, and she started to relax; it was then that an electrifying sound came from the darkness.

"No! Oh, no!"

A woman's voice, half scream, half moan, exclaimed with such anguish that Aimée sat bolt upright, wondering fearfully who had cried out. Suddenly terrified that her father had drawn his last breath, she leaped out of bed and ran across the room to throw open her door.

Across the hall the door was open wide, as it had been when she'd left her father's room earlier. The light from the fireplace outlined Jeannette's profile as she sat by Hilaire's bedside, a rosary dangling from her hands. Aimée stepped into the corridor, and the floor creaked.

Jeannette looked up at her. *"Ma petite,* why are you out of bed?" she asked in a hushed tone.

Aimée crossed the hall, hesitant to voice her fear and upset her mother even more. "I thought I heard something," she whispered. "Is—is he the same?"

"Oui, he's the same," Jeannette answered softly. "I heard nothing. You must have had a dream." Aimée nodded, still unconvinced; and Jeannette, understanding her daughter's fear, said soothingly, "Don't let a dream add to your worry. Go back to bed and get some rest, *ma fille.* I will need your help tomorrow."

Aimée turned away. It *had* been a dream, she repeated to herself; but the sound had been so vivid she couldn't shrug off its effect on her. She pulled the blankets close up under her chin, shivering at the remembered scream of grief, wondering how it had come so loudly to her ears from the darkness of her imagination, how she could have a dream when she knew she'd not yet been sleeping. Still shaken by the fading echoes of the remembered sound, she wondered if she'd heard her mother's first scream of grief.

"Non, non, non!" she whispered to the shadows of the room. "I can't hear a cry that hasn't been uttered. It isn't possible."

She closed her eyes, denying to herself that she'd heard any sound, wishing she could deny that the entire night had ever happened.

In the morning Aimée rose wearily from her bed, haunted afresh by her memory of the silent cry, still terrified that she'd somehow heard a sound from the future. Fear clung to her all through the day as she stood watch over Hilaire with Jeannette and Mignon. When they weren't busy attending him in some way, they took out their rosaries and prayed.

Victoire had heard no news about the severity of Hilaire's wound or his chances of recovery; and she knew Roget would be hesitant to send a message, and thus link his house with the Dessalines so soon after the incident between King Louis and Aimée. She worried continuously about her brother-in-law's condition. The Dessalines, although not of the nobility, were too prosperous to be considered ordinary merchants, especially since both Antoine and Hilaire had been personally honored by the king; therefore Victoire assumed that if Louis wanted to learn Aimée's whereabouts even to reprimand her, he would make sure the inquiries were discreet so as to avoid the embarrassment of a public scandal over his pursuit of the unwilling girl.

A number of visitors had chosen to call this day, and Victoire suspected that they at least wanted to learn about the commotion during the night. Each time she faced a visitor who had any connection with the royal court, however remote, she reminded herself of Aimée's confrontation with the king and took great care about what she said. By late afternoon her nerves had become claws tearing at the inside of her skin.

When the butler handed Victoire a calling card engraved "Valjean Étienne, Comte de la Tour, Marquis d'Auvergne," her suspicions were immediately aroused: might he be there under King Louis's orders? Was he seeking clues to Aimée's whereabouts? She remembered that the comte de la Tour had died leaving no male heirs; and although she'd heard of the d'Auvergne family—theirs was a very old and esteemed name—she had never met any of them because they seemed to eschew Parisian society with its attendant scandals, preferring to live quietly on their estate in the south of France. The butler stunned her with his announcement that it had been no other than the marquis who had rescued Hilaire and his family from the mob on the Versailles road.

The man the butler admitted to the drawing room had little resemblance to the mysterious—albeit dangerous—figure Jeannette had hurriedly described; and when Valjean greeted Victoire, his words were as refined, his manners as flawless, as the heir to such prestigious titles would be expected to have. Still, Jeannette had to wonder from where this unknown heir had suddenly materialized.

While Germaine poured tea, Victoire silently appraised the tall, elegantly dressed man seated opposite her, and wondered if his titles were, after all, genuine. Perhaps he had come out of concern for Hilaire and his family. Maybe the marquis hadn't identified himself the previous night to avoid notoriety; his, after all, was an illustrious name. She concluded that she could take no chances on his motives.

After Germaine had withdrawn, Valjean said, "I hope I'm not intruding with my visit, madame, especially in view of the strain you and your family have been under."

Speculating on which strain he referred to, she answered only, "*Non*, Your Grace. I was just sitting down to my tea anyway."

Her reply was so casually given Valjean wondered if in the darkness he'd mistaken this house for another. "Madame, this *is* the residence of the people who were accosted last night on the road to Versailles?" he inquired.

"*Oui*, Your Grace, it is." Victoire lifted her teacup and sipped slowly, delaying further conversation while she wondered what more she dared say. Finally, putting down her cup, she added, "We are very grateful for your help."

Valjean was silent a moment, speculating on the possible reasons for her tension. He raised his eyes to meet hers, then asked, "A gentleman seemed to be injured. Can you tell me now how he has fared?"

Inwardly praying that she was making the right decision, she answered, "I don't know, Your Grace. The entire family left my house immediately after the incident, and I haven't heard from them since."

"But the gentleman seemed unconscious when I arrived—the young lady had been roughly handled—the entire group was doubtless very upset! How could they have gone anywhere?" Valjean exclaimed in surprise.

Victoire lifted her hands in a gesture of perplexity and shrugged delicately. "I cannot answer your question; but that is, nevertheless, what they did."

"But where did they go?" Valjean asked in amazement.

"I don't know."

Sensing that Victoire was lying, Valjean settled back in his chair, for a long moment staring at the patterns in the carpet under his feet, wondering about the baffling situation. Finally he said, "Then, madame, you truly have no idea of the gentleman's condition or even whether the ladies had been injured?"

He seemed so concerned, Victoire decided to tell him that much. Her hand on his arm, she said, "Although my sister-in-law and her daughters were badly shaken and, I'm sure, remain very disturbed over Hilaire's condition, I can assure you that none of the ladies were otherwise harmed. I know that much because my husband and I returned home just before they drove away."

"They just drove away," Valjean commented softly, trying to absorb the perplexing news. He raised his gaze to regard Victoire with eyes clouded by worry. "I won't disturb you further by lingering, madame, if you'll answer only a couple more questions," he said, as if doubtful she'd agree. After Victoire nodded, he asked, "What is the name of the young lady who was jostled by those peasants?"

Puzzled by his question—for Victoire assumed that he would know her niece's name if he had in fact been sent by the king—she answered, "Aimée."

Valjean's heart turned over at the sound of the name. Though wanting to take this woman by the shoulders and shake her until she told him every detail of the truth he was certain she was concealing, he remained motionless and silent. Despite his frustration he reminded himself that if Aimée had married a high official of the court, her husband would surely have warned the family not to speak about the incident so as to avoid any base publicity arising from it. His heart finally resumed an irregular beat, and he said quietly, "When you do hear from the family, will you convey my wishes that the gentleman recover fully?"

Victoire nodded, then rose saying, "Your Grace, let me tell you again how very grateful we are for—"

His impatient gesture silenced her, and he too stood up. He lifted her fingers to his lips, and held them there as he impulsively said, "Will you tell Aimée that I inquired after her?"

"You know Aimée?" Victoire asked in surprise.

"If she doesn't remember my name, you may say we met briefly near Montreal almost a year ago." Releasing Victoire's hand, he said, "I bid you a good day, Madame . . ." He paused, waiting for her name.

"Dessaline," Victoire finished in a faint voice, now having grave doubts about her terse answers to his questions; but he turned away and left the room, giving her no time to call him back.

Victoire hurried to the window and, peering through the heavy lace curtains, watched Valjean as he entered a coach. "Have I lied to the real marquis d'Auvergne? Was it really he who rescued them? What have I done?" she whispered, noting the crests of both the de la Tour and d'Auvergne families on the door of the coach.

After the coach had moved out of view, Victoire turned from the window. She would discuss the matter with Antoine when he returned. She glanced at the clock on the mantel. It was late afternoon.

Surely Antoine would be home soon, she thought uneasily. That day her husband was being interviewed by Inspector Meusnier, a high official of the Ministry of Law who she understood had close personal connections with the king, and that was another source of worry. As she thought about the possible repercussions of her husband's lying to Meusnier, the mysterious marquis faded from importance in her mind.

Antoine arrived home an hour later, his troubled wife following him upstairs, asking questions about his interview all the way. The couple had barely entered their bedroom when a knock on the door sounded.

"Can a man have no peace? Come in, come in!" Antoine called gruffly.

Claude entered, looking surprised at his father's tone. "I wanted to learn how the interview went; but if you'd rather not talk about it now—perhaps after dinner?"

Antoine had been struggling ineffectually with the knot of his neckcloth. Victoire's fingers replaced his, and the knot was quickly undone. Claude came forward to help his father slip off his coat, and Antoine gave them a grateful look as he unbuttoned his waistcoat.

"I'm sorry for being snappish," he apologized. "I'm just weary of answering questions of any kind. Claude, call Philippe and have him pour a little brandy for me. Then I'll tell you about what Meusnier said."

"I'll get your brandy myself and save time," Claude promised, and left immediately. When he returned, his father, now clad in a dressing gown, was resting in a comfortable stuffed chair. He'd never before seen Antoine look so worried, and had rarely even glimpsed a display of his father's temper; so he guessed just how agitated Antoine must be about today's events.

Claude crossed the room to hand Antoine his glass of brandy, then handed Victoire a glass of claret. "If you want to rest . . ." Claude began.

Antoine looked up from his brandy. "Sit down, Claude, and take that worried look off your face. Meusnier questioned me most thoroughly, but I believe he's now convinced we know nothing about where Hilaire and his family went. Have you heard anything from them?"

"Not a word, *mon père*, but I'm sure that's because Roget is being careful," Claude replied.

"*Oui*, no doubt. Well, let us take that as good news. If Hilaire had died, Roget would have sent us some message despite the risk," Antoine said slowly. He took another sip of brandy, then added, "Meusnier, of course, never mentioned Aimée specifically."

"How could he?" Victorie exclaimed. "It would confirm His Majesty's purpose."

"His Majesty can do as he wishes, no matter how his purpose would shame another man," Claude pointed out.

"That's true, but to openly persecute the Dessaline family because he pursues an unwilling maid would be foolhardy even for a king, when his people are already so disturbed about his carousing." Antoine leaned back in the chair and closed his eyes. "The mob on the Versailles road is what Meusnier pretended to be interested in. He wanted to know if Hilaire had in any way agitated those peasants, if he or any of his family had acquaintances among the—"

"Acquaintances!" Victoire exclaimed. "What would Hilaire or Jeannette know of drunken peasants? Acquaintances who would stab him and rape his wife and daughters!"

"No one was raped." Antoine spoke soothingly. "Please lower your voice, Victoire. The servants need not know each detail of our business."

Thus gently chastened, Victoire resumed in a voice barely above a whisper: "Antoine, what more did the inspector ask?"

"How the mob managed to stop the coach. Who got out and why. Was anyone of them intoxicated and, if so, who. What hour of the night it was. What was said. If any threats were issued that further angered the peasants. Who was the man that rescued them . . ."

"A man came today inquiring about Hilaire. He said he'd rescued them," Victoire told him. "He claimed to be the comte de la Tour, marquis d'Auvergne."

"The count is dead. He had no heir," Antoine replied.

"What of the marquis?" Claude asked suspiciously.

"The last heir of the d'Auvergnes is the count's childless widow," Antoine replied. "Your visitor was a fraud."

"He said he'd met Aimée in Montreal," Victoire said slowly. "He was very well mannered, flawlessly dressed, handsome."

Antoine's eyes flew open. "Of course! Would His Majesty send a ruffian to impersonate a d'Auvergne? Everyone knows Aimée's from Montreal. He inquired about her specifically?"

"Everyone also seems to know about the mysterious man who saved Uncle Hilaire's family. One of the peasants the soldiers captured must have told them about the man," Claude reasoned.

"So His Majesty sent this imposter to question me at a time he knew both of you would be away from home," Victoire reasoned. "His Majesty thinks I'm an empty-headed fool who, without a man at my side, would chatter about everything he wants to learn. His handsome imposter went away with nothing he didn't already know."

Antoine patted her hand and managed a small, weary smile. "Meusnier learned nothing from me either; but that Louis would go to such lengths, however discreet, confirms that it was wise for Hilaire and his family to disappear."

"This affair is one more blotch on France's honor," Claude said disgustedly. "Everyone must think our government is a collection of irresponsible pleasure seekers."

"Don't speak that way so loudly or you may be accused of plotting a revolution," Antoine warned.

"If such a thing as revolution were possible . . ." Claude began vehemently.

"Hush!" Victoire said sharply. "We have enough problems now without having to worry about your getting arrested for such foolish ideas."

"I wish I knew how Hilaire is," Antoine said worriedly.

"Roget dares not send a message now," Victoire reminded.

"Roget's reputation of being a useless wastrel is what helps protect Uncle Hilaire and his family," Claude said.

"He must continue the farce and seem to shun our entire family now that Mignon has apparently disappeared."

"His house might be watched and any servants who leave could very well be followed right to our door," Victoire agreed.

"Servants, yes," Claude said slowly, thinking over an idea that had just come to him. "But what of a beggar who came on foot to the back of the house asking for supper?"

Antoine looked at his son in surprise. "What beggar?"

"Why, me, of course," Claude answered. "I could leave this house dressed for an evening out and take the coach. Then I could circle around on a back street and leave Paris. If I hide the coach in the forest near Roget's country house, change into rags, and walk the rest of the way . . ."

"That is an idea," Antoine said slowly, reluctant to put his son in danger.

"I couldn't return in the daylight. I might have to wait until tomorrow night," Claude said. Then frowning, he added, "It would appear that I'd spent tonight and tomorrow with a woman—like so many other men my age who have a little money."

Victoire shook her head in disgust. "I dislike your getting such a reputation."

"It isn't as dangerous as having people think I'm plotting revolution," Claude said lightly.

Victoire gave him a sharp look, knowing he referred to her previous warning.

"You must be very, very careful," Antoine reminded.

"I'll stop at a fashionable salon and an inn or two first. Everyone will think I'm drunk even before I turn toward the forest," Claude promised solemnly.

Early the same evening Roget drew up to the back door of his country house in a creaking old cart. Dressed like a farmer, he appeared to be trying to sell the last of his produce.

He'd spent the afternoon in a pub with a drinking crony from the court, pretending to match his friend's consumption of brandy, but in fact passing most of his drinks under the table to a ragged drunk who was happy to accept the largess. After Roget's friend had become too intoxicated to measure his words, Roget had coaxed him to speak freely about the king's reaction to Aimée's refusal; but he'd learned little more than that the soldiers sent from the palace after Aimée and her family had left had been dispatched to deal with the mob of peasants on the road. It appeared that King Louis was still annoyed by Aimée's refusal, but Roget had not a hint of the king's possible plans.

When Jeannette pressed Roget to speak of Alain, Roget admitted that a mutual friend had told him that Alain had remained at Versailles with the two companions Aimée had discovered him with in the mirrored room. Jeannette so determinedly questioned Roget that, although he didn't exactly admit his own guilt, it became clear that the mutual friend was a lady of the court with whom he'd spent the rest of the night after he and the doctor had left the Dessalines.

Aimée went to the kitchen, supposedly to make chocolate for them all, but she really wanted to escape Roget's presence. Disgust for his habits, anger at Alain's unconcerned carousing, fear and grief for her father—all welled up in her in a violent storm of conflicting emotions. She muttered angrily as she worked, carelessly banging pots together and kicking cabinet doors closed.

At last she sat down at the small worktable, cradled her head in her arms, and wept.

At first she ignored the soft tapping on the window, thinking that a tree branch moved by the wind was scratching the glass. It became louder and so persistent that she finally lifted her head to look toward the window. A face was peering through the glass, its features shadowed by a ragged hat.

"A beggar," she concluded, then got wearily to her feet and went to the door. "I'll give you a loaf and some cheese, but you must take it elsewhere to eat," she said as she opened the door.

"But, mademoiselle, won't you allow a poor man a few minutes of shelter from the cold?" the beggar asked.

"It's spring and not cold at all . . ." Aimée began, then finally recognized her cousin Claude. She stepped aside quickly, not speaking again until she'd closed the door behind him. "*Mon Dieu,* what a disguise you've made!" she breathed.

Claude pulled off his ragged cloak to reveal a suit as threadbare as his outer garments. "The chocolate is burning," he warned, sniffing the air.

Aimée gasped, then ran to remove the pot from the hearth. The boiling liquid spilled as she ran to the table to put it down. Watching chocolate puddle over the table, she sighed. "I hardly know what I'm doing lately."

"I'll make the chocolate while you tell me how Uncle Hilaire is," Claude said, rolling up his tattered sleeves as he set about performing the task more efficiently than she had.

Aimée told him how Jeannette had driven away the doctor, and how she and the girls had attended Hilaire. She confided her dream, and the fear that it was somehow a prophecy. Claude took a moment away from his chocolate making to put comforting arms around Aimée while she again wept.

After she had quieted, he told her that Antoine had been called to an interview with Inspector Meusnier that afternoon, and that Victoire had been bothered by a succession of visitors who seemed to be trying to learn where Aimée and her family had gone. Not wanting to upset Aimée even more, he spoke as if they'd all been neighbors seeking gossip; he did not mention the marquis, whom he regarded as an imposter and an agent sent by the king.

"I'm so sorry to have brought this scandal on your family," Aimée apologized, unconsciously wringing her hands. "I'm so afraid you too will be in trouble."

Claude took her hands, flattening them between his palms, hoping to calm her agitation. "My family is *your* family as well, Aimée," he said. "If further trouble comes of this, my father and mother would certainly stand behind you." When she looked up at him, he added, "What can King Louis do, after all, that won't cause him embarrassment?"

"He *is* the king," Aimée reminded him.

"The populace is already much distressed over his habits. If he hasn't the sense to recognize how all this appears, Madame de Pompadour surely will. I have no doubt, if he can't forget you, she'll advise him to do no more than make a discreet search and try to persuade you to come to him," Claude said. "You know His Majesty takes her advice always."

"To think that a courtesan must be my defender," Aimée said softly. She was about to say more when the door to the hallway opened. Mignon looked into the kitchen.

"Hello, Claude," Mignon said. "I thought I would help you with the chocolate, Aimée."

Claude released Aimée's hands and turned to Mignon. "Aimée has just been telling me about your father. My parents have been worried." He turned to pick up the tray where the pot of chocolate steamed, adding, "We'd best not delay joining Aunt Jeannette any longer."

As they entered the parlor they found only Roget sitting there. He looked up at their entrance and explained, "Madame Dessaline has gone upstairs to change her husband's dressings."

Claude's eyes ran over Roget's garments and, as he set down the chocolate, he commented, "We're a fine-looking pair of ragamuffins."

Roget smiled wearily. "If someone were to knock on the door now, they'd surely think the house had been taken over by vagabonds . . ."

"*No! Oh, no!*"

Aimée's heart stopped at the scream that tore down the staircase from the upper floor. "It's the same cry I heard last night," she whispered.

Roget leaped from his chair, and he and Mignon ran out of the room to dash up the steps. Aimée, shivering violently, turned slowly to face Claude.

"He is gone," she said faintly. "My father is dead."

Chapter 11

Monsieur Bossuet saw nothing unpatriotic about selling his company's merchandise to a shipbuilder in the British colony of Massachusetts, particularly when it was such a large and profitable order. He reasoned that Boston wasn't at war with France, and actually he was taking business away from a company in London, so his conscience was clear.

When Valjean had mentioned his intention of accompanying the cargo to Boston on the *Santa Luisa*, Bossuet insisted on traveling to Le Havre to see him off. Bossuet was to admit later that because of France's war with Britain, any errors made now in the Carleton shipyard's order might be difficult to correct, as blockades by either France or Britain could possibly hinder the movements of vessels—whether they flew the fleur-de-lis, the British jack, or any other country's flag. Bossuet intended to be present in the shipping office, thereby assuring that the proper cargo would be loaded on the *Santa Luisa*. Valjean privately realized that Bossuet's solicitous attitude was really motivated by hopes for future, equally profitable orders from the Carletons.

The coach arrived in the port city mid-morning; and as soon as the two men had checked into a hotel, Bossuet took Valjean to his company's warehouse to inspect the equipment his employees were preparing for shipment.

Bossuet brought Valjean to the office connected to the storage area, and there a clerk poured them each a brandy. Bossuet was called back to his warehouse on some other business. Valjean, temporarily left alone, lounged in a chair, sipping his brandy while he waited for Bossuet to return so they could go to lunch. The office consisted of only a few small rooms attached, seemingly as an afterthought, to the warehouse. Valjean, idly looking over the modest furnishings, comparing them with Bossuet's elegant personal office in Paris, was reminded of Andrew's workshop in Boston; and a pang of homesickness for Boston and the Carleton family stabbed him.

The thought of Andrew's and Julia's friendly warmth, the easy camaraderie of their sons, seemed like the beam of a distant lighthouse beckoning safe passage after the turbulence of these last months in France.

With Simone's death, Paris's glitter had seemed to tarnish; and after Valjean had decided there was no likelihood that he'd see Aimée again, France had lost much of its lure. He'd wondered often if his emotions had been so affected by grief for his mother and disappointment in Aimée that he was judging France unfairly. He recognized the necessity of deciding whether to take up permanent residence there as the comte de la Tour, marquis d'Auvergne—or to sell his French properties and reestablish himself in Boston.

While visions of Aimée still shimmered in his memory, he reminded himself that a month had passed since the incident on the Versailles road and his subsequent visit to the Dessaline house in Paris—enough time for the injured man to have recovered; more than enough time for Aimée's shock over the incident to have worn off. But whether Aimée had married or was still convinced Valjean was a British spy, she hadn't even sent a note to thank him for rescuing her and the others from the mob of peasants.

As he had done many times since the incident—with the fading of the last shreds of hope that Aimée would contact him—Valjean wondered if the injured man had been Aimée's husband. In the darkness and excitement he hadn't seen the man's face or been able to assess the extent of his injury; but he'd assumed the man had merely been knocked unconscious in the scuffle, because he knew the peasants owned no firearms. The possibility of a stabbing had never occurred to him. Having no idea of Aimée's difficulties with King Louis, neither had it occurred to him that Victoire wouldn't have told Aimée about his visit.

He remembered Simone's insistence that, after she'd died, she wanted to be a guardian angel to him, to lead him to Aimée. How sentimental Simone had been, he mused. How ironic it was that he should find Aimée only to learn she was out of his reach. He wondered if Simone's spirit was aware of the hopelessness of his dreams for Aimée, if Simone was as unhappy about it as he. She understood well enough how it felt to watch dreams dissipate like smoke until they vanished. She'd known about loneliness—the handful of mourners at her funeral were testimony to that. Aside from him, only her doctor, lawyer, a few servants and the priest had stood at her graveside. Since her husband's death she'd lived so solitary a life that no one knew Valjean was her heir until he gave them his calling card. Even Bossuet had no idea that Valjean had become a titled nobleman, and Valjean had never bothered to tell him.

Growing even more depressed with each turning of his wandering mind, Valjean got to his feet to gaze out the window at the *Santa Luisa* standing beside the dock.

During Captain Mareto's winter voyage back to France he'd encountered a storm so violent that the *Santa Luisa* had been damaged. The vessel had remained at Le Havre while repairs were made—a delay that had given Valjean the time he'd needed to remain with Simone until her death. Now the *Santa Luisa* was once again seaworthy and was taking on supplies and cargo. It would be only a fortnight more until the ship was ready to sail and Valjean was convinced they'd leave with no time to spare before Britain's probable blockade of Le Havre, as well as all the commercial French ports on the English Channel.

Valjean had recently learned that the war was going very badly for France. The news came from Captain Mareto, who shared with other sea captains information the general population seldom heard. While the Parisians were confident that King Frederick, Britain's closest ally, had nearly ruined Prussia with his costly campaigns, Britain already was beginning to attack the garrisons on the

French coast. Aside from King Louis's closest advisers, very few people were aware that the French colonies in North America were losing their long struggle against Britain. Quebec had fallen the preceding autumn; and as soon as the Saint Lawrence River thawed, the British were likely to threaten Montreal itself.

Valjean wondered if Aimée's family realized Montreal would probably soon be turned into a battlefield. In his depression he wondered cynically if Aimée would even care.

Roget's house wasn't as spacious as the country estates of other noblemen because it had originally been intended for use as a hunting lodge. It was furnished comfortably rather than elegantly. Instead of silk-covered walls it had wood paneling, and stone fireplaces rather than marble. Iron chandeliers inherited from earlier Dieudonnés gave light as readily as the crystal and gilt fixtures in other homes, and the effect was one of coziness. The warmth of the house did not touch Aimée's spirit.

Not only did the pain of Hilaire's death twist her heart with sorrow, but Jeannette's reaction to her own grief tore Aimée with worry and frustration.

Jeannette would remain where she was sitting until told repeatedly that there was some task she must do. Then she went woodenly to where, puppetlike, she attended to her business as directed. She never spoke until someone else asked a question persistently enough to penetrate her senses; and then she invariably spoke of Hilaire, ignoring the question posed to her. Mignon frequently dressed her mother and herself like servants so they could walk in the garden without being noticed. She hoped that the spring air, the budding trees, and the songs of the birds building nests would lift Jeannette's spirits. Jeannette seemed aware of little occurring outside her own mind; and that little, more often than not, caused her to speak of Hilaire—describing one or another spring they'd shared, the flower seeds and bulbs he'd ordered from France for their home in Montreal, the plum tree he'd had planted outside their bedroom window that bloomed each spring.

It seemed as if Jeannette had entered a glass bottle and

stoppered it—sealing herself in much like a model ship; she now existed beyond her daughters' voices or touch. To Aimée's own burden of grief was added the fear that her mother was becoming unbalanced.

Aimée was not altogether certain that the tension of her various problems wasn't affecting her own mind; for she was growing so nervous she was beginning to see suspicious-looking strangers each time she peeked around the drapes shielding the windows. If she had not imagined the figures standing in the grove of trees at the beginning of the Dieudonné lane, then she was as afraid of the possible alternative: Agents of Louis had located her despite Roget's precautions.

The first time a stranger had caught her attention was when she'd attended her father's funeral, a very simple, private ceremony in the churchyard of a nearby village. Jeannette, Mignon, and Aimée had dressed like servants, pretending Hilaire had been stable master for the Dieudonné household. Not even Antoine and Victoire had dared attend; they had sent Claude, also disguised as a servant. The only other mourners had been the priest and two kindly old nuns. But Aimée had noticed that a man, who appeared to be visiting another grave, was watching the funeral party with too much interest for mere curiosity. That afternoon she'd seen the same man—she'd thought—loitering in a field that adjoined the Dieudonné property.

Several nights later, after the lights had been put out, Aimée had found herself unable to sleep. She'd curled up on the seat formed in the space where the bedroom windows and doors before going to bed each night since, she'd glimpsed a shadowy figure moving stealthily in the garden. She feared King Louis had ordered her abduction; and although she'd made sure to latch all the downstairs windows and doors before going to bed each night since, she'd become afraid to sleep. Slumber came only after exhaustion claimed her, and she'd recently begun to wonder if her sleeplessness, added to grief and worry, was causing her to imagine the figures.

After dinner one evening, hoping to find a book to dis-

tract her from the fears haunting her nights, Aimée went
to the library; but two hours later the book she'd chosen
lay open in her lap, ignored while she stared at the dra-
pery-covered window wondering if the garden's shadows
concealed a possible kidnapper.

Roget quietly entered the room wearing a frayed jacket,
patched trousers, and a faded tricorn hat adorned by a
broken feather. Glimpsing his movement from the corner
of her eye, Aimée leaped to her feet and whirled to face
him.

"Forgive me for frightening you!" Roget exclaimed,
taking off his hat so she could see his face as he approached. The way I'm dressed, you must have thought a
tramp had gotten into the house."

Although memories of the stranger she'd seen in the
garden had stabbed her with fear, Aimée forced herself to
smile in greeting. "You look more like a pirate than a
tramp; but I'm getting used to your disguises, Roget. I was
deep in thought and you just startled me."

Roget turned to open a door to the cabinet, reaching in
for a decanter. "You've been thinking about all the things
that worry you. I see it in your eyes. Have a little brandy
with me. It will help you cheer up."

Aimée began to shake her head. Roget, it seemed, believed brandy cured all life's ills, because any time they
discussed a problem, he suggested having a drink.

"I have some news that won't lift your spirits, Aimée;
so have at least a glass of claret as I tell you," Roget
urged.

Aimée noticed that the usual humor in his eyes was
eclipsed by solemnity. She reluctantly nodded agreement,
then waited, apprehensive as he poured the drinks.

Finally Roget turned and began, "The news has been
suppressed for some months; but a friend, who is close to
the king, slipped and told me."

"Was it Alain?" Aimée guessed that it was he.

Roget looked uneasy. "I thought you wouldn't want to
be reminded of him." Aimée shrugged as if Alain no longer mattered. Roget remarked, "He's known this news for
some time. I don't know why he didn't tell you long ago."

"Because you caught him at a moment when he was too drunk to be discreet, and he never drank heavily in my presence," Aimée said tartly. "He hid many of his vices from me."

"*Oui,* I suppose he did," Roget agreed quickly, not wanting to discuss anyone's shortcomings when he had so many of his own. "But we must speak of this unhappy news now—not of Alain."

Aimée took a sip of her claret, then asked wearily, "What is it?"

Roget fortified himself with several swallows of brandy before he replied, "Shortly after you and your family left Montreal, Quebec fell to the British."

Aimée's shock was obvious as she breathed, "Quebec has fallen?"

"The city is a shambles," Roget said solemnly. "The British could make no other advances once winter had set in; but it's expected that as soon as the thaw comes they'll approach Montreal."

"The Saint Lawrence should be free of ice very soon," Aimée whispered fearfully.

Jeannette, accompanied by Mignon, was passing the open door on her way upstairs to prepare for bed. Overhearing Roget's voice, she paused. When the full import of the news penetrated her malaise, she exclaimed, "Sainte Marie!"

She hurried into the room, Mignon at her heels. As she turned to grasp Roget's arm her eyes bleamed with more spirit than Aimée had seen in her mother since she'd driven Roget's doctor away from Hilaire.

"Quebec gone? Montreal threatened?" Jeannette cried. "Why didn't Alain tell us so we could return home?"

"Madame, please don't upset yourself even more," Roget said in a soothing tone. "Probably Alain didn't want Aimée to leave Paris. He didn't want to lose her."

"He has done so in any case," Jeannette answered sharply, though her eyes were filling with tears. "The swine! Maybe my Hilaire would still be alive if we'd left," she said brokenly. "What about Marcel? He's alone in Montreal!" She turned to Aimée and, half weeping, declared, "We must pack immediately. We must go back!"

"But, Madame Dessaline . . ." Roget began.

Jeannette caught Aimée's wrist with one hand and Mignon's fingers with the other. "I can't lose Marcel as well as your father. I must go to him. We have to leave."

"I understand, Madame Dessaline, I *do*," Roget said quickly, "but you must realize a ship isn't so easy to find these days. It's possible that the Saint Lawrence has already been blockaded by British gunboats. A French ship would never get through."

"We came here on a Spanish ship," Aimée recalled. "Wouldn't it be possible for us to return on one—or a ship flying some other country's flag?"

"No ship would get to Montreal if the river is blockaded by British gunboats," Roget replied. He fell silent for a time, thinking how passage to the city could be managed. "Were you able to land at another port, perhaps in the British colonies, you might be able to make arrangements to travel overland. But, no, I couldn't promise that. I wouldn't want you to travel alone overland through that wilderness. It's full of savages, mostly unfriendly to the French."

"Is there another ship leaving France that could take us to one of the British colonies?" Aimée asked, ignoring the threat of hostile Indians.

"Josette brought a newspaper from the village when she did the marketing today," Mignon said. "Isn't there always a listing in the paper of the ships that are planning to sail in the not too distant future?"

"Yes, there is," Aimée said. "Where is the paper?"

"I think I saw it in the kitchen. I'll go and look for it," Mignon said.

"Don't you realize how dangerous it would be for three women to travel in that country alone?" Roget protested. "I can't let you do it!"

"Roget, as grateful as I am for all the help you've given us, I don't believe you can stop us from going on our way," Jeannette said firmly.

"I can't stop you, of course, madame. I can only try to

convince you that it would be very unwise," Roget replied. "Please, I beg of you, wait for a while until we learn more about what's happening in Montreal."

"We've waited too long already," Jeannette declared. "The situation in Montreal can only worsen. If we wait, we might not be able to get home at all."

Mignon reentered the room, carrying a crumpled newspaper, which she gave to Jeannette. Jeannette quickly found the ship listings, and her daughters peered at them over her shoulders. "God must be watching over us!" Jeannette breathed. "The very ship we came here on is at Le Havre now. It's ready to take on passengers and cargo, and it's due to sail for Boston in a week."

"That doesn't leave us much time to pack, to say goodbye to Uncle Antoine and Aunt Victoire," Aimée commented.

"Claude will be coming tomorrow. He can tell Antoine and Victoire our plans. Perhaps they could meet us at Le Havre. We can't return to Paris anyway or the king's agents will surely discover us," Jeannette said quickly.

Aimée gave her mother a sideways look, surprised that Jeannette in her grief had even remembered her problem with the king.

Jeannette glanced at her daughter. "Did you think I'd forgotten everything? *Non*, I have not—despite my sorrow about your father."

"We'd best board the *Santa Luisa* before dawn if we can. We could stay in our cabin when the other passengers arrive, and so none of the king's spies would know we were leaving until after we'd sailed," Mignon suggested. Then, remembering Roget's many marriage proposals, she fell into awkward silence.

Roget saw Mignon's expression and understood her thoughts. He reached out to take her hand. "I've asked you repeatedly to marry me and you've put me off without answering. I think your eagerness to return to Montreal is my answer."

"Roget, I don't know what to—" Mignon said faintly.

"But you're right, Mignon. You shouldn't marry me," Roget interrupted gently. He turned to look at Jeannette, who was watching him sharply. "Madame, you know I'm devoted to Mignon. I love her as much as is possible for me—but you also know I'm not capable of being the kind of husband she needs, any more than Alain would be capable of loving Aimée as she needs to be."

"What do you mean, Roget?" Mignon asked, puzzled by his sudden change of attitude.

"I mean, *ma belle fleur*, dear as you are to me, I have lived so different a life from yours, you would never be happy with me," Roget said quietly. "Like Alain, I'm too used to having my way; and you would never be able to live with my habits. A woman of this society could accept them—but you couldn't. Not any more than Aimée would be able to accept Alain's paramours."

"Paramours?" Mignon echoed.

"Yes, Mignon. There's not a man of wealth in Paris who doesn't have them, and I'm no exception," he confessed. "You couldn't accept that or my gambling or my drinking or . . ."

"Please stop!" Mignon exclaimed. "Tell this list to your confessor, not me. I don't care to hear about every sin you've ever committed."

"You see, Mignon? You think of my habits as sins. I think of them as pleasures. Wicked, perhaps, but not evil." Roget sighed. "Whatever you call them, I realize I'm not likely to change."

"I know that Mignon has given serious thought, especially during these last weeks, to accepting your proposal; and I'm grateful that you are being so candid," Jeannette said. "I admire you even more for telling Mignon these things than for taking the risk of hiding us."

Roget lifted Mignon's hand to his lips, kissed it tenderly, then said quietly, "That I have told you is a measure of how much I love you. I would rather lose you than have you be as unhappy as a husband like me would make you."

The next few days Aimée got even less sleep than she'd had before Roget's announcement. She had little time to dwell on thoughts of spies watching the house, or grief for her father, nor could she worry about Marcel. She, like Jeannette and Mignon, was kept too busy gathering their belongings and packing. In her condition of sleeplessness and worry the series of events occurring since her father's death began to seem like an unending nightmare. Even when Josette and Pomponne left them to return to Paris—Roget couldn't arrange passage for them on the already overcrowded *Santa Luisa*—their leave-taking didn't seem real.

Finally, when Aimée entered Roget's coach for the trip to Le Havre, she looked back at the house dully, too tired to think; and once she had settled in the coach, exhaustion caught up with her.

The trip to Le Havre was a blur of passing landscape watched from drowsy eyes, and meals so little noticed that she couldn't remember moments later what had been served. When they stopped at an inn overnight, her only thought was that of sleeping. She catnapped the second night, though they continued to travel; and when the coach was an hour away from Le Havre, she awoke to stare out at the darkness, finally alert enough to think about all that had happened to her since she'd arrived in Paris.

How different Paris had been from what she'd anticipated when she'd left Montreal, she mused. How different her present attitudes were from those she'd previously held. She'd learned too much since the previous spring to ever again be the same, and she viewed this change in herself with emotions as mixed as those she felt about leaving France.

She hadn't been able to see Paris one last time, not even to say good-bye to some of the friends she'd made. This saddened her because she doubted she would ever return to France. Although visiting Versailles and mingling with the nobility had brought her many problems, it had been exciting, she admitted to herself. As selfish and pleasure-seeking as were so many of the aristocrats, they were graceful, beautiful, and witty; and the fabulous luxury of their lives was something she would never know again.

Remembering King Louis, Aimée surprised herself

when she realized she now felt pity for him, rather than fear. Yes, it was very possible that he'd ordered her abduction, but she couldn't help remembering their first meeting: he'd pretended to be a huntsman. How often had he wished that he'd not been a king? She'd sensed his unhappiness just as she'd sensed the loneliness in Alain.

Alain filled his time with women who meant nothing to him. He dabbled in court intrigues as if playing a game of chess. He drank heavily and gambled away huge sums of money, filling his empty life with meaningless amusements to avoid thinking too much about what he lacked—love. Unlike Alain, Roget was aware of the hollowness of his life but refused to change it; and she puzzled over his attitude, finally realizing that both Roget and Alain clung to their barren life-style because they were afraid of love. They would risk fortunes on gambling, but not their hearts on women. How different they were from her father.

Hilaire had made his entire life a commitment to love. Even his death had been a pledge of love, for he'd died trying to defend his family. Aimée closed her tear-filled eyes tight, shutting out the darkness of the night. She thought about the courage of her father's relatively obscure life and the glittering but useless lives of Alain and Roget. She saw against her closed eyelids the little rectangle of fresh earth under which Hilaire's body now lay, and Jeannette's white face, drawn with pain when she'd gazed for the last time at her husband's grave before they'd left for Le Havre. It seemed impossible that her father was truly gone; the thought had come to mind so many times, even while she'd been trying to convince her mother to accept his death.

Aimée could understand Jeannette's need to rush back to Montreal. She too felt the urgency to rejoin Marcel, to help him in any way possible when the British came, and, if necessary, to die together.

The clattering of the horses' hooves on the cobblestoned streets of Le Havre jolted Aimée from her reverie; and she opened her eyes to see Jeannette watching her. She smiled wanly at her mother, knowing that Jeannette had sensed her thoughts as surely as if she'd spoken them aloud. She reached across the space between them and patted her mother's hand.

"I'm all right, Maman," she whispered. "We will manage as long as we're together."

Jeannette nodded and smiled fondly at Mignon, who had reached for her other hand. No one spoke again, but the three women continued to hold hands, forming a sort of circle against the world, until the coach rattled to a stop on the wharf, beside the *Santa Luisa*.

The driver helped Aimée out of the coach first; and as she waited for her mother and sister she turned to look at her surroundings. The eastern sky had just begun to lighten to purple, promising another hour before the sun's rim rose over the black line of the water. A few blinking lanterns on the deck of the *Santa Luisa* cast the only light they had to see by. The wharf seemed devoid of life. Not even a sailor could be seen, and Aimée wondered if she and her family were to march up the walkway or wait until someone from the ship came to escort them.

The only sounds were those the driver made as he unloaded their baggage from the coach, a horse's snorting, the brief click of Mignon's heels as she uneasily shifted her weight on the planks of the wharf. Then the driver bid them fair winds in a tone self-consciously hushed in the stillness. His whip cracked, and the horses leaped forward. The clatter of the moving coach faded in the distance until finally there was no sound other than the gently lapping waves.

"Antoine and Victoire were supposed to meet us here. I wonder if they were detained?" Jeannette said softly.

"Roget was supposed to be here too. I wonder where he is?" Mignon whispered, peering into the darkness.

"They all will come," Aimée said reassuringly, but she too felt uneasy standing alone on the wharf in the darkness.

Then a coach moved slowly out of the shadows where it had obviously been waiting. Aimée held her breath, not sure if the coach held Roget or her uncle or even agents of the king who had come to carry her off.

She sighed in relief when she saw Claude get out of the

coach. Antoine followed and turned to help Victoire. Finally Roget alighted.

Victoire immediately embraced each of them, murmuring condolences, for she'd seen none of them since the night Hilaire had been stabbed. Stepping back, she fell silent. She didn't know what more to say at this tragic ending to their stay in France. It was Jeannette this time who approached Victoire, put her arms around her sister-in-law, and lay her head on her shoulder while they both wept.

Antoine came forward to face Aimée and Mignon. "When someone you love is about to leave, you usually ask them to stay longer or at least urge them to return soon, but I can do neither," he said awkwardly. "Even if you could stay, I'm sure you wouldn't want to."

"We feel as if we should apologize for the king, for Alain, for the man who . . ." Claude began, then changed his mind and said angrily, "I wish I could hang Uncle Hilaire's murderer myself! I wish I could challenge Alain and King Louis and shoot them both!"

"Don't say such things!" Aimée exclaimed. "You could be arrested for treason!"

"And you could be snatched off this wharf and dragged away to Parc aux Cerfs," Claude returned. "You and Mignon and Aunt Jeannette have had to hide like criminals while you watched Uncle Hilaire die—all because of the corruption of our government."

"Claude!" Antoine said sternly. "If you don't learn how to hold your tongue, it will be you who will have to leave France."

"By that time you might have to swim to the colonies, because no ship will be able to leave a French port," Roget said dryly. He turned to Aimée and Mignon. "I can't wait to see you board the ship. The boat I'm taking back to Paris leaves at dawn, and I can't miss it."

Jeannette stepped away from Victoire, resolutely wiped her eyes, and, struggling to control her tears, dug into her reticule. She produced a small purse and pushed it into Roget's hands. "They're gold coins—Spanish—so you'll have no trouble using them," she said. Seeing the protest rising in his eyes, she firmly closed his fingers around the purse. "It's proper payment for the passage on the *Santa Luisa* and the time we stayed at your house."

"But, Madame Dessaline—" Roget began.

"*Non*, Roget," Jeannette interrupted. "My Hilaire never allowed himself to remain in anyone's debt, and I intend to follow his good example and try to conduct my affairs as wisely as he did." She wiped her eyes once again and straightened her shoulders, her attitude dismissing any further mention of the payment. "What arrangements did you make with Captain Mareto? Do we simply walk onto the ship?"

"One of Captain Mareto's officers is on deck with instructions to escort you to your cabins whenever you wish," Roget answered.

"We won't share one cabin?" Jeannette asked.

"Three single cabins were the only accommodations I could get," Roget replied.

Jeannette sighed in resignation. "I hope they're near to each other." Remembering the servants who had to remain in Antoine's house, she turned to her brother-in-law. "You will send Josette and Pomponne as soon as possible?"

Antoine assured her that he would arrange their passage on the next ship that could safely sail to Montreal.

Roget had been studying the eastern horizon. The dark edge of the sea was touched with watery gold. "I *must* leave you now, Madame Dessaline. I wish you a pleasant voyage and good fortune upon your arrival in Montreal."

"Thank you for all your help, Roget," Jeannette replied, clasping his hand warmly.

Roget turned to Aimée, brushed her cheek with his at the same time he whispered in her ear, "If your mother can't be dissuaded from this madness of traveling overland to Montreal, please be sure to obtain a trustworthy escort." Aimée nodded, and he released her shoulders to face Mignon. "*Ma fleur*, the best advice I can give you is to put this entire stay in France out of your mind as soon as possible—to forget me," he said quietly. He kissed her once and stepped away. "May God watch over all of you," he said, then turned to walk swiftly into the shadows.

Jeannette, her daughters, Antoine, and his family began to speak hurriedly, trying to condense what they had to say in the short time they still had together. All were near to hysteria. That disquieting thought came to Aimée as the group talked avidly about many unimportant matters—avoiding any mention of the heartache they shared. None of them noticed the man carrying a lantern as he came down the walkway of the ship and moved toward Antoine.

"Monsieur Dessaline?" the man said. "I'm First Officer Zurbaran. If the ladies wish to board the *Santa Luisa* while it is still dark, they must do so without delay," he said concernedly.

Antoine glanced at the sky, then cleared his throat and replied, "Thank you, monsieur."

Zurbaran moved a few paces away from the group to wait, and Antoine looked at Jeannette and her daughters from eyes bulging with tears.

Left with no more to do than say farewell, the two families stared at each other in silence for a long moment. Then suddenly Aimée was wrapped in Antoine's arms. She was so blinded by tears that when Victoire embraced her, she recognized her aunt only from her touch and the scent of the perfume she always wore. Aimée could not see Claude's expression when he hugged her, and his auburn hair was no more than a blot of dark fire in the light cast by Zurbaran's lantern.

Amid hasty wishes that their journey be safe, that they find their home in Montreal untouched by violence, that God guide and protect them, Jeannette and her daughters were led up the walkway and onto the *Santa Luisa*'s deck, weeping uncontrollably.

After one last glance at Antoine, Victoire, and Claude, who stood on the wharf below, Aimée followed a waiting sailor to the cabin that had been assigned her. He opened the door, told her in Spanish-accented French that her baggage would be delivered shortly, then, bowing courteously, left her alone.

Aimée's cabin was on the east side of the ship; and

while she waited for her baggage to be brought, she gazed at the sky, which now held a streak of crimson fire. The storm of tears had drained her of all energy, and she found herself praying for the strength to face whatever the future held. Roget had asked her to arrange for a proper escort when they began their overland journey to Montreal, which made her feel that the safety of her mother and sister was somehow her personal responsibility; but she was weary of responsibilities and decisions.

She wished fervently that Alain had been more reliable, that she could have married him—or *someone* who could manage the situation she now faced. She wished she had a husband at her side whose presence alone could still her fears, a husband who could make her feel safe and protected—as Valjean had done when they walked together through the forest near Montreal.

Realizing that the water she faced was the English Channel, and Britain lay somewhere in the distance, Aimée sighed.

"Valjean, Vale, whatever your true name is, I wish with all my heart that I had let you speak when I had the chance. I swear that if I should meet you again, I will listen," she whispered.

Wearily leaning back against the bulkhead, she closed her eyes. What, she wondered, might Valjean be doing now in England—or was he in England at all?

Chapter 12

During the first few days after the *Santa Luisa* had set sail, Jeannette and her daughters spent very little time outside their cabins. Although they no longer needed to fear that King Louis's agents might trace them, their energies had been depleted by worry and grief; and they saw the voyage as an opportunity to recover themselves. Jeannette had even thought of giving the cabin boy a gold coin, promising another upon their arrival in Boston if he would deliver their meals to their compartments.

Jeannette needed time to think, yet she did not want her daughters to worry about her moodiness as she knew they had done in the weeks immediately following Hilaire's death. Her withdrawal at that time hadn't been prompted only by grief, as they'd assumed. Although her heart had been—and still was—torn with sorrow, Hilaire's sudden demise had also showed her the fragility of life. She wanted privacy to absorb this and found herself reevaluating all that she had before accepted without question. She thought about the way that she and Hilaire had reared their daughters.

Their efforts to protect Aimée and Mignon from all of life's hardships, though well meant, had poorly equipped the girls for the struggles of living, Jeannette realized. Aimée and Mignon had made good decisions out of mere instinct, not wisdom; and it had been the buoyancy of youth—not really strength—that had brought them through the suffering they'd endured. Their resourcefulness of mind and spirit would enable them to deal with possible crises in their uncertain future. She resolved then to encourage and nurture their self-reliance and expand the scope of their thinking—an unheard-of idea in an era when girls were taught only the domestic and social skills necessary to make them good wives and mothers, who left all major decisions to husbands. So when Aimée and Mignon came to their mother's cabin for companionship, although they took out their needlework to busy their hands on measured, dainty stitches, Jeannette introduced into their conversations matters that hardly ever concerned other young women.

Instead of merely telling her daughters how she thought they could arrange to travel safely from Boston to Montreal, Jeannette asked them for suggestions. She speculated about the situation they would face in Montreal, even though those conversations centered painfully on their fears about Marcel. Jeannette knew that talking about it would help to prepare them for surviving in a war-torn or possibly conquered city.

Jeannette recalled with them the many adventures they'd had in France. They wept together for Hilaire; they discussed the corruption they'd seen; they remembered Alain's perfidy and Roget's profligate ways. But, not wanting the ugliness they'd witnessed, and the selfishness of some of the people they'd mingled with, to be her daughters' foremost memory of the culture that had borne them, Jeannette discreetly reminded them of the beauty they'd seen, the courtesies they'd been shown, and the wit that had stimulated their minds.

After a week had passed, their conversations were temporarily interrupted. Jeannette developed a fever accompanied by weakness that forced her to take to her bed. Unable to do anything more than raise her head high enough to sip the broth her daughters fed her by spoon, Jeannette was impatient with her helplessness. Aimée and Mignon took turns nursing her, so that one of them would always be at her side. Just when Jeannette's fever broke, Mignon too became ill. Aimée arranged a makeshift bed for her sister on a cot in Jeannette's cabin so that she could more conveniently look after both of them. By the time Jeannette was able to get out of bed, Aimée was exhausted; and Jeannette, though still a bit weak, insisted that her

daughter return to her own compartment to rest so she too
would not fall ill.

Aimée had been so absorbed in caring for her mother
and sister, she had lost all sense of time; and when she
stepped out of Jeannette's cabin, she was surprised to see
that darkness greeted her. She approached a lantern hanging from a hook on a bulkhead and held up to the light
the watch that hung on a chain around her neck—the only
one of Louis's gifts she'd kept. She was stunned to learn it
was well past midnight.

After days and nights of nursing Jeannette in her compartment the fresh sea wind was so revitalizing; so despite
her fatigue and the lateness of the hour she felt too alert
to go to her cabin immediately. She moved to the rail and,
facing the brisk wind, gazed at the moonlight reflected on
the waves, thinking about nothing other than the beauty
of the ocean and the star-shimmering sky.

A man walking silently through the shadows noticed the
solitary woman and paused. Eyes made silver by the
moonlight stared at her in disbelief for a long moment before the man, still hesitant, turned in her direction.

Valjean's soundless steps brought him to Aimée's side.
She was unaware of his presence as she stood at an angle
turned slightly away from him. He confirmed that it was
indeed her profile. Stunned that it was the auburn-haired
girl he'd met in Montreal, not the elaborately coiffed,
formally dressed lady he'd rescued on the road to Versailles, he wondered if the woman he'd snatched from the
mob had, after all, been someone else.

"Are you the lady I saw in Paris or is it possible I've finally found the girl I kissed in a Montreal forest?" he inquired.

Aimée turned slowly to stare incredulously up at
Valjean's moon-dappled eyes. She was too surprised to
speak.

"You *are* Aimée," he breathed. He lifted a hand and
lightly stroked the outline of her fiery curls with the back
of one finger as the shock of finding her subsided enough
for him to speculate on her situation. "But are you still

mademoiselle? Or did you marry that nobleman you went to Paris to meet?" he asked quietly.

Aimée's stunned mind hadn't registered his question. She was wondering if it was Valjean standing before her or the man who had taken her from the mob. He appeared to be a composite of them both. He was as elegantly clothed as her mysterious rescuer, his hair carefully dressed, his speech no less refined than Alain's. But his height and proportions, his features, seemed to be Valjean's. In the moonlight the smoky flecks of his eyes seemed to merge into shimmering silver.

"Did you marry?" Valjean asked again. When she still didn't answer, he recalled how she'd vanished from the Dessaline house in Paris immediately after the incident, and thought of a new possibility. "Perhaps you did marry and, discovering it to be a mistake, are trying to escape your husband?"

"I'm not running away from a husband," she replied in a faint voice. It was all she could think of to say.

Valjean took another guess. "Maybe your family was so alarmed by my appearance in Boston they wouldn't let you contact me, not even to send a note to thank me for your life or, at least, your virtue?"

"My life, monsieur? My virtue?"

"After that scene on the Versailles road, anyone would have expected a polite acknowledgment for his trouble," Valjean prompted.

"It was *you!*" Aimée breathed. "How could I know? I never saw your face!"

"Don't pretend you didn't recognize the name on the card I left at the Dessalines'," he said coolly.

"Card?" Aimée echoed blankly.

Valjean reached into his waistcoat and produced a calling card. "This card. I told the lady of the house—Victoire, I believe her name was—to mention that we'd met near Montreal last spring. Surely you haven't forgotten that as well."

Aimée's eyes lowered to gaze at the calling card he'd thrust into her hand. "Valjean Étienne, Comte de la Tour, Marquis d'Auvergne?" she whispered in disbelief. "But what of that other name I heard in Boston—Vale Kendall?"

"I *am* Valjean d'Auvergne. Everything else will require some time to explain, which I'll be happy to do, if you'll let me. I'd like you to answer some questions as well."

He leaned closer as he spoke, and she noticed the scent of brandy on his breath. Memories of Roget's and Alain's perversities were yet too near for her; and suddenly learning that Valjean was himself part of the French aristocracy, and doubly titled at that, made Aimée's temper rise from the confusion of her emotions.

"While you interrogate me, shall I address you as the Monsieur le Marquis or as Monsieur Kendall, spy?"

Surprised by her sudden flash of anger, he said curtly, "Valjean or Vale, whichever you prefer. I'm not used to the titles yet."

"But you dress like a nobleman. You sound like a nobleman. Did you fake that English accent in Montreal?" she demanded. She leaned closer to sniff ostentatiously at his breath. "You even drink like a nobleman."

His own temper rising, he grasped her wrist tightly and pulled her nearer. "I had some brandy while I was playing cards tonight."

Aimée tried to twist free and, failing, looked up at his narrowed, gleaming eyes. Although she knew he was angry, she said defiantly, "Gambling and getting drunk I've learned are two of a nobleman's greatest pleasures."

"I'd like to show you a third," he returned, bending toward her. His face was only a breath from hers. She turned her head to avoid him, but he pulled her closer, the warmth of his mouth covering hers, for an instant moving restlessly, hungrily, then abruptly withdrawing as he said, "But I'm sure your husband would object. Which is your cabin? I'll escort you safely back to him."

That brief contact sent a bolt of lightning streaking through her, and Aimée was so shaken that her irritation at herself sharpened her retort: "I have no husband! Why do you keep talking about a husband?"

Valjean was obviously startled. He remained silent a moment as he absorbed this news. Then she hadn't *wanted* to make contact with him, he surmised; and this he found even more depressing. Finally he said quietly, "You can't be traveling alone."

"With my mother and sister," she answered, perplexed at his suddenly subdued attitude.

He glanced down at the wrist he gripped so tightly, seeming surprised that he was still holding her. Releasing her, he said, "I'll escort you back to your mother and sister."

Confused by his mercurial moods, but still feeling the ache where he'd held her wrist, Aimée merely nodded. Far from being secure in his presence, as she remembered she'd felt during their walk through the forest, she decided not to correct his assumption that her mother and sister shared her cabin. It was safer, she was certain, not to tell him she had a compartment of her own.

As they began to walk he slid her arm through his—a gesture that with any other man would have been merely courteous. With Valjean it seemed peculiarly intimate. Aimée was sharply aware of the warmth of his touch, of the firm body beneath his coat, of the lithe walk that brought memories of the forest path and the sensation of sun-warmed doeskin. Exhilarated by his nearness, yet angered by her own reaction, she remained silent. Her awareness of his magnetism grew to such proportions that she felt the lack of conversation like a hand pressing down on her, shortening her breath, making her own movements clumsy. As they approached her door she saw through the curtain-covered porthole that the cabin boy had lit her lamp. It would, she hoped, appear as if Jeannette were waiting for her to return. But her heart sank at Valjean's next words.

"I can see your mother is awake and, no doubt, concerned about your disappearance. I'll explain that you weren't on a romantic tryst," he said, his tone tinged with sarcasm.

"You need explain nothing . . ." Aimée began hastily.

But Valjean was already tapping on the door. Receiving no answer, he knocked again, this time calling softly, "Madame Dessaline?" Silence answered him. For a moment he seemed perplexed. Then his hand reached for the handle as he commented, "Maybe she fell asleep. But I still think I should tell—"

"Monsieur, it isn't necessary!"

The alarm in Aimée's tone struck him as curious, and he asked suspiciously, "Are you traveling with your mother—or is there someone in your compartment whom you'd rather I didn't meet?"

"There's no one . . ." Aimée anxiously began, then stopped.

Valjean had opened the door and was stepping into the cabin. His eyes slowly scanned the small room, which obviously had been meant for a single passenger. He noted that the open door to the wardrobe revealed only her gowns; the tiny dressing table held one set of brushes and a few feminine toilet articles. He turned to look at Aimée, who stood at the entrance to the compartment. Without a word he again took her wrist and pulled her inside, closing and latching the door behind them.

"Why did you lie?"

"My mother and sister have separate cabins. It was all we could get," she answered, then added hastily, "But their compartments are nearby."

"Are you afraid of me?" he asked in surprise. When she was silent, he added quietly, "There's no need."

Aimée backed away slowly. "You've been drinking. You've behaved strangely, asking peculiar questions—as if you're accusing me of something—and I don't know why you should accuse me of anything when I've done nothing to you."

"I've only had a couple of brandies, hardly enough to make me drunk. I never allow myself to become intoxicated." He approached to lay his hands on her shoulders and added, "Except possibly by you." Noticing the alarm that flashed through her eyes, he withdrew his hands and sighed almost imperceptibly. "I would like to explain myself, if you'll listen; and as I said before, I have questions to ask you—if you're willing to answer them."

Remembering that he'd saved her from the peasant

mob, she said slowly, "I suppose, if only to be fair, I should listen to whatever it is you want to say."

Her aloof tone irritated him, and he inquired coolly, "Will you condescend to answer my questions as well?"

"I think I'll have to hear what they are before I can—"

"Damn it, Aimée! Stop behaving as if you were Queen Marie!" he burst out. "Can't you say anything without qualifying it? Have you become so practiced a coquette you can't simply answer yes or no?"

"I don't know what—"

Again his hands gripped her shoulders. "Never mind saying you don't know this or can't be sure of that. *Mon Dieu*, you're maddening!" He glared at her a moment, the lamplight making crystal streaks in his eyes. "You're the kind of woman who would put a man on his knees and keep him there forever while she decides his fate. But I'm not the sort of man who will get on his knees."

When Valjean released her shoulders, she was so surprised she didn't immediately move away. In her hesitation she'd lost her opportunity; for his flattened hands grasped her temples, his fingers twining in her hair, then he tilted her face to his. She knew he intended to kiss her, and her body tensed. For a fleeting moment she hoped he would feel her resistance and change his mind. Then she realized, if she pounded on his chest with her fists, it wouldn't matter.

Anticipating forcefulness, she was undone when his lips, barely brushing hers, moved softly around her mouth's perimeter, caressing her with a delicacy more exciting for its elusiveness. As his lips continued to move lightly over hers, she was stunned by the urge she felt to reach for him, to catch that mouth with her teeth if necessary. During that moment, though her lips had parted only slightly, his mouth firmly covered hers. A streak of fire shot through her blood, setting it alight.

His hands left her temples and slid down her sides to tighten around her back, and the hard body she'd so vividly remembered was suddenly pressed against her. Now his mouth compelled her response, his kisses enflaming her senses. A fire ignited low in her belly, as if a bubble of hot honey had burst in the core of her and spread its sweet fluid through her limbs.

His hands left her back, releasing her; but his mouth yet moved searchingly over hers. His fingers on her bodice, stroking her breasts through the thin cambric of her gown, sent a fresh torrent of sensations through her; and she gasped, feeling as if she'd been dipped in a pool of live sparks. She ached with the desire he'd aroused in her; but surprised at the sound, she opened her eyes.

Valjean's lashes parted, revealing eyes that were smoldering coals flickering with silver lights. His lips caressed her cheek as he murmured, "Don't think too much, Aimée. Don't think at all."

"But I must," she breathed. "I must!"

His mouth moved to her ear, the tip of his tongue tracing its whorls, his breath making her shiver; and she tried to move away. In a motion too fast for her to resist, his arms enclosed, then lifted her; and he carried her to the bed.

"No, Valjean. Please, no! I must have a moment—just a moment to—"

"I've decided for you," he said, then bent to brush his mouth to hers. His lips once more were elusive, fondling her with delicate little nibbles; he stroked her mouth with the tip of his tongue until she seethed with the need for his kiss. He covered her lips with his, carefully nurturing the passion he knew she contained until her hands, weakly pushing against his chest, stopped.

When he withdrew, she remained sitting on the bed where he'd placed her. Fate had snatched her into its current and would carry her where it chose. She stared up at Valjean as he tossed his coat, his neckcloth, his shirt—each item of his clothing—one by one to the floor. His body was as she'd expected it, as her instincts had told her it would be: long-legged, supple and lean, full of the power she'd inspired. This knowledge—that she had made him so, that her touch had aroused this desire, enslaving them both—swept aside all her fears.

He reached for her hands, drawing her to her feet; so she stood before him, enabling him to unhook her dress, release the several petticoats which now fell in tangled layers around her feet, and untie the ribbons of her chemise. Then he knelt at her feet, his caressing hands removing the stockings from her legs.

As he tipped her slipper from her toe, she said softly, "I thought you said you knelt for no woman."

Startled by her tone, he looked up at her; but his surprise vanished into a wicked smile as he stroked the inside of her ankle. He rose languidly, his fingers traveling up her legs with his movement, tracing a path of fire that ended at her breasts.

Facing her now, he asked quietly, "Would you say that I'm begging?" She was silent. "I thought not. Get on the bed."

Once again the impulse to defy him flashed through her; but at the same moment she found herself reclining, just as he'd asked. Amazed at her obedience, she lay looking up at him warily.

Valjean sat beside Aimée, watching her a moment. Her long fiery curls spread over the linens like a wreath of flames. He lifted a tendril shedding loose strands like a silky web; and with eyes locked on hers, he kissed the curl's spiraling end. "I told you I would explain myself," he said softly.

Surprised, she began, "But—" Not knowing quite what to say, she finished, "—but now?" "

His eyes glimmered with humor. "Don't you want to know if you're giving your maidenhood to a French nobleman or an English spy?"

She closed her eyes, overcome by conflicting emotions. "But I think I . . ." she began.

His fingertips were moving slowly, lightly over her skin, caressing the inside of her thighs. The sensation was subtly enticing. A gush of sweet warmth flowed through her, and she felt as if she had become no more than a fluid held in shape by her skin. She opened her eyes to stare up at him.

"Tell me now that you don't want love," he said softly. He watched her, knowing her answer, again caressing her thigh. She remained stubbornly silent while his fingertips slowly traveled up her body to tease her breast. She closed her eyes, frustrated beyond endurance. Finally she knew she must surrender.

"Now, is it you who wants me on my knees?" she panted. She opened her eyes to see that his face was tense, and his eyes were hard and bright with desire. "Like you, I won't beg," she breathed.

"I don't think I'd want you if you would," he answered as he leaned over her.

The last shreds of Aimée's defiance dissolved into gasping as his lips moved over her shoulders, then her breasts, lingering until she bit her lips so she wouldn't cry out. The tip of his tongue flicked along her midriff, down her side to her waist. She moaned and flinched away, trying to escape the sharply tantalizing sensation. He would not let her. Waves of exquisite fire ran through her, maddening her almost beyond endurance. After she'd been reduced to a shivering frenzy of impulses so piquant she could hardly bear them, he lifted his head to place a line of soft, startling little bites over her stomach. His hands on her waist—the fingers spread as if he would absorb every texture of her—had a peculiarly clinging sensation, as if they had conformed to her skin and become part of it. But she had no time to think about it.

The elusive touch of his lips, the kisses caressing her thighs, the delicate nips, were exquisitely measured, it was as if he were brushing her skin with the very tip of a feather.

His chest—muscular, male, unfamiliar to her body—pressed warmly against her breast. Once again his mouth reached for hers, rubbing, caressing, and teasing until she felt as if her nerves would soon disintegrate in a flash of sparks.

"I can't," she panted. "I just can't bear—"

"Yes, you can," he whispered; and shifting his weight, he began to become part of her. He felt her tense, and knowing that it was from pain, he stopped. His mouth reached for hers, kissing her as delicately as if they'd just begun.

Abruptly her lips groped for his; and this time it was she who lured him, moving restlessly, lingering hungrily, causing him—though she did not know it—to move with her as easily as two ocean currents slide over and through each other. Her kiss seemed to focus, becoming concentrated, arousing sensations in him so intense he felt as if she were drawing the life from his body through his lips. Only when he heard her sudden gasp did he realize that the power of their kisses had accomplished what earlier he'd hesitated to do.

"Aimée, little fire flower, shall we pause a moment?" he whispered concernedly.

"In Montreal you called me a wind," she murmured.

"A sweet wild wind," Valjean remembered.

"If I'm a wind, you're a fire. Neither winds nor fires pause," she breathed.

At her words his desire, waiting for almost a year in him, grew into an acute and terrible hunger, a longing that filled him with an unbearable need. He wanted to move slowly, though he felt he would explode with his joyous impulse.

His efforts to shield her from the intensity of his surging emotions made him awkward and in turn impatient with that awkwardness. A throbbing began in him; it seemed to him that the ocean that buoyed up the ship had withdrawn, and the earth beneath was convulsing with uncontrollable forces. He spoke to her, unconscious of the whispered love words falling into her darkness like silvery sparks lighting her way, leading her shuddering body toward fulfillment. The storm of his passion lashed him with sheets of fire, engulfing him with its heat. He heard Aimée's soft cry almost beyond the realm of his perception; so distant it was, he could hardly hear it, yet somehow it seemed to come from the center of his being. His own instincts erupted in a savage brilliance that blazed fiercely against the sunrise, then slowly dissipated in a sky now shimmering with the sparks of their love.

They lay quietly a long time, watching the morning dawn through the porthole; fingers of light touched their faces. Remembering that the cabin boy would come with breakfast, Aimée whispered her warning in Valjean's ear. He smiled, kissed her, and got out of bed.

Wondering if he would leave her cabin now, and hoping he would remain, she watched him cross the room. His naturally sinuous movements reawakened her desire. She closed her eyes, trying to deny the feeling, yet hoping he would guess. But if he did, would he think her insatiable? His weight on the edge of the bed surprised her. She looked at him now, wanting to say something—anything other than her true feelings. "What did you do?" she asked lamely.

Valjean nodded toward the dressing table, where a stack of gold coins gleamed in the new sunlight. "Those should buy the cabin boy's silence and blind his eyes to my presence in this room."

"That boy will end this voyage feeling wealthy," she commented. Silently appraising the amount, she asked, "Do you have so much that you can give it away that easily?"

"Not until I went to France and learned about my inheritance," he answered.

"Titles do bring wealth, and I'd forgotten you have two of them," she said. "Claiming such titles would be a good reason to travel to Paris. What did you do before that?"

"I worked in a shipyard," he replied.

"Sudden riches must make everything seem possible," she commented.

Valjean pulled his legs onto the bed and lay with his cheek on her stomach. He watched her face as they talked. His hands covered her breasts, holding them as delicately as if they were flowers. "Money can make life comfortable, but love makes it possible."

She was silent, wondering if he meant the emotion or the physical thing they'd just shared.

He read the hesitation in her eyes and understood its purpose. "I mean all of it, Aimée."

She raised her head a little to look at him warily. "Is it so easy for you?"

His lips dropped a kiss on her navel. "It's never been easy for me at all. I've always been too particular about women to fall in love easily. That's why our meeting in the forest affected me so much. I was surprised at how you made me feel. I knew from that first kiss I would want you always."

"Always?" she whispered.

"Yes," he answered firmly. He was silent for a long moment, as if wondering himself about this admission. Finally he said, "I suppose it's time—in fact, past time to tell you something about myself."

Realizing that she had spent the night with a relative stranger—yet lying naked with him this way seemed the most natural thing she'd ever done—she knew there was only one answer for it. "I guess I should know more about you than only that I love you."

At her confession his eyes softened to the color of a dove's wing. You've accepted me without knowing who I am—I could very well be an English spy. I suppose you really must love me." He paused a moment in thought. "Your attitude reminds me of my mother's. She fell in love with an English spy, but politics didn't matter and he became my father."

"Your father really was a spy?" Aimée asked hesitantly.

Valjean nodded and sat up. He drew up her knees and put his arms around her legs. Cradling his chin in his clasped hands, he rested his head on her knees. Looking steadily into her face, he told her about himself. Once he'd seemed to her as elusive as moonlight; and now finally she understood that he had the endurance of the snow-swept mountains. He had only finished speaking when the cabin boy knocked on the door.

Aimée looked shyly at Valjean. He knew she would be embarrassed for the boy to see them there, despite the gold he intended to pay for the boy's discretion.

"Just a moment!" she managed to call.

"Stay here and I'll take care of him," Valjean promised. Then he arose from the bed, quickly pulled on his breeches and shirt, and went to the door to let the boy inside.

Although not yet in his teens, the cabin boy had walked into many such scenes before. He betrayed no surprise at Aimée's indiscretion; in fact, he never glanced at her. He faced Valjean and merely asked if they wished a second

breakfast tray. When Valjean replied and handed him the
stack of gold coins, the boy's silence was assured; and he
left the cabin immediately.

Listening to the light footsteps running down the deck,
Valjean commented, "It sounds as if he'll be back with the
other tray pretty fast." He threw her a smile, picked up
one of her brushes and began to smooth his hair.

She watched him in silence—the smooth working of the
muscles across his shoulders, the golden lights the sun
made in his hair, the deft movements of his wrists and
hands, which reminded her of those long tapering fingers
on her body while they'd made love.

He was now tying his hair into a neat queue at the nape
of his neck. "For myself, Aimée, I would choose to spend
the rest of this voyage with you; but I assume that would
invite your mother's censure." At her silence he nodded
agreeably, then went on, "I'll spend as much time as I
discreetly can with you, but I hope you'll introduce me to
her as quickly as possible so she won't be concerned about
seeing us passing so much time together on deck."

"At the moment, both my mother and sister are recovering from a fever they developed earlier; so it probably
will be a few days before they'll even come on deck,"
Aimée said.

"I hope it wasn't too serious," Valjean began.

"If it was, I wouldn't have left their cabin and met you
last night. I'd been nursing them both, but my mother told
me to leave them and get some sleep."

"They'll be confined to their cabins for a few days, and
they expect you to stay in yours and rest," he commented
speculatively. "That would give us some time together, if
you want it."

A smile of delight broke over her face. "I'll ask the
cabin boy to deliver a note telling Maman I'm going to remain in my room, as she suggested."

Valjean moved closer to her, lifting her hand to his lips.
He looked into her eyes. "Your eyes are exactly as I'd
thought they'd be in love—like brandy warmed before a
fire." He heard the cabin boy's soft tapping on the door.
"After we've eaten, I'll go to my own compartment to col-

lect some things I'll need for the next few days. Meanwhile you should write that note."

Aimée remembered that she was going to have to get up and face the cabin boy after all. Blushing at the idea, she resolutely swung her legs from the bed and hurried to the wardrobe to pull out her dressing gown. As she hastily fastened the hooks her flush deepened.

Valjean gave his hair one final stroke with the brush and, turning, saw her expression. "Now you do look like a fire flower," he commented.

Knotting her sash hurriedly, she turned to seat herself at the dressing table. She wrote a quick note to Jeannette.

Alone again, they sat on the edge of the bed eating their breakfast; and she answered his still unasked questions by telling him about her own past. When she told him that her father was the man who had been wounded that night on the road to Versailles, and that he had died, she couldn't hold back the tears that ran slowly down her cheeks. He put his arms comfortingly around her; and she felt, as she had in Montreal, that those strong arms could protect her from the cruelties of the world she'd so recently been introduced to.

For the next few days the little cabin became the focus of a fantasy, a world where Aimée and Valjean existed only for each other; the brief visits of the cabin boy were their sole contact with the reality outside. There was nothing for them to do but talk, sleep, and love; and their lovemaking was wonderfully varied.

Aimée had been utterly innocent and so was unschooled in the techniques of passion. Valjean, by his own admission, had been too particular to give himself easily to love. They explored their sensuality like grown children who had never been told yea or nay by a sophisticated world.

They discovered that each of their moods gave a new design to the expression of their desire, and their lovemaking ranged from sweetly tender moments to recklessly wild abandon. Each kiss and every caress evolved into a bond between them, one even they couldn't at that time guess the strength of. They only knew the delight of their discoveries was an outpouring of emotions from deep within them; it was as if they had tapped the wellsprings of their souls.

Chapter 13

When Aimée told Jeannette she'd met the man who had rescued them from the peasant mob on the Versailles road, Jeannette perceived the excitement her daughter was trying so valiantly to control; and she realized Aimée was very attracted to the marquis d'Auvergne. Anxious to make her own assessment of the man, she readily agreed to join the couple in a promenade on deck that afternoon.

Jeannette and Mignon had left their cabin to keep the appointment; and now, recognizing Aimée as she stood with a man at the ship's prow, Jeannette paused in the shade of the bridge to inspect him from that distance, when he wouldn't be aware of scrutiny. The two of them were engaged in conversation, and though they weren't touching in any way, there was an air of intimacy about them—as if they were enclosed in an invisible bubble that separated them from everyone else. Aimée seemed to lean toward him—though she stood erect—as if magnetized. If Aimée did not yet realize how near to love she was, Jeannette herself wouldn't mention it and perhaps encourage an alliance she might later decide she didn't favor.

The marquis was taller than Alain and Roget, Jeannette observed. In order to look at Aimée he had to bow his head; but, Jeannette decided, his posture was otherwise that of a man who didn't easily bend under pressure. He also didn't seem to care as much about fashion as the nobility in Paris had; none of them would have appeared in public without a hat, even if they merely carried it. But his head was bare, his dark hair shining with gold highlights in the sun. He dressed well, however unintimidated he was by fashion's trends. Being the wife of a *pelletier,* she could judge, even across the distance, that the tan coat he wore was of superb suede. As a woman, she could admire the breadth of his shoulders, the flat stomach and narrow hips, the length of the legs his fawn-colored breeches fit just snugly enough to reveal their mold discreetly.

"When will we step out, Maman?" Mignon anxiously asked from Jeannette's side.

"We will proceed now, but we don't want to appear overeager." Jeannette opened her parasol and stepped into the sun. It was then that Aimée saw her and spoke rapidly to the marquis, who offered his arm and started toward them. Observing his supple walk, Jeannette resolved to keep an alert eye on Aimée's behavior; for she knew that men who moved in such a fashion—almost animallike— were reputed to be sensualists.

"*Ma mère,* may I present Valjean Étienne, Marquis d' Auvergne, Comte de la Tour? Valjean, my sister Mignon," Aimée introduced.

Valjean greeted them courteously, then expressed his sympathy for their grief over Hilaire's death.

"It is, I understand, because of you that we all aren't dead. I'm most grateful you came to our aid," Jeannette replied, privately continuing to assess him. The marquis had a stronger face than the other noblemen she'd met. His eyes on her were steady, and Jeannette wondered if they could read her inner thoughts, as it seemed. Whatever else he was, she decided, he was no weak-kneed dandy.

"I don't know that your lives hung in the balance, Madame Dessaline," Valjean was saying. "I doubt those men, however intoxicated, would have killed a woman. I'm only sorry I couldn't have arrived a bit sooner and, perhaps, have prevented your husband's tragic death."

Jeannette again expressed gratitude that no harm had come to her daughters, then fell silent as Mignon made a comment. While Valjean and Mignon were engaged in conversation, Jeannette again studied his features. Had she seen him somewhere else, other than on the Versailles road? At a pause in the conversation she said, "You seem familiar to me, Your Grace. Did we meet in Paris, maybe at a party or some other gathering?"

"I went to no parties and very few public gatherings, Madame Dessaline," Valjean replied. "When I arrived in Paris, my mother was ill. We attended only a very few entertainments before her condition deteriorated to the point where she couldn't go out."

"Is she with you on this voyage?" Mignon inquired.

"*Non*, mademoiselle. She died the night your father was stabbed," Valjean answered.

Once again sympathies were extended and appropriate comments made; but all the while Jeannette studied Valjean's face, still wondering where she'd seen him before. Finally she asked, "Do you travel a great deal, Your Grace? I confess I'm quite baffled about where I saw you last. Have you ever visited Montreal?"

Valjean had been aware of Jeannette's scrutiny. He'd been hoping she wouldn't remember him from Boston and so conclude, as Aimée had, that he was a British spy. At her persistence he realized he'd have to tell her; or she would later remember and be so distressed she might not give him a chance to explain.

"*Oui*, madame, last year in the spring, very briefly," he answered smoothly. "I was conducting some business for my employer. Perhaps you noticed when I escorted Aimée to your gate. She'd taken a fall with her horse, and I walked home with her. You may also remember seeing me on the wharf in Boston, when we were boarding the *Santa Luisa*."

Jeannette's eyes widened in shock. This was the man she'd wanted to distract Aimée from in Montreal because he'd appeared to be an impoverished trapper? He was the man on the wharf Hilaire had shielded Aimée from?

Valjean noted Jeannette's surprise. "My appearance was quite different, madame. I was not then a member of the French court. In fact, I had only just learned I was French at all. I grew up thinking myself to be Vale Kendall, the son of an English serving-woman. I was employed by the Carleton family, who are shipbuilders in Boston."

"I remember you from that day in Montreal!" Mignon

exclaimed. "Aimée told me about how she and Brandy fell and you walked home with her."

"Did she." Valjean made it a statement rather than a question as he watched Jeannette's changing reactions. "I'm afraid, Madame Dessaline, that my background is too complicated to be described easily; but perhaps one day, when you have time and if you wish to hear it, I can explain," he said warily.

"Indeed it would seem a complex story," Jeannette agreed. "I'd like to hear it in more comfort and privacy than a promenade offers. If you have the time now, let us retire to my compartment for a glass of wine. I'm sure the cabin boy can bring whatever we wish without too much bother."

Valjean felt a certain unease knowing that the boy who had brought Aimée and him meals for the last several days and nights was also attending her mother and sister. He nodded, then said with more ease than he felt, "I'll be happy to answer your questions now, Madame Dessaline."

Later in the cabin, after Valjean had related his history, Jeannette leaned back in her chair and said nothing for a long time as she considered his story. Although he was obviously intelligent and resourceful, she recognized that his nobility was so new to him that he was still in a period of transition: whatever he'd been in the past, he could yet develop into an adventurer who would never put down roots. Or, once he'd become accustomed to the advantages of his position, he might very well become as arrogant and amoral as Alain.

Now she commented, "Forgive my silence, Your Grace. Your background is so unusual one needs time to absorb it."

"And time to speculate on where it all will lead me?" Valjean suggested. Noting the startled expression that flashed across her face, he knew his guess had been accurate.

Jeannette said hurriedly, "I can understand why you would hesitate to mention your British background. It must be very difficult to be caught between the heritages of two countries so frequently at war."

Valjean smiled ruefully. "I feared I'd never be able to persuade Aimée I wasn't spying for Britain."

Jeannette glanced at Aimée. Her daughter certainly seemed to be persuaded now—of that and more. "Have you told Monsieur Carleton about your inheritance?"

"I said what was possible in a letter," he answered. "I can't know his reaction until I return to Boston; but, as I already said, the Carletons are like my own family. I suspect their greatest concern will be whether I'll decide to live in France permanently."

"It would appear to be the obvious course," Jeannette said slowly.

"I've lived in the colonies all my life, and Boston seems more like home to me than Paris. One of my purposes in returning is to discover how I feel about it now, but I think it will be a difficult decision, Madame Dessaline," Valjean returned. As he spoke to Jeannette he was aware of Aimée's increased tension. If he decided to make his home in Boston, would she be willing to live among the people she now regarded as enemies?

The following weeks were very unsettling for Valjean. Although he spent a great deal of time in Aimée's company, it was either under Jeannette's watchful eye, in Mignon's presence, or both. It was impossible for him to join Aimée in her compartment because Jeannette had developed the disconcerting habit of making unannounced visits to her daughter, or sending Mignon to ask Aimée some question or to borrow one item or another at almost any hour of the day or night. Nor could he even talk to her alone at any length; and so there could be no discussion of future plans.

The situation sharpened his desire for Aimée to a hunger that distracted his thoughts; at the same time he feared that their inability to speak privately might lead her to doubt his intentions. While Valjean understood Jeannette's motives, frustration was wearing his patience thin. The *Santa Luisa* was rapidly nearing its destination, and the Dessalines intended to continue to Montreal as quickly as possible; this he knew would give him and Aimée little time to discuss their future.

When the *Santa Luisa* was only a day out of Massachusetts Bay, Captain Mareto's first officer approached Valjean, who was strolling on deck with the Dessalines, answering a new barrage of Mignon's questions about Boston.

After politely greeting the women, Zurbaran began, "Monsieur d'Auvergne, forgive my intrusion, but I have a message from Captain Mareto." Valjean nodded for him to continue. "The captain hopes you can discuss the final details about your cargo transfer this evening over dinner in his quarters."

Recently so distracted by thoughts of Aimée, Valjean had forgotten about the Carletons' plan to avoid the tariff collectors in Boston. Startled at this reminder, he hastily accepted the invitation. After Zurbaran had left, he turned to Jeannette.

"I'm sorry I won't be able to join you and your daughters for dinner tonight as we'd planned. This will be the last evening Captain Mareto and I will have to discuss this matter," he said.

"Will you stop by my compartment for a glass of brandy later?" Jeannette invited.

"Thank you, but I'm afraid I cannot," Valjean replied. "I know the captain and I will be talking very late into the night."

Throughout the rest of the afternoon Valjean thought intently about how he could arrange to speak to Aimée alone; but he could see no way to manage it. He couldn't go to Aimée's cabin after dinner, however late the hour, because of Jeannette's seemingly perpetual vigilance. For the same reason, it wasn't likely that he could see Aimée alone in the morning; and during the afternoon he would have to supervise the man readying the Carleton order to assure that he wouldn't later turn over to Andrew's employees someone else's shipment of goods.

Valjean didn't leave Captain Mareto's quarters until well past midnight. Uncomfortably warm after the closeness of the compartment and stifled by the pungent odor of Mareto's cigars, Valjean was in no hurry to return to his own cabin. He pulled off his coat as he walked slowly along the deserted deck. He needed to review details of the plan to transfer the cargo from the *Santa Luisa* to the boats Andrew would send to the ship, the signals they must use, the need for secrecy; but thoughts of Aimée broke into his concentration. If he couldn't find a way to speak privately, and at some length, with her, the next day, would it be possible to arrange a meeting once they all were in Boston?

He paused at the ship's rail to gaze at the ocean. His shirt lay heavily against his body, and he untied his neckcloth, then tore open the buttons halfway to his waist to let the freshening breeze cool his chest. The sea wind caught at his wide sleeves, a sudden gust snapping the cloth against his arms, ballooning the body of the shirt from his skin; he closed his eyes in pleasure.

"Are you the marquis d'Auvergne, or is it possible I've finally found my own Valjean?" a voice beside him asked softly.

Surprised, Valjean turned slowly to look down at Aimée. The white lace of her dressing gown was gossamer in the moonlight, shadowing her body like a glowing web. The eyes in her upturned face glimmered like still wine. His kiss wanted to be where a long curl swirled in the valley between her breasts.

"If you wait as long to answer that question as I waited to answer yours when we last met this way, I'll begin to wonder if you're changing your mind about me," she added playfully.

"Never," Valjean answered quietly. He took her into his arms, burying his face in the silken curls that loosely framed her features, momentarily forgetting all his problems as he lost himself in the sweet warmth of her nearness. Finally remembering they could easily be seen in the moonlight, he released her and stepped away. "We might be discovered . . ." he began.

"By whom? That little cabin boy who has profited so handsomely from this voyage?" she asked saucily.

Longing to kiss the mouth that was pursed so tempt-ingly, to put his arms around her again, he restrained himself and only took her hands in his. "It isn't that boy's good opinion I've sought these nights I've lain tossing in my cabin, unable to sleep for want of you," he returned.

"All this time I've been tormented by dreams of your love instead of enjoying it, while you've been concerned about gaining my mother's favor," she commented imp-ishly.

"Don't joke about it, Aimée. She has used every device known to mothers, since time began, to make sure of their daughter's virtue."

"But mine is already gone," Aimée reminded. She slipped her hands out of his and reached up to clasp them behind his neck, adding in a more serious tone, "Despite her caution about our being alone together, I can tell she has grown to like you."

"You shouldn't do this, Aimée. I want you too much and might not notice if your mother or Mignon should come in search of you," Valjean warned, starting to un-clasp her fingers.

Aimée lowered her arms to slip her hands inside his shirt. She held his waist and smiled up at him. "Mignon comes only at Maman's direction; and Maman, having de-cided that you would be absorbed with business until it was late enough for you to be too tired to think of any-thing else, has gone to bed. She's been having trouble sleeping since Papa has gone, and I finally persuaded her to take a sleeping draft so that she can be rested when we reach Boston. I don't think she's likely to awaken much before noon."

Valjean listened to Aimée in wonder. When she finished speaking, he inquired, "Where is that shy little maid I met in the forest in Montreal? You've made your plans as art-fully as a courtesan."

Aimée's smile faded. "Maybe you prefer that shy maid and I shouldn't have approached you so boldly," she said, glancing down a little regretfully at the lace that barely veiled her breasts.

Feeling her grasp on his waist loosening, he covered her

hands firmly with his own and said quietly, "I'm not afraid of *courtisanes en déshabillé.*"

Valjean intended only to kiss her briefly; but as his lips sought hers her body swayed closer, then softly molded itself to his, her mouth reaching for his kiss. At her eagerness his own desire, smoldering in him these last weeks, ignited with new life.

He reached out to lock her body to him. His mouth on hers hardened, demanding and evoking a passion in her equal to his own. She trembled with the power of the urges he aroused in her; and he felt as if the sea wind had suddenly turned into a gale that shrieked around them, filling his body with its own heartbeat, sucking the breath from his lungs.

Suddenly Valjean broke away from Aimée's kiss to look down at her from eyes lit with pinpoints of silver. Without a word he took her arm and stalked so swiftly to her nearby cabin that he drew her half running behind him.

After Valjean had closed and bolted the door, he turned to pull Aimée into his arms, his lips reclaiming hers. The sudden power of his passion overtook his caution, which now faded into vapor. She moved against him, kindling every nerve to brilliance; and his mouth caressed hers eagerly, mocking any thought of denying the urges that drove him.

Wave after wave of passion spiraled through Aimée. Her lashes parted, and she saw that he was watching her. The crystal flecks glimmering in his eyes seared her, as if they'd caught fire from the stars and were live sparks glowing, burning into her soul. He moved against her; and she clung to him, reaching up for his lips and, once possessed by them, feeling as if she were drowning in a torrent of sensations. She moaned softly.

That small sound was like an alarm ringing in his ears. Abruptly he tore his mouth from hers and buried his face in the mass of her curls, breathing deeply while he struggled to regain his control.

Rubbing her temple against the soft texture of his hair, inhaling the subtle musk of his skin, she whispered against his cheek, "Are you afraid you're going to hurt me?" At his nod, she added, "Stopping is what would hurt me."

Valjean didn't answer. As the blaze of his passion lowered into a quieter fire, he was able to think again. Aimée realized his mind was focused on some future plan; and though she couldn't penetrate his thoughts, she asked nothing more.

After a moment Valjean's fingers cupped the sides of her temples, holding her tenderly as he kissed her eyelids, her cheeks and forehead, the outline of her face. The tip of his tongue brushed her skin thoughtfully, as if tasting its sweetness for the first time; and this sudden change of mood, these newly unhurried, lingering caresses began a pleasantly insistent fluttering in her temples that slowly grew and spread, until she felt as if her whole body were gently pulsing with need for his touch.

His mouth again sought hers, this time nibbling at her lips, coaxing them to softness; his tongue surprising the corners of her mouth with little thrusts of fire, drawing her senses further into the current of desire he was deliberately building in her. He bent to caress her throat with his lips; and as his mouth followed the opening of her dressing gown, she felt his hair brushing her chin, his lips exploring the curve of her breast. Although he began to untie the ribbon at her waist, it was her fingers that pulled at the gown, throwing it open to him, tugging at his shirt while he straightened to make her task easier.

When she looked up at him, his eyes were smoke shimmering with crystal lights as he said softly, "Continue, little courtesan. I won't mind your undressing me."

Suddenly she felt awkward, her trembling fingers nervelessly ineffective, struggling clumsily with the buttons at his cuffs, the fastening of his sash. She stopped, straightening to look up at him helplessly. "My hands are shaking," she breathed.

Valjean said nothing. His eyes still on her, he undid his buttons and sash, sweeping off his garments so quickly she had barely the time to let her dressing gown slip from her shoulders before he again circled her in his arms.

At the sensation of the warm, naked length of his body,

the fire of his lean hips pressed against hers, she wrapped her arms tightly around his back, wanting him even closer as his mouth possessed hers. She reveled in his kiss, returning his caresses one for another, knowing that he shared every sensation she felt, knowing that the level of her passion mirrored his.

He slowly moved his hips against her, and Aimée's little gasp of surprise brought a smile to his lips. He said softly, "Now it wouldn't even be necessary for us to use the bed. But I prefer to do more than is necessary."

So inflamed by their fusion, she wanted no delay. She moved her hips seductively, hoping she would lure him into the ecstasy that ended with fulfillment; but he stepped away. Surprised, she looked up at him, wondering what he intended. He took her hand and turned her toward the bed.

As she lay among the linens he gazed down at her a long moment before saying softly, "Sometimes even a courtesan need do nothing to satisfy her lover other than allow him to please her." He sat on the edge of the bed beside her; his eyes shimmered with smoky lights as he pulled his legs up onto the bed.

She expected that he would continue with the same urgency as before, and her heart beat faster; but he sat beside her, merely looking at her for a long moment as if he were deciding what he would do. Finally he knelt to bend over her. His lips caressed her throat, his tongue making a flame bloom where her neck and shoulder met. She tipped her head; but his mouth again became elusive, his tongue flicking down her body to her waist, where he left a line of soft bites along her midriff.

Valjean's lips leaped to her arm, and Aimée discovered the sensitivity of the flesh inside her elbow. He lifted her hand and, uncurling her fingers, planted a kiss in her palm, his tongue lightly stroking the cup of her hand until it seemed to glow with fire. His lips hovered over her breasts, then alighted to circle them with kisses; as the circles shrank, her nipples were transformed into shafts of fire.

When she was quivering with the exquisite sensations

he'd given her, he straightened to look down at her, his
eyes glittering with the knowledge of what he was doing;
but giving her no respite, he again leaned forward, this
time to tease the inside of her ankles, moving up her legs
slowly to linger sensually at the tender skin behind her
knees. Wondering how far he would go, she shivered with
delight as he kissed her thighs, his lips as light as butter-
flies' wings, surprising her with the soft brushing of his
teeth, then the stroking of his tongue. She writhed with the
passion that surged in her; but his hands at her waist held
her still as he continued. Propelled by the forces he'd in-
duced in her, she whispered urgently, begging him to take
her now. When he withdrew, her eyes flew open. A streak
of fire tore through her as, his eyes flashing warnings, he
swiftly knelt over her.

Certain Valjean would delay no longer, Aimée reached
up toward him; her movements were stopped by his weight
as he abruptly sat up, his hands tightly gripping her hips.

The eager waiting, the anticipation, was as seductive as
his kisses; but he would let her do nothing. She lay there,
powerless to ease her hunger, her frustration mounting.

Finally she burst out, "Why are you doing this to me?
I'm starving for you and you bring me to this—to nothing!"

"Your need is no greater than mine," he said, his voice
tense with the desire he controlled. "I want you to learn
something about yourself, Aimée. Stop struggling and acquaint yourself with this body that's so dear to me."

Impatient and angry at his enforced discipline, she tried
again to move; but he held her still, his eyes flashing ominously; and she knew, though his passion was as great as
hers, she could do nothing until he let her. She closed her
eyes, torn by conflicting emotions, helplessly experiencing
his quiet oneness with her. Gradually the fires that had
raged so wildly in her being tempered to a steadily burning, deeply glowing flame.

Aware of her new control, he ran his fingertips over her
body, as lightly as if he explored the petal of a flower.
Tingles ran along her nerves, little shocks of pleasure; and
yet she remained docile, absorbing and savoring what he

taught her she was capable of feeling. Each time he felt her body tightening with its old impulsiveness, he stopped, waiting for her tension to subside, forcing her to relax—for she would have nothing from him otherwise—before resuming.

He began to whisper to her, telling her what he was doing, making her understand, leading her slowly to ever higher plateaus of sensation, coaxing her to the edge of ecstasy and stopping to allow her need to descend while the passion he had led her to remained waiting to rise further. He moved his hips slowly, measuring her hunger and deliberately giving her less; so her senses reached out to him almost to be unleashed, then eluded her. Her arousal intensified to so great a pitch she thought she must scream. Fire ran along her nerves, cascading toward a chasm; but yet he held her from its edge.

Finally she opened her eyes and saw him watching her, the level of his own passion revealed in the tautness of his face.

"How can you wait this way?" she panted.

Suddenly he closed his eyes tightly, as if he must more securely leash his passion; but her body would no longer obey. Though he still held her hips firmly, a ripple of tremors ran through her inner being, eroding away his will.

Valjean sat up rigidly, making a soft noise; and the sound—like a smothered cry—became a flame that seared Aimée. It was not possible to stop the molten waves that seethed in her now. The slowly rising current broke into fiery sparks rhythmically coiling around him. His lashes parted, and he gazed at her from eyes luminous with desire, knowing that nothing, not even his will, could stop her now.

As his body went with her, she knew that this was what he'd sought for her. A flash of flame lit her, but this time he didn't slow. The impulses he'd unleashed had so magnified that the two of them now became wild, mindless creatures, with one raging need filling them. Their beings seemed to shudder, then erupted in an explosion of ecstasy that shattered their senses into clouds of shimmering fragments.

They lay as they'd been, silently bathed in a film of moisture while their lacerated wills struggled to regain their former shapes. Still they didn't move except for their breathing, until the furious pounding of their hearts slowed to a more regular beat.

Finally Valjean whispered, "Aimée, my love, I wanted it this way so that you would remember it through all the lonely nights that lay ahead."

"I know," she murmured. "There's nothing more to say about us now."

"When dawn comes, I must leave you; and tomorrow night I'll be getting off the ship. I know of no way we'll be able to share love while we're in Boston."

"Probably not until after Montreal," she said slowly.

"Whatever is in Montreal, I'll be with you. I'll take you there myself," he promised.

Aimée turned her head to rub his shoulder gently with her temple. "Perhaps on that journey . . ."

"No matter what that journey, or the end of it, holds for you, we'll find a way to be together," Valjean said softly.

"Your love already has made all the promises I need tonight," she breathed.

She felt him relax, his body on hers gradually lengthening; and she knew he was surrendering to sleep. Not wanting to disturb him, she touched his shoulder lightly with a kiss, picking up a drop of moisture on her lips. She licked at it, learning its flavor, savoring even this small part of him.

Valjean startled himself awake and lifted his head to look at the porthole. "The sky is already getting lighter," he said wearily. He turned his head to look at her. "I must get up and dress."

"I know," she replied regretfully.

He delayed moving while he gazed at her, his eyes traveling over each feature of her face as if he were memorizing every detail. Finally he kissed her, his mouth as tender now as it had been compelling earlier, lingering to seal the promises they'd just made. Not meaning to arouse either of them, when he felt a spark of desire begin to glow softly in him, he ended the kiss, caressed her cheek with his lips for a moment, then got up.

Aimée watched Valjean dress, following every effortless movement of his muscles, each supple step, her eyes loving the body that had commanded her obedience only to bind itself just as irrevocably to her as she was to him. He hurriedly brushed his hair, already intent on the task that night; but when he turned and saw her expression, he forgot all else. His eyes softened as he came to stoop beside the bed and take her hands.

"I must go now, *chérie*," he said solemnly. She nodded. He kissed her fingers, then suddenly groaned, leaned closer, and kissed her lips lingeringly. When he withdrew, he gazed at her a moment longer, then rose and reluctantly turned away.

Throughout the day Aimée's dread grew. What would happen to Valjean if somehow the British learned of the cargo transfer and sent soldiers to catch him? What was the penalty for smuggling? She no longer cared if her mother saw the emotions in her eyes when they sought out Valjean on deck.

He was dressed much as he'd been when she'd met him coming from Captain Mareto's cabin—coatless, his shirt opened at its neck revealing the throat she had kissed and caressed. His hair, though tied in a queue, had loose strands, ruffled by the wind; and she longed to smooth them. But more than anything else, she yearned to run into his arms, to be clasped against that warm, vital body— to beg him to send someone else to shore and avoid the risk he would face.

Long after darkness had fallen and the other passengers had gone to sleep, Aimée knew the hour had come for Valjean to leave the *Santa Luisa*. She told Jeannette and Mignon she was going on deck to bid him good-bye.

Mignon gave Aimée a look of sympathy, then glanced at their mother, wondering what she would do. Jeannette said nothing to restrain Aimée. She just watched her daughter close the door behind her and silently prayed for the safety of this man Aimée loved.

Aimeé stood quietly out of the way, watching Valjean murmur final instructions to a man she didn't recognize as one of the ship's crew; she realized he must be one of the Carleton employees who had come on the boat from shore. She moved to the rail to look down at the dinghy that already had made several trips to the *Santa Luisa*. Then she felt a familiar body brushing her back and turned into Valjean's arms.

His lips touched hers, capturing them with their warm caress. She realized he kissed her so lingeringly, despite the presence of the others, to smother the fears he knew had arisen in her. Finally he released her and stepped away.

"I *will* see you tomorrow in Boston," he promised, then turned to climb down into the waiting boat.

Aimée stood by the rail, blowing him a kiss when he looked up at her. She glimpsed the longing in his face before he hid it with a sudden smile of reassurance. She blew him another kiss; then with hands gripping the rail so tightly they ached, she watched as the boat pulled away through the shadowy water. She remained there, scarcely able to breathe for her fear, as she listened to the faint sounds of the oars dipping into the water, even after the boat had vanished in the darkness.

"Mademoiselle, come away," Zurbaran said beside her.

Aimée shook her head adamantly; and the first officer shrugged, then left her alone to stare into the night, waiting for another hour or more while she prayed she'd see no lights, hear no gunfire announcing discovery.

Finally, Jeannette came and, putting her arm around her daughter's slim waist, led her back to the cabin.

Chapter 14

Aimée knew she wouldn't be able to sleep for worry about Valjean, so she didn't even bother to turn down her bed-cover. She lay, fully dressed, staring at her opened port-hole and waiting for the dawn.

The danger of discovery was twofold, she realized. Even if no one on shore caught sight of the cargo being loaded onto the wagons, it was possible a sleepless passenger on the *Santa Luisa* itself might be suspicious of the dinghies that had visited the ship during the night. The *Santa Luisa* had immediately withdrawn from the inlet and sailed far out into Massachusetts Bay, so no one would have been sure of the ship's location during its pause; nevertheless Aimée feared that questions might be asked.

When it was finally time to get dressed for the landing, she took off her wrinkled garments and stared at her wan face in the mirror, wondering what she would wear when she left the ship; she needed something that would bring life to her complexion. She finally chose a gown she hoped would attract Valjean's eye in the crowd—a gold-colored serge trimmed with burnt-orange braid. A matching hat in the new pancake shape had its center filled with rust-colored plumes, one of them tipping over her brow to brighten her eyes. But as Aimée studied her appearance, rewinding over her finger one fat curl that lay on her shoulder like a spiral of dark fire, she decided that nothing except the sight of Valjean could erase the shadows from her eyes. She knew that, whatever happened, his fate was hers; he'd left his mark on her soul, as the sun had left streaks in his chair.

While Aimée stood on deck with Jeannette and Mignon,

watching the ship maneuver into its place at the dock, she
was so absorbed in thoughts of Valjean she didn't even notice the mid-morning sun beating on her shoulders. Jeannette finally took Aimée's parasol from her unfeeling
fingers and opened it for her, warning about the freckles
she might find sprinkling her nose. Aimée was too distracted to hear Mignon's efforts to make a little conversation
to cheer her, and Mignon soon became as silent as she.

Aimée paused before the opening in the ship's rail while
she waited for the passengers ahead to sort themselves out
before going down the walkway. Her eyes hastily scanned
the crowd, searching for Valjean. She didn't see him. She
stared at the faces below, more slowly, more carefully inspecting each one. Her heart seemed to have stopped with
fear. When a tall man in an unornamented dark blue coat
took off the black tricorn he wore, Aimée stiffened in
recognition. A smile broke over her face as she let out a
little cry of happiness, and her heart resumed its beat.

Once Valjean realized that Aimée had seen him, he
again clapped on his hat lest anyone else from the ship realize he was the French nobleman who had accompanied
them across the Atlantic. He'd particularly noticed one
man, the first passenger to disembark, who had hurried to
the small group of British soldiers waiting nearby to question the passengers about customs declarations. Valjean
didn't like the soldiers' expressions as the man, still talking
excitedly to them, turned to watch the other passengers
coming down the walkway.

When the Dessalines stepped onto the dock, the man
shouted, "That's them! The girl with the red hair! I
wouldn't mistake her anywhere!" He couldn't have
aroused more attention if he'd called Aimée a witch. A
crowd immediately began to gather around the three
women.

Paul Carleton, standing beside Valjean, saw the commotion and asked, "What's going on over there?"

"I don't know," Valjean answered, straining to see over
the heads of the people thronging around the Dessalines.
"Whatever it is, I don't like it at all. Aimée's terrified—
that much I can tell."

"Monsieur, you are mad!" Jeannette was saying in heavily accented English. "Spies, smugglers—us?" She turned to the nearest soldier, who was obviously in command of the others. "Captain, can *you* believe we are spies?" she asked in the most piteous tone she could muster. "Do we look like smugglers? Obviously we are French; but we are running away from King Louis, not working for him. My daughter, Aimée—*oui*, the red-haired girl—was in fear of being abducted by the king's agents. Such corruption, such decadence!" she exclaimed, rolling her eyes skyward. She sniffled and said with her voice breaking, "Even my dear husband was killed by a rioting mob near Paris."

"All of this is true, Captain," Aimée said, pulling at the soldier's arm. "My father *was* killed, and the king *was* pursuing me. Does it sound like we're spies? We fled at night with hardly time to give Papa a decent burial!"

The soldier, who was in reality a sergeant, looked from the half-weeping Jeannette to the beautiful girl tugging at his arm, then to her sister whose lovely face was frozen with fear. "Ladies, please calm yourselves," he begged. "I only want to ask about a man who was on the ship and was seen in your company. This gentleman, Mr. Timmins"—he indicated the other passenger—"swears he saw a man stealthily leave the *Santa Luisa* last night. If the man is a fugitive, surely you'd want him apprehended."

Jeannette dabbed at her eyes and commented, "We are all fugitives, Captain. Anyone coming from France these days is fleeing something."

"I don't mean that kind of fugitive, madame," the sergeant returned, disturbed by the women's distress. He wasn't a rogue, who enjoyed tormenting women, but a soldier of His Majesty King George trying to do his duty. "Can you tell me anything about that man?" he asked.

"What *is* happening here?" Andrew Carleton demanded imperiously as he approached the sergeant, who was unnerved that the head of one of Boston's most respected families should now be bearing down on him.

"Sir, this passenger, Mr. Timmins, has questioned the propriety of another passenger's motives, raising the possibility of his being a spy or a smuggler," the sergeant began.

"I don't carry spies and smugglers on my ship." Captain Mareto, who had just approached, seemed affronted.

Mr. Timmins glanced at Valjean, who was standing beside Andrew and Paul Carleton. Startled, the man pointed at him. "That's the man I saw those women talking to on the ship. It's him!"

Valjean feigned surprise. "I, a French criminal?" he inquired coolly.

"Absurd!" Andrew declared. "This is Vale Kendall, who manages my shipyard. I've known him all his life. He's like one of my sons. A criminal—that's ridiculous!" he ended disdainfully.

"The man Mr. Timmins saw leaving the ship was a French nobleman," Captain Mareto put in. "He was a diplomat traveling secretly—or so he told me. He didn't want to be detained by a scene such as this, which would have been embarrassing."

"Where was this French diplomat going?" the sergeant demanded.

Mareto shrugged. "I assumed Philadelphia. I fly a neutral flag, and I can't question passengers acting as official messengers between countries. Mine was the last ship to leave Le Havre before the blockade sealed every port on the French coast. Maybe the count had his own reasons to leave France. Who can tell where he went? Perhaps to New Orleans."

Aimée turned to Jeannette. "Maman, didn't I say the count seemed secretive?"

"*Oui, ma fille*," Jeannette agreed. She moved closer to Valjean, scrutinizing his plain coat, the worn hat, and the slightly frayed edge of his neckcloth. "Captain, I can understand why Monsieur Timmins might mistake him at a glance, because this man has some similarity in height and proportions; but the count was more—how can I say it—*sophistiqué*, more the *bon vivant*." She turned to the sergeant, her attitude apologetic. "Being a man of the world, you understand what I mean."

"*C'est ridicule!*" Aimée exclaimed, seeming to inspect

Valjean as her mother had, and at the same time privately wishing she could throw herself into his arms. "This man looks nothing like the count."

Julia Carleton, who had recognized Aimée from Valjean's description earlier that morning, had taken all this in silently. Now she stepped forward, brushing past the perplexed soldier to grasp Jeannette's hand. "Madame, forgive this fool Timmins," she said. "Is someone coming to meet you and your daughters? No? Come away with us, then. You look pale. You're welcome to come to our home and recover yourselves after this wretched experience." She looked up at the sergeant and scolded, "Shame on you, sir! A new widow at that!"

"It's obvious Mr. Timmins was mistaken about Mr. Kendall's being a French count, and this lady and her daughters certainly aren't spies." Andrew addressed the sergeant. "Perhaps we could take these ladies out of the sun before they start fainting and cause further disturbances?"

The sergeant sighed at the thought of including such a situation in his report for the day. "Yes, Mr. Carleton, do take the ladies out of here," he said wearily.

Aimée drew in a breath of relief and, clasping Mignon's hand, turned to follow Julia and Jeannette. She felt Valjean's arm brush her shoulder; and although she hungered to turn into his arms, she didn't allow herself even a glance at him.

He walked beside her all the way to the carriage. His were the hands that caught her waist to lift her into the vehicle. Gazing into his eyes for a moment, she saw the love she felt for him reflected in their dappled depths. But she dared say nothing. After she was seated in the carriage, she discovered that he would not join them. He, like Paul Carleton, had a horse tethered nearby. But Valjean guided his mount to Aimée's side of the carriage; and although she kept her eyes demurely lowered as they drove through Boston, from under her lashes she could glimpse his hands holding the reins, his leg resting against the horse's side.

It wasn't until after the group entered the Carleton

house that Andrew turned to Jeannette and said warmly, "Welcome, Madame Dessaline. You played your impromptu role superbly."

"Yes, Madame Dessaline, thank you for saving me from detection," Valjean said.

"What else could I do? Let them arrest you?" Jeannette asked, shaking her head to indicate that such a thing was unthinkable to her.

"May I call you Jeannette?" Julia asked, taking Jeannette's hand in hers. "Please call me Julia. We're informal here."

"We aren't formal in Montreal either," Mignon said. "Please call me Mignon."

"Thank you, my dear," Julia replied with a smile. She turned to Aimée. "I knew who you were the moment I saw you. Vale told us about you."

Still unused to Valjean's being referred to as Vale Kendall—but realizing it was of the utmost importance that she not forget it while they were in Boston—Aimée looked at Valjean speculatively. "What did you tell everyone about me?" she inquired, wondering how she should behave toward him before the Carletons.

He came closer to take both her hands in his and answered simply, "That I love you."

Valjean had never declared his love even in front of Jeannette and Mignon, and Aimée felt as if someone had stolen her breath. Knowing everyone was waiting for her reply, she couldn't speak.

The man who had been standing behind Valjean came forward. He flashed Aimée a smile and tactfully said, "Vale's always been like part of our family, and mother wouldn't allow one of her sons to keep such news a secret. I'm Paul Carleton, Aimée—if I may call you that."

Aimée took the hand he extended, and managed to smile. "Of course, please call me Aimée, Paul," she said, then paused. She looked around at the others, then added, "I don't know what to say. All of you are so kind."

"We never expected so warm a welcome. *Merci*," Jeannette said quietly.

"Any further greetings will have to wait until after

we've had some refreshments," Julia declared. "Jeannette, would you like a glass of claret or a cup of tea?"

Jeannette, still pale, answered, "I believe, after that fright on the wharf, a small amount of claret would be soothing."

Julia nodded to the serving-maid, who had entered the entrance hall. "Please get claret for the ladies and brandy for the men, Abigail," she instructed, then put her arm companionably around Jeannette's waist and led the group into the parlor.

By the time the women had seated themselves, the serving-maid returned with a large tray holding the decanters and glasses.

"Of course you must be our guests while you're in Boston," Julia said as Abigail handed her a glass of claret. "This house has plenty of space—you each can have your own room."

Seeing that Jeannette was of a mind to refuse, Andrew asked, "Where else would you and your daughters stay? The hotel? That would be ridiculous when we have empty rooms—and you don't know how long it will be until you can go to Montreal."

Jeannette glanced at Vale, who said, "I told Andrew about your plans this morning."

Jeannette sighed and turned to Andrew. "I intend to leave as soon as transportation can be arranged. Please understand, it isn't that I don't appreciate your kindness. We had to leave France without even taking the time to buy mourning clothes. My Hilaire was killed, and I'm afraid I could lose my son as well."

"I realize that, and you have all our sympathy; but I shouldn't think you'd want to expose your daughters to such a risk," Andrew said solemnly.

"I know there's always some danger in traveling, but is moving overland really that perilous?" Jeannette asked, alarmed that she could reach Montreal only by ship, and that couldn't be done until after the blockade was ended.

"Are you familiar with the Indian situation?" Paul asked. "The Iroquois have sided with the British, and the Algonquins with the French." When Jeannette nodded, he added, "The razing of so many French forts, followed by Quebec's fall, has seemed to arouse the Indians that much more. Lately it isn't safe for anyone—French, British, or Indian—to travel in small groups through the territory north and west of here, all the way to Montreal. It's become a bloodbath."

Noting Jeannette's delicate shudder, Julia said, "Surely you don't want to lead your daughters into that!"

Recalling stories she'd heard of the tortures the Iroquois had inflicted on captured white women, Jeannette squeezed her eyes shut and shook her head. "But what about my Marcel?" she asked anxiously. "Is there no way for me to go to him?"

"I've already promised Aimée I'd escort you to Montreal." Vale approached to lay his hand comfortingly on Jeannette's shoulder. "I intend to fulfill that promise as soon as I possibly can." He removed his hand and turned away, adding, "The danger to Montreal seems not acute at the moment. From what Andrew has told us, the fort is still intact, and the French are keeping the British back. With the Indians as dangerous as they are, I think we should wait a little longer."

"You're probably right." Jeannette agreed with obvious reluctance. She lowered her eyes to stare silently at the glass of claret she held poised halfway to her lips. She was contemplating Aimée's possible future. Finally she asked, "Valjean, have you decided whether to return to France or remain in the colonies?"

"You'll have to take your time making a decision as important as that," Julia remarked.

Vale nodded agreement, knowing Julia longed to have him promise to stay in Boston. "No, Madame Dessaline," he replied. "Where I finally live depends on a number of factors, some of which still aren't settled."

"You certainly don't have to hurry on my account," Andrew said. "I still can use your help at the shipyard, though you obviously no longer need the job."

Vale turned to Andrew and smiled. "I'm glad to hear that, because I do need at least the façade of having a job. Now that Mr. Timmins has publicly accused me of smuggling, it wouldn't do at all for me suddenly to appear too prosperous." He put his brandy glass on a small table and picked up his hat. "After having been away for so long, I have a lot of things to do at home. I should leave now," he advised.

"I'd assumed you lived here," Aimée said in surprise as she got to her feet.

"Bess and I rented a cottage from Andrew. I kept it after her death," Vale explained. "Maybe you'd like to see it tomorrow."

"Oh, yes, I would," Aimée quickly answered.

Noticing Jeannette's warning glance, Vale said, "Madame Dessaline, I thought you and your daughters might enjoy a tour of the shipyards tomorrow morning. Then we could visit my house afterwards."

"It would be interesting to see how ships are put together, Maman. Why don't we all go?" Mignon urged.

"I think I'd like a little more time to rest; but you and Aimée can go if you wish," Jeannette replied, satisfied that Aimée wouldn't be alone with Vale in his house.

Vale nodded, wished them a pleasant afternoon, and said he'd let himelf out. He turned toward the door to the hall.

"I'll walk with you," Aimée said, and eagerly followed him.

When they were in the entrance hall, she closed the door to the parlor before turning to him. He reached out to take her hands, but she threw her arms around him. He bent to put his cheek to hers.

"I was so afraid you'd be discovered last night," Aimée whispered. "My heart didn't beat until I saw you waiting on the dock."

"Everything went smoothly," Vale said reassuringly. She felt his smile against her cheek as he added, "I would have done credit to a real smuggler—just as the role you played on the wharf would have been the envy of an actress."

"All the while I pretended to be indifferent to you I wanted so desperately to hold you this way," she murmured.

Vale loosened the arms that encircled him, and withdrew slightly to face her. Then he laid his hands along the sides of her face and brought his lips to hers for a long, tender kiss—even sweeter for having to be so furtively given. When he released Aimée, her eyes remained closed and her face was tilted to his, inviting him to kiss her again.

"To linger would be to invite discovery," he said, straightening.

She laid her head on his chest, remaining close for as many precious seconds as she could. When his hands told her to move away, she whispered, "Valjean, I love you so!"

He embraced her for a brief moment, then stepped back and opened the outside door. "You must remember to call me Vale, especially now that Mr. Timmins has pointed me out as a smuggler," he warned. "Although no one believed him at the moment, the thought has been planted in the mind of everyone who heard him; and if I have to do anything similar in the future, I don't want my name to be the first that everyone remembers."

"You won't hear me say Valjean again unless we're alone with no chance of being overheard," Aimée promised. Thinking about all the possibilities such an occasion might hold, she commented wistfully, "I guess the most we can look forward to for a very long while is a hasty kiss from time to time."

"Maybe not," Vale said speculatively. Aimée looked up at him in surprise, and he added softly, "My house is within walking distance. If you should ever see an opportunity to get away without being discovered, I'll be home every night. I have no servants, and I'll leave my door unlatched. When I show you and Mignon my garden tomorrow, I'll make sure to point out the shortest route you'd need to follow." Then he turned to go down the steps.

Aimée stood inside the open doorway, watching Vale walk swiftly down the path until he turned a corner and vanished. Then she composed herself, closed the door, and returned to the parlor, where Julia was urging her guests to enter the dining room for lunch.

The group had just been seated when a man who appeared to be Paul's age, entered the room. He was accompanied by a youth in his teens. Aimée guessed they were the youngest Carletons.

Benjamin was tall and dark-haired like his father; his hazel eyes ran over the Dessalines in brief, but penetrating appraisal. Aimée felt sure that he'd fathomed her character in that one glance. But it was Mignon on whom his gaze lingered. Timothy, like Paul and Julia, had light brown hair, and his bright blue eyes immediately warmed Aimée with their friendliness.

After Benjamin and Timothy had settled in their places and the meal had begun, Andrew began to question Benjamin about the legal advantages of a contract he was considering signing. Aimée could tell from Benjamin's answers that he was not only knowledgeable about the law but shrewd. Noticing Aimée's interest, Andrew explained that Benjamin was employed by a Boston law firm and hoped eventually to begin his own practice. While Andrew talked briefly about his son's promising career, Aimée noticed Benjamin's eyes were again on Mignon, as if measuring her reaction. Although Mignon's gaze remained on the food in her plate, Aimée knew her sister was aware of Benjamin's attention and was pleased by it.

When Andrew's comments became praise for Benjamin's accomplishments, Benjamin modestly turned the conversation to discussion of a friend's criticism of the tariffs the colonies were having to pay Britain for imported manufactured goods. Timothy made some brash comments about King George's government of his North American colonies, and Benjamin skillfully changed the subject to something less volatile. Aimée saw that this English family was more loyal to their colonial governors than to the ruler of their ancestral land, although Timothy was the only one who would openly say it. He reminded her of her cousin Claude, despite the difference in their ages.

As the conversation moved to homier subjects Aimée found that no one pressed her for an opinion on anything; but if she did speak, she was listened to as attentively as Paul or Benjamin—a refreshing change from France where women were usually expected to be charming, decorative, and silent, whatever power their dainty fingers held. Aimée began to feel truly comfortable in the company of these relative strangers who had taken the Dessalines into their house, completely ignoring the fact that their separate backgrounds should have made them enemies. The sound of the quiet voices around her became a hum in the air that she could listen to or not, and the last lingering remnants of her tension faded.

Aware of Aimée's long lapse into silence, Julia noted the shadows under her eyes and finally asked gently, "Are you feeling well, dear?"

Not wanting to appear bored by their company, Aimée quickly straightened her shoulders and replied, "Forgive me if I seem distracted. I sat up all last night worrying if Vale would be arrested or hurt."

"Worry about Vale?" Timothy exclaimed in surprise.

"If anyone else had been put in charge of transferring the shipment last night, I would have worried," Benjamin commented.

"Vale has always been able to take care of himself," Paul said.

"Yes, he is indeed very competent," Andrew agreed.

"As to his being harmed in any way, I only have to remember the times we roughhoused as boys and he beat me," Paul said.

"Vale was only twelve when he and Bess came to us," Andrew recalled. "He did get into some terrible scraps with the neighbor boys." Noting Aimée's expression, he explained, "You know how children will behave when a new boy comes into the neighborhood. They must test him."

"Test him!" Julia exclaimed. "They taunted him mercilessly about having lived with the Abnakis. He had nothing but respect for his Indian stepfather and wouldn't tolerate any of the remarks. Heavens, I hope never to see again such furies as he went into! He caused many a lad to go home with blackened eyes and a bleeding nose."

"He's always seemed so well mannered, so restrained," Jeannette commented. "Of course, when he saved us from that mob on the Versailles road, he was quite forceful—

and I'm thankful for it; but he seemed very controlled even then."

"Vale has always appeared calm on the surface; but it is, I believe, a *discipline* he's taught himself," Benjamin said thoughtfully.

"Violence is hardly a congenial subject after the Dessalines have so recently experienced more than their share of it," Julia observed. She peered at Aimée and Mignon in turn. "Both of you girls look weary. If you've finished your lunch, perhaps you'd like to go to your rooms and have a nap."

Aimée had not slept for two days, and now she wanted to be alone to think over the new insight she'd gained into Vale and to rest. "I believe the excitement of these last days has finally caught up with me."

Mignon, having noticed Benjamin's many glances in her direction, was torn between remaining in his company and taking the nap she sorely needed. When he said he must return to his office, her decision was made. She turned her eyes from Benjamin—he had decided those eyes matched the shade of a wild iris—and arose to follow Aimée and Abigail upstairs.

Once inside the room Abigail had indicated, Aimée found that her baggage had already been unpacked and a fresh pitcher of water awaited her. She undressed quickly, then rinsed her face and hands and put on her dressing gown to lay beneath the flower-sprigged canopy covering the bed.

The windows to the garden were open, and she gazed at the eyelet-flounced curtains moving with the breeze as her body sank comfortably into the fluffy coverlet she hadn't bothered to turn back.

Aimée recognized the passions the Carletons had described as being hidden under Vale's surface. His love-making certainly wasn't inspired by a moderate heart, but she supposed that anyone with such deep wells of emotion must find a way to control them so his actions would be acceptable to polite society.

Although initially it had disturbed her to hear that Vale was capable of great violence, she realized that from the beginning it had been this quality that had sharpened her desire for him, however gentle he was when they made love. It excited her to reflect on the powerful impulses Vale so carefully controlled; and she knew, if she was attracted to him all the more because of this, her own passions must be similar. She considered this and decided that that might be why her mother watched her and Vale so carefully. Jeannette knew her daughter well enough to recognize the depth of emotion she contained.

Julia's clear voice floated up from the garden and through Aimée's window, carried on the rose-scented breeze: "I hope our discussing Vale that way hasn't made you worry about him and Aimée. He's as dear to me as one of my own sons, and I believe I know him as well as I do any of them. I can assure you, Jeannette, you need have no misgivings."

Aimée's closed eyes shot open at the mention of Vale's name, and she sat up, alert.

"You have sensed feelings I've tried to hide." Jeannette's voice had a softer quality than Julia's, and Aimée found herself straining to hear what her mother would say about Vale when she thought Aimée was not listening.

"I suspect I'm more critical than I should be, but both Aimée and Mignon had admirers in Paris. I wouldn't have wanted to see either of them marry."

"Such beautiful girls will attract many men. Some of them suitable, others not," Julia agreed.

"Both those men had seemed to me to be very satisfactory until we learned one was a womanizer, who would never change, and the other a wastrel, who drank heavily," Jeannette said sadly. "I blame myself for encouraging their friendships. I was impressed by their titles and taken in by their charm and excellent manners. I thought they were decent."

Suddenly Aimée realized that Jeannette had been as completely fooled by Alain as she had; and her mother's admission of her own vulnerability made Aimée's heart swell with affection.

"Some of them can fool the wisest of us—and that includes the girls who pursue my sons," Julia confided. "It isn't easy to bring up three boys. I always wanted to have a daughter, but now I can only hope the boys will give me daughters as their wives." Julia fell silent for a moment, then added, "That's one reason I'm so glad to have you staying with us. It's pleasant to have other women in the house besides servants." Again Julia paused; but when she continued, her voice was hesitant, "Of course, I can't decide Vale's future; but because I do love him, I'll hope that he and Aimée's romance leads to marriage."

Jeannette, obviously pleased, thanked Julia for her good opinion of Aimée.

"It's hard to think of Vale being in love now," Julia remarked. "To the best of my observations, he's never avidly pursued any girl. He quite surprised me when he told us straight out that he loved Aimée."

"You can never really know what these children think," Jeannette agreed.

"It always was difficult to predict what Vale was planning. Bess commented on that many times," Julia replied. "There were occasions when Vale would behave as the other boys did, rollicking with them. Then the moment would pass, and he'd be just as reserved as he is now. Perhaps it's because he spent all those early years with the Indians."

"You admit he's difficult to understand, but you trust him anyway?" Jeannette asked.

"I'd trust him with anything, including my daughter, if I had one," Julia declared.

"Your praise of him relieves me of some of my worries," Jeannette remarked.

There was a pause in the conversation, then Julia said, "Before I forget it, Jeannette, we've been invited to a party the evening after next."

"Don't be concerned," Jeannette quickly replied. "You and your family must not alter your plans because of us."

"I won't be concerned, if you'll agree to go with us." There was another pause in Julia's conversation while Jeannette's murmuring voice seemed to decline the invitation. But Julia exclaimed, "Oh, no, Jeannette! You must not worry that you or your daughters would be ostracized because you're French. I'm sure your confrontation with those soldiers on the dock has been described all over town, and you'll be regarded as a heroine. Not all of us in Boston are so enthusiastic about being policed by imported soldiers."

Aimée lay back again, considering Julia's words. These colonials regarded the soldiers from their ancestral land as imported, and seemed to have begun to think of themselves as something other than British. She wondered if they would ever openly object to being governed by a British king. Turning her mind from that extraordinary idea, she contemplated the coming party, wondering which of her gowns Vale would find most attractive.

Once she had fallen asleep, her dreams had nothing to do with parties. They were vivid with the figure of a silvery-eyed man who stood outlined against the flames of many torches, a whip in one upraised hand and a pistol in the other; and Aimée—her gown hanging from her shoulders in tatters, barely concealing her nakedness—pressed her face to his chest, terrified by the unseen danger he held away from them both.

The next morning Vale arrived after breakfast dressed in a sedate dark gray coat that matched the deeper tints of his eyes, a white shirt with a carefully arranged cravat, and black breeches. His smile was so warm and his manner so cheerful as he took Aimée on one arm and Mignon on the other; there was nothing about him to remind any of them of yesterday's discussion.

The carriage ride to the shipyard was brief, but Aimée did catch a glimpse of streets shaded by oaks, neatly whitewashed fences, stone and brick houses surrounded by gardens she'd been too upset to notice the day before.

At the shipyard Vale took the girls to inspect three vessels in varying stages of progress, pointing out that the main parts of any sailing ship—whether it was meant to carry passengers or wage war—was its hull, its rudder, and its sails. Looking up at the great hulks surrounded by scaffolds on which crews worked, Aimée and Mignon felt even more dwarfed by these ships out of water than they'd been the first time they'd set eyes on the *Santa Luisa*.

The tang of the sea wind blowing out of Massachusetts Bay whetted their appetites for lunch, and Paul readily agreed to accompany them to a large, but cozily furnished restaurant. Later, when they were seated, Benjamin strolled in to join the group; and Aimée knew from his many glances at Mignon that his arrival there was not the chance occurrence he claimed it was.

Aimée noticed that throughout the meal other diners were glancing at the group in discreet curiosity. When she mentioned the attention they were drawing, Benjamin remarked that it was because of the girls' beauty. Mignon, who was dressed in a gown in the same blue as her eyes, blushed prettily as she thanked him. Aimée, who wore a gown of cream batiste trimmed with green ribbons, merely smiled. She knew Benjamin meant the compliment for her sister, but she was content to bask in the light of Vale's eyes. Paul remarked humorously that although the girls were charming, the group was drawing stares because Vale had been accused of smuggling and pirates weren't often seen in that establishment. Vale commented smoothly that Paul was jealous there wasn't a third Dessaline sister for him, and Paul unabashedly agreed.

Finally Benjamin, having stretched his lunchtime longer than would please his employer, confessed he had to leave them; and Paul reluctantly admitted that he too had to return to work at the shipyard's office. Watching Paul go, Vale reflected on the many admiring glances Paul had given Aimée over lunch, and glad that he didn't have to return to work, he silently decided there were advantages to being a marquis that he hadn't considered before.

Vale drove the carriage down a lane pleasantly shaded by a line of tall old elm trees that spread their branches like parasols to the sun. The farmer who owned the field bordering the Carletons' land drove past, waving and calling out greetings.

Noting the easy friendliness of Vale's reply, Aimée could hardly believe that only the night before last he'd smuggled a valuable cargo past the British soldiers. He chirped to the lagging horse; and watching his profile, she wished she could kiss the lips that were pursing in a second signal to the mare. He glanced at Aimée and smiled, then looked away to guide the carriage around a pothole; his smile lingered, softening the line of his mouth. His eyes were as serene a gray as a lazy cat's. She recalled the terrifying confrontation with the mob on the Versailles road and Vale wielding the whip that had held the peasants at bay. France seemed so distant, and her adventures there so like a dream, that she had to remind herself that Vale was a French aristocrat and the son of an English spy. As she reflected on this she realized that he was both, yet neither. He was part of a new breed of people just as she recognized she was; because she knew, despite her ancestry, her attitudes were as unlike those of the women she'd met in France as Vale's differed from the attitudes of the British soldiers she'd seen in Boston.

Vale drew the horse to a stop before a stone house. Hollyhocks marched in a cheerful line around the sides of the house, the red of the flowers matching the color of the shingles. Window boxes held a tumble of petunias and snapdragons, and Aimée noticed a blanket of morning glory vines falling over the low stone wall surrounding the garden. This was the home Vale had grown up in, she realized. How, she wondered, had Bess, the woman he'd thought was his mother, altered his future by concealing his background from him all those years?

Vale invited Aimée and Mignon into the parlor and poured them each a glass of sherry. While she sipped the wine, Aimée looked about the modestly furnished room. The walls were merely painted; the stained wood floors were covered by an occasional hooked rug. But it was comfortable. The large brick fireplace would wink cozily on a winter night, she decided, envisioning Vale as a boy studying by its light.

"It's a cheerful house," Mignon remarked. She took a sip of sherry and leaned back in her chair. "It's so peaceful here everything that happened in France seems like a dream."

"If it wasn't for the danger Marcel is in, I wouldn't

even care if we never went back to Montreal," Aimée said, glancing at Vale.

"Everything in Montreal will remind us of Papa; and though I don't want to forget him, I know Maman's grief for him will be sharpened there," Mignon commented.

"I don't want to upset either of you, but you should realize that many things could be different when you return," Vale said quietly.

Mignon sighed. "I know that. Maman has discussed all of it with us." She looked up at him, adding, "Maman and Papa used to hide bad news from us; but now that he's gone, I think she realizes we can accept it, so she's much franker."

"After your experiences in France she probably recognizes your strength," Vale observed.

"Perhaps, though she watches as carefully after our virtue as if we were still schoolgirls," Mignon remarked.

Mignon—Vale had decided—was a very proper miss, so he was surprised that she would make such a comment. He looked at her narrowly, noting that she was biting her lip. "She's concerned about you," he said, wondering at Mignon's agitation.

Two small patches of color appeared on her cheeks, and she lowered her eyes as if embarrassed. "Nevertheless, I didn't want to chaperon you and Aimée on the *Santa Luisa* any more than I do now." She glanced up at Aimée, her eyes briefly falling on Vale; and the pink of her cheeks spread to delicately tint the rest of her face as she resolutely continued: "Aimée has said nothing to me, Vale; but she and I are too close for me not to have sensed that you're lovers."

"Mignon! You've known all along?" Aimée exclaimed.

"Yes," Mignon answered, her blush deepening.

Vale was silent a moment as he absorbed this news, then said quietly, "It would upset your mother if she realized this."

"Maman isn't all that certain you aren't," Mignon replied softly. "She's hoping you aren't; but if so, she wants to minimize the chance of—" She searched for a word and could think of nothing, so she finally finished, "— Aimée's becoming *enceinte*."

Vale revised his previous opinion of Mignon. Like her sister, she wasn't as naïve as first impressions would have one think. "I too wish to avoid that," he said.

Mignon breathed in relief, then was silent for a moment before raising her eyes shyly to meet Vale's. "Did you mention before that this house is in walking distance of the Carletons'?" she asked.

"Yes, it is," he acknowledged.

Mignon put down her glass of sherry and slowly, as if measuring every word, suggested, "Don't you think you should take this opportunity to show Aimée how to find her way here—on the chance she might be able to slip away to visit you sometime alone?"

Aimée crossed the room to put her arms around Mignon. "Thank you, Mignon," she said fervently.

Vale finished her sherry and put down the glass, wondering what Benjamin would think if he heard Mignon saying such things. If Benjamin and Mignon had enough time to get better acquainted, Benjamin would have a happy surprise in store.

As Aimée and Mignon followed Vale through the garden, Mignon was still so disconcerted by her words that Aimée deliberately paused to admire the roses climbing the back wall, hoping to distract her sister. When Mignon pointed out the profusion of other blossoms in the garden, Vale recalled that Bess had loved flowers and had kept him busy digging up new beds. Aimée noted the incongruousness of a marquis working in a garden with a shovel, and they all laughed. The tension was relieved.

Vale led them past the stable into a dense grove of trees and down a path overgrown with shrubbery on both sides. They stepped out of the shade onto the lawn that stretched to the rear of the Carleton house.

"As you can see, we are close neighbors, after all," Vale said.

Having finally put aside her previous hesitance, Mignon peered through the sunlight at the windows that marked her own bedroom. "Why, it wouldn't take ten minutes to walk."

Aimée looked up at Vale with a kiss in her eyes and said softly, "Only five minutes if one were to run."

Chapter 15

Aimée and Mignon had decided to get dressed for the party in Jeannette's room to save Abigail the trouble of running from one room to the other. Aimée sat at the dressing table while she and Jeannette studied her coiffure, deciding where among the flaming pile of curls a small hair ornament should be placed. Julia knocked on the door. Noting that Abigail was absorbed in fastening the hooks of Mignon's gown, Jeannette called for Julia to enter.

Julia paused at the threshold to exclaim, "Jeannette, you look beautiful!"

Jeannette put Aimée's hair ornament on the dressing table and turned with a whisper of lavender silk. "I have no black gowns, and this is the only one that's even a little subdued. Even so, I feel that a new widow shouldn't attend such a party."

"Nonsense," Julia responded. "No one will criticize you unless it's one of the ladies who criticizes everyone—and no one listens to such people anyway." She came closer to study the lace trimming the gown. "Such fine work, such a lovely color," she commented. Then she turned to look at Mignon, who was fluffing out the tissue silk flounces at the hem of her gown. "That color reminds me of wild irises and matches your eyes exactly," she said warmly. "I'm sure that Benjamin will follow you around all evening." At Mignon's beginning protest Julia shook a finger. "Don't deny he's attracted to you, Mignon. Anyone who watches his face when you come into a room can tell how he feels. But perhaps I shouldn't be so enthusiastic. Maybe you don't feel the same way about him, and I don't want to seem pushy."

"I suspect Mignon welcomes his interest," Jeannette remarked. Noticing that the door was still partly open, she asked, "Do I see someone else in the hall?"

"Oh, yes," Julia said distractedly. "I had to make sure everyone was dressed first. Do come in, Timothy!"

The youngest Carleton entered the room, glancing at each of the women in turn, his blue eyes lighting with pleasure. "You all look so pretty," he said.

"You look quite splendid yourself, Timothy," Jeannette commented, running her eyes over his light blue brocade suit.

Timothy flushed; then remembering the boxes he was holding, he mumbled his thanks and said, "Vale sent these for each of you. He's going to be a little late and wanted to make sure you got them before you left, so the Parkers just dropped them off on their way to the party." He handed each of the women a ribbon-tied box.

Mignon undid the white bow on her box, opened it, and took out a nosegay of white camellias. "How lovely!" she exclaimed. "I shall wear them tonight—perhaps in my hair."

Aimée watched as Julia and her mother also revealed gifts of white camellias. Timothy handed her a box, the only one tied with a gold ribbon. Inside she found several small yellow tea roses.

"Did someone tell Vale the color I planned to wear?" Aimée asked as she took out the roses and held them against the champagne moiré gown.

"Put them in your hair," Julia said eagerly, taking the flowers out of Aimée's hand. She separated the blooms, placing them one by one against Aimée's locks. "Like that, don't you think, Jeannette?"

Jeannette nodded readily. "Here, *ma belle,* let me fasten them," she offered, leaning closer.

Aimée bowed her head so her mother could pin the flowers in place; and her eyes fell again on the tissue paper in the box. "Oh!" she exclaimed softly.

"Did I pinch you with the pin?" Jeannette asked in concern, stepping away.

"*Non, Maman,* but look at this," Aimée said wonderingly. A circlet of gold and topaz lay over her hand. "The stones form the petals of each flower—mayflowers," she breathed.

Jeannette stepped around Aimée to peer at the dainty necklace; the others too gathered closer. "It's beautiful," Jeannette commented. She took the necklace from Aimée and held it against her throat. "Shall I fasten it for you? It goes perfectly with this dress." Glancing suspiciously at Julia over her shoulder, she commented, "I believe someone did tell him the color of the gown you planned to wear tonight."

Aimée nodded and watched in the mirror as Jeannette deftly closed the clasp. The necklace looked like a single garland of golden mayflowers against the base of her throat.

Julia smiled and lightly tapped Aimée's bare shoulder with her closed fan. "Vale is in love with you for certain," she said teasingly, then directed, "Step away and let me look at you now."

Although Aimée's bodice was cut daringly low, the champagne lace frilling across her skin partly concealed the creamy curve of her bosom. There was no ornamentation other than the shadowy swirls of the moiré of the dome-shaped skirt that flowed out from her tiny waist.

"Charming, charming," Julia commented, looking from one girl to the other. "Vale and Benjamin won't be the only men to have lost their hearts by the time this evening is finished."

Aimée insisted on delaying their departure until the last minute in the hope that Vale would arrive in time to escort her to the party; but at last she gave up and got into the Carleton coach with Paul, Mignon, and Benjamin. Andrew, Julia, Jeannette, and Timothy went in a second carriage. Disappointed that she couldn't thank Vale immediately for his gift and for his remembering the special meaning mayflowers had for them, Aimée hardly heard Paul's compliments during the drive to the Thornton home.

The coach moved up the lane toward the house, and they could see lanterns strung cheerfully among the trees. The party would spill into the garden. When, at Paul's urging, Aimée turned her eyes toward the house, she could do nothing but admire the clean white frame and stone building, which had a wide veranda running the length of its front.

Adam and Sarah Thornton welcomed the Dessalines to their home with no less enthusiasm than the Carletons; and if they had any misgivings about entertaining guests from a country at war with England, they never revealed it. When Jeannette complimented them on the elegance of the ballroom that glittered with two crystal chandeliers and a marble-surfaced floor, Sarah proudly offered to show the women through her home.

The house had two parlors; the larger one, and the more elegant, was opened only for guests of special distinction. Its furnishings were of dark green velvet and rosewood. A rich Aubusson carpet was at the center of the shining parquet floor. The main dining room gleamed with crisp white linens, fragile flowered china, and silver. French doors opened onto the garden, and the perfume of flowers filled the room. The smaller, family dining room held the coziness of oval hooked rugs and maple furniture and had cream and blue linen curtains. The visitors were allowed only a glimpse of the well-equipped kitchen, where the cook poked down lobsters that tried to escape an iron kettle hanging in the great stone fireplace. Her helpers bustled about arranging dishes of vegetables, stacked napkin-lined baskets filled with steaming muffins, fresh baked bread, and popovers, sliced succulent hams, and cut pies fragrant with raspberries.

"There's a side of beef being roasted outside, and potatoes and yams are baking under the ashes," Sarah informed them, as if the food in the kitchen might not tempt them enough.

Aimée decided this was the sort of house she would like to give parties in—to plan menus and choose china and crystal. As she walked from room to room, she tried to imagine how it might be to live with a husband in such a house; and the man she envisioned seated opposite her in that cozy family dining room each morning was Vale.

As they looked into the library—with its brick fireplace, oriental rug, and glass-paneled bookcases—Aimée could picture Vale sitting in one of the upholstered chairs, reading during the evening while she embroidered.

Seated at the rosewood desk in Sarah's sitting room, Aimée imagined herself planning menus, doing her correspondence, or preparing her household lists.

Moving up a wide flight of oak stairs, she admired the long stained-glass windows on the landing, visualizing the rainbow-colored light that would stream through them on a sunny day. Long windows at each end of the hall had lace curtains pulled gracefully back. The doors opening onto this corridor revealed seven bedrooms and a now unused nursery. It was obvious that each of the chambers had been decorated by an expert, with an eye toward warmth and comfort; but it was the master bedroom that Aimée loved best.

At one end of the large room a silk love seat, a velvet upholstered chair, and an occasional table were set before the marble fireplace. The walls were covered with cream and gold damask. The comforter on the bed and its canopy were of ivory silk with inserts of ruched lace. The drapes, dust ruffle, and pillow shams, made of gleaming ivory satin, were trimmed with the same ruched lace.

"*Très élégant,*" Jeannette commented as she turned slowly. "*Très, très élégant.*"

"It's very tasteful, Mrs. Thornton," Mignon added, her eyes shining with her own dreams.

"There are rooms upstairs for a couple of maids, Adam's valet, and our butler; but there are additional servants' quarters separate from the house. Of course, there's also a smokehouse, a laundry building, a bake house, a root cellar, and a stable," Sarah said. "I'll sorely miss it when Adam and I move to Philadelphia."

"How can you bear to leave?" Aimée exclaimed.

"My husband's work must take us away," Sarah replied.

"Will you close the house or will you sell it?" Aimée asked. Then realizing that she was prying, she apologized, "Forgive me, Mrs. Thornton. It's just that I would want to close the house and keep it—so I could move back some day, if possible."

"I do feel that way, but I regret we must sell it," Sarah said. "A man is considering buying it, but he's unmarried at present and must wait until next spring to learn if the girl he's courting will accept his proposal—or even like the house."

"It must be inconvenient for you to wait so long," Jeannette remarked.

"No, Mrs. Dessaline," Sarah replied. "It will fit into our plans very nicely, as my husband won't take up his new business until then—and I'm not in a hurry to leave the house where our children grew up."

"It holds many pleasant memories, I'm sure," Julia agreed.

"If that potential buyer you mentioned does marry, this will be a fine home for him and his new wife to make their own memories in," Jeannette said slowly.

"Yes, indeed it will," Sarah agreed, brightening at the thought of the prospective buyer's pleasure. Wishing she hadn't solemnly promised to keep his identity a secret, she took Aimée's arm. Her eyes then fell on Aimée's bodice. "What a lovely necklace," she commented.

"It was a gift from Vale," Aimée replied. "Mayflowers have a special meaning for us."

"Do they?" Sarah remarked thoughtfully. "There's a meadow full of mayflowers bordering our property, and Vale did comment on the scent." Sarah threw Aimée a quick smile, adding hastily, "He stops in to visit once in a while." She caught Mignon's arm with her other hand and said, "Come, my dears. We'd best join the others."

Aimée and Mignon were enthusiastically welcomed by Boston's young gallants; but Benjamin's constant presence at Mignon's side effectively deterred many of her would-be suitors. Paul had other friends to greet and frequently left Aimée alone. Although she repeatedly told her admirers she was waiting for Vale to arrive, two men in particular paid court to her. While she anxiously kept glancing at the door hoping to see Vale, she couldn't help but be flattered by their compliments.

Patrick Drake, a tall, black-haired horse breeder, had manners to match any nobleman's in King Louis's court. Though he said nothing Aimée could criticize, his dark eyes unabashedly told her he desired her. Tom Griggs, a sandy-haired, green-eyed silversmith, was more playfully flirtatious, asking Aimée to run off with him or at least take a solitary walk in the garden's shadows. Aimée refused both offers, which were so charmingly given that she couldn't avoid smiling.

Dinner was announced. With Paul on one arm, Tom on the other, and Patrick watching her with darkly provocative eyes, Aimée went to the table wishing even more fervently that Vale could be there to escort her.

After dinner some of the guests decided to stroll in the garden, while others entered the ballroom, lured by the sound of the musicians beginning to tune their instruments. Paul led Aimée into the ballroom; and her first dance—the one she had especially wanted to share with Vale—was with Paul. As Patrick led her onto the floor for the next dance, she glanced at the open doorway; but Vale still hadn't appeared. Aimée had spent the day dreaming about how it would feel to have Vale's arm around her waist, however briefly, and how she would dip in a curtsey and raise her eyes to meet his. Now she began to wonder if he would come at all.

When Tom approached Aimée for the next dance, she accepted. He was disappointed that his charms seemed to have no effect on her. Another man danced with Aimée, yet afterwards went away thinking her unable to speak enough English to understand his remarks; because she invariably answered him with the same artificial smile. Although Patrick's eyes were difficult to ignore, he asked little from her in conversation; but she was so distant he decided she must be distracted by other thoughts. While the men who tried to catch Aimée's attention seemed to meet with little success, they were magnetized by her beauty and decided her aloofness was a challenge they'd like to overcome. Aimée wasn't completely immune to their compliments; and her worry about Vale slowly began to change to annoyance in exact proportion to the attention she was getting from so many attractive and charming admirers.

Sensing a gradual change in Aimée's attitude, Patrick and Tom were encouraged. Neither man was inexperienced in winning a young woman, and their unflagging efforts began to bring responses from Aimée. She finally decided that if Vale had been delayed for a good reason, it would do no harm to have him see other men paying her court. She smiled up into Patrick's dark eyes. She laughed at Tom's teasing quips. With the loosening of her tension, her eyes sparkled mischievously, her skin took on a new glow, and her smile was so bewitching that even Paul forgot about Vale and fell under her spell.

No one noticed the tall figure in the pearl-gray brocade suit pause in the doorway before entering the room. His eyes, catching silver lights from the prisms of the chandeliers, flickered over the dancers, stopped at Aimée and Patrick, and watched for a long moment. The elegantly clad long lean body tensed as Aimée threw back her head to laugh gaily, baring her creamy throat. Muscles tightening like a spring, Vale made his way through the fringes of the crowd, still casting glances at the dancing couple. A servant bumped Vale and, brushing aside his apologies, Vale took a glass of brandy from the tray he carried and drank it with a speed unusual for him. Then he threaded through the guests to approach Jeannette.

"Good evening, Vale," Jeannette said. Though he returned her greeting and asked if she was enjoying the party, Jeannette noted his narrowed eyes were focused on something beyond her shoulder, and guessed accurately that he was watching Aimée. "You *are* very late," she said, offering a subtle reminder.

"It was unavoidable, Madame Dessaline," Vale replied, taking another glass of brandy from a passing tray.

Hoping to distract his attention from Aimée and Patrick, Jeannette observed, "The people here have been very

cordial to us, and we're making many friends. The evening
has so far been very pleasant."

The dance had ended; but as Patrick led Aimée off the
floor Tom interrupted, taking her on his arm. Still
watching, Vale said softly, "I can see that."

"Have you had dinner?" Jeannette inquired uneasily.
When Vale shook his head, she suggested, "I'll be happy to
ask a servant to prepare a plate for you."

His stomach was the least of Vale's concerns at that
moment, and he replied quietly, "Thank you, Madame
Dessaline; but I'm not hungry."

"The seafood is truly superb," Jeannette said faintly.

Aimée held an opened fan before her face and was looking provocatively over the top of it at Tom. Even from his
distance Vale could sense that she was smiling warmly at
the silversmith. He tore his eyes from the couple and
looked down at Jeannette. "I have some bad news for you
and your daughters, Madame Dessaline," he began reluctantly.

Jeannette put her hand on his arm. "Montreal has
fallen?" she whispered fearfully.

"Not yet, madame," he replied. "However, the British
army has captured most of the outlying area. The British
are promising peace to the people in the villages who
swear allegiance to King George. Those who won't are
seeing their houses burned. Your home is in an outlying
stronghold. Do you think Marcel would have sworn such
allegiance?"

Jeannette, who had listened with bowed head, gasped
softly. Unable to speak, she shook her head.

"Then your home might already have been destroyed,"
Vale said tightly. He took both her hands in his and added
comfortingly, "There's considerable confusion in such circumstances, so it's possible Marcel escaped. If he has been
captured, then he is being treated decently, as I am told all
such prisoners are."

Jeannette looked up at Vale, her eyes filled with tears.
"Is there any way we can find him—go to him?" she whispered.

Vale was silent a moment, hating to give Jeannette even

more distressing news. Finally he said, "General Amherst is taking the main body of his troops down the Saint Lawrence; Murray has begun up the river from Quebec; and Haviland will follow on Lake Champlain. Their progress is slow because they're stopping to inspect the villages, but I'm afraid Montreal will soon be under full siege."

"No doubt the city's supplies are low." Jeannette sighed.

"The people are hungry, frightened, and confused. I suspect many men are deserting to protect their families," Vale said frankly. He paused, then added, "My source of information said the city's walls aren't strong enough to resist the kind of cannon fire they'll face."

"*Mon Dieu*," Jeannette said softly, fervently, as if in prayer. Her face had become so pale that he motioned for Julia, who had been standing nearby watching them, to come to their side. "*Non*, I won't faint," Jeannette said. "Get a glass of brandy for me and let me sit down a moment." She took several deep breaths, lifted her head, and added, "We must discuss what we can do."

Vale and Jeannette, accompanied by Julia and Andrew, promptly withdrew to an adjoining room where they could speak without interruption. Aimée therefore did not know that Vale had arrived. She didn't notice Paul and Benjamin circulating among the men in the crowd of guests, pausing to speak hurriedly and earnestly to a number of their friends.

She was again dancing with Tom Griggs when Vale reentered the ballroom. Already tense, Vale stopped to watch the couple while he wondered how to approach them. He preferred not to break into the formal double line of dancers. When Tom drew Aimée away from the other dancers, Vale saw his opportunity; but as Tom put his arm around Aimée's waist, Vale was annoyed that Tom would handle her so intimately in public, as if they were engaged. When Tom began to guide Aimée toward the doors that opened to the garden's shadowy paths, Vale knew his purpose was to steal as many kisses and caresses as Aimée would allow. Thinking of another man kissing Aimée, or touching her intimately in any way, caused

Vale's temper to glow red. Struggling to control himself, he strode purposefully toward the couple.

"Aimée promised this dance to me, Tom."

Hearing the quiet, tense voice, Aimée felt as if an icy finger were tracing a path down her spine. She turned quickly to look up at Vale. His eyes were filled with crystal pinpoints of light.

"Aimée didn't mention it," Tom replied, reluctant to give her up, though he took his arm from around her waist.

"Nevertheless, it is so," Vale said coolly.

Tom glanced at Aimée, momentarily considered protesting, then measured Vale's determination and changed his mind. "Thank you for the dance, Aimée," he said as he stepped away.

Aimée assumed Vale was jealous; and immediately after Tom was out of hearing, she began, "Please don't be angry with him, Vale . . ."

He put her arm through his, tightly holding her wrist with his free hand. "I need to talk with you," he said curtly and steered her toward the door.

Aimée hurried to keep pace with him as he crossed the room answering several greetings to which Aimée herself gave only a distracted nod. She was thinking about what she could say to Vale when they were alone. She'd known that Tom would try to kiss her once they were in the garden, and she felt guilty. How long had Vale been watching? Had he seen her flirting with Patrick too? She was certain he had, and this angered him; his grip on her wrist would surely leave marks on her skin.

Once they'd entered the garden, he stopped a few steps from the door and turned to face her. Although he drew her arm from his, he still held her wrist.

"I'm sorry I behaved so foolishly," she said, turning her wrist and trying to loosen his grip on her.

Vale looked down at his hand, surprised that he still held Aimée. Releasing her, he said brusquely, "I hope I haven't left any bruises. I didn't realize how tightly I was holding you."

"Please don't be angry with me," she begged. "I'd begun

to think you weren't coming at all, so I danced with him and—"

"You don't have to explain," Vale interrupted, surprising her. "People are supposed to dance at a party." Gently taking her hands in his, he hurriedly continued, "I was late because I learned that a man I know had just returned to Boston from Montreal, and I went to talk with him."

Aimée caught her breath and asked anxiously, "What did he say? Is Montreal under siege? Has it surrendered? Oh, please tell me!"

"He's a sailor and the ship he was on was confiscated by British troops. He had to work his own way back," Vale began. "Although Montreal may be surrounded by the British army now, it wasn't when he left. In any case, it's just a matter of time. The British aren't moving very fast because they're stopping at the outlying villages." He paused to give her a moment to grasp the implications, then said softly, "If the villagers don't swear allegiance to King George, the soldiers are burning down their houses."

"Marcel . . ." she breathed, then looked up at him. "Does Maman know?"

"I've already told her and Andrew," Vale replied. "Maybe Marcel escaped; but if he was captured, I understand that prisoners are being treated decently. In any case, I expect Montreal will have to surrender, whether they try to last out a siege or not. Food and ammunition are very low because of the blockade, and the British outnumber them many times over. Also, the city's walls won't be able to withstand the cannonade." He paused for breath. Aimée lowered her head. Putting his fingers under her chin, he tipped her face toward his. "Aimée, your mother wants to leave as soon as possible. Andrew has promised to start arranging for the supplies we'll need, and Paul and Benjamin have volunteered to go with us. They're asking their friends if any of them can join us."

Quivering, Aimée took a deep breath and whispered, "My only comfort in all this is that you'll be with us."

Vale's hands slipped to her shoulders. "I can't stay at this party, Aimée. I have to leave so I can get a little rest tonight, because early tomorrow morning I'm going to

Providence." At her startled look he explained, "You, your mother, and Mignon will have to travel by coach, and I'm going to Providence to see a man whose coaches are particularly made for long trips. We don't want axles breaking or wheels falling off along the way."

Aimée nodded in agreement. "How long will you be away?" she asked.

"A fortnight or close to it," Vale answered, then added regretfully, "I expect I'll return just about the time Andrew will have arranged for everything else we'll need."

"Then we'll go immediately," Aimée concluded. "I guess I'll have no chance to visit your house as we'd hoped." Realizing she was being selfish to think of her own happiness when Marcel had possibly been imprisoned or even wounded, she looked up at Vale and said lamely, "I just wanted to spend one night with you before we left. I just wished . . ."

Vale put his arms around her, holding her close. "I know, *chérie*," he said softly. "I wished it too. If there was any possibility you could slip away from the others tonight, I wouldn't care if I didn't sleep at all; but Andrew has already mentioned going home; and everyone will be awake far into the night making plans."

Aimée raised her arms to slide her hands around his shoulders. With her movement she felt the topaz garland shift against her skin. "In the excitement I almost forgot to thank you for your gift," she said. "It's a beautiful necklace."

"It looks beautiful on you," he replied. "I only regret it isn't perfumed like real flowers."

"Live mayflowers wilt very quickly if one picks them, but the ones you've given me will never die. They remind me of the way I feel about you, that my love won't ever fade," she said softly.

He gazed down at her for a moment before he stepped away. Then taking her hand, he guided her farther down the path to stop in the deeper shadows, and there he drew her into his arms.

Vale's lips touched the side of Aimée's neck and caressed her tenderly. They moved along the line of her jaw, brushing over her chin to seek her lips. A poignant ache rushed through Aimée as he kissed her softly, careful to restrain himself. She knew he was deliberately withholding his fire so as not to excite them too much before he had to leave; but even his careful kisses infused her with passion, and her arms around him tightened. His lips responded, becoming insistent, lingering for more than a light caress; and the need in her moved closer to the surface, tempting her to forget restraint. Her mouth caressed his hungrily, eroding his will; and his lips parted. As his tongue began to trace the outline of her mouth, she felt his desire rising; and wanting him desperately, needing to prolong this moment as much as possible if it was all they could have, she moved against him sensually. The sweet aching in her sharpened as his hands on her back slipped lower, holding her firmly against him. Then abruptly his grasp on her lightened and he stepped back.

Though his smoky eyes yet swirled with passion, he said firmly, "I must leave."

Realizing his desire was as acute as hers, she nodded and whispered, "I'm sorry for what I did."

Vale looked down at Aimée a moment, realized she was apologizing for flirting with Tom, and said quietly, "There's a difference between being jealous and being possessive, *chérie*. Jealousy is suspicion born of the fear of losing, while possessiveness is looking after what's yours." He bent to brush his lips to her forehead as he added, "I'm not afraid that your dancing with Tom or anyone else is going to change your mind about me." He straightened, finishing, "You're mine and you know it."

Then he turned and left her standing in the shadows. As she looked after him the breeze enveloped her with the scent of the mayflowers in the nearby field.

The days following the party were crowded with social calls and invitations. The Dessalines, despite Jeannette's fears of possible social rebuffs, were warmly welcomed by the Carletons' friends. News of their impending journey to Montreal spread like fire through the neighborhood. Admiring the Dessalines for their courage and respecting their determination to be with Marcel in such perilous times, the Bostonians streamed into the Carleton house with offers of help for Jeannette and her daughters. There was however nothing that Vale hadn't already done or arranged for, so the most they could offer was invitations designed to distract the Dessalines from their troubles.

Aimée found herself dressing every day to have lunch in someone's home, to do last-minute shopping with one of Julia's friends, to attend a picnic, a quilting bee, even a horse race. The evenings were filled with dinner engagements in someone's home, the meal often followed by musicians playing chamber music or sometimes a local singer. Aimée was at first surprised at the number of amusements Boston had to offer; and though the *soirées* weren't as elaborate as those in Paris, she found the relative lack of sophistication refreshing. One night the Dessalines and the Carletons attended a play, another evening a musicale on the commons under the stars. One night they even saw *Alcina*, an opera by Handel, a composer Aimée had never heard of before, though he was popular in England and its colonies. The earthiness of the rousing music struck a chord in her own spirit and temporarily distracted her from her loneliness without Vale.

During the first few days of his absence she had stoically endured the lingering fiery impulses aroused by his kisses in the garden; but as her physical need passed its piquancy it was replaced by a longing to be in his presence, merely to know he was nearby.

Although the social gatherings and outings the Dessalines attended with the Carletons frequently brought Aimée into contact with the men she'd danced and flirted with at the party, her mind was focused on Vale; and the men invariably went away puzzling over her newly distant attitude. Both Tom Griggs and Patrick Drake visited the Carleton house; and although Aimée was pleasant to them, she seemed unaware of Tom's flirtatiousness and eluded Patrick's covert advances with a skill even Alain would have admired. Yet, rebuffed as they were, they didn't give up; and wanting to impress her favorably, hoping to make better progress during the trip to Montreal, both men volunteered to act as escorts for the Dessalines. When Andrew announced this offer, Aimée made no comment. All she looked forward to was Vale's return from Providence.

Finally, only two days before the Dessalines planned to leave Boston, without waiting for Abigail to announce his arrival, Vale marched into the dining room where the Carletons and Dessalines were having breakfast. Startled, they looked up from their dishes to stare in shock at his appearance.

Vale's face was smudged with soot, and his hair was covered with a film of gray ash. He was coatless, his wide shirt sleeves were torn and blackened, and his wet breeches clung to his legs.

"What's happened to you, Vale?" Andrew cried in alarm as he leaped up from his chair.

"I just got back from Providence; and as I was driving through town I decided to stop at the shipyard for something. I discovered that the scaffolding around the ship for the Southern Atlantic Lines had caught fire," Vale said hurriedly. "The men are trying to save it, but I doubt they'll be able to."

"Damnation!" Paul exclaimed, throwing aside his napkin.

Benjamin quickly got to his feet, tearing off his coat. "We'd best get over there and make sure the flames don't spread to the rest of the shipyard."

Aimée, too, had leaped up from her chair. Visions of the huge ships engulfed in fire made her heart pound with fear. She followed the men as they hurried from the dining room. Andrew was asking Vale questions and firing off directions to his sons all the way to the front door.

"Can we help?" Julia begged, tugging at Andrew's arm.

"Surely we could so something," Jeannette offered.

"Every man in the area of the shipyard has come to help," Vale said quickly, shaking his head.

"Don't even think of coming," Benjamin declared. "We don't want to have to worry about you."

"Can't we do anything?" Aimée persisted.

Vale turned to face her. His hands on her shoulders

were firm but carefully gentle as he said, "Ben is right. Sparks and burning timbers are falling everywhere—and if the fire spreads, the entire shipyard could become an inferno."

The thought of such a catastrophe sickened Aimée. "Please, *please* be careful," she breathed.

"I will," he promised, bending to brush his lips to hers. He quickly straightened, then turned to follow the Carletons outside.

Aimée stood with the women, watching silently as Vale and Andrew and his sons got into the coach Vale had brought from Providence. He turned to look one more time at her before he snapped the whip over the horses' heads and they plunged forward. The women remained staring after the coach until it turned out of the lane.

No one even thought of finishing breakfast. Julia distractedly turned into the parlor and asked Abigail to bring tea. Aimée stood at the window looking at the black smoke billowing from the direction of the shipyard; she prayed for the safety of the men.

The women passed the day in relative silence, each one so concerned with her personal fears she could think of little else.

Aimée continued to stand by the window as the hours crept by, staring at the roiling smoke, thinking of all the crippling injuries fires caused, the hideous deaths. Her heart pounded; she was living a nightmare. The mute terror on her face was reflected in the features of the other women.

When the sun finally sank over the trees, its scarlet merged with the glow of the fire, now more visible in the early evening sky. The smoke still rolled darkly over the housetops. Aimée wondered fearfully if the fire had spread.

"Don't you think we could help in some way?" Jeannette asked Julia.

Julia shook her head. "I've considered taking coffee or food to the men, but I doubt they'd have time to stop for anything. We'd only be in their way," she said slowly.

"Don't worry, Jeannette. They have plenty of help. I'm sure every man in town is there."

"It's wonderful that they would all risk their lives to help fight a fire that isn't really their concern," Jeannette commented.

"When the first colonists landed in Boston Bay, they had to help each other just to survive," Julia said. "This attitude, that all our fortunes are bound together, hasn't left us."

"Maybe that's the reason—this loyalty you share with one another—I and my daughters have been accepted here," Jeannette said thoughtfully.

Julia replied, "It may have been the reason everyone was willing to get acquainted with you, but you've been accepted because everyone likes you."

Aimée, who remained silent, thought about what Julia had said; and she understood why Vale was so reluctant to move to France. Although in France Valjean would be revered as the comte de la Tour, marquis d'Auvergne, he would find few friends in King Louis's court. Had he been a wastrel like Roget, he would be dismissed as harmless and ignored. Had he been a schemer like Alain, there would be many who would fear him because he wouldn't hesitate to use his power to harm others, even ruin them, if it amused him or brought him more wealth. He was neither, so he would probably live like his mother had—very privately, an outcast of his own choosing. But here in Boston a man could earn the kind of respect and affection that made friends risk serious injury, if not their lives, fighting his fire. Here in Boston Vale Kendall would always have loyal friends, whether he was an employee of the Carletons or a man who'd inherited enough money to invest in an undertaking of his own.

Whatever the future held for Vale, whichever decision he finally made, Aimée knew she would be equally happy being the comtesse de la Tour, marquise d'Auvergne, or Mrs. Vale Kendall. She would even be willing to be his paramour if necessary. If all the world would point accusingly at her, she could endure the scandal. She could endure anything at all if he loved her—if he survived the inferno the shipyard surely had become.

Aimée lifted her eyes to stare at the sky. The orange light beyond the treetops was like a wound in the now darkened heavens. The stars were no longer white but yellow, like sparks that had escaped the blaze. Even the moon was red, as if smeared with blood. She remained at the window staring at the ominous glow, praying that it wasn't Vale's blood that was to flow.

Aimée was oblivious of the monotonous sound of Mignon's incessant pacing behind her, of the soft clicking of Jeannette's knitting needles as she busied her fingers to ease her tension. Aimée didn't even hear Julia's frequent grumbling about tearing out more stitches than she sewed as she distractedly embroidered.

After another hour had passed, Aimée began to wonder if her eyes were deceiving her or if the light in the sky was in fact fading. She continued watching for a time, hesitant to arouse false hopes in the others; then the glow abruptly vanished.

"Look, look!" she cried.

Mignon whirled and ran to Aimée's side. Julia's embroidery frame fell, scattering her threads in bright rivulets on the carpet. Jeannette stood up to join her daughters, her knitting crushed in her clenched hands.

"Thank God," Julia said fervently, then turned to call in a voice shaking with emotion, "Abigail, Abigail! Warm up that stew! Slice some bread! Cut up those pies you baked this afternoon!" She paused as the maid rushed into the room smiling and weeping at once. "Make some coffee for Mr. Carleton—the boys—yes, I'm sure Mr. Kendall too!"

"I only hope they all are safe," Mignon whispered, voicing the fear that tore at Aimée's heart.

Jeannette dropped her knitting on a table, then put her arms around her daughters' waists. "Don't worry, *mes petites belles*. I have a feeling everything is all right now."

The women waited anxiously until they heard the coach rattle to a stop before the house. Then they ran out into the night to greet the men. Julia flew into Andrew's arms. Mignon caught Benjamin's hands and stammered out the questions that had waited so long on her lips. But while Jeannette simultaneously hugged Timothy with one arm and squeezed Paul's waist with the other, Aimée stood helplessly by, as silent and motionless as if she'd been turned to stone. Vale wasn't with them.

Noticing Aimée's forlorn figure, Paul freed his sleeve from Jeannette's grasp and hurried to Aimée's side.

"You're looking for Vale," Paul said to her. Aimée nodded numbly, her eyes brimming with tears; and Paul hurriedly explained, "Vale is safe. He went directly home. He asked me to tell you not to worry about him. He's just tired. We're all tired, Aimée; but he fought the fire longer than any of us. If it hadn't been for his quick action this morning, the whole shipyard would have been lost."

"I thought it was, from the light I saw in the sky," Aimée murmured. The fear that had filled her eyes became tears of relief, and she bowed her head as she wept. "All that matters is he's safe."

She appeared so solitary, so helpless in her weeping. Paul put his arms around her comfortingly. "Don't blame Vale for not stopping here to see you. We're all tired. By God, *so* tired." Paul held her away from him so he could look into her face. "None of us even wanted to be bothered with bathing when we got home. We just drove over to the beach and walked into the water." He smiled sheepishly. "We must have looked like madmen, the lot of us standing there in the moonlight, the waves washing over us fully clothed."

"Are your clothes still wet?" Julia asked, feeling Andrew's sleeve. "You'll have lung congestion if you don't get into the house. Yes, you are damp. Madmen, indeed!"

"You'd best go inside," Aimée urged, wiping away her tears. "Abigail is setting out supper for you."

Timothy, who had noticed Aimée's tears, came to peer at her in the light coming from the doorway. "Will you sit with us? I suppose you already ate."

Aimée shook her head. "None of us had an appetite. I still don't feel like eating, but maybe I could have a cup of hot chocolate."

*   *   *

Andrew's description of the fire was frequently interrupted by comments from his sons, who added things he'd overlooked, or by questions posed by Julia, Jeannette, or Mignon. The entire incident seemed more like an adventure as the men told it, than the dread catastrophe Aimée had envisioned. She listened in silence as she sipped her chocolate, needing to ask nothing. Andrew's account of the event was richly threaded with praise for Vale: Vale's immediate decision to launch the nearest half-built ship because its hull was watertight; Vale's idea that the scaffolding around the third unfinished ship be covered with the cloth that was to have been used for its sails, then soaked with water; Vale's decision to send a messenger to a nearby pub, even before he'd told the Carletons, because he knew some retired sailors who spent their mornings there would help fight the fire.

The end result was that, aside from the Carletons' office building, only the one ship had been lost, along with its scaffolding, rigging, and the sailcloth.

Finally the men's yawns became too insistent for them to disguise, and Jeannette declared they all must go to bed. They all said their good nights and made their way upstairs. But Aimée, once she put out her candle and got into bed, found she was no longer tired.

Although bursting with pride at Andrew's descriptions of Vale's role in the conquest of the fire, she wanted desperately to see Vale herself and confirm that he wasn't injured.

She got out of bed and went to the open window to look in the direction of Vale's cottage. Wondering if he'd already put out his lamp, or if the trees obscured any light still in his windows, she peered through the darkness. Vale had told her he'd leave the doors unlatched every night, she recalled. The Carleton household was sound asleep. The servants had been told not to awaken them before noon, which meant the servants too would sleep later than usual. If she went to Vale's house tonight, discovery was unlikely, she realized.

The need to put her arms around Vale, the longing to be close to him even if he was already sleeping, was too strong to resist; and she left her room to tiptoe down the hall to the back stairway.

With the full moon to guide her Aimée easily found the place where the path began. Silvery light sprinkled through the treetops, dotting the path—and reminding her of the flecks of color in Vale's eyes.

She approached the house warily. When she reached for the door handle, she held her breath; but as Vale had promised, the latch was off. The moonlight pointed out the stairway; and at the top of the steps she found a short hall that contained two doors. He'd said there were two bedrooms, she remembered, and wondered which was his.

The first door she tried opened onto a room obviously furnished for a woman's use—Bess's former room. Glancing at the bed. Aimée found it neatly made; a small black cat sprawled on top of the coverlet stared curiously at her. She closed the door softly and turned to the one across the hall.

As the door swung soundlessly inward Aimée peered through the shadows. Hooked rugs were scattered over the wooden floors. Moonlight flowed through the curtained windows to reveal slanted rafters, a wardrobe closet, an armoire, a washstand, a rush-backed chair, a canopied bed. The coverlet had slipped to the floor, and Vale's body, covered only by a sheet, was silhouetted in the moonlight. He was lying on his side, his back to her—so still she supposed he was sleeping. She crept across the room, ignoring the slight squeak of the floor, grateful after the coolness of the grass for the soft rugs that warmed her bare feet. She sat down, careful not to disturb him, then slid gingerly under the sheet.

Discovering Vale was naked, wanting their closeness not to be hampered by even her thin batiste nightgown, she slipped it over her head and dropped it to the floor. Then like an animal needing the comfort of its mate's sensation, she nestled against his back. Even her legs wanted to touch him again, and they folded against his limbs. Inhaling his warm familiar scent, feeling the soft texture of a tendril of his hair lying against her cheek, she contentedly closed her eyes and sighed happily.

Vale wasn't in a deep sleep. Completely relaxed, he was drifting in the area where his senses were aware of Aimée's presence while his mind was too near slumber to question it. He lay unmoving for a while until, without a word or even thought of a word, he turned and put his arms around her, his face against her cheek, burrowing his nose into her hair.

The perfume of her curls, the silky texture of her skin, the contours of her breasts against his body, confirmed her identity. His lips brushed across her cheek searching for her mouth. Finding it, he merely put his lips to hers, not kissing, not caressing, the contact enough for him at the moment. His hand slid to her waist, then moved slowly along the curve of her hip, renewing its recognition of her proportions before returning to her back and gently pulling her closer.

Aimée, who had quickly fallen into the same half-sleeping state as he, wasn't awakened by his touch, though she was aware of it. She responded instinctively, languidly twining her legs with his, curling her arm around his hips, moving nearer. With this contact their senses were content, and they drifted deeper into sleep.

Neither one had any perception of waking or sleeping, or the passing of time; so when their consciousness rose a little higher, each one was again instinctively aware of the other's being.

Vale's lips on Aimée's began a subtly caressing movement that was just the beginning of a kiss, arousing her only enough to bend her knee and draw up her leg between his, her thigh against his echoing the soft rubbing of his lips, awakening a spark of desire in them both. His arms slid around her, the movement of his chest making her breasts bud into firm little points against him—two more sparks of awareness luring their sleeping minds.

His mouth fondled hers until her lips parted, and the tip of his tongue traced the round softness between, producing a glow within both of them. Their bodies responded by lazily moving against each other, the firm length of him warming. Her instincts recognized his reaction, but this knowing didn't impose on either of them the need to do more. Lips together, bodies all but joined, they drifted again into deeper slumber.

Through the tunnels of Aimée's darkened mind was spiraling a sensation, a tingling too insistent to be ignored; and her consciousness rose a degree. Without her direction, her body moved accommodatingly and the warmth smoldering in her nerves was stirred into glowing sparks. The tantalizing contact became a single tongue of flame flickering restlessly as it gradually impressed itself on her awareness. Her hips moved yieldingly against his, her body melting into pliancy, their separatenesses flowing easily into one.

A piquant ache coaxed them through the veils of their slumber; their fusion kindled the fires that drew them to awareness.

Aimée opened her eyes. Vale's lips were searching the contours of her mouth with growing urgency; and though his eyes were still closed, tension was written on their lids. She discovered that her leg was folded over his hip; her arms around his shoulders locked him to her. In her surprise her arms slackened, and Vale's eyes opened. The smoky shadows in them were streaked with silver lights. He held her shoulders a little away from him, causing her back to arch; and with the movement a flash of flame drove through her, shocking her to breathlessness. When she gasped, he gathered her shoulders closer, cradling them in his arms, his teeth gently catching her lips, urging them to softness, his tongue hungrily licking their roundness until his mouth finally possessed them. The fire again took command and moved her body tightly against his, her pliant softness loosing forces that compelled them on.

The sudden flaring of Aimée's passion seared her and, even after several moments, didn't fade. The ecstasy remained, making a torch of her senses, continuing until she made a sound—half cry, half moan; and still it went on, becoming a wild fire beyond their control, seemingly without end. The sounds of Vale's gasp, of his ragged breath, unleashed a new wave of sensation of such intensity that her pleasure seemed more than her flesh could endure, drawing her to the edge of madness until the prolonged

ecstasy emptied their minds of all consciousness and finally withdrew from their scorched nerves.

When Aimée at last came to her senses, she found that
they were still locked together, their arms wrapped around
each other; and her surfeit was so great, her exhaustion so
total, that she had not the strength to move even a finger.
When Vale's lashes parted, she knew that the still stunned
look of his eyes was a mirror of her own. Neither could
speak, not even to whisper pledges of love. Their eyes
communicated their wonder; the weariness of their bodies
was eloquence enough. Too tired to separate, each knew
the other wanted not the smallest space between them anyway. They both knew they'd reached into a different level
of their beings. Another bond had been forged, stronger
than any before; and each could effortlessly read every
thought, every emotion, that passed through the other's
eyes as if it were his own.

Neither slept again, but they didn't stir until the moon-
light faded, giving way to the glow of the coming dawn.
Finally, knowing Aimeé should return to the house before
the sun rose over the trees, they reluctantly drew apart.
Aimée pulled on her nightgown and stood up to watch
Vale throw a dressing robe loosely over his shoulders.

They padded down the stairs to the door without speaking. As Aimée stepped over the threshold, she paused, offering her lips to Vale. His mouth caressed hers softly,
sweetly, lingering with the knowledge that it could be
many weeks, if not months, before they would again
share love. Finally he withdrew; and she turned away.

In the stillness of the coming dawn she moved like a
wraith across the dew-sprinkled grass. He watched her
pause at the beginning of the path, the rosy glow of the
sky shining softly through her slip of a gown, turning her
limbs to golden shadows. She looked back at him over her
shoulder, her lips not needing to form a kiss, her fingers
not having to fan a gesture toward him. All that was
promised by kisses or caresses was in her eyes. She turned
away, her hair catching the first shaft of the rising sun, for
a moment becoming a flame, before she vanished among
the trees.

* * *

Late in the morning, the Carletons and Dessalines straggled into the dining room for brunch. It was then that Jeannette asked Andrew if, because of the damage the fire had caused at the shipyard, the start of their journey to Montreal, scheduled for the next day, would be delayed. She knew, if the trip was postponed too long, the early-arriving winter in Montreal could prevent their traveling before spring. Andrew assured her that Vale, Paul, and Benjamin could escort the Dessalines as they'd promised. A number of Andrew's friends had sons who'd volunteered to help clean up the shipyard, and a sea captain friend of Vale's was willing to act as temporary manager while his own ship was being repaired. With Andrew personally supervising the work, and with Timothy as his assistant, they could manage without Vale's and Paul's presence.

Because everyone had awakened so late, the time they needed for last-minute preparations for the journey had been shortened; so the household was thrown into a flurry of activity that made everyone except Aimée feel harried. An air of calm surrounded her as she went about her tasks, which seemed to separate her from the others. Jeannette frequently glanced at her daughter, perplexed by her unruffled attitude—never imagining that Aimée's serenity came from Vale's love the night before.

Everyone retired early for the night, and Julia instructed the servants to awaken them at three so the travelers would be able to leave at sunrise.

Abigail, expecting to have trouble arousing Aimée at such an hour, was surprised by the girl's immediate response. As tired as Aimée was, her heart was singing that Vale would soon arrive, they would spend the next several weeks in close company day and night; and even if they never had a moment of solitude during the journey, they could look at each other, hear each other's voice, sometimes touch in passing.

Aimée had laid out a sturdy dark green worsted gown that required a minimum of petticoats and the narrowest of hoops. She dressed quickly, continuing to think about Vale as she tucked her lustrous hair into a chignon. But when two footmen carried out the last of her baggage, she gazed wistfully at the room that seemed to have become her own, and thought of the friends she must leave behind. She resolved to return to visit the Carletons even if Vale decided to take her to France. She glanced at herself in the mirror for a final inspection before she hurried downstairs to the dining room.

Abigail had laid out a hearty breakfast, but Aimée passed the steaming dishes without lifting one lid. She asked only for a muffin and coffee to help wake her up.

Although Vale's walk was soundless, she sensed that it was he standing in the dining room doorway; and as he greeted everyone she turned to look at him briefly over her shoulder, sending him a message in that one glance that he alone could know the full meaning of.

Vale made sure to sit opposite Aimée at the table; and though he drank his coffee hurriedly while answering questions and describing some of the conditions he anticipated they would experience, his eyes touched Aimée's as often as he dared. To the others it was a casual glance; to her it was life.

Finally the tension and excitement that had filled the Carletons and Dessalines emptied out. The servants had loaded the coach with the supplies and baggage, and it was time for the journey to begin. Everyone walked slowly toward the front door, unhappily anticipating their farewells.

"Did you boys take along your rifles? Enough powder and shot?" Andrew inquired. "What about your pistols?"

Vale, Paul, and Benjamin all had pistols; but only Paul and Benjamin had rifles. Attached to Vale's saddle was a long bow and a large container of arrows.

"Are those effective enough?" Jeannette asked, eyeing the feathered shafts doubtfully.

"The rifles take some time and bother to reload between each shot, Madame Dessaline," Vale explained, "but firing a succession of arrows is much faster if one knows how."

"And Vale does know how," Timothy eagerly added.

"We've all gone hunting together, Madame Dessaline,"

Paul reassuringly said. "Vale's bow is not only accurate but deadly—and silent if we need to be stealthy."

Jeannette studied the wicked point of the arrow Vale had drawn from its container; and she agreed it appeared deadly enough. She said nothing about the fear arising in her when she thought of the reasons they might need stealth.

"Do be careful," Julia begged as she hugged Jeannette.

Jeannette hugged Julia even more closely and answered, "Whichever way this war goes, we'll always be friends, Julia. When everything is settled, I hope you'll come to Montreal and visit us."

Andrew embraced his sons, then turned to Vale and gripped his shoulders affectionately.

Finally Jeannette, Aimée, and Mignon settled themselves in the coach while Paul and Benjamin climbed up into the box. Vale mounted his horse, and they were ready.

"May God watch over you and bring a happy conclusion to this adventure," Andrew declared.

"I love you all!" Julia cried.

Mignon reached out of the window to clasp Julia's hand a last time. "We love you too!" she cried.

"Thank you for all your help," Jeannette said brokenly.

"We'll visit you again," Aimée promised.

Paul cracked the whip, and the team of horses moved forward. The women waved handkerchiefs from the coach windows until they knew the Carletons could no longer see them.

Aimée settled back in her seat, drew a long breath, and thought of Marcel alone and perhaps imprisoned in Montreal. She dabbed at her eyes and knew that however she would miss Andrew and Julia, finding Marcel was what she must concern herself with now.

Patrick Drake soon guided his horse onto the road to join Vale. A few minutes later Tom Griggs added himself to the group. Although Patrick's dark eyes seemed to penetrate the shadows inside the coach to find Aimée, and Tom frequently made quips designed to amuse her, she could see only Vale.

He was dressed in a sturdy shirt and breeches such as the men working in the shipyards had worn, and his calves were encased in well-worn riding boots. Although he looked straight ahead as his horse trotted placidly beside Aimée's window, she knew he was aware of her eyes on him.

Chapter 16

The Boston area was now well behind them, and the countryside was dotted with farms. The growing season was at its end; and throughout the morning the coach and its escorts followed roads bordered by the varying greens of vegetable fields partly harvested. Trees bowed under the weight of blushing pears and rosy apples, and fields of ripe wheat rippled in the breezes like shimmering golden lakes while cattle and horses browsed contentedly behind low walls made from stones the farmers had dug from their land.

Having heard so many times about the dangers they would face during this journey, the women were surprised that the region, though far from populous, contained as many houses as it did; and their fears were eased even more when the coach rattled into a village where they had lunch in a tiny pub.

The farms became fewer as they traveled through the afternoon, giving way to occasional forests of white-barked birch mixed with spruce and stretches of grassland flaming with fireweed; but by the time the sun was hovering low over a field of daisies, the coach entered another settlement and stopped at an inn, where Vale arranged for the travelers to spend the night. The inn was so small that the five men had to share one room while Jeannette and her daughters had to be satisfied with another that contained only one large bed.

Aimée settled under a fluffy quilt between her mother and sister. Vale, she knew, had volunteered to spread his blankets on the floor so that the other men could more comfortably share the two beds in their room. She wished

fervently that she and Vale could have stolen out of the
inn to sleep in each other's arms among the daisies; and
her slumber was filled with dreams of being wrapped in a
patchwork quilt with him, with the stars revolving in the
frosty sky as their only ceiling.

Vale, who had followed this route when he'd first gone
to Montreal, had asked the inn's proprietor to have a basket of lunch packed for them the next morning; so the
Dessalines weren't surprised when they noticed the
growing distance between the farms they now passed. The
increased jouncing of the coach testified to the rougher
roads, which soon dwindled to two tracks worn in the
earth. There was no inn to sleep in that night; but an ami-
able farmer, glad to have company, welcomed the travelers. His wife made a bed for Jeannette and her
daughters in the loft of the small house, while the men
burrowed into the hay piled in the barn.

The next day found the Dessalines' coach winding
around the edges of oak forests too dense to drive
through. The trees' normally dark green boughs had been
touched with rust foretelling the nearness of winter. Clusters of black-eyed Susans, bright goldenrod, and dusty wild
asters at the foot of the yellowing trees made a warm tapestry, which was crowned by the deep asure sky.

Aimée sensed a change slowly taking place in Vale.
Despite his promise that they would again enter a more
populated area—they would pass near Concord the next
day—his attitude took on a subtle alertness that warned
Aimée of potential dangers in this now isolated region.
She recognized the expression on his face, recalling that
she'd seen it first when he'd walked with her in the forest
near Montreal. He was like an animal testing the wind, his
ears attuned to the faintest sound. When he urged his
horse ahead of the coach and disappeared into the whispering forest, she knew he was searching for signs of hostile Indians; and she waited anxiously for his return. He
finally reappeared when the sun was low in the sky; several
pheasants were draped over the front of his saddle.

"Madame Dessaline, do you know how to cook wild
birds over a campfire?" he called into the coach.

"Certainement. Marcel frequently brought wild birds home. I've never cooked outdoors, but a fire is a fire," Jeannette answered.

"I'll tell Paul to stop the coach on the riverbank ahead, then I'll drop back to clean and dress the birds," Vale advised, and moved his horse ahead so he could tell Paul the plans. Afterwards he again slowed his horse, preparing to turn away from the coach.

"May I come with you and watch?" Aimée called, eager to seize any opportunity to be alone with him.

Vale looked at her speculatively for a moment. "It's too much bother to stop the coach's team," he replied. "Do you suppose you could swing up behind me while we're still moving?"

"If I take off my hoops, I can," she answered. Hearing her mother's quickly indrawn breath at the suggestion that she might slip off her underskirts with Vale watching, she hastily added, "Will you look the other way for a moment?"

Vale turned to fix his eyes on the trees. Despite the noise of the coach's wheels his ears were focused on the tantalizing rustle of Aimée's skirts. He caught Jeannette's whispered warning to Aimée to be careful, her halfhearted scolding at the impropriety of Aimée's riding astride, of being pressed against Vale so closely in the saddle, of being alone in the forest with a man; and he smiled. But when Aimée called that she was ready, his smile vanished; and he turned a solemn face toward them.

Opening the door wide, he maneuvered his horse close to the vehicle and directed, "Put your hands on my shoulders to brace yourself while you swing your leg over the back of the saddle."

Aimée nodded and waited while he tucked his reins under his thigh before turning to her again. Catching her waist with both hands, he swiveled around to help guide her into place. He released her, advising that she put her arms around so she wouldn't slip off the horse.

As Jeannette reclosed the door Vale looked up at her and said reassuringly, "Don't worry, Madame Dessaline. I won't let Aimée fall off."

"*That* isn't what will worry me," Jeannette replied tartly, and reseated herself.

As Vale turned the horse away from the coach, Aimée laid her cheek against his shoulder and whispered, "It feels wonderful to have my arms around you again."

Intoxicated by the sensation of her body warmly pressed against his back, Vale said softly, "Last night I dreamed of our riding away from the others like this. I awakened to spend the rest of the night thinking of how it would be to share my bed of hay with you."

"Will fallen leaves do as well?" she asked, a provocative huskiness in her voice.

Vale considered that possibility for a moment, then answered regretfully, "I doubt we'll be alone that long. Your mother is certain to send someone after us, and I have no doubt Pat or Tom would volunteer before the words were half out of her mouth."

"They would have to find us first."

"A task that wouldn't be too difficult because this is a horse likely to announce its presence to any other horses approaching," Vale replied unhappily.

She remained silent until after he'd stopped the horse in a little clearing. Then, unable to contain her disappointment, she commented, "I thought you suggested we separate from the others to dress the pheasants because you wanted us to have a chance to be alone."

"It's never wise to clean game close to where you'll camp for the night. The smell of blood can attract predators," he explained as he carefully swung his leg over the front of the saddle to slide down. He turned and reached up for her, adding, "But we are alone."

When Aimée slid down into Vale's arms, he didn't release her immediately. She looked up at him, a shaft of light from the lowering sun catching fire in her hair and making orange-gold sparks in her eyes as she asked hopefully, "Maybe you were teasing me when you said Tom or Pat would come too soon?"

"No," Vale answered. Recalling Tom's and Pat's attentiveness toward Aimée, he added, "I wouldn't be surprised if they come hurrying to find us on some pretext or another as soon as Paul stops the coach. I've noticed how they've been trying to attract your attention—Tom with his double-edged humor, Pat's eyes following your every move."

"As long as they don't say or do something offensive, I can't accuse them; but I haven't encouraged them," Aimée quickly replied.

"I know you haven't." Vale's hands moved up her sides, his outspread thumbs caressing her swelling breasts. "You aren't to be blamed for having a body with the kind of curves a man's fingers just yearn to explore."

His arms slid around her back, drawing her to him. She tilted her face to his, closing her eyes in anticipation of his kiss; but when it didn't come, she looked up at him in surprise. His face was a breath away from hers.

He said softly, "I think one day, not too distant, I'll have to explain to them that you're mine—and I suspect they'll force me to do it in some unpleasant way."

It wasn't how quietly he said it, but how the flecks of color in his eyes suddenly blended into an opaque mass, like a sheet of slate, that suddenly struck fear in her. "What do you intend to do?" she breathed.

"That will depend on them."

As he leaned closer she anticipated a kiss reflecting his annoyance; but his lips barely brushed hers as he threaded his fingers through her hair. She opened her eyes and found that he was watching her.

"Surely you didn't think I'd take you into the forest with me and refuse even to kiss you," he murmured.

Again he put his mouth to hers, caressing her lips with restraint that aroused her ardor as readily as would a more lusty kiss. The edges of his teeth coaxed her lips apart; and his mouth covered hers, the tip of his tongue stroking the parting with a sensual eloquence that filled her with a sweet aching.

The horse nickered softly, and Vale tensed. He stepped back a little from Aimée, his narrowed eyes swinging over the perimeter of the glade. Noting that the horse had returned to its browsing, he relaxed.

"It's just as well he interrupted us. If we went any fur-

ther with this, stopping would only be that much more difficult." He took a deep breath and nodded sideways at the
pheasants still attached to his saddle. "I'd best get on with
cleaning the birds."

Aimée stepped aside to let him pass; but she turned to
watch his lithe strides as he walked toward his horse. Her
eyes lingered on the mold of his legs beneath his snug-fit-
ting breeches, his flat hips, the trim span of his waist, the
breadth of his shoulders. She moved a few steps closer to
watch his fingers deftly loosen the twine he'd used to bind
the birds to the saddle; and aware of the renewed clamoring of her body, she turned away.

Vale approached so soundlessly that Aimée was startled
at the nearness of his voice as he remarked, "I'm beginning to regret having gotten these birds."

She turned to face him and saw in his eyes the desire
that seethed just below the surface. Gathering together the
resolve that so precariously leashed her passion, she asked
in a tone calmer than she felt, "Can I help you pluck out
their feathers?"

He looked at her a long moment, wanting her so acutely
he could hardly bear it, then shook his head. "I think I
can do it much faster," he said, and turned away, careful
not even to brush against her. He chose a level place at
the far edge of the clearing and stopped to begin working
on the birds. She remained where she was for a time,
then followed him, sinking down to sit on the grass
and watch.

Aimée found herself noticing the turn of Vale's lashes
against his cheeks; and she lowered her eyes only to watch
his hands, remembering how they felt when they caressed
her. She struggled to focus her attention on the bird.

By the time Vale had finished dressing the first two
birds, Aimée had become so absorbed in his technique,
she'd leaned forward without realizing it. As he began
working on the last pheasant she bent even a little closer.
A dark strand of hair falling over his forehead softly
brushed her cheek; and as he looked up at her she became
sharply aware of his warm breath on her shoulder. A

streak of fire passed behind his eyes, and he put down the bird.

In one smooth motion Vale stood up. He turned without a word, went back to his horse, and, taking a cloth from his saddle, wiped his fingers with careful deliberation. When he returned, he extended his hands, silently offering to help Aimée to her feet. Then, as if he'd changed his mind, in a sudden swift movement he scooped her up in his arms and strode across the glade to the other side to set her down in the dusky shadows beside a giant fir tree.

"I want you to crawl under those branches to the center of the tree. You'll find an open space around the trunk," he said. He straightened to stand over her, his eyes shifting along the edge of the clearing, looking for any movements in the foliage that would hint of discovery or danger. "The branches will at least partially conceal us," he added softly.

Aimée's pulses were humming with excitement, but she asked, "And if someone glimpses us anyway?"

Vale lowered himself to sit beside her; and when he looked at her, his eyes were lit as if by live sparks. "I'm at the point where I don't care," he replied. He separated the branches of the fir, then nodded for her to enter the space within.

As she huddled beside the trunk she watched as he followed her in. Despite the great size of the tree the clearing she sat in didn't allow him to raise his head fully; and still on his hands and knees, he gestured for her to lie down. The fallen needles were a cool, soft carpet beneath her shoulders, and the fragrance of the tree was a heady perfume showering down on them.

Vale moved over Aimée. The familiar weight of his warm body, even if only partially resting on her, was so welcome she trembled with anticipation. He slid his arms under her shoulders to frame her temples with his fingertips and stroke the pulses that were already beating so joyously for him.

His lips moved slowly over her face, kissing her forehead and her eyelids, then following her hairline. She felt his warm mouth against her throat, lingering there while his lips moved over hers, deliberately building the fires they both contained. His mouth covered hers. Her fingers sought the opening of his shirt, and slipped beneath the cloth, they traced fiery patterns over his chest, sliding down his sides to his waist, tugging loose the shirt tucked into his breeches.

He slid his hands down her sides, his fingertips making little bunches of her skirt, inching the hem up her legs. When it finally would go no farther, he moved to one side so he could free the gown's folds.

Against his lips she murmured wistfully, "I wish we could be naked. I want so much to feel your skin against mine."

Her words were liquid fire pouring through his veins, and he replied, "If you say more, you'll return to the coach in rags. I'm just about ready to tear—"

His words were stopped by a distant shriek so piercing that Aimée started with fear. Vale instantly moved away, and Aimée rolled to her side only to be stunned by a second cry. Her eyes followed the direction the sounds had come from, though she dreaded to see what had made them. A third cry, joined by several others, tore through the forest. She shivered with fright.

"*What* is that?" she whispered.

Her answer was his palm firmly pressed over her mouth as he rose into a crouch, his eyes darting among the shadowy brushes surrounding the glade.

Finally he released her; and in a voice so hushed he put his mouth to her ear so she could understand his words, he said, "Those are Iroquois war cries, and they're coming from the river. I'm afraid they've discovered the coach."

Aimée heard a gunshot, then another and another. Though rigid with terror, she put her mouth to his ear and breathed, "What will we do?"

"The Iroquois can't know we're here or they would have killed us before attacking the coach. I'm going to get that horse out of the clearing, hide both of you, then I'll go and help the others," he whispered.

Aimée grasped Vale's arms, and at another wave of shrieks followed by more gunfire, she gripped him so tightly her nails dug into his flesh. "If everyone but me is killed, what would I do alone in this wilderness? Let me go back with you! Marcel taught me how to fire a pistol. Maybe I could hit one of them. If not, I might surprise them with the sound of another gun."

Vale was thoughtful for a moment. Aimée had given him an idea, yet he didn't like to think of her anywhere near the Indians. He finally decided she was right; she couldn't survive alone in the forest.

"You can come with me," he said reluctantly, then paused, letting his eyes sweep along the edge of the clearing to make sure no one was near. "We won't be able to talk later, so listen to me carefully now."

She nodded hastily, her attention riveted on his next words.

"I want you to follow me as quietly as you possibly can until I've looked the situation over and know where I want you to stay. I'll give you my pistols—I have two in my saddlebag—but I want you to use only one of them on the Indians." He paused, listening to the distant gunfire, lowering his eyes while he gathered the strength he needed to say, "You must keep the second pistol loaded and close at hand; because if the situation becomes hopeless, you'll have to use it on yourself." At the sound of Aimée's indrawn breath he took her hand. His eyes, hard as slate, met hers, and his words came out slowly, like bitter seeds found repugnant and spat out in anger: "If the Iroquois were to capture you alive, they'd kill you later; but they'd take as long a time doing it as your body could endure."

Aimée laid her cheek against Vale's for a brief moment to whisper, "I've heard stories in Montreal about rape and hideous tortures."

"Those stories are true," he said grimly. He lifted her hands to his lips, not kissing them, just speaking against her fingers. "Don't do it if there's any chance at all for you. As long as I'm still alive, even if I'm wounded, I'll try to help you."

Horrified to think of the possibility of his death, Aimée nodded, speechless.

Vale lowered her hands and continued, "After I've left

you, you must remain absolutely quiet until you hear another cry. Don't worry—you'll not mistake it for the Iroquois cry. It will be me speaking in Abnaki. The Abnakis are deadly enemies of the Iroquois, and I want them to think I'm an Abnaki hunting party. I'm going to use my bow and arrows, and I'll be moving around constantly, so you'll hear the sounds I make in different places. You can begin shooting anytime after you first begin to hear me." He paused, considering the slim chance he had of sounding like a dozen angry Abnakis, and sighed in resignation. He couldn't think of another tactic.

"What about Paul and Ben and the others? How much help will they be?" she whispered.

"Ben and Patrick are excellent marksmen, Paul and Tom fair," he answered. "With them shooting from the coach and you from the forest—if I keep moving fast enough—we might drive the Iroquois off." He paused to look at her appraisingly. "That red hair will be like a banner against the trees. If I give you my shirt, can you use it to cover your hair?"

"Yes, I'll do it," she replied. She watched as he pulled off the shirt, faded from many launderings to an anonymous dun color.

"I'm going to get that horse and tie him in the cover of the trees," Vale said softly, and turned away to slither on his stomach out from under the drooping branches.

Aimée watched until he'd stood up; and noticing her attention on him, he gestured toward her hair, and she nodded. But after he'd turned away, she bunched the shirt against her face, silently praying he would be safe; then blinking back her tears, she turned her thoughts to concealing her hair. Glad she'd arranged it in a chignon that morning, she wrapped the shirt around her head and tied the sleeves at the nape of her neck to secure it. Her eyes followed Vale's sun-darkened back as he approached the newly nervous horse to stroke its neck and soothe it. She wished it were Brandy, who obeyed a command to be silent, not this horse Vale had said was likely to make noise. When Vale took the bridle and turned to walk back toward the fir tree, Aimée flattened herself to the ground to wriggle out from under the branches.

After she'd gotten to her feet, Vale bent close to whisper in her ear, "I'll take the horse now and look for an area where I can leave him to feed. I hope he'll be too absorbed with eating to make any noise."

Vale led the horse into the forest, where both disappeared. Aimée waited nervously until he returned a few minutes later.

A fiery lock had escaped the shirt to curl around her temple, and now he tucked it back under its bindings. The light touch of his fingertips so gently coaxing her lock into place brought new tears to her eyes. Wanting to raise her spirits, knowing he dared not speak to her later, he looked at her for a long moment, trying to think of something he could say; then suddenly he bent to brush his lips to hers in a brief caress.

"I love you," he whispered. Before she could answer, he turned away and started into the trees.

Aimée followed Vale, carefully avoiding dry leaves, twigs, or stones that might move under her weight, putting her small slippers into each soundless step he vacated. Her senses seemed unnaturally acute. Without glancing away from the path he took she was aware of each bush they passed; and she heard not only the gunfire and shouts of the battle by the coach but the sighing of the wind in the treetops. A low embankment rose on one side, a result of the spring floods, and, she knew, the river wasn't far away. Stacks of boulders that had fallen from the embankment were walls for the unwary to bump into, but she dared not raise her eyes from his feet if she was to remain as silent as Vale. Perceiving little more of the battle than the flashes of gunfire, she realized he was somehow scrutinizing the entire scene while he decided their own approach.

Finally he faced her, motioning that he intended to help her to the top of the pile of rocks before them. She nodded and turned away, studying the best footholds she might use. He put out his booted toe to indicate the first step she should take. Immediately upon placing her foot

securely, she felt his hands at her waist lifting her so rapidly, as she chose other steps, that she scrambled to the
top of the stones faster than she'd thought herself able.
She turned to look down at him; and he handed her the
pistols one by one, gesturing they were already loaded. After he'd given her the powder and shot she would need, he
motioned her to lie on her stomach so that anyone passing
below wouldn't readily see her. She nodded; and wanting
desperately to reach out and touch him, she watched him
back away, then turn and melt into the shadows of the
forest.

Aimée sighed and lay down as Vale had directed, propping herself up on her elbows to wait. From her height she
could see above the shrubbery that lined the edge of the
forest; and the coach was so distant she could see no details of the struggle. Her disappointment was mixed with
relief as she realized Vale had purposely placed her so far
away to protect her. At each gunshot she wondered who
had fallen—an Iroquois, Vale, her mother, Mignon, or any
of the others. She shivered with terror for them all.

Vale tried to turn his mind to the battle ahead; but
memories of Aimée, who only moments before had lain in
his arms, and of the warmth of her eager body beneath his
blazed in his thoughts. There was a tightness in his body,
an aching tension that aroused a dark anger. Suddenly he
realized that despite their grim situation his passion for
Aimée was a living thing, a primal urge that hungered for
fulfillment—or revenge on those who would prevent it.

Vale paused in his steps, assailed by memories of a
campfire glimmering in the night, of painted bodies writhing in a soul-stirring dance to drums whose beat matched
the throbbing in his body. He understood at last, as a boy
then couldn't, the purpose of the drums and the war
dance. The Abnakis never slept with their wives on such a
night, for their love would have given them peace. But
Vale's passions had already been aroused, his fulfillment
dashed away; and he realized his motives now were the
same as those of any male animal interrupted during mat-
ing—his desire changed into lust for violence. Walking-in-
Honor, his adopted Abnaki father, had seen the wisdom

of going into battle in this state of mind; and now he too would use his frustration to similar advantage.

Walking again, Vale gave himself over to his feelings; and the parts of him that were Valjean d'Auvergne and Vale Kendall faded to be reborn into Lightning-of-the-Winter-Moon. His steps were infused with the supple strength of a lynx on the trail of its quarry; his eyes glowed with the strange lights that had inspired his Abnaki name; and when his sharp ears perceived someone moving stealthily through the foliage, he bent in a half crouch and began to stalk him.

Just a few steps beyond the tall weeds that veiled his own presence, he saw the outline of a dark shape. Realizing that he might be able to kill an Iroquois or two and diminish their numbers before he risked open attack, he stepped out of his boots and slipped off his stockings. His fingers carefully tied the two stockings together, pulling them to make sure the knot was firm. His eyes did not leave the Indian. Now he twisted the cloth several times to give it strength and crept closer to the figure. When he stood immediately behind the warrior, he dropped the knotted stockings over his head and raised his knee to plant it in the Iroquois's back, simultaneously jerking the stockings tight against his throat. The Indian made an effort to struggle free, but Vale held him until he felt the inert body sag against him. He waited a moment more, then eased the Iroquois to the ground.

Vale arose immediately and continued on through the bushes. A little farther ahead he heard soft footsteps coming in his direction, and he backed around a tree trunk. As the Iroquois approached, Vale poised himself. When the Indian passed the tree, Vale's coiled muscles lengthened and he sprang. Vale struck the warrior squarely and they both fell. The Indian yelped but was only halfway to his feet when Vale plunged after him: and even before he touched the warrior, his knife was swinging in a low arc to spear the Indian's heart.

Knowing other Iroquois had heard the dead Indian's cry and not wanting them to discover he was their only attacker, Vale leaped up to dash into the undergrowth. As he ran silently through the shadows, he pulled the leather container strapped to his back around to his side. From it he took his bow and an arrow; and pausing in the shelter of a giant oak, he fit the shaft to his bowstring. As another Indian came trotting warily along the line of trees, Vale drew the bow taut. The missile sang to its mark, and the warrior fell.

Vale raised his head and, taking a deep breath, let out the cry of an Abnaki victorious against an enemy. The sound echoed through the air, momentarily silencing the startled Iroquois attacking the coach. Vale followed with a string of threats traditional to a warring Abnaki, knowing that even if the Iroquois could not understand his words, they would recognize his meaning. Then he turned and trotted into the dusky shadows, searching for another enemy, letting out further cries to mislead the Indians: they would now think that he was many instead of one.

Aimée had watched the warrior who stood only a dozen paces from the base of her hiding place, holding her fire for Vale's signal, her hands cold and wet against the pistol's handle. When she heard Vale's cry burst from the forest, the blood momentarily froze in her veins. He had been right: that cry in no way resembled the sounds of the Iroquois. The warrior in her sight had stiffened, seeming as frightened by it as she; and when the string of threats followed the initial cry, she was near enough to hear him softly exclaim, "Abnaki!"

She fired the pistol. The recoil jerked back her hands, and her elbows scraped against the rock she lay on; but she didn't notice. Her attention was on the Indian who crumpled to the ground.

"One less to shoot at Vale," she whispered, and reached for her container of powder to reload the pistol.

During the few moments it took her to prepare the pistol for another shot, she heard the Abnaki war cry come from another location, then another, and still a third. She smiled at the swiftness of Vale's movements; it did sound as if an entire Abnaki war party were converging on the Iroquois. She gripped the pistol tightly and prepared to fire again; but no Indians came into view. Aware that she was so far from the fight that she might not need to fire again, she still watched alertly. She heard more Abnaki threats and a renewed burst of gunfire from the direction of the coach.

Her fingers seemed welded to the pistol when finally an Iroquois burst from the trees—then another and another. They were running toward her! For a moment she was stunned with fear that she'd been discovered, that they were coming to avenge the warrior she'd shot. She flattened herself against the boulder, her cheek pressed tightly to the rough stone, afraid to breathe. But no wiry body scrambled up the side of the rock, and she knew that if one did, she'd best have her pistol at the ready. She cautiously lifted her head just enough so she could see.

The Indians paid no attention to the body of the dead warrior. They were running past and into the deeper forest. They were fleeing!

Aimée trained her pistol on their receding backs in case one of them should turn; but they continued into the undergrowth. She was afraid to move lest she reveal herself if this was in fact a ruse.

"They aren't coming back."

The quiet voice stunned her, and she spun around, scrambling to a sitting position to turn the pistol on Vale, who had climbed high enough to see over the boulder's top. At the unexpected sight of the gray eyes watching her she let out a breath of relief and lowered the gun. As she crawled to the edge of the rock she remembered what he'd said and whispered, "Are you certain?"

Vale nodded and put out his arms to help her down. When she was standing beside him, he bent to rub his cheek against her hair as he took the weapons from her.

"I see you shot one of them after all," he commented.

She nodded and put her arms around his waist, clinging to him a moment before they turned to make their way to the river.

As Vale and Aimée approached the clearing where the coach had stopped, he said, "I think you should take off that shirt now. If Paul or Ben glimpse us through the trees, they won't mistake us for Iroquois and fire at the sight of that hair."

Aimée tugged at her improvised head covering with such force that she loosened half the pins holding her chignon. A wealth of fiery curls were freed to the fading sunlight as she pulled away the cloth.

Vale reached up to touch her hair, then after a moment whispered, "Damn those Iroquois!" At her startled expression he added vehemently, "I want to take you back to that fir tree to finish what we started before the Indians attacked."

"How do you think I feel with you walking around half naked?" she breathed. She thrust the shirt into his hands, adding, "Maybe we'll have another chance when we go back for the horse and the pheasants."

But they never got that chance. When they neared the coach, they found Paul hastily wrapping a strip of muslin around Tom's chest while Ben knelt beside Mignon, who was frantically tearing apart the rest of a petticoat. At Vale and Aimée's appearance, Mignon leaped to her feet.

"Aimeé, Maman has been wounded by an arrow!" she cried.

Only then did Aimée see Jeannette lying beside the coach wheel. "Maman!" she gasped, and ran to throw herself to her knees beside her mother.

Jeannette turned her head to look up at her daughter. "It's just an arrow in my thigh," she said. "I believe one of my hoops deflected it."

Vale, now standing over the prone woman, commented, "If so, it's the first good purpose I've seen for whalebone—except, of course, for the whales' own use of it." He lowered himself to kneel beside her, reaching for the fold of her skirt. "I'd judge it would have struck you in the abdomen had it not been for that hoop," he commented.

"*Non, non, non,* Vale!" Jeannette exclaimed in horror. "You cannot disrobe me!"

Vale looked at her in surprise. "Do you intend to preserve your modesty by traveling to Montreal with an arrowhead festering in your thigh?"

"My daughters will remove it. They've seen me tend trappers, and they helped me nurse Hilaire."

"Were any of those trappers impaled by an arrow?" he asked patiently. When Jeannette reluctantly shook her head, he said, "Madame Dessaline, I'm not a doctor, but has either of your daughters ever seen an arrow wound?" Again Jeannette reluctantly shook her head; but as she opened her mouth to argue Vale took an arrow from the case he yet wore, and held it to her view. "The barbs at the back of the arrowhead are embedded backwards in your flesh. Would you like to have an arrow like this simply pulled straight out of your leg?"

Jeannette eyed the deadly-looking barbs and shivered. "*Non*, you're right. I'll put aside modesty. You do it, Vale."

Vale nodded and, without further comment, swept up Jeannette's skirt hem. He touched her thigh carefully, feeling the flesh beside the wound, his eyes noting the amount of blood puddling under her leg. Finally he looked up. "I believe it missed the artery or there would be more blood; but even so, when I take out the arrow, you'll bleed a great deal." He took a deep breath, adding, "Madame Dessaline, this is going to be very painful."

"I expected that," she said calmly. "I'm sure I'll be able to bear whatever's necessary."

Vale slowly got to his feet. He looked at Mignon. "When you're finished ripping out that petticoat, tear up a couple more."

"Shall I start heating some water?" Aimée asked.

Vale looked down at her. "I won't use water to clean this wound," he said quietly.

Surprised, she asked, "But how will you clean it to avoid infection?"

Vale regarded her a moment, as if making a decision, before he finally said, "She's going to bleed so profusely I'm going to have to use a knife to stop the flow. That will clean her wound at the same time."

"A knife? How would that stop her bleeding?" Aimée asked. Suddenly realizing he meant to heat the knife in the fire and lay the tip of it into the wound, she paled. *"Mon Dieu,"* she whispered.

"Before I do that, I'll make sure she's drunk some of the very good rum I know Patrick has brought with him," Vale said.

Hearing his lowered voice, Jeannette remarked, "I do not ordinarily care for rum; but I suppose, before this evening has ended, I'll be intoxicated with it."

Vale squeezed Aimée's hand and commented, "She knew before I said it what would have to be done. Get Patrick's rum while I see how Tom's chest looks."

"Monsieur Griggs was slashed with a knife and needs some stitches," Jeannette said. "I was inspecting his wound when I was hit with this arrow."

Vale shook his head in disgust. "My sewing ability is sadly lacking. I know I'll make a clumsy job of it."

"Mignon has a fine hand at embroidery and watched me do what I could for my husband," Jeannette said. "Mignon, do you think you could take care of Monsieur Griggs while Aimée helps Vale attend to me?"

Mignon came closer. "I could try, Maman," she said in a faint voice, uncertainty clearly written on her face.

"I'll stand right next to you." Benjamin had made that offer, and she glanced at him gratefully. "But I think we shouldn't delay tearing up those petticoats for bandages. I'll help you, Mignon."

"Merci, Benjamin," Mignon said. Though grateful for his help, she was nonetheless embarrassed to have him handling such intimate articles of her clothing; and she began to blush. He took her elbow and smiled reassuringly. Her blush grew even deeper as they turned away.

"I suspect I am losing both my daughters to Boston men," Jeannette breathed, looking not very disturbed at the prospect as she added, *"Sacrée mère de Dieu,* what next?"

Patrick Drake came forward to put a flask into Vale's hands. "I have more rum, if you think Madame Dessaline needs it," he said. "Someone should fetch that horse and those birds you got for dinner before it gets too dark. Tell me where you left them, and I'll go, Vale."

Remembering Aimée's previous hopes that they would be able to go back themselves, yet knowing regretfully that it was impossible now, Vale thanked Patrick and gave him the directions.

"I'll get more firewood and set up our camp for the night," Paul said, and turned to walk toward the shrubbery growing at the edge of the forest.

Mignon had to set her jaw and use all her determination to approach the task of stitching Tom's chest, but Benjamin's calm presence at her side gave her strength. Whenever her lips began to tremble, he would make some comment to distract her from her fear; and each time the blood obscured her work, his was the hand reaching with a cloth to sponge it away. By the time the last stitch was tied, his hands were as familiar to her as her own. She was only too glad to accompany Benjamin to the river to rinse away the blood that stained them both.

If Mignon's task was distressing for her, Aimée's was a nightmare. Jeannette had been given a quantity of rum and now no longer grimaced at the taste of it; her words had become slurred. At that point Vale asked Patrick to hold Jeannette's arms, and Paul to sit on her feet, so she wouldn't flail about. Although Aimée was achingly aware of her mother's anguish, she couldn't help but admire the careful delicacy of Vale's touch as he spread the wound open and cut it a bit wider, bringing a fresh flood of crimson that Aimée quickly wiped away. The arrowhead was stubborn, and Aimée blotted the perspiration running down Vale's forehead several times before he triumphantly pulled out the missile, which was barbed as he'd predicted. All through the operation Vale had spoken softly to Jeannette, giving her encouragement, even apologizing for the pain he must cause as he worked. Despite his care Jeannette tried to flinch away many times; but she was held securely by Paul and Patrick.

It was Aimée's fingers that pressed the edges of flesh together in an effort to slow the bleeding while Vale got the knife that had been lying on the fire. With a look he warned Paul and Patrick to hold Jeannette even tighter before he laid the ominously glowing blade, dull side down, into the wound. Jeannette's body grew rigid with agony, and she cried out, then became limp and silent. Vale took the knife blade away, quickly cleansed the surrounding skin, and studied what he had done. The blood flow had been completely halted. He wrapped the wound, then stood up and directed Patrick to put Jeannette in the bed they'd made for her on the floor of the coach.

Later, after Vale and Aimée had rinsed the blood from their hands and arms, neither could eat a morsel of the pheasants Paul had roasted. They just sipped their coffee as they sat by the fire, staring silently into the flames.

"Do you think the Iroquois will return?" Finally Tom voiced the question they'd all had on their minds.

"I counted at least fourteen of them," Benjamin said. "That was too big for a hunting party, but they weren't painted for war."

"It wasn't a war party," Vale confirmed. "I think they were just going somewhere together and happened on us. Thinking we'd be easy prey, they planned to steal our horses. They won't be back tonight, but I think we should leave tomorrow as soon as we have enough light to see what we're doing."

"You sure curdled my blood with that war cry you let out," Tom commented.

Vale smiled ruefully. "It was Abnaki."

"It was more than a war cry. It sounded like you were warning them," Paul said.

"I was," Vale replied.

Fascinated, Tom persisted. "What did you say?"

"Some rather traditional threats mostly, though I did add a twist or two that might have been a little surprising," Vale answered. He glanced at Aimée and Mignon, then added, "I don't think I should go into details."

"If what you said was that fearsome, I'm not sure I'd want to hear it anyway," Tom said.

"I saw the expression on that one Iroquois's face when he heard you. I know you frightened him," Aimée commented.

A small smile played about Vale's lips as he recalled what he'd said. "I guess they just caught me in a rather violent mood." Taking a sip of his coffee, he decided to change the subject: "I think Madame Dessaline should be taken to a doctor. Noting Aimée's and Mignon's alarm he quickly added, "I have no reason to think anything went wrong as far as what we could do is concerned; but she did lose a lot of blood and I don't see how we can dream of taking her the rest of the way—she'd be jolted about in the coach, and we'd have to carry her whenever she had to get out of it. If we were attacked again, what could we do if we had to move quickly? Besides, that burn was in itself severe; and the way we're traveling, there's all the better chance she could become infected."

"We're only a day's ride from Concord," Benjamin pointed out.

"That's what I was thinking," Vale said. "Someone could drive the coach to Concord, then take her back to Boston when she's recovered." Vale paused and looked at Tom. "I think you should go too." As Tom opened his mouth to argue, Vale quickly continued, "You don't have to be carried around, but you've lost a lot of blood—and if Madame Dessaline's wound could become infected, your chances of doing so are even worse. What could we do for you if you got gangrene?"

At the mere mention of gangrene Tom couldn't help but shudder. He'd once seen someone die of that dread disease. He nodded in silent acquiesence.

"Someone else must go with them," Benjamin said. "Tom can't drive the horses with that wound. Who will do it?"

"I don't know the country around here very well," Patrick admitted. "I've never been to Concord."

"I have," Paul said with a sigh. "I suppose that means I'll have to go."

"Then it's settled," Benjamin said, relieved to know that he would remain with Mignon.

"It is, unless Aimée and Mignon will agree that we all return," Patrick said.

Aimée shook her head. "We must do what we can for Marcel," she insisted. "If we went back, Maman would be sick with worry."

"So would I," Mignon said. "*Non*, we must go on if you men still are willing to take us."

"We're going to have to take two of the coach horses to carry our supplies," Vale said quickly. "You girls will have to leave all your baggage behind and take along only what you'll immediately need. You'll have to ride double with us on the horses. It's easy enough to hold on to someone else when a horse is walking or cantering, but if anything should happen and we have to run, or if we should have to jump over a stream or something, I know Aimée can ride. But what about you, Mignon?"

"Marcel taught us both," Mignon said firmly.

Benjamin got to his feet, tossing the rest of his coffee into the nearby bushes. "If all our decisions have been made, I think we should go to bed." He looked up at the girls and smiled. "You'd best enjoy sleeping in the coach. After tonight you'll have to make your bed on the ground like the rest of us."

Chapter 17

Despite all the rum Jeannette had consumed, fiery fingers of pain reached through her slumber, and she slept fitfully, whimpering from time to time like a small, hurt animal. Dawn had barely begun to light the sky when Vale tapped on the coach door to arouse Aimée and Mignon; and Jeannette surprised him by reaching back over her shoulder to push the door open.

When she heard what had been decided the previous night, she couldn't argue. She yearned to continue on to Montreal with the others, but her leg was a blaze of agony she knew would make her a burden. Like Tom, she had seen cases of gangrene; and she too was terrified to think of contracting it.

After the leavings from breakfast had been put away, the supplies carefully divided, and the horses prepared, Aimée and Mignon embraced their mother.

Jeannette's eyes swam with tears, but she didn't hesitate to whisper, "*Mes belles filles,* you will be alone with those men in very intimate circumstances. You must be careful to behave properly."

"Aimée will watch over me and I'll watch over her," Mignon promised.

"I've seen how you look at Benjamin, and Aimée at Vale, so I have my doubts about how much attention you'll pay to each other," Jeannette said dryly. "Don't forget Monsieur Drake will also be accompanying you, and such an arrangement can lead to trouble of many kinds." She gave each of her daughters a long searching look; and though aware of the many awkward situations that could arise on their trip, she decided she would just have to hope and pray for the best.

The girls gave their mother a last hug, then withdrew.

Vale leaned into the coach and said, "I seem always to be reassuring you that Aimée will be safe in my hands; but, Madame Dessaline, I promise I'll watch over her—both of them."

Jeannette sighed. "It's true you've been very reliable and no harm has come to Aimée in your company—at least none my eyes can see—but . . ." She raised a finger as if to wag it at him. Then tears refilled her eyes and, instead of scolding, she touched his cheek gently and whispered, "Take care of them—and yourself."

Vale nodded, then caught her fingers and brushed them with his lips. Finally reminding her to be careful to keep her wound clean, promising to send a message about the situation in Montreal as soon as it became possible to do so, he backed out of the coach and closed the door.

Vale waved to Paul and Tom up in the box, Paul cracked his whip over the team's heads, and the horses bounded forward. Vale slipped his arm around Aimée's waist and watched the coach follow the riverbank until it disappeared around a bend.

"Do you think the Iroquois will come back and follow them?" Aimée asked uneasily.

"This is the last stretch of wilderness they'll have to travel through. By mid-morning they'll begin to see farms. If the Iroquois do return, when they see the direction the coach has taken, I doubt they'll bother to try to catch up with it. They'd be more likely to follow our tracks because they'll know two of the horses have double riders." Vale released Aimée, then turned to the others and said, "We'd best mount and be on our way too."

After Aimée was seated on the horse, she leaned back against the firm warmth of Vale's chest and whispered, "Riding double with you is the best result of the Indians' attack."

Vale arranged the reins in his hands and answered under his breath, "I'll enjoy your nearness, it's true; but I doubt I'll sleep another night through for the rest of this journey. When I do sleep, I know I'll have dreams. I hope I don't speak aloud during such dreams; or if I do, let's hope it's in Abnaki. That's the only language no one else here will understand."

Vale no longer had to search for a route through the wilderness suitable for a coach to travel, so the small group of riders was able to progress faster than before, and they didn't pause until noon.

After a makeshift meal Aimée and Mignon removed their corsets and remaining petticoats—they had already left their hoops in the coach so that they could ride horseback. They packed the garments in the saddlebags, grateful to be free of confining stays and troublesome flounces. Once they'd remounted, the sensation of unfettered feminine bodies brushing against theirs with each step the horses took was a constant titillation to Vale and Benjamin. It disturbed them—as it did Aimée and Mignon.

Patrick had noticed that there had been no discussion that morning about which of the men Aimée and Mignon would ride with, and he wondered what the situation was between the couples. Having been enamored of Aimée since the night they'd met at the Thorntons', he had hoped this trip would give him an opportunity to rekindle the interest she'd seemed to show at the party. He was irritated that she appeared to have made her choice long ago. Vale seemed to be winning her without any apparent effort. During the afternoon Patrick's dark eyes wandered often to Vale and Aimée. He wondered what it would be like to have her perched on the saddle in front of him, her body leaning against his, swaying to the horse's rhythm, his arms enclosing her as he guided the animal. Recalling Aimée's eagerness to go with Vale when he'd left the coach to dress the pheasants the previous afternoon, Patrick speculated on what might have happened when they'd been alone; and his jealousy, like the deadly nightshade on the forest's floor, budded toward poison.

Aimée and Mignon weren't used to spending long hours riding horseback; so when they came across an area suitable for making camp, Vale suggested they stop early this first day. When no one's attention was on Patrick, his eyes followed Aimée as she went about her tasks. Although the sun was at a low angle, it still shone brightly through the clear autumn air and made shadowy impressions of her legs—no longer shielded by petticoats—through her skirt. Because Patrick wasn't ordinarily a talkative man, no one thought it odd that he spoke so little after dinner; but Vale noticed he lifted his flask of rum disturbingly often to his lips during the evening.

Vale made a bed of pine boughs for Aimée and Mignon to share close to the fire; for even though the days were comfortably warm, the nights had taken on the chill of coming winter. When he rolled up in his blanket a discreet distance away, he found his predicted sleeplessness was only too real; and he lay awake far into the night staring at the silhouetted mound the girls' blanket-swathed bodies made against the glow of the fire.

Although sleepless, Vale lay still; and he listened to Benjamin's restless turnings with a sympathetic ear. Through the slits of his half-closed eyes he could see Patrick, who had taken the first watch, pacing at the edge of the clearing, stopping too frequently to raise his hand before his face in a gesture that revealed he was taking yet another swallow of rum. Vale speculated on the reasons for Patrick's agitation, and not liking the possible answer, indeed not even sure of it, he was further disconcerted.

Aimée lay on her side with her back toward Mignon, as sleepless with frustration as Vale. Although she didn't want to disturb Mignon's rest by moving, she finally turned to lie on her back. Glancing guiltily at her sister to make sure she'd not been awakened, she found that Mignon's eyes were as wide open and troubled as her own. They smiled wanly at each other, both knowing they were sleepless for the same reason, beginning to understand the warning Jeannette had given them about the complications that could develop during their journey.

The next morning found all of them uneasy and withdrawn. They had only to look at each other's faces to see the weariness written in their eyes. Breakfast was taken in silence. Vale stared into his coffee indifferently. He would, he decided, turn the travelers at an angle to the northwest. He'd previously planned to follow the banks of the Connecticut River directly north, which was an easier ride; but he hoped cutting across the lower mountains would shorten their journey.

For the next several days the riders were partially distracted from their personal problems as they guided their horses into the foothills, then threaded their way through passes between the mountains. Vale was cheered only by the knowledge that they would soon approach a village, where he hoped they could finally spend a night in an inn with solid walls to separate them and ease their tensions.

Before anyone could say a word about their desired accommodations, the proprietor of the tiny inn they found looked accusingly at the ringless fingers of the two women and blandly told them he was horrified that the danger of Indian attack was forcing many unmarried people to travel together under conditions so tempting. But no couples who couldn't prove their marriage would sleep in the same room under his roof. He had only two rooms to let, each with one bed; so Vale and Benjamin could sleep in one of them, and the women in the other. Patrick, he sternly advised, would have to be satisfied with the loft.

The hostel was little more than a farmhouse, and the travelers discovered they had to share dinner, as well as their table, with the proprietor and his family. Despite the innkeeper's loud boasts about the high moral standards of his establishment, he served a strong ale and was willing to refill his customers' tankards as many times as they put a coin on the table. Vale noted uneasily that Patrick hesitated not at all to drink more than his share.

At bedtime the innkeeper's wife escorted Aimée and Mignon to their room, and Vale and Benjamin to another, leaving Patrick in the dining room below. While the innkeeper was obviously happy to delay his own rest in serving Patrick, his wife made several trips to each room upstairs, with chamber pots, warming pans, quilts, pitchers of fresh water, and towels for the morning.

By the time she'd finished her tasks, Vale felt as if he could fall asleep standing up; but he turned to Benjamin and said wearily, "I think I'd best go back downstairs to see to Patrick or he'll be too drunk to get up in the morning."

Benjamin yawned and nodded. "I always knew him to be a hard drinker, but I've never seen him drunk. I vow it will take both of us to haul him up to that loft."

When the two men entered the dining room, to their relief the innkeeper had disappeared. Patrick's shoulders were slumped over the table, his forehead resting on his arms.

Assuming he was asleep or unconscious, Benjamin whispered, "I'll take his legs, you his shoulders, and we'll carry him between us."

Patrick slowly lifted his head to stare at them through unfocused eyes, and after a moment he spoke slurring his words: "Leave me alone."

"Come on, Patrick, we'll help you upstairs," Benjamin said coaxingly.

"Thought you'd be too busy by now to bother with me," Patrick muttered.

Although a warning was ringing in the back of Vale's mind, he said amiably, "If you'll get on your feet, you can hold on to our shoulders."

"Suppose you're getting anxious to go up to your girls," Patrick mumbled.

"What are you talking about?" Benjamin asked suspiciously.

"He's too drunk to know," Vale said. "Let's just get him up to bed."

"Vale doesn't want to talk about what he's doing tonight, but it's the same thing as when he was supposed to be cleaning the birds." Patrick spoke again. "Same thing you're going to do with Mignon."

Benjamin's eyes flashed with anger as he reached down to grasp Patrick's shirt and pulled him halfway to his feet. "One more word about Mignon and I'll ignore your drunkenness," he warned.

"I saw how she looks at you all the time, how Aimée's running after Vale. None of you asked if one of the girls should ride with me, I noticed. Everybody had his plans made before the mother got out of sight," Patrick muttered.

"Aimée and Mignon are sleeping in their own room, and Vale and I will be sharing the other one," Benjamin rasped. He pulled Patrick even higher off the chair and invited, "Exchange rooms with me, if you wish—or come upstairs and see for yourself, if your eyes can see that far."

Exercising every bit of restraint he had left, Vale pried Benjamin's fingers from Patrick's shirt and said tightly, "You can't reason with him, Ben. Leave him here if this is where he wants to stay. Let's go back to our room."

"Suppose what tricks those Indians you lived with didn't teach you about loving the Frenchies did. Suppose you and Aimée were carrying on all the time you were in Europe," Patrick muttered.

Vale, who had halfway turned to leave, whirled around to face Patrick and said in a deceptively soft tone, "Drunk or no, you'd better realize that I love Aimée. If I hear you insult her one more time tonight—or at any time in the future—I believe I'll kill you, so you'd best turn back to Boston tomorrow and not risk this happening again."

Despite Patrick's besotted state, he understood the light that glowed ominously in Vale's eyes, and he wisely remained silent. He stood bent beside his chair, bracing his hand on its back as he swayed slightly, staring after Vale and Benjamin.

In the morning, when the two couples came downstairs for breakfast, Vale noted that Patrick was nowhere in sight; and when Mignon asked where he was, Benjamin said only that he'd decided to return to Boston.

Mignon was no more satisfied than Aimée with Benjamin's terse explanation for Patrick's sudden disappearance; but they noted the anger in both Vale's and Benjamin's eyes and asked nothing more.

The river that ran near the village cut through the worst of the mountains, Vale explained as they left the inn. Because it made a natural pass through the rocky walls, he suggested they follow its banks to the foothills beyond. Everyone agreed with his reasoning; but all questions about Patrick were forgotten when they discovered that the rocky ledges along the river were slimy with moss from the splashing water. Their attention was solely concentrated on each step the horses took as they silently prayed none of the animals would lose their footing and plunge either one of them or the remaining supplies into the treacherous-looking river.

When they paused for a welcome midday rest, Vale changed into the doeskin shirt and breeches he'd worn in the forest near Montreal, and told them he'd be gone for an hour to hunt their dinner. Aimée watched him walk away, bow and quiver of arrows over his shoulder, his hunting knife sheathed at his waist—reliving the day they'd met. He walked with the lithe, silent step of the people he'd spent his childhood with; he moved so effortlessly that the speed of his moccasins was revealed only by the distance he covered. No longer was there anything about him of the elegant marquis she'd met on the *Santa Luisa,* she reflected. He seemed as comfortable in the wilderness as he'd been in his little house near Boston.

After Vale returned carrying a string of fat trout, they resumed making their precarious way along the riverbank. It took the rest of the day to get through the worst area, and Vale promised they'd be clear of all the mountains by the following noon. When night came, they found the day's tension had exhausted them; and they slept beside the rushing river, as soundly as if they were children too young to be affected by each other's nearness.

The next morning Vale again wore his doeskins and moccasins, giving Aimée's heart a fresh wrench with the flood of memories the sight of him evoked. After they had mounted and his arms enclosed her, the soft sensation of his sleeves brushing her skin and the pleasant scent of sun-warmed doeskin made her almost weep from longing—if only everything could be now as it had been that day in Montreal. Her father would be conducting his business instead of occupying a lonely grave near Paris. Marcel wouldn't be in prison or hiding from British soldiers. Her mother wouldn't be in Concord suffering from a hideous wound.

Aimée closed her eyes, dreaming of how happy they all could be if she'd only had the power to design their destinies. She would have brought Valjean home to meet her family that first afternoon. He would have courted her in Montreal, and none of them would ever have traveled to France. She envisioned their marriage and their wedding night in a cottage like Vale's little house near Boston. She knew that such dreaming was senseless, that the hard knot in her chest was the realization that she didn't want to return to Montreal and learn Marcel was dead and the home she'd spent her childhood in destroyed. She didn't want to see Montreal ever again, and the thought of living in a city reduced to rubble by the cannonade she assumed the British army had already loosed on it was unbearable.

Aimée's thoughts had been inspired by the touch and scent of Vale's doeskin garments, and the perfume of mayflowers she'd accepted as being part of her memories until she finally opened her eyes, startled to discover they'd left the mountains behind and the foothills really were covered with a blanket of mayflowers.

Vale had assumed that Aimée had fallen asleep when her body had relaxed against his chest; and when she suddenly sat up alertly, he said, "Beyond these foothills is a lowland that stretches to Lake Champlain. We won't go anywhere near the lake because there may still be sporadic fighting, but these foothills are pleasant enough to ride through for a few more days till we reach Montreal."

Again Aimée leaned back against Vale. She didn't want to tell him that she dreaded the end of their journey and what she expected to find there, that she wished she could simply turn around and go back to Boston.

Chapter 18

The travelers met no British patrols during the next few days; but when they entered a small village south of Montreal, they were immediately aware of the presence of soldiers, their scarlet coats making bright splashes against the duller-hued houses. Although several buildings had been burned—Vale assumed these were owned by the people who had refused to swear allegiance to King George and stop fighting—the rest of the village seemed intact; and the people appeared to be conducting their normal business. Because the inn was filled with military personnel, Vale arranged to spend the night in a private home. Their host and hostess readily gave them all the news about the recent events.

Hungry, confused, and disheartened, the people of Montreal had been surrounded by British soldiers outnumbering the city's entire population; and the marquis de Vaudreuil had finally surrendered without a fight nearly a month previous. He, the French soldiers, and nearly all the officials of his government had already been shipped back to France. General Amherst, commander in chief of the British army in Montreal, had surprised everyone by issuing strict orders that there be no plundering and that all his forces behave properly in every respect.

Amherst and the governor he'd appointed, General Gage, seemed intent on keeping order as peacefully as possible. Established French laws weren't changed; no customs had been interfered with. The result, thus far, was that the government was at last orderly and seemingly uncorrupted. Although the villagers were compelled to billet soldiers in their homes, the money they were allowed for food was welcome. If anyone had a complaint, he was heard by the militia captain in charge of his parish.

In answer to Aimée's and Mignon's anxious questions the couple assured them no mass arrest of citizens had taken place; and from all accounts they'd heard, anyone arrested had been fairly tried. It wasn't likely that Marcel was languishing in a dungeon or had been severely punished, even if he'd refused to swear allegiance to King George. Most of the people who had in the beginning resisted the British advance had already been freed with little more than light penalties. Although Aimée was much encouraged by this news, she still was aware that the village wasn't part of the city; and these people possibly didn't know the full truth but had merely accepted what the British had chosen to tell them.

When they left the village the next morning, they were briefly questioned about their destination and purpose by soldiers stationed in the road. They were not detained, however, and this reinforced what they'd been told.

Although they were again stopped at the gates to Montreal and asked the same questions as those they'd answered when when leaving the village, they were allowed to pass inside. Like the village, the city seemed peaceful, its inhabitants appearing to conduct their daily business without fear; and the British soldiers, although numerous, seemed concerned with their own affairs.

By the time the group had seen enough of the city to be satisfied that conditions were as the villagers had described, the mid-afternoon sky was clouding over, and a moistly chill wind had begun to rise. The Dessaline house and business were still some distance away across the Rivière des Prairies on Île Jésus, in the Lavaltrie district north of Montreal; and since they couldn't know if the house had been damaged or destroyed, Vale suggested they wait until the following morning to visit that area. The city was so filled with militia it might be difficult to find accommodations, so they immediately went to the Hôtel Dieu.

A harried desk clerk informed them there were no rooms available that night, but Aimée promptly asked to speak to the manager. Vale and Benjamin learned how respected the Dessaline name was when the manager apologized profusely for not having a place in the hotel that night but added that two British officers had been reassigned to Crown Point and were leaving in the morning. The manager vowed he'd reserve their rooms for the Mesdemoiselles Dessaline and their protectors to occupy the following night and for as long as they wished afterwards. The travelers had to be content with this. Vale suggested they continue on toward the Lavaltrie district with the hope that in this less populated area they would be more likely to find somewhere to pass the night.

After inquiring at three inns and being turned away, they approached a fourth with great uncertainty. The inn was larger than the others, though it was seedy-looking.

Vale raised his eyes to the sign that seemed to wail softly as it swung in the wind. "Le Mouton Noir, 'the black sheep'—it seems a suitable name for this place." He turned to regard Benjamin. "It isn't the inn I'd choose, but maybe we don't have a choice."

"I suspect we'll have to be grateful if there's room available even here," Benjamin agreed. "I see there's a stable in the rear, so maybe we'll find ourselves sleeping with the horses."

Aimée's eyes followed a man, who approached and entered the inn. "I'd rather sleep with a horse than under the same roof with that man, unless a stout door with a heavy bolt stands between."

"*Oui*, he's a blackguard if I ever saw one," Mignon remarked.

Vale tilted his head skyward. The clouds gathered ominously. "I would even consider sleeping in the forest on Île Jésus, but it's going to storm. Any roof over our heads would be preferable to sleeping in an icy rain."

"At this time of year the rain could be half ice," Aimée agreed.

Vale bent closer to look at Aimée over her shoulder. "Then you wouldn't mind too much staying here tonight, if there's a room for us?"

Enclosed more snugly in his arms when he leaned

nearer, Aimée turned her head so her lips lightly brushed his cheek as she answered, "I wouldn't mind any place as long as I know you're nearby."

Aimée felt Vale's cheek tighten in a smile. He straightened now and looked at Benjamin. "Shall we inquire?"

Benjamin turned his horse toward the inn.

After Vale and Benjamin had dismounted, Mignon glanced suspiciously at a disheveled-looking man who was loitering on the corner. "I think I would prefer to go inside with you," she announced.

Benjamin extended his arm to help her dismount, and Vale promptly reached for Aimée. The men entered the inn with Aimée and Mignon firmly holding their arms.

The proprietor, a grimy little man with the features of a weasel, told them he had only one room left. His narrowed eyes traveled from Aimée to Mignon so appraisingly that Aimée felt Vale's arm slide possessively around her waist. The man suggested that the ladies could stay in the room, while Vale and Benjamin could make a bed for themselves in an empty storeroom at the end of the hall. Vale looked at Benjamin questioningly. Benjamin nodded and Vale agreed.

After Vale and Benjamin had brought Aimée and Mignon the bundle of items they needed for the night, Aimée was even more tempted to ask Mignon if she would agree to the four of them spending the night together. The door to the room had a latch a kitten could displace, and the storeroom where Vale and Benjamin would sleep appeared so musty she wondered if rats would disturb them when they rolled up in their blankets on the floor. She could hear the rumble of thunder and hoped the roof wouldn't leak during the impending storm.

When the two couples went downstairs for dinner, Aimée was silently appalled at the appearance of the inn's other patrons. Resigned that she would have to eat her dinner with a gang of pirates and thieves, Aimée took a firmer hold on Vale's arm as he wove his way among the disorganized assortment of tables to the one most distant from the others.

The meal was a thick stew of greasy vegetables and a mixture of meats Aimée didn't care to identify. She was so hungry she picked out one of the more presentable morsels to taste, then decided to concentrate her attention on a basket of bread and cheese. The others, she noted, had come to the same conclusion. The inn served no wine, so Aimée and Mignon settled for tea while Vale and Benjamin decided to try the spruce beer. Although the beer was sharp and had a sour taste, the men knew it would be useless to complain.

The couples spoke very little during their meal, not wishing to shout to make themselves heard over the din in the room; nor did they want to arouse the ire of anyone in the rough-looking crowd with uncomplimentary remarks about their surroundings. Although none of them were enthusiastic about going to their respective beds, the increasing drunkenness of the others around them made it seem wise to retire for the night. Vale and Benjamin escorted the girls to their room, reassuring them that they'd be just down the hall if the girls needed them for any reason, and then waited until Aimée had latched the door before they left.

"The bed appears to be reasonably clean," Mignon commented as she inspected the linens. Holding the lamp nearer, she bent to look more closely at the sheets and, after a moment, straightened to advise Aimée, "I see no vermin."

"I'm grateful to hear it," Aimée replied as she unhooked her bodice. "I only hope Vale and Ben don't have trouble with rats."

Mignon pulled her dress over her head, her voice muffled as she commented, "When I saw that this room had two beds, I considered suggesting that Vale and Ben sleep in one of them; but I didn't have the courage."

"Hearing you say that tempts me to go down the hall and ask them now, but I'm afraid to step out of our door," Aimée declared.

Mignon came closer to put her hand on her sister's arm. "Aimée, it is difficult for you and Vale to see each other every day as you have, then have to separate at night, isn't it?" she whispered.

Aimée's face took on a pink tint as she sat on the edge of her bed and looked up at Mignon. "I suspect, even if Vale were far away and I couldn't see him at all, I would still feel like this."

Mignon smiled ruefully at Aimée and confessed, "Riding all day enclosed by Ben's arms has been tempting for me too."

As Aimée lay down and pulled the blankets up to her chin, she said thoughtfully, "Many times during this journey I've thought of Maman's saying we could have problems in such intimate circumstances."

Long after Mignon had blown out the lamp, both girls remained awake, listening to the rain falling in sheets on the window, watching the lightning flashes on the wall. Though they said no more, each knew the other was thinking about the man who had won her heart.

For a while the storm added to the heavy footsteps going up and down the corridor. The peals of loud laughter and raucous voices outside the door disturbed Aimée, but as she slowly became accustomed to the noises weariness began to overtake her. Finally she closed her eyes and drifted into sleep to begin a dream about Vale; and her senses didn't register the soft scrape as the latch was lifted. In her dream she was caught in Vale's embrace; and the bed shifting with added weight didn't alarm her, the fingers touching her becoming part of her dream until they caressed her roughly.

"*Qu'est-ce qu'il y a?*" she mumbled, still half asleep. She opened her eyes and stared at the crooked face the lightning revealed hanging over hers. "*Le diable!*" she cried. Struggling to escape the arms that now pinned her to the bed, she screamed, "*Méchant! Le bas méchant!*"

Hearing Mignon's sudden cry and the sounds of her sister's body thrashing around on the bed across the room, Aimée curved her hands to form claws. Her nails raked her attacker's face so ferociously she drew blood as she screamed, "*Laissez-moi!* Get away from me!"

The door flew open to crash against the wall. The sour-smelling face before Aimée's was plucked away, and she leaped out the opposite side of the bed. A flash of lightning lit Vale as his fist slammed Aimée's attacker against the wall. Another man in the room launched himself at Vale's back; but before his flying body struck, Vale had stepped aside and turned, his arm driving down to strike the attacker as if swatting a fly, knocking it down midair. A third man approached, but Vale caught his shoulders in both hands to hold him for the instant it took to drive his knee up into the would-be assailant's groin; and as the man screamed and bent double in pain, Vale's hands, knotted together, swept up under his chin and snapped his head back, the force of the blow sending him sprawling to the floor.

In a streak of lightning Aimée glimpsed movement in the shadows behind Vale and opened her mouth to call a warning, when she heard the ominous click of a pistol being cocked.

"I'd advise you against doing that," Ben said from the doorway. He stepped into the room; and taking advantage of the moment it took Ben's eyes to adjust to the darkness, the man who lay almost at Ben's feet caught the wrist that held the pistol, pushed it aside, and raced past him. An explosion of thunder shook the inn, and a second silhouette, still half crouching, ran stumbling into the hall.

More concerned about Mignon than about catching the intruders, Ben hurried to her side. "What did he do? Are you hurt?" Ben asked concernedly. Mignon began to sob, reaching up toward him; and he put his arms around her comfortingly.

Still standing with her back to the wall and holding her torn nightgown together, Aimée blinked in the light from the lamp Vale lit. "He was in bed with me when I awakened," she whispered, shuddering at the memory of the man's touch.

Vale quickly put down the lamp and enclosed her in his arms. "What did he do? Did he have time to . . ." He couldn't form the words.

"*Non, non, mon amoureux,*" she said hurriedly. "He only—he just bruised me, I think."

"What's happening here? What's all this noise?" the innkeeper demanded from the doorway. "What are you men doing in this room? I'll have none of that!"

Not lessening his grasp on Aimée—though he stepped in front of her to shield her from the innkeeper's stare—Vale looked over his shoulder with eyes that matched the lightning-streaked sky, and snarled, "Get out of here and take that man on the floor with you. He won't be interested in raping any women for some time after what I did to him."

When the two men flanking the innkeeper entered the room, Benjamin gathered a blanket around Mignon to cover her tattered nightgown, then raised his pistol menacingly. The men hurriedly bent to grasp the unconscious intruder's ankles and start dragging him toward the door.

"But you men can't stay in here," the innkeeper began.

"Get out," Benjamin snapped.

The innkeeper backed into the corridor, hastily closing the door after him.

"*Mon amour*, my dressing gown," Aimée whispered. Vale bent to pick up the garment that had slipped off the foot of the bed, and handed it to her. She plunged her arms through the sleeves, then ran across the room, hurriedly tying the sash. "Mignon, Mignon, what did he do? Are you hurt?"

"I think not, Aimée," Mignon answered, lifting her head from Benjamin's shoulder. "Vale and Ben arrived in time."

"*Dieu merci!*" Aimée took a deep, shuddering breath, then turned to Vale. "Please don't leave us alone here again," she begged, and put her arms around him.

"Nothing could make me leave this room unless you came with me," Vale promised. He looked at Benjamin over Aimée's shoulder, "What do you say, Ben? Do you mind sharing one of these beds with me while Aimée and Mignon sleep in the other?"

"Is that all right with you, Mignon?" Benjamin whispered into her hair.

"*Oui*, Ben. Oh, yes!" Mignon breathed.

"Would you mind letting go of me for a few minutes so

I can get my things from the storeroom?" he asked softly. Feeling her body tense, he added, "We'll leave your door open while we're gone. We'll be only a few steps down the hall."

Mignon nodded and released him.

Vale and Benjamin returned a short time later to find Aimée sitting on the edge of the bed beside Mignon. Both women appeared calmer.

"Are you certain you're all right?" Benjamin asked cautiously. They answered that they were, and he turned to Vale, who was carefully latching the door. "Then I suppose we can put out the lamp?" he asked. How he wished he could snatch Mignon from Aimée's side and hold her close to him all night.

Vale glanced at Aimée, sending a message of love and longing in that brief moment, then turned to Benjamin. "Yes, you can blow it out. I can see in the dark."

Because the men had previously planned to sleep in the storeroom, they'd remained fully clothed. Aimée listened as they got into bed. She wished that she herself could lie next to Vale all night, even if it meant only to be enclosed in his arms—to feel the warmth of him. Nothing more, she thought. Just that much—holding him. She felt Mignon's fingers creep into her hand and squeeze her fingers.

"I'm not sure I'll sleep at all tonight with Ben so near," Mignon whispered in her ear.

"It won't be easy for me either, but we must try," Aimée breathed. She said nothing more. How strange it would seem in the morning to have Vale in the same room but in another bed and so out of her reach.

Aimée awakened to the sensation of Vale's lips brushing her forehead. When her eyes opened, he straightened; and after gazing longingly at her a moment, he finally reached out to touch Mignon's blanket-covered shoulder. He told them mugs of hot chocolate awaited them on the little table in their room. Benjamin was preparing the horses, and they would leave the inn as soon as Aimée and Mignon were dressed. Then he turned away, his moccasined feet moving silently through the sunlight that slanted from the window. Before he stepped into the hall, he paused to assure them he would wait outside their door so no one would bother them.

Later, as they rode down the cobblestoned street, they found a *boulangerie* where Benjamin bought a sack of *croissants* still warm from the oven; and they ate the simple breakfast as they continued toward Île Jésus. Although the sun was bright, there was a distinct chill in the air. Aimée knew that this foretold an early winter. The storm had stripped the leaves from many of the trees, creating a gold and amber carpet on the road.

Aimée and Mignon stared incredulously at the charred timbers still standing upright, the slanting fragment of a blackened roof that had collapsed into the center of the building where Hilaire had run his *pelleterie*.

"Why should they burn Papa's *pelleterie*?" Aimée whispered. "Everywhere else it was the houses of resisters that were put to the torch. They have destroyed our family's livelihood."

"Maybe the fire was an accident that had nothing to do with Montreal's surrender," Vale said. "When we locate the British headquarters for Lavaltrie, we'll learn what happened."

Aimée took one more long look at the sodden ashes of the business her father had built from the line of traps he'd once tended in the forest, and said angrily, "Let's see what happened to our house. If it too has been destroyed, I'll confront the commandant with more than mere questions."

Mignon took a deep breath and began, "Perhaps Marcel . . ." Overcome with horror at her thoughts, she paused, turned to look at Benjamin over her shoulder, then forced herself to continue: "Maybe Marcel's ashes are in there."

Benjamin's arms tightened around her, and he leaned closer to say soothingly, "Don't anticipate the worst. As Vale said, we'll learn what happened from the commandant."

Mignon nodded and, not wanting to look again at the ruin, lowered her eyes as Benjamin turned the horse away.

When the Dessaline house first came into view, it appeared not to have been damaged; but as they drew nearer, Aimée and Mignon were stunned to see that a British flag had been hoisted next to the entrance and a pair of scarlet-coated soldiers were stationed beside the door. Vale and Benjamin drew up their horses. The Dessaline house itself appeared to have been made into the commandant's headquarters.

One of the horses standing before the gate shifted its position; and suddenly Aimée recognized a deep reddish-bronze coat blazing in the sun. Brandy was standing with his proud head lowered; his nose almost brushed the ground, though he wasn't nibbling at what was left of the grass. He looked listless, dejected, as if he were sick. Gathering her skirt, Aimée swung her leg over the saddle and leaped down.

"What are you . . . ?" Vale began, but she didn't answer.

Hearing approaching footsteps, Brandy turned his head to look dully in Aimée's direction. When he saw not a soldier, but his mistress coming, his head went up and his eyes grew bright again.

"*Mon grand cheval, mon* Brandy," Aimée said softly, and put her arms around his glossy shoulders. The horse nickered softly and arched his neck to touch her hair gently with his nose. "What have they done to you that you stand with your nose to the ground?" Aimée whispered; and remembering he obeyed no one's orders but hers, dreading what she might find, she stepped back to look at his body.

It was as she feared. He wore marks from the spurs that had raked his side, the still swollen welts of a crop viciously used on his withers. She touched him gently as she walked slowly around him to discover blood still oozing from the cut near his eye, raw gashes on both his knees. Though she spoke softly, soothingly, an anger was rising in her that made her forget her own possible danger. She tore open the buckles that held his girth, ripped off the saddle, and let the pad fall to the dust.

Feeling Vale's presence behind her, she rasped, "Look

what they've done. Just look! Do you have a piece of rope? A strip of hide? Anything I can use?"

One of the soldiers loitering nearby saw the saddle fall, and hurried over. "Say, now, miss, you can't do that," he said anxiously. "That's Colonel Morehead's mount."

Aimée spun around to glare at him. "Thank you for telling me. Now I know whom to accuse," she snapped as she began to unbuckle the bridle.

"No, miss! Don't do that!" the soldier exclaimed in genuine alarm. "That's a vicious beast!"

Aimée pulled off the bridle, dashing it too onto the road. "Stay." The word was spoken softly to the animal, then she turned to the soldier. "This is not a vicious beast, but your Colonel Morehead is," she declared. She took the coil of twine; which was all Vale had found to give her, strung it around Brandy's neck and tied it to the fence.

"You can't expect that bit of string to hold him," the soldier said, aghast at the idea.

"I expect my word to hold him." She gave the horse one more pat, then turned to the soldier to warn, "You'd best not try to take Brandy off somewhere now that I've told him to stay—or he'll certainly trample you."

The soldier stared after her, incredulous as Vale, who strode behind her to the house.

Aimée marched past the sentries at the door and into the entrance hall. "Where is Colonel Morehead?" she demanded of the handful of men she found there.

A voice behind Aimée said, "I'm Colonel Morehead, commandant for Lavaltrie district, mademoiselle."

Aimée whirled to face a stockily built officer not much taller than her. His dark hair was sprinkled with gray. Piercing blue eyes ran over her figure, making her anger rise even higher. "You can take our house and destroy my father's business; and for all I know, you might even have murdered my brother—but I will not let you have Brandy too."

"Mademoiselle . . ." a tall sandy-haired officer behind Morehead began.

"If you think you can confiscate Brandy, I will go out-

side, put a pistol to his head, and kill him rather than let
you torment him because he's loyal to me," Aimée vowed.

"I'm Major Stewart Templeton, mademoiselle," the officer said. "Who is Brandy and, if I may ask, who are
you?"

"Brandy is that Thoroughbred outside who's been liter-
ally beaten to his knees," Aimée shot back. She returned
her attention to Morehead. "I'm Aimée Dessaline, and
you, Colonel, are dirtying my carpet with your muddy
boots."

Morehead's expression changed to amusement as he replied, "Come into my office, Mademoiselle Dessaline, and
we'll discuss your complaints." He nodded to indicate a
door.

"You mean my father's study, not your office," Aimée
snapped. She glanced at Vale, who took her arm to accompany her, but the major's hand on her shoulder
stopped her.

"Who is your companion?" Morehead inquired, looking
derisively at Vale's doeskin garments.

Morehead obviously thought him a lowly trapper, and
Vale had no intention of allowing the colonel to be alone
with Aimée. He brushed Templeton's hand from her
shoulder, then answered in his crispest English, "I'm
Valjean Étienne, Comte de la Tour, Marquis d'Auvergne.
Mademoiselle Dessaline is my fiancée. General Amherst
has issued certain orders regarding the governing of this
colony; and if anything in Lavaltrie is amiss, I shall be
sure to bring it to his attention."

Assuming then that Vale was one of the few French
leaders in Montreal who had not been shipped back to
Paris and so must have extraordinary friendly ties with the
British government, Morehead nodded at Templeton and
turned to lead the couple into the office he'd com-
mandeered.

Aimée took the chair that Jeannette had often sat in,
embroidering while Hilaire worked at his desk on afternoons. She waited not a moment to demand, "What has
become of my brother, Marcel? Why did you destroy the
pelleterie? And what, Monsieur le Colonel, are my sister

and I to do with winter coming and you occupying our house?"

Colonel Morehead's head raised in annoyance at the sound of another feminine voice just outside the office door. "Where is my sister, you scoundrel? If you think you're going to secrete her in some dungeon, you'll have to lock me up as well; and I'll scream so loud King George will hear me in his palace!"

"Let her in too, Corporal!" Morehead called to the man he'd stationed outside his office.

The door opened, and Mignon entered, her eyes blazing with blue fire. Benjamin followed her.

Morehead sighed in resignation. "I take it you're another Dessaline? No doubt you're some duke or another," he said, looking at Benjamin. "Come in and sit down, both of you."

Templeton silently followed Mignon and Benjamin into the room and stationed himself in a corner. Morehead seated himself in the chair behind Hilaire's desk and looked at Aimeé. "You may certainly take that animal of yours whenever it pleases you," he said coldly. Then his eyes moved to Mignon. "Mesdemoiselles, in all truth I have no idea where your brother is. He vanished almost immediately after we occupied this town. As far as I know, he wasn't injured in any respect."

Mignon took a deep breath of relief; but Aimée, still actively suspicious, remarked, "How convenient for you that Marcel has disappeared and cannot tell us what happened to the *pelleterie*—that he, in fact, can tell us nothing at all."

"Do you think I murdered him and hid his body?" Morehead demanded, his eyes flashing.

Vale's fingers closed over Aimée's in silent warning, and she glanced up at him worriedly as he commented, "I don't believe my fiancée has accused you of anything at all, Colonel Morehead. I also don't believe you can blame her for being distressed by the situation we've found. Perhaps you can give us more details."

Morehead looked narrowly at Vale. "It's quite impossible to keep account of everyone's whereabouts when you first occupy a town," he said coolly. He was quiet a moment, thinking over what he might tell them about the destruction of the *pelleterie*. Finally he said, "As far as the business is concerned, I can say only that one of the chemicals used in tanning the skins must have caught fire. The building burned very quickly, possibly because of all the various oils and fats it must have contained.

A plausible explanation, Vale thought; but he still didn't like the vagueness of it—or the expression on Morehead's face as he spoke. The flecks in Vale's eyes blended into an opaque mass as he said in a deceptively calm tone, "Perhaps you would be so good as to describe how long you intend to occupy the Dessaline home?"

"It's the only house in the area that's large enough to contain my headquarters. I have no choice but to remain here until I and my men are assigned elsewhere," Morehead replied in a lofty tone.

Undaunted, Aimée said hotly, "What are my sister and I to do while you and your men tramp around our house scratching the furniture and scraping our walls, smashing our china and ruining our carpets?"

"If you and your sister wish to occupy one of the rooms upstairs and act as our housekeepers, you're welcome to do so," Morehead replied.

Aimée's mouth fell open at the idea. *"Mon Dieu!"*

"I will not allow my fiancée to sleep under the same roof as a dozen soldiers, however gentlemanly they're supposed to be; nor will she be forced to clean up their mess," Vale said coldly.

Major Templeton took a step forward, his green eyes apologetic. "If anything is damaged or destroyed, compensation will be made for it. Certainly the ladies meanwhile can take any of their belongings to another location, if they choose—with the colonel's permission of course."

Morehead gave the major a sharp look, but he realized the officer was only reciting the orders General Amherst had issued. "Yes, of course, the mesdemoiselles Dessaline may take anything they wish," he said with false magnanimity.

"Then, *chérie*, I believe we must continue to accept accommodations at the Hôtel Dieu," Vale said.

"That does seem the most discreet course," Templeton agreed, but Morehead remained silent.

Aimée got to her feet and, turning to Mignon, said, "Let us go upstairs to our rooms and pack what we can. At least we will be able to have some of our clothes and jewelry." She looked at the commandant and asked sarcastically, "You haven't confiscated our jewelry, have you?" To her amazement Morehead opened one of the drawers of Hilaire's desk and drew out two gilt-covered boxes.

"I kept your jewels locked in here so that if thieves broke into the house, they would be safe," Morehead explained.

"I wouldn't have thought thieves would break into a military establishment to steal my modest jewels," Aimée said tartly.

They did not discuss the interview with Morehead and Templeton as they headed back to the Hôtel Dieu, as they didn't want their remarks to be overheard by passersby, especially soldiers. At the hotel Benjamin arranged for porters to carry up to their room the items Aimée and Mignon had taken from the house. Mignon promised to unpack everything herself so Aimée could attend Brandy's wounds. Vale helped Aimée with this task with the stable master looking on, clucking over Brandy's condition. Again they avoided all talk of Morehead and recent events in the stable master's presence. When Vale escorted Aimée to her door, he purposely reminded her of the bath Mignon surely had waiting, and so he distracted her from troubles. He left her more cheerful than he'd seen her for several days.

By dinnertime her hair had been freshly arranged and perfumed, and she had put on an indigo velvet gown with white lace ruffles caught up at the hem by narrow satin ribbons. Aimée went down to dinner on Vale's arm feeling more equal to dealing with her problems.

Vale had arranged for a small private dining room; and so they were able to discuss the situation after dinner.

"The thought of leaving that man sitting at Papa's desk in Papa's own chair as if he owned it turns my blood cold," Aimée said angrily.

"If anyone is to sit there, it should be Marcel," Mignon agreed. "If Maman saw them sitting at her table while we must have our dinner in a hotel, she would chase them out with a broom, soldiers or no."

"Morehead said there's no place else they can set up their headquarters, but that isn't true. The village has a building used for public business that's large enough," Aimée said bitterly. "Morehead just finds our house more comfortable—and he can ransack it at his leisure. Did you see how he had our jewelry at his fingertips? Not for one moment did I believe he was simply keeping it safe from thieves. He was keeping it safe for himself in case we didn't return."

"Neither do I believe Marcel simply disappeared," Mignon declared. "Marcel wouldn't go away when he expected us to come back anytime." She paused, her lower lip trembling as she thought of the alternative. "I only pray he hasn't been murdered—his body hidden in that convenient fire at the *pelleterie*," she whispered.

"Now, Mignon, you must not assume such things," Benjamin said, reaching across the corner of the table to take her hand. "It's true there's something disquieting about Colonel Morehead, but we can't accuse him of murder. It's very likely Marcel had his own reasons for disappearing this way."

Vale took a sip of brandy, then put down his glass. "Although I don't trust Morehead, I have a feeling that Major Templeton is honest. If all our suspicions are right, Templeton's being second in command would make Morehead cautious."

"Templeton did promise to make inquiries about Marcel, but I doubt he'll learn anything," Benjamin said thoughtfully. "I suspect, if anyone has a hint about Marcel's disappearance, they wouldn't tell one of the soldiers or even anyone associating with them. Perhaps we can discover something, though. If I were to dress like one of the sailing men, I could perhaps learn if Marcel had smuggled himself aboard a ship. With my father's business being what it is, I can talk to sailors in their own jargon and impersonate one of them easily enough."

Vale nodded in agreement. "And being as familiar as I am with the wilderness, maybe I could learn something from a trapper."

"We would be so grateful if you could stay and help us," Mignon said softly.

"Really, Mignon, do you think we could possibly take off for Boston and leave you alone?" Benjamin asked in surprise.

"Well, no," she admitted. "I just thought . . ."

"Not only would your mother have our heads for it, but it certainly isn't the way for a proper fiancé to behave, now is it?" Benjamin asked offhandedly.

Mignon glanced up at him in surprise, wondering if his light tone was only meant to soothe her or if he was preparing the way for a marriage proposal. At the thought of the second possibility her heart suddenly began to beat with a new rhythm.

Aimée's mind was on another matter, and she didn't pay attention to the turn the conversation had taken. She stared down at her glass of sherry for a long moment, then finally lifted solemn eyes to meet Vale's.

"I didn't mention this before because I thought I was imagining things in my agitation, but I do believe that one of the men—a civilian—I saw standing in the corridor leading away from my father's study was the man who attacked me last night at Le Mouton Noir."

Vale stared at her. "Are you certain of this?" he asked softly.

Aimée again carefully considered the possibility a moment before replying, "He was standing in the shadows and I only had time to catch a glimpse of him, but it isn't a face I'm likely to forget. It's twisted as if he had been born that way."

"Possibly he had been taken prisoner for some other wrongdoing?" Benjamin offered.

Aimée shook her head slowly. "No one else was with him. He appeared free to come or go as he chose."

"What would a ruffian like any of those we saw at Le Mouton Noir be doing strolling around the commandant's headquarters?" Benjamin asked speculatively.

"That's something I certainly would like to know the answer to," Vale said softly.

Chapter 19

The passing days became a week, then two; and although Vale and Benjamin searched diligently for Marcel, they learned nothing about his disappearance. While the men were gone, Aimée and Mignon would go riding, play cards or alter the dresses they'd taken from the Dessaline house to resemble more closely the fashions they'd seen in Paris. Once they hired a coach and went out to look in the stores, but the occupied city offered a dismal selection of wares and the gloomy skies of the steadily colder days did nothing to lift their spirits.

They were riding near the ruins of the *pelleterie* one day; and seeing the scarlet coat of a soldier who was poking about in the ashes, Aimée stopped Mignon from approaching closer. She recognized Colonel Morehead and wanted no further conversation with him, though she wondered why he was personally investigating a fire that had occurred so long ago. The next day they were surprised to receive a message from Morehead inviting them to dinner. They sent the courier back with a cool little note saying it wouldn't be proper for engaged women to attend a private dinner party if the invitation wasn't extended to their fiancés as well.

As sisters who were also close friends, Aimée and Mignon often discussed their love for Vale and Benjamin; but the sharp edge of their desire was blunted by fear for Marcel's fate, concern over Jeannette's recovery, and anger that the destruction of the *pelleterie* and Colonel Morehead's continued use of their house made them as impoverished and homeless as orphans.

Vale had decided to visit the farther outlying villages

with the hope of hearing something that would lead him to
Marcel. Before he left, he warned that he might be gone
for more than a week. After several days had passed, Benjamin invited Mignon and Aimée to lunch and an outing
afterwards; but Aimée declined, knowing that Mignon and
Benjamin would enjoy being alone. Instead she put on a
wool-lined riding habit and took Brandy for a canter. Still
curious about why Morehead had been searching the ruins
of the *pelleterie,* she decided to do her own investigating.

The *pelleterie* had been built on the edge of the forest
outside of town because the odors from preparing skins
would have disturbed the townspeople. Aimée approached
the lonely ruins from the forest; so if Morehead happened
to be there again, she would see him while her presence
was still hidden by the trees. Confirming that she was
alone, she guided Brandy closer. She remained in the
saddle for a few minutes, scanning the ashes from her
height, trying to imagine what Morehead had been looking
for. Finally, still perplexed, she dismounted; and lifting her
hem to avoid soiling her skirt, she entered the ruin.

The ashes were so fine her boots sank almost to her
ankles with each step. She walked slowly, cautiously, trying to avoid a certain area where she knew the cellar extended, though it was now disguised by the rubble that
had collapsed to fill the hole. The long worktables she
remembered had disappeared, and the only evidence of the
huge vats the workers had used was an occasional curved,
blackened fragment. She picked her way to the office
where her father had worked and, pausing at what used to
be a doorway, surveyed the area sorrowfully. Hilaire's
desk, his cabinets, the tables where furs had been spread
for assessment, had all vanished into anonymous piles of
gray. If she who was familiar with the *pelleterie* could now
recognize nothing in it, how could Morehead possibly have
hoped to learn anything from the ashes? Finally she
turned to leave, each step raising a powder so fine her
skirt was, despite her care, covered with a gray film.

"Don't you know how dangerous it is to enter this
place, mademoiselle?"

Startled, Aimée looked up to see Morehead standing at

the edge of the ruin. "I am quite aware of it, Colonel Morehead," she answered stiffly.

"You shouldn't be allowed here at all," said Morehead, who wore civilian clothes.

Aimée lowered her eyes as she carefully traced her steps around the rubble disguising the cellar's stairs. "Despite its condition the *pelleterie* still belongs to my family; and you have no right to tell me whether or not I may walk here." Ignoring his extended hand, she stepped over a charred timber and out into the open. She looked up to meet his eyes with an angry gaze. "That is, unless you have confiscated my father's business as well as our house."

"Perhaps I should, if only to keep you from being injured," he said slowly. "Then you do seem to know your way around in there."

"Of course I know. My sister and I played here many times as children. But if you choose to issue an edict proclaiming this ruin another spoil of war, I suppose I couldn't prevent it," Aimée replied coldly.

"What were you looking for?" The question was posed so matter-of-factly Aimée realized her answer was of great significance to him.

Although it was on the tip of her tongue to retort that it was for him to explain what he'd been searching for, she decided to avoid the subject. Instead she said sadly, "I was remembering how it used to be when my father was here—reminiscing, I suppose."

"I presume your father has died?" Morehead asked, his tone thoughtful. "And your mother?"

"My mother was wounded by an Indian arrow on our journey here and had to return to Boston to recover," Aimée replied.

"So you and your sister are alone in Montreal except for your brother—and of course no one knows where he is."

Aimée realized that Morehead was actually trying to find out if they'd learned anything about Marcel, which might confirm that he'd done nothing to her brother after all. She shrugged and said, "It is a mystery." She paused a moment, then added, "Mignon and I aren't really alone as long as our fiancés are our protectors."

"Your fiancé is neglectful of your welfare if he allows you to come here," Morehead commented.

"Valjean is away for a few days and doesn't know I'm here." The words were out of Aimée's mouth before she realized it might not be a good idea to let Morehead know Vale had left Montreal.

"It seems less than attentive of him to go off—not the way for à devoted lover to behave, I'd think," Morehead said speculatively. "I wonder if you and your sister were telling a little lie when you said those men were your fiancés—perhaps to make it appear more acceptable for you to travel through the wilderness with them all the way from Boston."

He looked questioningly at Aimée, stepped closer, and took her arm in a firm grip. Only then did she detect the odor of rum on his breath—she realized then that he'd been drinking heavily. She raised her head to say in an aloof tone, "What you've just said is insulting, Colonel Morehead, and untrue as well. I fail to understand why our personal lives should concern you in any event."

"It occurs to me that neither you nor your sister are as decorous as you'd like everyone to believe; and if that's the case, it is also possible your so-called marquis is a fake, which means he has some reason to hide his identity from the authorities and isn't likely to hurry to General Amherst to complain about anything." Morehead's grip on Aimée's arm tightened as he spoke, and his eyes became chips of blue ice.

Aimée's anger and fear were so thoroughly blended, all Morehead could discern was that she was very agitated. He assumed she was afraid that he would expose her pseudo fiancé. "I don't have to mention these suspicions to anyone if you'd give me some encouragement not to," he said insinuatingly.

"What are you talking about? Colonel, I really don't understand . . ."

His mouth enveloped hers, stopping her words. She tried to turn her face away from the reek of rum, from the tongue digging at her lips to force them open; but his hands caught her chin and held her so tightly she thought he might raise her off the ground. His tongue filled her mouth, half choking her; and she gasped for breath. Desperate with fear, she lifted her foot, sliding the narrow little heel of her riding boot down his shin. He stiffened with pain, and she wrenched free of him.

"Quel salaud! Cochon!" She spat out the words. "Don't ever dare touch me again!" She turned and ran to catch Brandy's bridle; but before she could put her foot in the stirrup, she felt Morehead's hand on her shoulder.

Aimée's fear vanished, and she turned to face Morehead. Amber swirled through her eyes as he put his other hand on her waist, intending to draw her to him again. Suddenly she let loose the anger that until then had hovered like a falcon awaiting her command. Her riding crop whipped across his face once, then again and again. He backed away, hands covering his face to protect his eyes, his fingers growing welts from her blows.

"How does it feel when it's used on you, you swine?" she demanded as she swung up into her saddle.

Morehead was looking at her from behind his still upraised hands, his eyes burning with hatred. He started to take a step forward, but she raised her riding crop threateningly and he remained where he was.

Lowering her voice, she said more calmly, "Consider that only a small payment for what you did to Brandy. If you ever touch me again, I'll repay the balance—providing Valjean doesn't kill you first."

She turned Brandy away and galloped off, leaving Morehead staring furiously at the flaming banner of her hair, silently vowing to tame her one day.

After Aimée returned to the hotel, she splashed her face with cold water until the slight swelling of her lips had diminished enough not to be noticeable. Finally, having calmed her temper, she took off her riding clothes, bathed, and put on a fresh gown.

. She was sitting in the window seat, staring unseeingly at the few flakes of snow that floated lazily from the bleak sky, when there was a knock on the door. She answered it and found Vale standing in the hall.

Aimée immediately threw her arms around him and forgot about Morehead. After a brief moment he released her, guided her into the room, and closed the door. Noting that they were alone, Vale again took Aimée in his arms.

"Where's Mignon?" he asked.

"She and Benjamin went out," Aimée murmured against his shoulder.

He drew her closer, enjoying the feel of her. "It's been a long time since we've been able to hold each other this way."

Aimée sighed. The scent of a wood fire, pine needles, and the earth was in his shirt, reminding her of when they'd lain together under the fir tree just before the Iroquois attack. "I wish Mignon and Ben would stay out for dinner, but they'll think of me and be back soon."

"We haven't loved since that night I awakened to find you'd stolen into my bed," he said quietly. "It seemed so much like a dream then that sometimes when I dream about you now, I'm not sure if you haven't come to me again that way."

"I would if it were possible," she promised. "I often wonder how long we'll have to wait—sometimes it seems like forever. Mignon knows I can't sleep at night; but she understands because she lies awake thinking about Ben."

"If it's any consolation to her, Ben is just as restless as she," Vale said softly, his arms tightening around Aimée. "I've been tempted to tell him and Mignon that we should make new sleeping arrangements. We want each other, they want each other; yet we stay apart for convention's sake. The Abnakis would think us all fools. I agree with them that each day spent without sharing our love is a bit of love we've wasted."

"I think those Abnakis are wiser than our own people," Aimée agreed as she tilted her head up to him.

He bent to touch his lips to hers in a kiss that was searchingly tender, achingly sweet. It was the taste of their shared loneliness flavored with more love than desire.

The door behind them opened, and they parted hastily to turn and face Benjamin and Mignon.

Disconcerted at having interrupted their kiss, not sure what to say or do, Benjamin finally commented, "You're back sooner than we expected, Vale."

Thinking that rather it was Benjamin and Mignon who had returned too soon, Vale replied, "That's because I might have learned where Marcel is."

"Marcel! You think he's still alive?" Mignon exclaimed.

"I've never thought otherwise," Vale answered, realizing Mignon all along had feared that Marcel had died in the fire at the *pelleterie*. He put his arm lightly around Aimée's waist and said, "Let's all sit down while we talk about this."

Mignon asked excitedly, "Where do you think he is, Vale? What is he doing? Do you have any idea why he disappeared that way?"

Benjamin, who had seated himself beside Mignon, took her hand and said, "Let Vale tell us what he knows, darling." At Mignon's startled glance Benjamin realized what he'd called her before the others, and a brief smile tipped one corner of his mouth as he looked up at Vale. "Please just tell us what you've learned."

Vale leaned back in his chair. "I spent last night in a little village where the people seem to be shy or suspicious of strangers and pretty much avoided me. I ate my dinner alone in the inn's dining room; but afterwards a man who also was a stranger in the village came to my table. He's a trapper and thought, because I was wearing my doeskins and moccasins, I was a trapper too. He said, after all the weeks he'd spent in the wilderness, he needed to pass the evening in someone's company. We treated each other to an ale, and I told him what I was doing there. I was surprised when he told me he'd known the Dessalines for years."

Taking Aimée's hand, he continued, "He met your father when he too was a fur trapper, then dealt with him after he'd opened the *pelleterie*. Your mother once set his ankle when he'd broken it in a trap. He was shocked that your father had been killed and the *pelleterie* destroyed.

He said to tell you both that he remembers you as children and hopes your mother recovers fully."

Vale took a breath before going on: "He told me there's a cabin deep in the forest about a day's ride west of Montreal. Your father used that cabin when he was tending his line of traps. This man had visited the cabin a week or so ago and said that though he saw no one, it looked like someone was living there, and he'd assumed it was another trapper. He suggested that it could be Marcel."

"It's strange that Marcel would conceal himself from this man," Aimée said slowly.

"Not necessarily," Vale said. "Marcel could have been afraid of a stranger in such a desolate place. Or if Marcel has a line of traps of his own, he could have been out tending them." Vale paused, then said slowly, "If there is some reason Marcel wants to avoid people, it would serve no one's purpose for me to visit him alone. He would just conceal himself. But if you and Mignon were to come with me, I'm sure Marcel would welcome you."

"Of course we'll go with you!" Mignon said immediately.

"How soon can we leave?" Aimée asked.

"Tomorrow morning if you wish," Vale replied. He looked questioningly at Benjamin.

"After I've traveled all the way from Boston, I certainly intend to go to this cabin with you," Benjamin declared.

"We'll have to take a few supplies with us—just a little food to eat along the way and blankets in case Marcel isn't living in the cabin and whoever is refuses to let us stay the night," Vale said.

"We still have the supplies left from our journey to Montreal," Aimée said.

"Ben and I can get things ready; but you and Mignon should plan on awakening before dawn," Vale warned.

Aimée thought of how little sleep any of them appeared to be getting anyway, but tactfully said, "Mignon and I grew so used to waking early on our trip to Montreal we can hardly keep our eyes closed past sunrise."

Once again they set out at dawn the next morning, but

this journey had little else about it to remind them of the trek to Montreal. Now Aimée rode Brandy, and Mignon one of the horses they'd previously used to carry supplies, so there was none of the physical tension of before. Although they avoided trails the Indians had long ago established and frequently traveled, they weren't as fearful of attack as they'd been in the past. With the British having secured this territory, their allies, the Iroquois, considered themselves also as having triumphed; and one had only to hail them in English to win their friendship. The Algonquins, regarded as conquered, secreted themselves in the forest, avoiding contact with Indian and white man alike.

Vale led the little group of travelers through groves of pine trees that sighed in the wind, and through forests of naked trees. As they moved along paths covered with deep piles of crackling golden leaves, Aimée's thoughts were plagued by questions about why Marcel had decided to leave Montreal to live in such isolation.

Aimée despised Colonel Morehead, but the Lavaltrie area appeared to be governed in an orderly fashion. The *pelleterie* had burned and the Dessaline home had been confiscated, yet Marcel could have stayed at the Hôtel Dieu as they were doing. Surely he had some money from the business that could have paid his expenses; and if all had been lost in the fire, he had friends who would have taken him in, she reasoned. Yet he had vanished at a time when he would have begun to expect his family to return from France.

It seemed to Aimée that Marcel had deliberately erased all clues to where he'd gone because he was hiding, and she wondered why. What could he be afraid of? The question blazed in her mind like a torch; and no matter how she tried to persuade herself that she was letting her imagination run free, she couldn't ignore the fact that Marcel had disappeared so completely even his own family couldn't find him.

Vale finally found the cabin in a clearing backed by a line of cliffs overlooking the Ottawa River. The sun had sunk behind the spruces that surrounded the clearing's other sides; and long violet shadows crept out of the forest like fingers pointing to the little house. Reminding himself that the cabin's occupant might greet visitors with gunfire, he halted the group while they were still concealed by the trees.

"You in the cabin!" Vale shouted first in French, then English. "If your name is Marcel, I have your sisters, Aimée and Mignon, with me! Whoever you are, we mean you no harm! Don't fire on us!"

There was no reply or sign of life in the little house. Vale turned to the others. "It's possible he's gone out; but just in case whoever lives there has a gun pointed out the window, you stay here while I investigate."

"If it's Marcel, he'd never shoot me. If not, don't you think whoever's there would be less likely to fire at a woman?" Aimée asked.

"Maybe so," Vale conceded, "but I don't care to take that chance." He prepared to dismount.

Aimée watched until Vale had one foot on the ground and was taking his other foot out of the stirrup, then her heels sharply bumped Brandy's sides and she called, "I'm coming out, Marcel!" Brandy sprang from the cover of the trees and bounded toward the cabin.

Vale leaped back into the saddle and raced after Aimée; but before his horse got halfway into the clearing, he saw the cabin door open. A lean, fiery-haired man hastily stood his rifle against the log wall, then ran toward Aimée. Vale stopped his horse a few feet from the couple, who had thrown their arms around each other, and watched silently while Mignon too hurled herself into Marcel's arms. He swung his younger sister around as he hugged her. Finally glimpsing Vale, he put Mignon down, his smile fading.

"May I ask who you are, monsieur?" Marcel inquired warily.

"A friend of Aimée's who has searched long and hard to find you." Vale replied.

"He's much more than my friend, Marcel," Aimée declared. "Oh, Mignon and I have so much to tell you!"

Marcel's eyes began to lose their suspicious look. "Then

step down, monsieur, both of you gentlemen." He glanced at Benjamin. "Come inside and welcome."

From the shadows of the trees a man with a lopsided face watched Aimée and Mignon joyously greet Marcel, then backed away, very satisfied with this day's results. If he rode fast until it grew too dark to see, then awakened before dawn, he thought he might very well be back in Montreal by mid-afternoon.

Chapter 20

After Marcel had greeted Aimée and Mignon so affectionately, Vale expected him to take his sisters' hands to lead them into the cabin. Vale dismounted, reminding himself to pick up Marcel's rifle; but when he faced the Dessalines, Marcel stepped aside and took Vale's reins.

"All of you go ahead into the house," Marcel said. "I'll take your animals around to the barn."

"Let me take care of the horses," Benjamin said. "I'm sure you're anxious to visit your sisters."

"*Merci,* monsieur, but I won't be long," Marcel replied. He looked at Aimée and smiled fondly. "If you would make a pot of coffee, I would appreciate it, *ma soeur.* It will be such a pleasure for me after having to drink my own. All of you just make yourselves comfortable."

Although Marcel spoke cheerfully, Vale noticed he seemed anxious to get them into the cabin. There was an air of tension about the man Vale couldn't help but wonder at.

When Marcel, still holding the reins, bent to retrieve his rifle, Vale said, "I'll help you. Two can do the work in half the time." Recognizing the protest rising to Marcel's lips, Vale turned away to gather up the reins of the remaining horses and began to lead them around to the side of the cabin.

The barn was actually an extension of the house, built to shield the cabin from the winter winds coming off the river. Like the cabin, it was made of logs, the chinks between filled with a kind of mortar made from mud clay and moss. Inside the barn Vale observed a pair of horses, a cow, and here and there a scurrying chicken. From the loft wisps of hay occasionally sifted down to land on a wagon parked in a corner. The barn was of modest size, but it was so carefully organized that it would easily accommodate the extra animals.

"Whoever built this barn certainly designed it to advantage," Vale commented as he began to unbuckle the first horse's girth.

"My father planned it, and some friends helped him build it. My parents lived here for a while before I was born," Marcel replied. He turned to the horse he'd led, and began to take off its bridle. Although his sisters obviously trusted these men who had accompanied them to the cabin, they were strangers to him. He was sure they'd ask questions about why he'd left Montreal so suddenly, and he wondered how much he dared say about his problems. This man, who had come into the barn with him, was a peculiar mixture. He was dressed in doeskins like a trapper and walked like an Indian; but his speech was as refined as that of Vaudreuil, the former governor, while his mannerisms were decidedly not French. Marcel didn't speak again until he'd finished taking off the saddle. Then hoping to learn something about this puzzling stranger, he ventured, "Aimée mentioned that she considered you to be more than a friend?"

Vale turned to regard Marcel. "We love each other," he said. "I believe the same may be true of Mignon and Ben, though they haven't announced that yet."

Marcel was silent a moment as he absorbed this news. "Ben, I presume, is the gentleman with you?"

Realizing that in the excitement no introductions had been made, Vale smiled and put out his hand. "After what I've just told you, you should at least know our names," he said apologetically. "I'm Valjean d'Auvergne. If you hear Aimée or Mignon call me Vale, it's because I grew up in Boston thinking my name was Vale Kendall. Your sisters stayed in Boston for a few weeks before we started to Montreal. Everyone there knows me as Vale Kendall, so Aimée and Mignon have gotten used to the name." At Marcel's obvious confusion Vale quickly added, "Be assured I'm not hiding my identity for any nefarious purpose. I'll be happy to explain everything whenever you wish. The man accompanying us is Benjamin Carleton. He's an attorney by trade, and the Carletons are a highly respected family of Boston shipbuilders."

"The idea of your double name is rather curious, and I would like to learn more about it later," Marcel admitted. Then having silently reminded himself that he was a fugitive through no fault of his own and so shouldn't prejudge Vale, he said, "I suppose my father and mother are concerned about what happened to me."

Vale did not know whether Aimée would want to tell her brother herself what had happened to their parents, or would prefer that Vale give him the sad news. "They aren't in Montreal," he answered evasively. "But Aimée and Mignon, of course, were very worried."

Why hadn't Hilaire and Jeannette accompanied their daughters to Montreal? The question sounded like a warning bell in the back of Marcel's mind. "It's very unlike my father and mother to send Aimée and Mignon on such a long and dangerous journey, especially when they couldn't know what the situation in Montreal would be; so I must conclude they have great confidence in you and Monsieur Carleton." He turned to begin unsaddling a second horse as he added, "Only something very important would cause my parents to decide to remain in Boston. What was it?"

Vale laid aside the second saddle and turned to help Marcel with the remaining horse before he began, "Your mother traveled with us part of the way, but we were attacked by the Iroquois and she was wounded." At Marcel's look of alarm he quickly added, "She was struck in the leg by an arrow. I removed it myself and, with Aimée's help, cleaned the wound. It was obvious your mother couldn't travel the rest of the way with us, so she went to Concord in the coach we'd been using. Benjamin's brother, Paul, and another friend, who had accompanied us, went with her. They're probably all back in Boston by now."

"You're certain my mother is well? You aren't just telling me so? I want to know the truth, monsieur," Marcel warned. Vale nodded solemnly, and Marcel took a deep breath of relief. "This is stunning news, of course. I apologize for behaving so suspiciously toward you. You and Monsieur Carleton have indeed been more than friends to us all."

"Please call me Vale—or Valjean, if you prefer," Vale invited.

Marcel nodded. "You will, of course, call me Marcel." He was silent for a long moment. When he lifted his eyes to meet Vale's, fear shadowed their amber depths. "Vale, there's some reason you haven't mentioned my father. Is he ill? Has anything happened to him?"

Vale looked into eyes that matched Aimée's, and said quietly, "I'm not sure I should—"

"Your hesitance forewarns me of disaster," Marcel interrupted. "I'm ready to hear whatever you must tell me."

Vale laid his hand on Marcel's arm. Remembering from his own experience that there was no way to soften such a blow, he said regretfully, "Your father died in France, Marcel."

Despite his suspicions Marcel discovered he wasn't prepared to hear the words spoken aloud. He paled and turned away. Feeling as if his body couldn't contain the anguish that was pouring into it, wondering if he would explode with grief, he sank down to sit on an overturned basket and put his face in his hands.

Vale waited quietly. Marcel didn't weep; he just sat silent and motionless, his head bowed, looking as vulnerable as a child. Compassion rushed through Vale and he took a step forward to put his hand on Marcel's shoulder and squeeze it.

"I lost an adopted father and mother as well as my real mother, so I know what you're feeling now. Please don't hold back your sorrow because I'm here," Vale said gently.

Marcel remained silent, giving no indication he'd heard Vale or even felt his hand; but finally, overwhelmed with pain, he whispered, "*Mon Dieu, Papa est mort.*" Then he turned to rest his brow on Vale's arm while his grief welled up from deep inside him to tear his breath with wrenching, uncontrollable sobs.

Vale laid an arm around Marcel's shoulder while he waited for this first shock of desolation to pass. He remembered the despair he'd felt when Walking-in-Honor had been killed.

Finally Marcel's sobs lessened, then quieted; and he turned from Vale's arm, wiping his face with his sleeve, trying to regain some semblance of dignity. "How did it happen?" he asked brokenly.

Marcel listened silently as Vale summarized the incident with the mob of peasants on the Versailles road. Then he got to his feet slowly, like an old man weary of living, and said, "Thank you for doing what you could then—and for telling me now. It was better not to renew such unhappy memories for my sisters by leaving them to recount all this and have to witness such an outburst as you've just seen."

"Don't apologize for your feelings, Marcel. I'm familiar enough with grief," Vale replied in genuine sympathy.

Marcel straightened, took a deep breath, and said, "I think I'm ready to rejoin the others now."

When Marcel entered the cabin, Aimée and Mignon saw his reddened eyes and immediately realized why he and Vale had been delayed. They stood up, not knowing what to say in the face of his grief, then finally said nothing. They just hurried to put their arms around him. He lowered his head to brush his lips to the tops of their heads, and whispered, "I don't wish to speak of what happened to Papa just now, *mes soeurs*." He raised his head to note the coffeepot on the hearth. "Aimée, would you be so kind as to serve us a little *café au lait*? I have a cow, so there's a pitcher of fresh milk we can use."

Aimée nodded and, without a word, went to her task. Marcel released Mignon and turned to extend a hand to Benjamin.

"Vale has told me, Monsieur Carleton, something of what you've done for Aimée and Mignon. I owe you a debt nothing can repay," Marcel said.

"Please don't talk about debts and just call me Ben," Benjamin said warmly, taking Marcel's hand firmly in his.

After Benjamin had released him, Marcel sighed and said apologetically, "What a thoughtless host I must seem to you. I'm afraid I haven't yet begun to prepare a meal even for myself."

"That's our good fortune if your cooking compares to the coffee I found in the bottom of that pot," Aimée commented as she poured milk into a pan.

"I'll make dinner," Mignon said. "Just tell me what you have on hand, Marcel."

Later, as the men lingered over their coffee, Aimée and Mignon cleared away the remaining scraps of a ragout they'd managed to assemble from a leftover venison roast and some of the vegetables Marcel had brought from the Dessaline garden.

Mignon took Marcel's plate and commented, "You've gotten thinner since we left Montreal, Marcel. You should have eaten more."

"I have little appetite tonight, *ma petite soeur,* despite the miracle of a meal you made from mere scraps," Marcel replied.

She bent to kiss his cheek. "Of course, you have no appetite tonight, Marcel; but I don't want you to get ill with winter so near—especially if you insist on living in such isolation."

Aimée turned from her task to approach her brother. "Why did you leave Montreal for this cabin? I realize you couldn't stay in our house; but you could have lived at the Hôtel Dieu as we've been doing."

Marcel glanced at his sister, then stared for a long moment at the coffee still in his cup. Finally deciding that he would have to trust both Vale and Benjamin, as it seemed his mother did, he answered, "I'm a fugitive from Colonel Morehead and his men, Aimée."

"A fugitive! Marcel, what happened?" Mignon exclaimed, almost dropping the stack of dishes she was carrying. She put them down and hurried back to the table.

"I admit I have no affection for Colonel Morehead, but why should he pursue you?" Aimée asked fearfully.

"What did you do?" Benjamin inquired in a calmer tone.

Marcel raised eyes blazing with anger. "I committed the

crime of defending my family's property from the thieves Morehead has working under his direction," he snapped.

"Do you mean you tried to prevent the soldiers from confiscating the Dessaline house?" Vale asked. "If that's all, you don't have to worry about being punished—at least not from the reports I've heard."

"I think you could safely return to Montreal, unless you've actually killed someone," Benjamin said. "General Amherst has been very lenient about resisters and seems to be mostly interested in keeping a decent peace."

"If General Amherst wants a decent peace, why is that rogue Morehead in command of Lavaltrie? Have you seen the *pelleterie*?" Marcel demanded. "If any one of them is inclined toward decency, how could Morehead feel free to burn our family's business? I'm lucky to have escaped alive—not only from the fire, but most of all from Morehead's cutthroats."

"Morehead told us the fire was an accident," Vale said thoughtfully. "Are you sure he ordered the *pelleterie* burned?"

"I was standing right beside him when he said it!" Marcel declared. "I wasn't there out of choice either. Two of his men were holding me captive while another was beating me. They were trying to make me tell them where I kept our money."

"*Sainte Marie,*" Mignon whispered.

"I wouldn't put such a thing past him!" Aimée exclaimed.

"Aimée's hated Morehead ever since she discovered that he'd beaten her horse," Benjamin explained.

"That's only one thing I've hated him for," Aimée said angrily. "The second happened yesterday. When Mignon and Ben went out for the afternoon, I decided to go back to the ruins of the *pelleterie* to see if I could learn what Morehead was searching for that day we saw him poking about in the ashes. While I was there, he came by. He'd been drinking, and he insulted me with lewd suggestions. I escaped his hands only by kicking him in the leg, then striking him with my riding crop."

"He tried to molest you?" Benjamin asked in shock.

"Oui."

"Why didn't you say something when I came back to the hotel? You must have just returned," Vale demanded, in his anger getting halfway to his feet.

Aimée turned to look at him and, seeing the crystal lights flashing in his eyes, answered, "I didn't tell you because I knew how you'd feel. I didn't want you to get into any trouble."

"Ma soeur, did he harm you in any way?" Marcel asked concernedly.

"Non, mon frère, unless his kiss carries contagion," Aimée replied. "But I did some damage to him. His hands got the worst of it from my crop or I would have had his eyes. As it is, he will carry my marks for at least a week."

"I'd like to put a few marks on him he'd carry all his life," Vale rasped.

"We should bring these charges to General Gage," Benjamin said solemnly.

"Why would he listen to us? He's probably the man who appointed Morehead to his post," Marcel said contemptuously.

"Not necessarily," Benjamin disagreed. "But Gage is under specific orders from General Amherst to enforce justice. You think he wouldn't hear your complaints because you consider yourself one of the conquered people, but I don't believe this is true. Even if it was, you would have Vale and me to reinforce your charges." He paused for a moment, considering the case he might build against Morehead. "Tell me, Marcel, were those men who beat you soldiers?"

"They were in uniforms, but I must admit I've wondered about them since," Marcel answered slowly. "I've always heard that British officers were very strict about discipline and appearances; but the men I saw were slovenly, actually unshaven and dirty."

"Maybe they weren't really soldiers," Vale suggested. "Perhaps they were only dressed that way; so if anyone came upon the scene, Morehead could pretend he was on an official errand."

"Did you give them the money, Marcel?" Mignon asked hesitantly.

"*Non!* They couldn't get Papa's savings from me!" Marcel declared. "That was why they set fire to the *pelleterie.* They thought, if the money was inside, I would say so before it was destroyed. I remained silent. When the roof fell in, there was such a blaze—with sparks flying everywhere, flames leaping out, they let go of me as they leaped back from it. I ran into the forest. I'd played in that forest when I was a little boy and I know it so well I had no trouble finding a good place to hide, even in the dark. They searched for me all night; but when dawn came, they had to go. I came out and went into the *pelleterie* and got Papa's savings."

"But, Marcel, how could you find anything in that rubble?" Benjamin exclaimed. "You're lucky you didn't fall through the floor!"

"I did fall through the floor, but the cellar was where the money was, and I wasn't hurt in the fall." Marcel paused, remembering how he and his father had so carefully planned for the emergency. It seemed as if that evening had happened in another lifetime. He blinked away the tears that had welled up in his eyes at the memory. "Papa had feared Montreal would be taken while you were in France. It was one of his reasons for going—to keep you and Maman safe." Marcel took a deep breath before continuing. "We converted the paper money to silver and gold and buried it beneath the cellar floor. He told me how to get to this cabin and instructed me to take all I might need from the garden if I foresaw trouble. I did as he'd asked some weeks before Montreal surrendered. That's why this cabin and that barn are so well stocked with supplies."

"Papa would be so proud of all you've done," Mignon whispered through her tears.

Marcel lifted his eyes to look at his sisters. "He would be proud of how you've both come through all this too," he said softly.

Benjamin rubbed his chin thoughtfully. "We should think of a way to get Marcel safely back into Montreal to prefer charges against Morehead," he said slowly. "That man must not be allowed to continue in command of Lavaltrie."

"I'm still not convinced Morehead would dare commit such crimes unless he's sharing his spoils with someone even higher in authority," Marcel insisted.

"If one official is taking bribes, it's possible others are as well," Vale reasoned. "Aimée and Mignon have already said they want to move in with you; so when Ben and I go into Montreal to collect their things, maybe we can learn if anyone else is paying the authorities to close their eyes to wrongdoing." He paused a moment before saying, "I don't like to think of staying at the hotel in Montreal while the three of you are so isolated here. If this cabin were larger, I would suggest Ben and I also move in."

"I don't feel exactly comfortable about being Aimée's and Mignon's only protection. If Morehead should somehow learn about my father's having owned a cabin out here, he might very well send someone after us," Marcel agreed. "There is another cabin just a little more than an hour's walk away. One of Papa's friends used to live in it. It's been deserted for a long time; but I took a walk there one afternoon and it appeared to be intact. I could see that the furniture, which was roughly made and very bulky, had been left behind. If you and Ben would care to live there, I would be grateful for your nearby company."

"That's exactly what we'll do," Ben quickly said. "While Vale and I are in Montreal, we can buy whatever we might need to make that cabin livable until we can decide what to do about Morehead."

Relieved that at least one problem had been resolved, Vale turned his thoughts to a more pleasant subject. He looked at Aimée and Mignon and reminded them, "Now that we've found Marcel, we should send a message to your mother. You'd better write a letter before you go to bed tonight."

"Do you think you'll be able to find a way to get it to Boston?" Aimée asked a little doubtfully.

"I'm sure the blockade has been lifted by now—certainly at least to British ships sailing to Boston. My speaking English without a French accent should convince even a hesitant ship's captain to carry your letter," Vale assured.

"Let me address the letter to my family. No one will think it a message between spies, and no one who might be resentful toward the French will be aroused by a letter sent from an Englishman to his parents in Boston," Benjamin declared.

The cabin consisted only of three rooms: two minute bedchambers and the main room that served as both kitchen and conversation area. After a cursory dusting of the room they would occupy, Aimée and Mignon made up the single bed, which they would share. Vale and Benjamin refused Marcel's offer of his room and insisted on sleeping on the floor near the hearth; so despite the sisters' efforts to make no noise the next morning, the men were awakened early by the tempting aroma of bacon frying, coffee brewing, and pancakes baking. So pleasant a beginning to the day was dampened when they looked out of the heavily frosted windowpanes and discovered it had snowed during the night.

Later, after hitching the horses to the wagon, Vale and Benjamin returned from the barn. The snowfall was too light to cause them problems in their journey to Montreal.

When they were ready to leave, Aimée's and Mignon's good-byes were brief—and cheerfully given, for Marcel had warned repeatedly that Vale and Benjamin must limit their stay in Montreal to a few days. The next snowfall could come at any time, and that one could be heavy enough to prevent the men from returning until the spring thaw.

Colonel Morehead's frown deepened into a scowl as his eyes moved down the lines of the message Major Templeton had just given him. Watching his commanding officer, Templeton lifted a sandy brow briefly, almost imperceptibly—revealing his inner speculation. As a major, he could understand that General Gage's inspection of Lavaltrie district would cause everyone under Morehead's command a certain amount of extra trouble; but he wondered why the colonel was this upset about the announcement. Templeton had always had a penchant for analyzing the motives and personalities of others, but Morehead was a particularly fascinating enigma.

Before Templeton had been assigned to serve under Morehead's command, he had never laid eyes on the man; and after almost a year he still felt as if Morehead were a stranger. Morehead could one moment be as cold and aloof as a hanging judge, and the next clap one on the back and invite him to the pub for a tankard of ale. If a man accepted this invitation, he could find himself with a colonel become as easily a roaring drunk merrily pinching the barmaids' bottoms as a disapproving prig pinch-faced as a Puritan. Morehead rarely accepted invitations to the homes of his married officers, though he always attended the social functions of his superiors; so he had no friends among his own staff, though he appeared to maintain a circle of civilian acquaintances who were mostly of a low order. Like Willie Ugland—a footpad if Templeton had ever seen one. Morehead had commented many times about what an excellent source of information Willie was; and though Templeton knew Morehead wanted him to believe Ugland was merely a peacher, Templeton had a hunch that Willie, like Tommy Millbank, Jake Woolsey, and a few others, was more than an informer.

There wasn't anything in particular that Templeton could single out, yet a combination of seemingly unrelated factors had made him suspicious of Morehead's motives. He was careful never to ask Morehead any pointed questions or make comments that would reveal he was even idly curious and warn Morehead of his distrust. After the so-called accidental fire at the *pelleterie* and the sudden disappearance of the Dessaline man, Templeton's wariness had increased; and ever since the Dessaline daughters' stormy visit, Templeton had noticed that Morehead had become unusually tense.

As a child, Templeton had been teased about his insatiable curiosity; and since he'd grown up, his family had repeatedly joked about his having the instincts of a police investigator; but it was exactly because of these qualities that he'd attained so high a rank at an age at least ten years younger than that of his peers.

Finally Morehead raised his eyes to meet Templeton's and remarked, "One would think the general could be more specific about when he'll visit us. None of us will be able to call a moment our own until he shows up."

"It will be a bother," Templeton blandly agreed, wondering what plans Morehead had made that General Gage's imminent visit might interfere with.

"Ah, well, we'll just have to adjust ourselves to the general's schedule," Morehead said, as if resigned to a necessary nuisance. He leaned back in his chair and directed, "Inform Captain Sharp, Lieutenant Crowell, and Sergeants Mason and Hunter that we'll meet here first thing in the morning to discuss how we're going to tighten up our organization and straighten out the ranks."

"I'll have Corporal Webber tell them immediately, Colonel," Templeton replied.

Morehead shifted a few of the papers spread on his desk. "All sorts of civil complaints here, the usual petty things; but I suppose I must clear them up before the general comes," he said, as if weary of such annoyances.

"Captain Sharp and I could expedite some of them," Templeton said, knowing Morehead kept such cases lying on his desk to maintain a façade of official busyness.

As Templeton had expected, Morehead declined his and Sharp's help, then said, "It's late, Templeton. Why don't you finish whatever you still have to do tonight and go on about your own affairs? A handsome young rake like yourself surely can find something more pleasant to do with an evening than work."

Aware that his being a bit of a coxcomb helped maintain Morehead's impression that he'd gained his rank through charm, social connections, and his father's money put in the right hands—rather than through brains or ability—Templeton allowed the smallest hint of wickedness into his smile as he wished Morehead a pleasant evening.

He had taken only a few steps down the hall when he met Willie Ugland, who scuttled sideways and nodded effusively as he passed on his way to Morehead's office. Templeton wished the Dessalines hadn't used such stout doors even inside their house, making it impossible for him to eavesdrop on what Ugland had to tell Morehead; but he resigned himself to waiting in the shadows outside the house, then following Ugland after he left.

"Blast! You couldn't find that Dessaline whelp until I'm tied up here for possibly another fortnight twiddling my thumbs waiting for Gage to decide to make his inspection!" Morehead exploded.

"If you're going to wait that long, the snow may come; and nobody's going nowhere then," Ugland whined. "Maybe me and Jake and the others should just go to the cabin and take care of things ourselves."

"I could just imagine what a mess you'd make of it if I'm not there," Morehead said contemptuously. "Marcel would escape with the money while your men were busy chasing the girls. You'll wait until I can go with you—or you'll find that I'll set my soldiers after you and your cutthroats with orders to hang you all by the roadside. You know, with Montreal under martial law and my being commander in Lavaltrie district, I can do that, don't you?"

"Aye, Colonel. 'Twas just an idea," Ugland said hastily, though he was aware that one of Morehead's reasons for wanting to go personally to the cabin was the wenches, especially the red-haired one. He added ingratiatingly, "We been making too good profits working together for me to complain now. Just let us know when you can go and we'll be ready."

Morehead smiled coldly at Ugland's capitulation. Willie knew he and his gang of thieves would never have the brains between them to get the kind of loot they'd gathered from the conquered people without Morehead's help—especially if they had to worry about official pursuit.

" 'Tis a chance the general will be done with his business with you before the snow," Willie said placatingly.

"If not, the Dessalines will be as unable to leave that

cabin as we'll be unable to get to them once the blizzards
start," Morehead said slowly.

"That toff, his money, and the wenches'll be there come
spring," Ugland agreed.

Marcel glanced warily up at the gathering clouds as he
trudged through the forest. That first snow had melted the
day after it had fallen, so he had taken Aimée and Mignon to the deserted cabin on his way to inspect his traps.
He smiled, remembering how his sisters had begged to
clean the cabin and surprise Vale and Benjamin when they
returned from Montreal. Both girls had to be in love if
they wanted to take on what Marcel considered the mam-
moth chore of getting that cabin in order, but he'd had to
agree that between the two of them they could accomplish
the job during the several days he'd take to see to his trap
line; after all, they would have little else to do if they remained alone in their own cabin.

Marcel stepped carefully through a welter of half-rotted
logs, then again paused to examine the sky beyond the
naked tree branches. He was thankful the weather had remained relatively clear since Vale and Benjamin had left—
another reason he had agreed to take Aimée and Mignon
to the deserted cabin, but now a storm appeared to be
brewing, and he was anxious to check the bait on the last
of his traps so he could rejoin his sisters and escort them
safely back to their own snug little cabin. The darkness of
the gathering clouds, the shifting of the wind, were sure
signs that the coming snow would be much more than a
mere dusting; and the cabin where he'd left Aimée and
Mignon had only the small supply of logs he'd hurriedly
chopped to last them for the time he'd be gone. If the
storm got too bad and he were forced to take shelter
somewhere, they would be cold and frightened, he knew.
As he neared the area where he'd laid his trap, he began
to whistle to frighten away any predators that might be
lurking close by, as well as to cheer himself.

Skirting a thick clump of fir trees that shivered in the
wind, Marcel half walked, half slid down an embankment
in the rocky gully where the trap lay. He stopped whistling

when he stood over the mechanism, then quickly stooped to examine it more closely. The rabbit he'd used as bait had been mauled. He stood up to scan the area for tracks but could see none between the rocks. It had probably been a lynx that had fled at his coming, he decided. He turned, looking warily at the top of the embankment, fingering his rifle appreciatively. Although lynxes were relatively small, he'd seen some that had brought down deer. They made up for their size with ferocity, becoming fearless, vicious fighters when they thought they had good enough reason; and one such reason could be this rabbit. If a lynx considered it its own prey, it would surely resent giving it up if it were hungry enough.

Finally satisfying himself that the lynx was no longer nearby, Marcel stooped and began hurriedly to reposition the rabbit; if the lynx should return, it wouldn't be able to steal its meal and escape. The long, silky fur of a lynx pelt brought a nice price on the market, Marcel recalled; and if he could get several lynxes, their pelts would make jackets for his sisters. If they stayed with him all winter, they would surely welcome the warmth of such jackets. Pleased with his idea, Marcel smiled to himself, hoping the lynx would return after he'd left.

When Marcel heard the shriek, much like a woman's scream of terror, he could do little more than fling himself to the side and roll away from the cat that had launched itself from the embankment. Marcel's feet were under him when he finished his roll, and he was ready to spring to his feet immediately; but he had only a moment to see the gleam of narrowed eyes, the fangs under curled-back lips, as the cat again leaped at him. He flung out his arms to ward the animal off, to protect his face; but the lynx's momentum threw him backwards against the stones.

Claws like razors worked furiously against his chest and abdomen. The sensation of wet warmth told Marcel that the lynx's hind feet had torn right through his heavy jacket at the same moment that he struggled to keep the cat's fangs from his throat. The lynx's shoulders twisted in Marcel's grasp; and while one set of claws raked his face the cat's fangs ripped into his shoulder. Marcel screamed in pain and, with supreme effort, threw the lynx away from him.

"*Diable!*" Marcel shouted a string of curses so vehement, the startled cat remained where it had landed, its eyes balefully studying the man for a moment.

Marcel took a cautious step toward his rifle. A harsh clank sounded; and a sudden, excruciating pain shot through Marcel. He fell on his side, his ankle caught in the trap, his hand reaching frantically for the rifle before the lynx charged. Again the cat's claws tore at him, its fangs ripping into his flesh. He couldn't reach the rifle. He couldn't shield himself. His hand shot out to grasp the lynx's head, twisting its ear, plunging a finger into its eye. The cat screamed and sprang away.

In the moment it took for the pain-maddened lynx to charge Marcel again, he had pulled his hunting knife from the sheath at his waist; and the cat's own momentum impaled it on the blade. It collapsed, sprawling across Marcel's chest. Marcel pulled out his knife, then angrily pushed the dead lynx away. He took a moment to catch his breath; then wiping away the blood that obscured his vision, he struggled to sit up.

His ankle was broken, he noted, and wondered at his calm acceptance of the injury: was he in a kind of shock? His rifle lay only a short distance away. Suffering the unendurable agony of the trap's metal teeth grinding against his shattered anklebone, as well as his various wounds, he managed to roll onto one side and stretch his arm to grasp the edge of his rifle butt. He worked his fingertips frantically until he finally was able to grip the stock and draw it to him. Then he pushed the barrel tip between the trap's jaws and pried it open. The sight of his lacerated ankle sickened him; but knowing he must somehow get to his feet, he clenched his jaw and made the effort. The pain that tore through him made him cry out, then curse at his own failure. He tried again several times until he could no longer bear his anguish, and lay sprawled across the rocks panting.

Finally, resigned to remaining in the gully, Marcel dragged himself across the stones to gather some branches so he could make a fire. In his pack was the blanket he'd used the night before, a few biscuits, and strips of dried meat. If he wasn't bleeding too badly inside, maybe he could survive until someone found him.

He lit the fire in a place under the embankment that was shielded from the wind, wrapped the blanket around him, and, grating his teeth in pain, huddled against the rocks. As he listened to the wind whistling through the branches above, he prayed that Vale and Benjamin, having realized a storm was coming, had left Montreal that morning. Aimée and Mignon could tell them he'd gone out to check his trap line. Vale, he was certain, would know enough about trap lines to search in the right places. Then tears of despair rose in Marcel's eyes as he suddenly remembered that Aimée and Mignon were in the deserted cabin waiting for him. Even if Vale and Benjamin did come back from Montreal, they had no idea where that cabin was. He wondered how he could have forgotten, even momentarily, where his sisters were.

Marcel lifted his gaze to the sky, mutely begging for a miracle; and a snowflake fell on his face, stinging his lacerated skin.

Chapter 21

"Now that we've taken care of the animals, we can see to ourselves." Aimée panted over the stack of wood she held precariously in both arms.

Mignon threw open the cabin door and stepped aside so her sister could pass. "It's as cold in here as that other cabin was. I feel like one of those desserts—*frappés*, they were called—at King Louis's buffets."

"I'll get a fire started and we'll be warmer soon," Aimée promised, her teeth chattering as she knelt on the hearth to arrange the logs on the grate.

"When I think of Marcel's being out there all night—maybe—maybe he'll . . ." Mignon stopped, overcome with fear.

"As soon as we're warmer we can pack some things we may need when we find him, then we'll go back out. He isn't—I know he isn't dead." Aimée tried to keep the tears from her voice as she forced herself to pronounce the dread word. She watched the little flame she'd lit in a tangle of twigs grow until it reached for a larger log. Satisfied that the fire wouldn't go out, she stood up and turned to Mignon, pulling off her cloak as she continued: "We couldn't possibly search for Marcel dressed this way. We had to come back to see if we could find something more suitable to borrow from his wardrobe, something like what he was wearing to inspect his traps." She dropped her cloak over a chair and rubbed her hands together.

Mignon hurried to Aimée and anxiously took her hands to help warm them with her own. "He was supposed to be back yesterday afternoon! He promised we'd return in time to have our supper here! What would stop him, Aimée? He knew his way in the forest," she cried.

Aimée put her arms comfortingly around her sister. "I don't know, Mignon. Maybe he just found shelter from the storm. Maybe he's at the other cabin right now worrying because we left."

"*Non,* Aimée. He isn't there, and you know it as well as I," Mignon said more quietly. "If he'd been that near the cabin yesterday, he would have continued even through the storm to spend the night with us there. If he was so far away he couldn't get to the cabin, something went wrong. He must have had an accident."

"I wish Vale and Ben were here. They'd know better than we how a trap line is laid out. Vale would know where to look for Marcel." Aimée sighed, then lifted her head and said determinedly, "We'll just have to find Marcel ourselves. I only hope we don't get lost."

"You found our way back to this cabin, but I don't know how. The woods all look the same to me, especially now, with all that new snow," Mignon said.

"At least the sun is shining this morning and we won't have to hunt for Marcel in a blizzard," Aimée said, then added only half jokingly, "Maybe we should take all the ribbons off our petticoats and tie them in the bushes and trees so we can find our way back."

Mignon managed a small smile despite her fears. "Imagine how the forest would look with satin and velvet ribbons hanging in the trees."

"Friendlier, I should think," Aimée commented. She released her sister. "You go through Marcel's clothes and find us some warm breeches and shirts, mittens and heavy boots, if you can. Maybe we can wear our own winter cloaks if we wrap mufflers around our heads under our hoods. Don't forget blankets for Marcel and some brandy to help warm him. Meanwhile I'll make some breakfast for us. We haven't eaten a scrap since noon yesterday and we'll need our energy."

Mignon turned away to go into Marcel's bedroom and do as Aimée had directed. By the time she'd collected the assortment of items, Aimée was filling their plates.

"I've cooked some extra bacon and biscuits and put them by to take with us later," Aimée said over her shoulder as Mignon reached for a cup of steaming coffee even before she sat down.

She was just raising it to her lips when she heard rustling and stamping sounds outside. She lowered the cup, her heart pounding wildly with hope, and turned to see the door open and Benjamin step into the room followed by Vale.

"Vale! Thank God you've returned!" Aimée cried, and ran past Mignon into Vale's arms.

Weeping with joy, Mignon put her cup down with a clatter and threw her arms around Benjamin.

"We started out yesterday morning and would have been back last night, but that storm came faster than we'd anticipated, and we had to find shelter," Vale explained.

"Marcel is still out there somewhere," Aimée said anxiously. "Mignon and I were just going to eat something, then go and search for him ourselves."

"Where did he go—on his trap line?" Vale asked concernedly, releasing her.

"We all went to the other cabin a couple of days ago. Mignon and I wanted to surprise you by cleaning it while you were gone. Marcel left us from there," Aimée said hastily. "He was supposed to come back yesterday afternoon. We waited all night, then came back here to get some other clothes."

"Can you tell us where that cabin is?" Benjamin asked worriedly.

"*Oui*, Aimée can," Mignon answered, stepping back from him. "But your clothes are wet and you must change first."

"While you're dressing I'll make something for your breakfast," Aimée said.

Ready to refuse the food, Vale remembered they hadn't eaten since they'd left Montreal. He nodded agreement.

Later, as they ate a hurried breakfast, Vale asked for directions to the cabin in case the tracks Aimée and Mignon had made in the snow had been drifted over.

Aimée described the route they'd taken using oddly shaped trees and rock formations as guides.

"Did either of you notice which way Marcel went into the forest?" Vale asked after she'd finished. "Trap lines are almost always laid in a more or less circular pattern, and it would help if we knew where Marcel's started."

"Better than that, I can tell you where it was likely to end," Mignon declared. "Marcel told us he would approach the cabin from its rear when he returned. He didn't want us to be frightened by someone entering suddenly through the back door."

"Knowing that will be a great help," Vale said, finishing his coffee. He stood up and hurried to get his coat. "How did your horses manage in the snow?" he asked. "Ours are pretty tired from the trip from Montreal."

"Ours have had a chance to rest," Aimée answered. Then remembering how Brandy had surprised her by obeying Vale when she had first met him in the forest, she added, "Take Brandy if he'll let you. He's strong in the snow even if he doesn't like the cold."

Vale nodded as he finished fastening his coat. Then he came closer to take Aimée's hands and say reassuringly, "We'll find Marcel, *chérie*. Don't worry."

She turned away to give him a bundle. "I've put some food and brandy in this, several blankets in case you have to stay out overnight, and bandages if you need them."

"Let's hope we find him before dark," Vale said slowly, and set the bundle at his feet to take her into his arms.

"You don't have to tell me why," she whispered. "He'll be frozen if he has to stay out there another night—especially if he's hurt and can't move."

Vale nodded reluctantly, kissed her cheek, and turned away.

Aimée and Mignon didn't speak while they watched for the men to come around the house with the horses. When they appeared, Aimée pulled a shawl around her shoulders and opened the door. Brandy, distastefully putting one dainty hoof before the other into the snow, glanced at her as he walked docilely behind Vale. Aimée stepped outside, then hurried through the trampled-down snow to pat her horse's shoulder.

"You be good with Vale," she whispered, hoping Brandy wouldn't give Vale trouble once they were out of sight. She turned to Vale. "Please be careful, *mon amoureux*," she begged.

Vale slid his arms around Aimée and bowed his head so his cheek rested against hers a moment. "Don't worry about us. I won't get lost out there, *chérie*," he said softly. Then he stepped back, pulled his hood over his head, and turned to the horse.

Aimée was relieved that Brandy allowed Vale to mount him without the slightest protest. She lifted her hand to blow Vale a kiss before he turned away. Then she felt Mignon's chilly fingers twine with hers as they stood silently looking after the men until they disappeared into the forest.

Mignon watched Aimée pace restlessly for a while, then decided to get some apples from the cellar to make a pie for supper. This would at least distract her from her worries. Aimée came to help her peel the apples, and they worked in silence, each one caught up in her own thoughts.

Finally Mignon stood up to begin preparing the dough for the crust. "Since it looks like we'll all be staying here in the wilderness for the winter, I was thinking I might tear up a couple of my petticoats and make shirts for the men for Christmas presents. Do you think two petticoats will be enough for three shirts?"

Aimée stared in surprise at her sister. Marcel, after all, might not be alive to need a shirt. Suddenly she realized that that was exactly why Mignon had been planning what she might give their brother for Christmas: she was denying his death. Aimée took a breath and managed to smile encouragingly. "How clever of you to think of it! When you've gotten that pie in the oven, we should measure the shirts Vale and Ben left here."

"Perhaps if you have a wool dress you don't care for

anymore, you could unravel it and knit them stockings or mufflers," Mignon suggested.

Aimée briefly put her arm around her sister's waist. "We can measure stockings too while we're at it," she agreed.

Mignon looked up from the dough she was cutting, and said softly, "We do need something else to think about this morning besides what might have happened to Marcel."

Aimée nodded, her eyes glazed with tears. "I said you were clever, but I was wrong. You're wise, Mignon, wiser than I knew." She wiped her eyes and went on more brightly, "After we've gotten the measurements, we can take our things out of the wagon. Maybe we can have everything put away before they come back home."

Aimée and Mignon went about their tasks more cheerfully than they inwardly felt, yet each tried valiantly to bolster the other's courage with her own seemingly good spirits; but as the sun sank nearer the horizon, their bravado began to sag.

Mignon at last turned to Aimée and asked quietly, "Do you think we should start making supper? If they don't come back tonight, I know I'll have no appetite."

"I have no appetite just thinking that that's becoming a better possibility with every passing hour," Aimée admitted. Gathering up the last shreds of her resolve, she said firmly, "You had the right idea this morning, Mignon. We must hope for the best. What if Marcel merely got lost somehow and needs warming and food? How will all three of them feel if they come back hungry and tired and find nothing to eat?"

"Oui, that's true," Mignon agreed. "I'll put on my cloak and go out to the barn and milk the cow. The poor thing probably is suffering by now anyway."

"In the meanwhile I'll start supper. *Mon Dieu,* what would Maman say if she could see us sitting here doing nothing? She would have had a pot of soup cooking over the hearth since this morning."

The sun had disappeared beyond the trees, and darkness had enfolded the little cabin like a shroud before the sisters were relieved to hear a horse nickering outside. They raced to the door, threw it open, and saw Vale and Ben struggling to take Marcel off the horse he'd ridden.

"Here, Vale, you catch his waist when he comes down," Ben was saying. "I'll take care of that leg from this side."

As Ben moved his leg Marcel gasped with pain, raising his head so the light from the doorway fell on his face.

"Mon pauvre frère! Son visage est sanglant!" Aimée breathed when she saw the blood on his face. She hurried forward. "Can I help somehow?" she begged.

"Just keep the door open," Vale directed.

"Mes soeurs, don't be so frightened. I'll be all right." Marcel panted as Vale folded him over his shoulder.

Vale turned and, carrying Marcel like a sack of flour, walked quickly into the house. Aimée followed Vale into Marcel's bedroom while Mignon ran into the kitchen to fill a basin with the water they'd been heating for coffee.

"We would have been back sooner, but we had to set his ankle before we dared lift him on the horse," Vale explained after putting Marcel on the bed. He turned to Aimée and saw Mignon come into the room carrying the basin. He nodded approvingly and said, "We'll need a lot more water than that to wash him, bandages too. Is there a sheet you can tear up while I undress him?"

"Certainement!" Mignon declared, then put down the basin and ran back out.

Aimée leaned closer to study Marcel's wounds. "What did this?" she whispered.

"A lynx—a big one. You'll see it for yourself. Marcel insisted we bring back its body," Vale replied tensely.

"I thought we might put it to some good use," Marcel said painfully. "The pelt will make fine mittens—something warm for you and Mignon."

"Mittens indeed!" Aimée declared as she gently touched Marcel's clawed cheek. "We'll need more than water to cleanse these wounds so they don't get infected, perhaps some of that brandy," she noted. She lifted away the shreds of Marcel's shirt to look at his chest and, trying not to let her horror show in her expression, added, "Mignon will have some fancy stitching to do, I can see."

"There are others on my stomach," Marcel said. He

tried to smile but failed. "I suppose I'll look like a pirate after all this heals."

"I'll go out to the woodpile and see if I can find something better to splint Marcel's ankle with than these branches we used," Vale advised as he stepped away from the bed.

Aimée bent to kiss Marcel's forehead, the only part of his face that wasn't blood-smeared. Then she turned to follow Vale from the room. Once she was out of Marcel's view, she whispered anxiously, "Was any part of his body frozen? His feet? Toes?"

"No," Vale answered to her relief. "I looked for that immediately. He got caught in his own trap when the lynx attacked. Later he pried the trap open, dragged himself to a hole in the side of the embankment he was near, and built a fire in the hole to heat it. Knowing he didn't have the strength to gather more wood for the fire after it went out, he scraped out the ashes, wrapped himself in his blanket, and crawled into the hole. That's where he was when we found him, huddled in that hole like a chipmunk. He'd even pulled that lynx's body in with him to lay over his feet."

Mignon, who had approached to hear the last of Vale's account, whispered, "Thank God he had the wits to do all that. At least he won't be crippled with frozen feet."

"Gangrene is the killer after frostbite," Vale reminded them. "You should realize his wounds—especially those bites—are pretty deep. I don't know how much damage might have been done inside."

Aimée nodded solemnly. "His muscles are torn. If they don't heal properly, he might be crippled anyway."

Mignon's indrawn breath was audible. She was silent a moment as she digested this news, then finally murmured, "I'll have to try to stitch what I can of them too, I guess." She looked up at Vale. "It's going to be very painful for him. I suppose you and Ben will have to hold him still while I work on him."

Vale shook his head. "Marcel won't have to suffer the way your mother did when we took that arrow out of her leg. I bought some laudanum while Ben and I were in

Montreal. You'll find it as well as some disinfectant in my pack, so you won't have to use up the brandy to clean him."

At that news both Aimée and Mignon threw their arms around Vale out of gratitude that Marcel would be spared that much pain. Surprised at Mignon's impulse, Vale grinned and stepped back. "I'll get that wood to splint his leg, then help Ben with the horses," he said.

When Aimée and Mignon returned to Marcel's side to tell him about the laudanum, he said, "As quietly as you were talking, I overheard you." He took a slow, painful breath. "You can't hide from me what's wrong with my own body, *mes belles*. I knew all that last night when I was lying in that hole trying to stay warm." He reached out to squeeze Mignon's fingers weakly. "Do the best you can with me. I'm just grateful Vale got the laudanum." He released her hand and now looked at Aimée. "If you don't mind, I'd like to have some of that laudanum as soon as possible."

Without another word Aimée went to search hurriedly through Vale's belongings to find the drug.

Later, while Aimée with Vale's help gingerly pulled off Marcel's tattered clothes, Marcel began to say drowsily, "I feel like a child having someone else undress me . . ." His voice trailed off as his body surrendered to the combined effects of exhaustion, blood loss, and the laudanum; and his eyes closed.

Only then did Mignon, watching silently from the doorway with her hands clutching a pile of bandages, finally allow herself to weep. Benjamin took the bandages from her, put them down on a lamp table, and slipped his arm around her waist.

"Do you think you'll be able to bear doing all that sewing on him?" he asked gently.

"I'll do it," she answered resolutely, though tears continued to run down her cheeks.

Aimée dipped a cloth into the disinfectant Vale held out to her, and said, "It will be a job to last the night; but when Mignon gets tired, I'll take the needle."

Aimée's prediction was accurate. She and Mignon alternated stitching Marcel's wounds, each working until her fingers were cramped from holding the needle and her eyes were blurred from strain. Vale stood at hand to wipe away the blood and sponge the wounds with disinfectant, while Benjamin bandaged the areas as they were finished, held the lamp nearer when necessary, and replenished whatever supplies were needed. Dawn finally found all four of them finally trudging off to their respective beds, so weary they hadn't even been able to finish the cups of chocolate that cooled on the kitchen table.

Aimée awakened suddenly, wondering if she'd heard a strange sound or been dreaming. She sat up, noting that there were no shadows on the floor near the window, realizing it must be close to noon. The noise came again—a low, moaning sigh from Marcel's room. Alarmed, Aimée leaped out of bed and, forgetting she wore only her batiste nightgown, ran barefoot into the main room, then around the corner to Marcel's bedside.

Vale, who had already risen and gone outside to get more firewood, returned in time to glimpse Aimée. He hurried to the hearth to put down the load of wood, then, still pulling off his coat, followed her.

Aimée was leaning over Marcel, her hand on his forehead. At Vale's entrance, she glanced over her shoulder and said, "He's feverish."

Vale took one look at Marcel's flushed face, turned, and left. Aimée heard the outside door open and, after a few moments, close before Vale hurried back carrying a bowl heaped with snow.

"I'll get more in a moment," he said, dousing the snow with water from the pitcher on Marcel's washstand.

Aimée needed no directions. She picked up one of the unused bandages, dipped it in the snow water, and, wringing it out, laid it over Marcel's brow. He opened his eyes. They had a hard, unnaturally bright gleam, but he said merely that he had a headache, and thanked her for the cloth.

Despite their efforts Marcel's fever increased; and with each passing hour he became more restless, his movements inhibited only by the pain from his wounds. By nightfall Marcel's entire body seemed afire; and Benjamin took a bedsheet outside to heap it with snow, returning to help Vale spread it around Marcel from chin to toe. Still Marcel's fever raged on; and although no one spoke of his fears, each knew that some contagion in his wounds had spread through his bloodstream, and that they were helpless to do more than try to stop the fever.

Marcel lost consciousness, slipping into a delirium that made him oblivious of the pain from his wounds and broken ankle; and Vale and Benjamin found themselves holding him down so his thrashing wouldn't cause new bleeding or make his broken anklebones grind together and splinter. When dawn finally came, his fever dropped enough so his delirium became a fitful sleep. By the next nightfall again his temperature had begun to soar; but this time it didn't go so high as to make him delirious. For the next two days the fever continued, at sunrise dropping to near normal, and when evening approached rising—but seemingly a little less each night.

On the fourth evening they waited to see how high his temperature would rise that night; but his forehead cooled and was dotted with moisture. Marcel smiled up at them wearily and fell asleep. The fever had broken at last.

All through this crisis Vale and Benjamin had remained with Aimée and Mignon, neither going farther from the cabin than to the woodpile or to the barn to care for the animals. This night was Vale's turn to feed the animals; so he began to put on his coat to go out.

"I need some fresh air. Let me go with you," Aimée said, and hurriedly drew on her cloak.

Although Aimée had felt the need to escape the cabin that had contained her for almost a week, once she stepped outside the door, she didn't pause to enjoy the moonlight or the crisp air but walked rapidly toward the barn. There, with the cozy warmth of the animals, the fresh smell of hay, the sweet nutlike scent of the horses, she felt her anxieties begin to slip away. She helped Vale feed the animals and care for the horses; and Brandy greeted her so affectionately the last of her tension dissipated.

When they were ready to leave the barn, Aimée paused in the doorway and commented, "Brandy needs a run, but there's no fenced-in area here. If I let him loose in the clearing, even though he'd ordinarily come at my call, something in the forest could frighten him. He may run away and get lost."

"If you wish, I could take him out on the *longue rêne* tomorrow," Vale said. "I should do that with all the horses anyway."

"We could do it together," Aimée suggested. "But I'd still like to take care of Brandy myself after I've neglected him so much these last days."

"He's high-spirited like most of his breed. Like you too," Vale said as he closed the door. "You're well suited to each other."

Aimée smiled, turned to walk toward the cliff that lined the riverbank, and Vale followed.

A full moon with the luster of old silver spread its cool radiance over the hushed landscape. Through the shadowy lace of the tree branches stars like diamond dust were sprinkled in the calm black arch of the sky. A silent wind blew softly along the top of the cliffs, causing the powdery snow to rise in shining little swirls, the ice coating the branches clicking softly, as if the trees were talking to the night.

Aimée lifted her head to breathe deeply, absorbing the scent of the luminous air, the sensation of it.

Watching her, Vale said softly, "You're behaving as Brandy would if we'd led him out here."

She glanced at him from the corner of her eye and admitted, "There's part of me that's like him—that is one with him."

"I knew that when I saw you riding him out of the forest that first day. You were like one creature," Vale agreed. His hands on Aimée's shoulders turned her to face him. "I knew then no matter how decorous you appeared on the surface, you had a spirit as wild and free as that horse's. That's what you and he understand in each other.

You both do what's expected of you by the world—what you must do—but that secret part of you is only waiting for its chance to come out, just as Brandy seems to be docilely standing in his stall while he's only waiting to be freed so that he can celebrate his aliveness."

She looked up at him solemnly and said, "That's something I can only do when I'm with him—or with you."

Vale laid his cheek against hers. "It's the way I am too, and that's probably why Brandy allows me to be his friend. But none of us have had the chance to set that part of us free for too long a time."

Aimée sighed. "The cabin is too confining, and we can only go a short distance from it. You and I, like Brandy, can only make the best of the situation and wait out the winter until spring, it seems."

"And when spring comes, we'll return to Montreal to bring charges against Morehead. In the excitement with Marcel, I forgot to mention that when Ben and I were in Montreal, I found nothing to indicate widespread corruption among the authorities," Vale told her. "The government appears to be dispensing justice, except for Morehead's administration in Lavaltrie."

"So when we return to Montreal, we'll prevail upon General Gage or someone on his staff to investigate Morehead," Aimée said.

"It would hardly be just—especially after she's already lost your father—to expect your mother to accept the confiscation of her house and the destruction of the *pelleterie* without hope of being compensated in any way," Vale said.

"After our home has been restored and perhaps some sort of reparation made for the *pelleterie*, what will you do?" Aimée asked slowly. "Are you planning to return to France or to Boston?"

Wanting to know what Aimée personally would choose, Vale answered obliquely, "If you were in my place, if the choice were yours to make with nothing and no one else to consider, what would you do?"

Although Vale had told Aimée he loved her and had even pretended, when it was convenient for their purpose, they were engaged, she reminded herself that he had not yet asked her to marry him. She turned away to look at the frozen river. In the moonlight the ice had taken on the color of the melted heart of a pearl. She decided she couldn't tell him to make a decision that would change his entire future.

"I can't put myself in your place," she finally said. "You'll have to follow your own heart."

Vale was silent for a long moment, thinking of the mountains surrounding the d'Auvergne house he'd visited briefly in southern France when he'd been searching for Simone. The sun had slid off the tiled roof to warm the garden, then slanted into the long narrow windows to touch the wood-paneled walls with light. His thoughts moved on to the Thorntons' house near Boston. He'd told Adam and Sarah Thornton to postpone selling it to anyone else until they had first spoken to him; because if he decided to conclude the sale, he'd meet any other offers they might receive while he was in Montreal.

Leaning closer to kiss Aimée lightly on the forehead, he said, "I am following my own heart—just as I've done since the first time I saw you. Perhaps, if you're having trouble making a decision, we should take Brandy with us to France and see if he likes it."

She looked up at him, startled. "Take Brandy with us . . ." she began.

"I suppose, when I marry you, I'll be adopting him as well," Vale commented. At Aimée's expression the silver flecks in his eyes caught glints of crystal from the moonlight, and he smiled. "I told you before I was too particular about women to fall in love easily. Don't you think now that I've found the woman I can love I would want to make her mine in all ways?" He paused, his smile fading as he added, "Unless, of course, you don't want to marry me."

"Imposssible!" she breathed.

"Then that's one problem we've solved"—he leaned closer to put his lips to hers—"if it ever really needed solving."

He kissed her carefully, trying to control his need for

her, which had been so long denied; but her lips responded
with all the hunger she'd withheld during the past months.
Without his wanting them to, his hands slipped between
the folds of her cloak, seeking the warmth of her nearness.
He was filled with a sweet longing he knew only too well,
and he caressed her possessively. She moved softly against
him, her arms tightening around him until he almost lost
himself in the piquant feelings she always aroused in him.

Abruptly he stepped away. Although his eyes swirled
with gray smoke rising from his inner fire, he said, "I can't
hold you like this, kiss you, want you as I do, knowing all
the while we have to wait at least until spring to do
more."

Aimée bowed her head in thought. She shivered and
hugged herself, trying to ward off the cold air, trying not
to think about what his kiss had reawakened in her. A
rush of warmth ran through her, and she lifted her eyes to
look up at him as she said, "You're right, *mon amoureux.*
Neither of us is made to steal one kiss and part content
with that."

They'd all thought they'd known the degree of Marcel's
illness, but they soon realized they'd underestimated the
effects of the infection's poison on him. It took several
days before he regained enough strength even to sit up in
bed; and then he was pale and drawn from the effort. Because of his weakness and shattered ankle, Vale and Benjamin continued to live in the cabin, only one of them
going out to tend Marcel's trap lines so the other could remain with Aimée and Mignon if they needed help managing their brother. Despite his extreme physical weakness,
Marcel was mentally alert and so spent many long hours
thinking about all the changes recent events would make
in his life. One day he told his sisters he'd decided that
with their father gone he didn't want to rebuild the *pelleterie;* he wanted to use whatever money they had left to
begin some other kind of business. They agreed with his
decision, and Vale gathered up the traps Marcel had made
to store them in the barn. From then on, when Vale and

Benjamin went into the forest, they simply hunted for meat to stock the larder.

One day Vale returned with a bear; and after he'd treated the pelt, he gave it to Marcel along with the lynx skin. Having no privacy in which to prepare surprises, Marcel admitted he wanted to make Christmas gifts for them from the pelts; and Vale gave him some suggestions based on how the Abnakis had made various items from animal skins.

The days fell into a routine, each one going about the tasks he'd volunteered to take up. Marcel became a little stronger, and Vale and Benjamin now carried him— wrapped in a blanket—from his bedroom to spend the evenings talking with them by the fire. They spoke about serious matters, the sorrows they'd all endured; but their talks were lightened by liberal infusions of humor. Benjamin and Vale joked about their adolescence in Boston; the Dessalines teased each other with memories from their childhood. During these evenings they all came to know each other far better than before. While they talked, Benjamin carved a piece of wood he'd brought in; and though they all asked what he was making, he would say nothing until it finally took a clear enough shape that they guessed. It was a crutch for Marcel to use when he was finally strong enough to get out of bed by himself.

There was little for any of them to do outside the cabin, and neither Aimée nor Mignon went farther from the door than the barn or the necessary until Vale asked if they would like to learn how to ice-fish. He and Benjamin cleared the snow from a small area of the frozen river near the shore; and the women, having no appropriate clothes for spending any length of time outside, had to borrow from the men. The effect of their assorted garments produced laughter and teasing: Marcel managed to hobble over to the window and watched as Aimée and Mignon, stumbling in their oversized boots and persistently unrolling cuffs of their too-long breeches, each took tumbles in the snow. They lay helpless laughing at their clumsiness until Vale and Ben helped them up. Then seeing Marcel at the window, his eyes glowing with humor, they exaggerated their problems with the bulky garments as they heaped snow in front of the cabin, sculpting it into a rotund man, who grinned back at Marcel. Vale and Benjamin finally dragged the still laughing girls toward the river to try their luck at the fish.

When Christmas was approaching, both Vale and Benjamin began to forage away from the cabin; and returning after an absence of several hours, they would give no explanation. The girls were mystified by their disappearances because there was no immediate need for them to hunt, as the bear was still supplying them with meals. Although they suspected the men were somehow preparing gifts, they had no idea what such presents might be; but they used the absences to their advantage—Aimée knitting as rapidly as possible while Mignon doggedly stitched the shirts she'd cut from her petticoats.

Vale and Benjamin were gone for the entire day before Christmas; and Marcel and the girls speculated about their purpose, until the two men returned carrying a fat pine tree and set it up in the center of the main room. The ribbons Aimée had previously thought she and Mignon might have to hang in the forest to point their way back had they needed to search for Marcel were now hastily pulled off their petticoats and used as decorations for their Christmas tree. Vale and Benjamin had filled their pockets with various winter berries and seed pods they'd found in the forest, so all five of them joined in stringing them on threads to adorn the tree. Finally, exhausted by the merriment, Marcel went off to bed, leaving the two couples sitting by the fire, tying the last of the mistletoe into bunches to decorate the rafters of the cabin.

Benjamin noticed that Aimée was standing beneath one of the little bouquets, and he caught her by the waist to plant a cheerful kiss on her lips. Observing this, and knowing Benjamin's gesture was only a prelude to kissing Mignon, Vale surprised Mignon by suddenly turning to sweep her off her feet, lifting her small frame till her face was level with his and kissing her laughing mouth before setting her down. As Vale had thought, Benjamin immediately came to take his turn with Mignon; so Vale turned to Aimée.

Feeling shy about kissing Benjamin before Vale and her sister, Mignon glanced up at the mistletoe she stood under, and commented self-consciously, "We've hung so many bunches of this kissing berry it seems there's nowhere in the room a girl can stand without being caught."

"That's why Vale and I gathered so much of it," Benjamin replied, and put his arms around her.

Remembering only too vividly what Vale's kiss could arouse in her, Aimée looked up at him hesitantly.

"This is a very acceptable custom in Boston," Vale said, and smilingly slid his arms around her.

"There is a similar custom in Montreal, but it's observed at the new year," Aimée answered softly.

Vale bent a little closer. "Do you think, *chérie*, that you'd be less affected by my kiss then?" he murmured as he nuzzled her cheek.

"*Non, mon amour*, not even at Christmas a hundred years from now," she whispered.

His lips brushed her skin caressingly as they moved to her mouth, then claimed it. She needed no coaxing. Her arms slid around his waist, her body moving closer. Her lips were soft and ripe for love, warm and silkily moist; and momentarily forgetting the other couple—who, locked in their own embrace, were unaware of them too—Vale lingered over the kiss, nibbling at Aimée's mouth. His heart accelerated as his lips again possessed hers, and a streak of fire raced through him, setting him alight. Only when he heard her soft gasp against his mouth did he release her and step away, his eyes glowing like silver lightning. He took her hand and led her toward the carpet that was spread near the hearth.

At Vale's wordless invitation to sit on the carpet with him, Aimée glanced fearfully back at Mignon and Ben, who stood facing each other, tightly grasping fingers to avoid another embrace that would only prove more tormenting than the last.

"I mean nothing more than to sit close to you, to gaze

into the fire and see among its flames what I dream of doing," Vale said softly.

Aimée sank to the rug beside him; and when he put his arm around her waist, she leaned her head on his shoulder, as he'd suggested, visualizing in the writhing flames how they might have been together. Like Benjamin and Mignon, who had finally found their way to the couch, they were unable to bear the thought of going to their separate beds; and finally both couples fell asleep locked in their sweet but achingly restrained embraces.

Marcel awakened in the morning and hobbled out of his bedroom to find what he'd anticipated: his sisters sleeping on the shoulders of the men they longed for. He smiled sympathetically and, moving as quietly as he was able, took the coffeepot from the cupboard and began to fill it.

Vale's eyes opened immediately; and while Marcel discreetly kept his back to the couple, Vale looked down at Aimée, still wishing the night had been spent as those he remembered on the *Santa Luisa*—or that last night in his cottage when Aimée had come to him after the fire. It seemed as if centuries had passed since they'd been able to love. He sighed regretfully, carefully disengaged himself from Aimée, and, propping several pillows behind her shoulders, stood up.

"It isn't easy, this business of being so close to the woman you love and not being able to do something about it," Marcel said softly as Vale approached.

Vale glanced narrowly at Aimée's brother, then quickly splashed his face with water from a basin. He groped for the towel, felt it being thrust into his hands; and as he dried his face he wondered about Marcel's feelings toward the man who'd sat up with his sister all night, his desire for her impeded only by the presence of others.

"Certainly I wish to see my sisters properly married before they give their innocence to a man—I want this for their own sake—but I can understand how you feel," Marcel said softly when Vale put down the towel. "There was a girl in Montreal before all this happened—Lisolette—whose parents watched me like hawks ready to swoop down on a mouse to insure my proper behavior. And they had good reason to watch me too."

"What happened to you and Lisolette?" Vale asked quietly.

"After all that trouble with Morehead I went to Lisolette's parents, explained what had happened, and asked them to hide me until I could decide what to do." Marcel shrugged his shoulders and sighed. "Once the *pelleterie* had been destroyed and they thought me penniless, not only Lisolette's parents but she herself was less interested in my future, or even whether I had one."

"That's a very difficult situation to face," Vale commented.

"*Oui,* but better to know before a marriage than afterwards, when there's no escape," Marcel answered philosophically. "Since then I've found there were even worse situations I've had to face than the shallowness of a girl. I'm still free to find another, I hope, trucr love."

"What are you two whispering about?" Aimée asked as she approached.

"Love and its many difficulties," Marcel replied.

"Oh," Aimée said, flushing as she remembered how she had so passionately wanted Vale last night, even though her sister was in the same room and her brother only a few steps beyond the doorway.

Noticing Aimée's discomfort, Marcel quickly explained, "I was telling Vale how Lisolette Marais was no longer interested in me once the *pelleterie* had burned."

"You'll find another girl," Aimée assured him.

"I shall try," Marcel answered, as if the possible problems that involved didn't greatly worry him. He handed Aimée the canister of coffee he was holding. "I suspect we'll all enjoy breakfast more, if you'll make the coffee," he quipped, then turned away to hobble back to a chair.

Although the holiday celebration in the little cabin was of necessity simple, it was warmed by the genuine friendship and love that was shared among the five in their varying relationships with each other. The men were delighted with Mignon's exquisitely stitched shirts; and though they had nowhere to use the carefully tailored garments that were obviously meant more for a party in the city than a cabin in the woods, they all put them on for the festivities. The locket that Aimée gave to Mignon matched the cameo Mignon gave her because each had always admired these pieces jewelry in the other's wardrobe.

Vale, Benjamin, and Marcel could readily appreciate the warm stockings and mufflers Aimée had knitted from the fluffy cashmere cape she'd unwoven; and Benjamin and Vale on their part had gifts of doeskin blouses and skirts for the girls and buckskin shirts and moccasins for Marcel and each other, explaining that in one of their long absences from the cabin they'd visited a tribe of Ottawas Vale had discovered, and had traded with them.

Marcel presented the girls with lynx mittens and bear-skin boots, and for the two men he'd fashioned mittens from the bear pelt. Aimée and Mignon thought of all the afternoons he'd spent painstakingly sewing the gifts behind his closed door; and both hugged him so enthusiastically he almost lost his balance on his crutch. Vale had to rush to steady him.

Working together, Aimée and Mignon prepared a Christmas dinner; although it was different from what they might have eaten in either Montreal or Boston, the men all swore that the meal was at least the equal of any Christmas dinner they'd had in the past. They began with a *purée de pois*, followed by a haunch of roast venison, sweet potatoes baked under coals, little onions simmered in cream, beet salad, corn pudding, and crusty bread. For dessert the girls made *crêpes* filled with honey and thickened cream that Benjamin declared were no less than a triumph.

They spent the evening before the fire, sipping what was left of the brandy, roasting chestnuts, and singing carols.

Later, after Marcel and his sisters had gone to bed, Vale and Benjamin lay sleepless before the fire. Both men were still acutely feeling the strain of living in the same cabin with Aimée and Mignon, and so they quietly agreed to move out the next morning.

*   *   *

Vale was assured that Marcel was able to get about on his crutch now that the most precarious stage of his recovery had passed. Still, Vale told Aimée that if they needed help of any kind, whatever the hour, she must ride Brandy to their cabin and let him know. He and Benjamin might not return for several days while they got themselves established in their new quarters; but they promised to stop by as soon as they were able, to make sure all was well. None of them had a clock, so they couldn't plan on marking the arrival of the new year at midnight. Instead the Dessalines invited Vale and Benjamin to come for dinner later on that day.

The excitement of the Christmas celebration had tired Marcel more than he cared to admit even to himself; and although he said nothing to his sisters, he fell into the habit of sleeping later in the mornings during the following week.

Aimée had anticipated that with Vale gone from the house her frustration would be eased; but she found it was not. Loneliness for his company was added to her desire, and her own sleeplessness made her volunteer to get up before sunrise and go out to the barn to tend the animals, a chore that now fell to the Dessalines.

Mignon remained in bed for another couple of hours, then got up to dress and make breakfast; so by the time Aimée returned, bathed, and changed her clothes, all three were ready to sit down at the table together.

The morning of the first day of the year began the same as all those of the previous week. The rooster crowed over the first streaks of pale light on the icy horizon; and Aimée, who had spent the better part of her night restlessly turning, promptly got out of bed to tie back her tousled hair with a ribbon, pull on the bearskin boots Marcel had given her, and put her heaviest cloak over her nightgown. Once in the main room, she took a twig from the lowering fire, lit a lamp, and trudged out the door.

In the still dark sky the moon was a fading sliver. Fingers of pale orange stretching over the cliffs by the river seemed to reach through the violet shadows on the snow and found the path where Aimée walked. The circle of light from her lamp, like a warm bubble enclosing her, was her only guide. The call of a distant wolf ready to give up his night's hunt reverberated through the crisp air; and Aimée paused in her steps to listen as his family answered, while the little puffs of vapor her breath made settled around her hair, frosting her auburn curls as she resumed walking.

She pulled the heavy door open and stepped inside the barn, then turned quickly to reclose the door so the warmth of the animals didn't escape. Her entrance was greeted by the lowing of the cow and the horses' soft nickers.

"Happy year, Brandy, Tonnerre, Bonheur, Soleil," she said to the horses. She paused by the unconcerned cow: "I'll take care of you in a moment, Princesse." Then she shuffled her way past the several cats crowding her feet and turned toward the grain bin.

With Aimée's movement the light from her lamp flickered over a tall shadow near the wagon in the corner. She momentarily froze. The memory of Morehead's creeping up on her at the ruins of the *pelleterie* flashed through her mind. Reminding herself that Morehead didn't know about this cabin, she wondered if an Indian had sought shelter in the barn. Slowly she turned back. "Is someone there?" she asked faintly as she lifted the lamp.

"I'm sorry I frightened you—that's exactly what I wanted to avoid," Vale said as he stepped away from the wagon.

Relieved her visitor was neither Morehead nor an Iroquois, Aimée didn't answer for the moment it took Vale to move soundlessly to her side. Finally she asked, "Why have you come at this hour? Is something wrong?"

"I thought I'd begin my new year with you," he replied. Though his arms hung limply at his sides and he was motionless, his body held a certain tension, like a coiled spring. She looked up, hoping to read something of his thoughts in his eyes; but they were obscured by the shadows falling from the rafters as he added, "You won't have to tend the animals. I've already seen to them."

"You must have left your bed in the middle of the night," she commented.

"I couldn't sleep," he said quietly. "I'd thought, when Ben and I moved to the other cabin, if you weren't just a few steps from me in the next room each night, it would be easier. If I didn't see you all the time during the day, I wouldn't be constantly reminded of how I want you. But it hasn't worked. I want you just as much as before; and added to that, I miss you."

He didn't move as he spoke. He just looked at her; but his tone of voice, the simplicity of his confession, were like a flurry of sparks rising from her ashes to singe her spirit with dots of light.

"It's been the same for me," she admitted. "That's why I said I'd do the morning chores." She tilted her head in inquiry. "And if it had been Mignon who had walked through that door?"

"I'd have been disappointed, but I'd have wished her a year of happiness." He shrugged. "She would have offered me breakfast, and I would have come into the cabin at least to see you." He moved closer and put his hands on her shoulders. "This is the holiday when, I believe you said, according to Montreal custom it's proper for a suitor to kiss the daughter of the house?"

Aimée nodded. "But that isn't usually done in the barn before everyone else has awakened."

"Since the moment we first met, we've had nothing but unusual situations to deal with," Vale said.

"You know the way we always feel, how it will only torment us that much more to turn away after we've kissed," she whispered.

"It wasn't my intention to turn away," Vale said softly.

"But someone might come!" Aimée breathed.

"When Ben awakens and finds me gone, he'll think I went hunting. Even if he thought about anything else, he wouldn't follow me any more than I'd follow him. Mignon won't leave Marcel alone in the cabin with his broken ankle."

Vale reached for the end of the ribbon that bound Aimée's curls; and his fingertips brushed her cheek, sending an airy little tingle through her. She felt the gentle tug that drew her hurriedly made bow loose, and a bright coil of hair fell over her shoulder.

"If this cabin was our own house, if we were properly married and lived here alone, I couldn't promise that I wouldn't do exactly what I'm doing now. Would you object to making love in the hay then?" he asked softly. Seeing the brightening amber lights in her eyes, he concluded, "I thought not." The loose ribbon slipped from her hair, and he wound it loosely around her throat to tie it in a bow, commenting, "Now we won't misplace it."

Again his fingers rested lightly on her shoulders, and he leaned closer to put his cheek against her hair. Inhaling the perfume of her curls, he said quietly, "Do you think I like having to steal a moment of love with you, hiding this way as if what we're doing is shameful? No, Aimée. I'm proud of wanting you, proud that you want me as well. If we were married, I would be happy to have your family, our friends, or neighbors sometimes call on us, only to learn we've latched our door mid-afternoon and guess why."

"Would we do such things?" she whispered, wondering at the passion in him.

She felt his smile against her cheek as he answered, "Not would, Aimée, but *will* when all of this is over." He drew away a little to look at her. His eyes were the soft gray of a cat's as he said, "We haven't been together since that night in my cottage in Boston. I think that's longer than heaven can expect of anyone. To think of continuing our wait until spring, until after all this business in Montreal is settled, is more than I can endure. And you, *chérie*? Could you wait so long?"

She thought of all the lonely days and empty nights that lay ahead, and they seemed as endless as the ocean seen from the *Santa Luisa*. "*Non, mon amour*," she whispered. "I can't bear even the thought of it."

Vale turned away to pick up the lamp; then twining the fingers of his free hand with hers, he led her toward the ladder that climbed up to the loft. She had never been in the loft. Its ceiling was so low, Vale couldn't stand upright without bowing his head. He blew out the lamp, carefully hung it from a rafter, then led her to the far end of the loft where a small window let in the golden beginnings of dawn. He took off his cloak, arranged it carefully over a soft mound of hay, then turned to look at her a moment before reaching out to unfasten her cloak. When he saw that she wore only her nightgown beneath it, he smiled.

"Sit down on my cloak, *chérie.* I'll cover you with yours so you aren't cold until I join you under it."

"What will you do meanwhile?" Aimée asked as she followed his suggestion.

Vale didn't answer but spread her cape over her, then moved to her feet, knelt, and pulled off her boots. She lay back and closed her eyes, inhaling the scent of hay sweetened by clover.

"Your legs are like ice," he commented, and began gently to rub one of her feet in a caress that moved tantalizingly up her thigh.

She felt his lips lazily following his hands as they warmed her; he kissed her newly warm toe, then tucked that leg under her cloak so he could rub the other. There was a long pause when he seemed to do nothing more; but she didn't open her eyes, knowing that even then he must have his purpose. Finally she felt his lips on her ankle, then traveling up her leg to her side; the hem of her nightgown flowed higher until kisses crisscrossed her breasts and his long body lay naked beside her. She looked into his eyes, which had deepened to dark smoke speckled with the light coming through the window.

He lay on his side; and his arm, burrowing under and around her shoulders, turned her to him, drawing her to his chest, his other arm completing the circle of his embrace. He held her close to him as if shielding her from harm—as if the touch of her were so precious he hesitated to move away even to caress her. She clung to him, feeling every contour of his body against hers, glorying in the strength of him, the love in him that made all that he was hers. She wished time could stop with this perfect moment, but she was aware that the light was growing in the window.

As if he'd read her thoughts, he said softly, "I came to make love with you, not merely to ease our frustration; but we have so little time."

She lifted her face from the hollow of his shoulder and offered her lips to him in answer. His mouth took hers gently, carefully, his rounded lips moving softly against hers, playing with her thoughtfully, teasing her until her lips parted and his own covered them, kissing her with a sudden rising of passion that turned her senses into layers of light, as the sun sparkles coming through the window awakened the world to dawn.

His hands, spread like burning stars on her back, slid forward to the sides of her breasts, bunching them against his chest; and his own movements became a caress that made her flesh into cones of fire between them. His leg folded over her hip, curving her to him.

He paused and her clamoring senses quieted so she could hear him whispering of love in a mixture of French, English, and finally lilting Abnaki while his mouth moved over her face, exploring her features as if he had no eyes and learned her identity through the touch of his lips, lingering as he caressed the smooth satin of her forehead, the silk of her hairline, the pulses fluttering at her temples. He traced the outline of her eyes, measured the length and texture of her lashes, and ended again at her mouth, stroking its curve, sensing its opening with his tongue, then possessing it.

His fingers slid down her side, over the mound of her hip, and, spreading against her back, quietly coaxed her to him. His hips moved in deliberate persuasion, giving one sudden little thrust that made her catch her breath.

She opened her eyes to see his face so close to hers that his eyes were but smoky whirls of light. His mouth moved against hers, matching the slow undulations of his hips, sending waves of passion through her; and all the while he watched her steadily through half-closed eyes. The sun became a stream of molten silver that filled her body with heat; crystal sparks flashed along her smoldering nerves, lighting the shadows in her soul; she felt as if all the light in the world, all its warmth, came from the power of his eyes.

Suddenly his body tensed and she trembled with anticipation; but instead of plunging into the emotions sure to explode their senses, he twisted, turning her to her back and swinging over her. As impulsive as his movement seemed, it was carefully calculated not to separate them. She saw his face tighten with desire, his eyes streak with warnings that he was near his limit. Yet he withheld himself, moving with her as if he would explore the very height and breadth of her soul, until she was at the brink of her endurance and sliding ever closer to the edge. She was only vaguely aware of his flattened palms under her shoulders; but just as she was taken by the powerful forces he'd aroused in her, abruptly he lifted her toward him, curling her body up against his. A bolt of silver fire seemed to explode in her, igniting even the breath he drove from her lungs, her own senses so shocking her with their intensity that her mind slipped into another dimension of shifting lights and fiery fading shadows.

Aimée lay against Vale's chest, trying to catch her breath. One of his hands left her back to grope for the cloak that had been swept aside. When she felt its soft folds settle warmly around her moist body, she opened her eyes to gaze up at him in awe. His arm again encircled her, and he dipped his head to look at her. His hand lifted to cup the back of her head, his fingers gently stroking her hair.

There was nothing left to tell her in words. He just held her closer as he gazed through the window at the awakening day, thinking the sweetness of this wild little wind in his arms had charged him with a love that must prevail over anything that would threaten it; for without her he knew he had no life.

Chapter 22

The river seemed as if, impatient to complete its freedom, it deliberately rushed around and over the ice slabs floating on it, forcing them to grind themselves smaller while the currents drove them toward oblivion. Aimée, standing on the riverbank, wondered if Marcel realized how much the river had thawed in the last few days, or if he was too excited about the arrival of Vale and Benjamin that afternoon to take off the splint he'd worn to brace his ankle all these months.

Vale had already removed it once, then replaced it because Marcel's ankle had still been too weak. The bones had knitted together, but Vale had feared he'd turn it and break it again. If Marcel's ankle was finally strong enough, now that the deepest snow had already melted, making it possible to travel through the forest again, they would soon go back to Montreal.

Aimée was anxious to return because Morehead's conviction would restore the Dessaline properties to them, but she anticipated the process would be neither simple nor promptly completed. Afterwards they would take a ship to Boston to get Jeannette and return her to Montreal, covering the distance in less time than they'd taken to travel overland when the Saint Lawrence had been blockaded. Aimée estimated that she and Vale wouldn't be able to get married until autumn. All the activities in Montreal and Boston weren't likely to afford them any privacy, she thought, remembering how seldom they'd even been able to steal an hour for love since the year had begun. Although they'd met several times in the hayloft at dawn, they'd had to limit these occasions lest Benjamin become suspicious of Vale's disappearance, or Marcel wonder why, so often when Vale accompanied her into the cabin for breakfast, Aimée's chores seemed to have taken so long.

Should she persuade Vale to marry her in Montreal immediately upon their return, despite her mother's absence? Aimée wondered as she turned to start her climb up the cliff.

The rocky path, dangerously steep at midsummer, was now so treacherous with icy patches that she had to concentrate all her attention on her climb; so she didn't hear the hoofbeats stopping at the cabin. Near the top she almost lost her footing when she looked up to discover the crooked face that leered down at her from over the lip of the cliff.

"Willie Ugland at your service, miss, whether you like it or not," the man said, extending a grimy hand to grip her wrist.

He pulled Aimée over the top of the cliff so roughly her momentum sent her sprawling. As she got to her hands and knees, she was additionally horrified to see another of the men who had broken into the room at Le Mouton Noir. He was standing nearby grinning at her.

"This here is Jake Woolsey, another admirer of yours, who came with your old friend Colonel Morehead for a visit," Ugland said as he took Aimée's arm to jerk her to her feet.

Aimée glanced at Woolsey as Ugland pushed her toward the cabin, saying nothing as she absorbed this information. She did not stop to think how Morehead had learned of the cabin's existence. She was too shocked, too terrified at their presence to think of anything other than their purpose: to take the gold Marcel had brought from Montreal and silence all three Dessalines forever.

Ugland's hand on her back sent her flying through the cabin door with such force she stumbled against a third man, whose grin displayed a set of snaggled, yellow teeth, as pointed as fangs.

"You're right, Willie, the vixens both are as pretty as you said. Wish I'd known that night at Le Mouton Noir." Aimée quickly began to step back; but his arm suddenly enclosed her waist, locking her body against him as he added, "Would have visited that room myself."

"That's enough, Millbank," came a familiar voice.

The man with the yellow teeth released Aimée, and she hurriedly backed away to turn and face Morehead. The colonel had replaced his bright scarlet uniform with civilian clothes as drably anonymous as the others', though he at least was clean.

"Mr. Millbank's mention of the inn reminds me of your fiancés," Morehead commented. "It was they who intervened that night at Le Mouton Noir, I take it. Where are they?"

Aimée's first impulse was to scream that Vale and Benjamin were coming soon and would tear Morehead to pieces if he harmed her or Mignon, but she realized that Morehead would only prepare a trap for them; so she said, "They had to return to Montreal before that first blizzard came, and I suppose they haven't been able to come back yet." The hesitance in her answer gave it just the element of doubtfulness she wished.

Morehead was silent a moment, then turned to regard Mignon and Marcel, who stood tensely near the kitchen table watched by two other men. "I would have thought such devoted gallants as they'd seemed would have braved the snowdrifts to return—unless the ladies were regarded not as fiancées but as mere *amourettes*," he said smugly. "It appears to me, mesdemoiselles, that you've been misled."

"I don't believe that," Aimée quickly retorted, but she lowered her eyes as if she too had her own doubts.

Morehead came closer to put his fingers under her chin and tilt her face to his. Unable to mask the revulsion in her eyes, Aimée pulled away; but he only smiled at her reaction. He noticed Aimèe's eyes flick over Marcel's rifle hanging beside the door, and he nodded sideways toward Woolsey, who picked up the weapon to cradle it possessively in his arms.

"Really, Aimèe, your face is so expressive as to make your thoughts transparent to me," Morehead commented, then turned to stroll toward Marcel.

More lightly than the other men could guess, Marcel was leaning on the crutch he no longer needed. He had really caught it up to use as a weapon when the men had burst into the cabin; and when he'd seen their guns leveled on him and Mignon, he'd pretended merely to get to his feet with the crutch's aid. After Mignon had seen Marcel deliberately disguising the extent of his injury, and heard Aimée's lies about Vale and Benjamin, she decided to add to the deception.

She quickly stepped forward to stand in front of her brother, crying, "Leave Marcel alone! Can't you see he has a broken ankle?"

Morehead paused in his approach. "Indeed I can, which should make my men's task that much easier if they have to break it again to get the answers I wish," he said coldly, pushing Mignon roughly aside.

Marcel, making a show of standing on one foot, lifted his crutch, intending to break open Morehead's skull if he could. The two men flanking him immediately caught his arms, dragging them behind his back, the crutch clattering uselessly to the hearthstones. Morehead faced Marcel seemingly as unperturbed as before, though when he lifted his finger to trace the scars the lynx had left on Marcel's cheek, his eyes gleamed as keenly blue as the edge of a sword.

"A lynx attacked him in the forest! That's how he broke his ankle! Hasn't he suffered enough without your adding to it?" Mignon screamed as she struggled with the man who had caught her around the waist and pulled her back against him.

Ignoring Mignon as if she hadn't made a sound, Morehead continued to peer at Marcel's scarred cheek, commenting, "These marks give a suggestion of wickedness to your face. Should be quite popular with the ladies, I'd think. Women seem to be attracted to men who appear a little dangerous. I've seen them flock around men who were actually quite plain, simply because they'd acquired a scar in a rapier duel."

"There's no point in my thinking about what effect I'll

have on women, because you'll never let me return to Montreal after this," Marcel said grimly.

"Not Montreal, of course, but I might consider putting you on a ship bound for the Indies—if you answer my questions without causing us further trouble," Morehead replied. Remembering now that Major Templeton had command of his office while he was gone, he added, "It is, after all, almost a full day's ride here, another back; and I can't be away from my post too long."

"What about my sisters?" Marcel asked warily.

"They would accompany you."

Marcel suddenly realized Morehead's intention. His face drained of color, and his lips parted in shock. "*Mon Dieu,* you're talking about a filthy slave ship!" he exclaimed. "You mean to sell us to some West Indian trader!"

Morehead nodded. "At least you'd be alive and have a chance to escape—or possibly you could find some way to buy your freedom. I should think that would be preferable to being tortured until you tell me what I want to know anyway. In that event I wouldn't bother smuggling your sisters aboard a ship. I'd just give them to the Iroquois—as a token of my friendship with them, you know."

Marcel's eyes narrowed and darkened with fury. "*Diable,*" he said softly. Reminding himself that Vale and Benjamin were on their way, wondering how long he could endure whatever torture Morehead's men might inflict on him—if he could buy enough time for Aimée and Mignon—he said contemptuously, "I'll tell you nothing."

Morehead had been so confident Marcel would agree to his proposal that for a moment he couldn't believe his ears. Rage flooded him, and he lost his composure. He viciously kicked Marcel's splinted ankle and said tightly, "I won't have the time to use the more refined methods I'd like, and prolong your torture. I'll just have to let Zack at you."

Marcel bent forward in pain, and the shaggy bear of a man who had sat hunched in a corner now got to his feet to approach him. The man's lips parted in a dingy smile in the moment before his fist crashed into Marcel's midriff. Marcel gasped and doubled up only to see the same fist swinging up in front of his face. A blinding light seemed to flash in Marcel's eyes as his head snapped back from the blow to his chin.

Aimée gasped in horror when Zack took a handful of her brother's hair to hold his head up so he could hit him again. Blood was trickling from the corner of Marcel's mouth. She stooped to snatch up the discarded crutch and darted forward wielding it like a cudgel. The crooked-faced man called Willie ducked under the crutch to twist one of her arms behind her back until she thought he'd tear it loose. She cried out in pain and dropped the crutch.

"Sacrée mère du Dieu! Marcel, tell them where you hid the gold!" Mignon cried.

"Yes, do tell us, Marcel," Morehead said as if the entire proceedings were beginning to bore him.

Marcel slowly shook his head, and Zack resumed pummeling him. It wasn't so bad, Marcel was thinking groggily. After Zack's last blow to his head, he was so close to unconsciousness he hardly felt anything more. It wasn't nearly as painful as that lynx's bites—or Vale's setting his ankle—he decided, half in a stupor.

Morehead's voice seemed to come faintly, as if from a great distance, as he ordered, "Horton, Melvin, let him drop!"

Marcel assumed Morehead meant him, but he didn't feel his body hit the floor. Zack's kicks were like little taps absorbed by the layer of fog that seemed to surround him. Someone dashed water over him, but he hadn't the energy to react immediately. He just lay quietly until the water dripped off his lashes, then he opened his eyes to realize his vision was blurred by blood as well as water.

"Throw another pitcher of water on him, Woolsey. I want him to understand exactly what I'm going to say next," Morehead directed.

Again water splashed over Marcel's head, flooding his nose. He coughed himself back to consciousness, then rolled over on his side and slowly pulled himself up on one elbow to gaze unsteadily at Morehead, who squatted beside him.

"Can you hear me?" Morehead inquired. Noting Marcel's faint nod, he said, "Something quite important to you hangs on your decision, Marcel. Are you certain you understand what I'm saying?"

Marcel struggled to a sitting position and gingerly wiped the water and blood from his eyes. Again he looked at Morehead as he answered disdainfully, *"Oui, salaud,* I understand you."

"Even if you think you care more about that money than about yourself, perhaps I can suggest something you hold dearer than either," Morehead said softly. "Did you previously notice the attraction your sister, Aimée, seems to hold for Mr. Ugland? Mr. Ugland, in case all these names confuse you, is that gentleman with the lopsided face who's holding Aimée now. Or did you happen to take note of Zack's equally avid interest in Mignon?" At Marcel's increasing pallor Morehead continued, "Zack needs a rest from this tiresome business and I'm considering suggesting he amuse himself with Mignon. Zack, as you might guess, isn't particularly modest, and the matter would go as far as I allow it."

Marcel's eyes widened in renewed shock. "You would have him beat my sister?"

"Not at all," Morehead replied. He lifted his head to regard the bearish man who earlier had beat him. "Give Marcel a sample of what I mean, Zack—just a sample, mind."

Before Marcel could speak, Zack caught Mignon by the arm; and lowering himself to the floor, he dragged her down beside him, pinning both her arms with one of his beefy hands. She let out a little cry of disgust as Zack threw one leg over hers and, tearing open her bodice with his free hand, began to fondle her before them all. Mignon's wide, hyacinth-colored eyes turned to look helplessly at her brother as she tried to squirm away, making little whimpers like a trapped puppy.

Afraid to move too quickly lest Morehead or one of his henchmen guess his purpose, still seeming to watch fixedly as Zack clumsily caressed his sister, Marcel rose to one knee. Suddenly he leaped to his feet, simultaneously twisting to catch the lamp that was standing at the edge of the kitchen table. He dashed the lamp against Zack's broad back; oil splashed in a fiery pool between his shoulders, running in burning rivulets along his buttocks.

Roaring in pain, Zack sprang away from Mignon to dash around the room like a blind animal, igniting everything flammable he passed.

Marcel leaped at Morehead, but Woolsey had picked up the discarded crutch. The first swing caught Marcel's side and deflected his attack; but when Woolsey lifted the crutch over Marcel's head and brought it down with a crash, Marcel dropped where he stood.

"All of you tear this cabin apart before that fire gets worse!" shouted Morehead. "Find that gold!" He drew his pistol and, carefully aiming at Zack, shot the burning man, who fell over the back of the couch. A curl of smoke immediately rose from the cushions.

Mignon and Aimée had thrown themselves down beside Marcel's inert body wailing that he was dead, though they both knew he was merely unconscious and lay on a rug that concealed a trapdoor to the cellar. One of the rooms below extended past the wall of the cabin and would be safe even if the cabin burned to the ground. If he could regain his senses without Morehead's seeing him, he might be spared even if they weren't.

Aimée looked up at Morehead and cried, "If I tell you where I suspect Marcel hid the money, will you just leave us alone?"

Morehead's eyes glittered with avarice, but he said, "So you can run back to the authorities?"

"How would we do that if you took our horses? We'd be alone in this forest now that Marcel is dead," she lied through her tears.

"Where do you think it is?" Morehead demanded.

"Marcel spent a lot of time in the barn before he broke his ankle. Maybe it's buried in there." Aimée sobbed, then returned her attention to Marcel.

Mignon's cheek was pressed to Marcel's back, but her fingers were stealthily pinching his cheek trying to rouse him as she added, "Maybe under the loose chinking between the logs!"

"We'll see about that," Morehead said, taking Mignon's arm to pull her away from Marcel. "Willie!" he snapped over his shoulder.

The man with the crooked face caught Aimée under the shoulders, pulled her away from Marcel, and dragged her backwards toward the door. Aimée didn't want to leave Marcel unconscious in the burning cabin but dared not let Morehead know it. Hoping Ugland would get disgusted with her seeming hysteria and drop her, she raked his arms with her nails, screamed and thrashed around, and struggled to catch her foot around a piece of furniture. But he doggedly hauled her after him. Just before he heaved her over the threshold she saw Marcel's foot move—only a little, but just enough to give her hope.

Once outside, determined to distract her captors from any further movements in the cabin, Aimée struggled to her feet; but Willie held her as securely as before, and she couldn't break free.

"Woolsey, Melvin, Horton! Search through that barn before it catches fire too," Morehead ordered. "Millbank, get those horses out of there! Put them in that paddock!" He pointed at the enclosure Vale and Benjamin had only recently erected.

Millbank ran into the barn and came out moments later with Brandy, who fought him at every step, rearing high enough to take Millbank off his feet, pulling back against the bit with a force that Aimée knew was tearing his sensitive mouth.

"Gawd, Colonel, this one's a devil!" Millbank shouted over his shoulder.

"Get over there and calm that horse down." Morehead pushed Aimée toward Brandy.

She didn't need a second order. She ran to brush Millbank aside, throwing her arms around the horse's neck, pressing herself against his chest. Brandy suddenly stood still—as if his legs had turned to stone—not wanting to hurt his mistress; but he kept his head high, his eyes flashing with anger at the strangers. Aimée slid her hands up his neck, her fingers talking to him in a language only the two of them understood; and he lowered his head to allow her to unbuckle his throatlatch. When she raised her hand to the top of his head, seemingly to soothe him, her fingers dug under his mane behind his ears to locate his crown piece. Then suddenly jerking it over his ears, she freed him from the bridle.

"*Va-t'en! Va-t'en, mon ami!*" she cried, and slapped Brandy smartly on his hip.

Stunned that she'd struck him, he raced away; but at the edge of the clearing he whirled around and stopped, looking back at Aimée as if wondering if it had indeed been his gentle mistress who'd slapped him.

"Blasted beast," Millbank said, and raised his pistol.

Aimée threw herself against him so his shot went harmlessly into the air. At the sound of the gunfire Brandy wheeled around and disappeared into the cover of the trees. Aimée sighed with relief, knowing that if she survived this day, her call would bring him back to her.

A roaring, tearing, squealing noise made Aimée and Mignon rigid with fear. They both turned stiffly to stare at the cabin's roof crashing down into the flames.

Mignon screamed, "Marcel! *Mon frère, mon frère!*"

"He's dead anyway," Ugland snarled as he hurried out of the barn to Morehead's side. "The wall attached to the house is gone, and the hay has caught!" he exclaimed. "We ain't looking in there no more. I don't want to be a roasted goose no matter how much gold is in there. No siree."

"At least we've silenced Mr. Dessaline," Morehead said, looking at Aimée and Mignon, who, after hugging each other consolingly, had sunk to their knees, tears continuing to stream down their faces as they crossed themselves. "We still can sell them to that slave ship. A couple of pretty virgins like that will bring a nice price."

"Virgins! I thought we was going to have a little fun with them!" Willie exclaimed.

"Back at Lavaltrie you can waylay one of them farm girls going to milk the cows now that spring has come," Woolsey said as he approached. "I'm for getting these two on the ship in the same condition they're in now."

"Then again, I suspect we'd be doing ourselves an even

bigger favor if we took them both to Stalking Bear," Morehead said thoughtfully. At the other men's rising protests he reminded them, "We have a little task for him and his renegades to do, if you remember. Handing him a pair of white-skinned virgins would make him agree to anything I ask."

" 'Tis a shame that an Iroquois should get those girls," Millbank said regretfully. "Ruin them he will. A month from now no one will be able to recognize them."

"Aye, but think of how happy he'll be with their red and yellow scalps to display after he's tired of them," Ugland said.

"Get them up and we'll bundle them off," Morehead ordered.

Still staring at the flames roaring through the top of the roofless cabin, Aimée prayed that Marcel had escaped. If he hadn't, then she hoped he hadn't regained consciousness before death had taken him, and had been spared at least that much pain. She remembered how he'd looked, scarred and bloody, beaten because he'd hoped his silence would buy them time. She bowed her head, burying her face in her fingers as she wept. She was so immersed in her grief she didn't even notice Willie Ugland's hand on her shoulder urging her to get up. Finally he gripped her arm and dragged her to her feet.

"Can't I even pray for my brother, you murderer?" she spat.

"Pray for yourself. You're going to need it more," Willie said slyly.

"What do you mean?" Aimée demanded, trying to twist out of his grasp. "What more can you do to us?" Seeing his leer and misunderstanding, she stamped her foot in hopeless rage.

"Ain't me who's going to get you," Willie said regretfully. "Morehead's got you and your sister in mind as a present to an Iroquois buck."

"Dieu! Mon Dieu!" Aimée moaned in horror. "I'd rather die!"

"Don't blame you," Willie agreed. "But you ain't going to have a choice. Not you nor your sister. She's going now with Millbank and Woolsey." Willie twisted Aimée around, meaning to drag her to one of the horses.

Aimée stared after Mignon, who was walking with bowed head between the two men, as docile as if she had given up all hope and resigned herself to her fate. "Mignon, *ma soeur!*" Aimée cried.

Mignon lifted her head, glanced back over her shoulder, tears streaming down her face; then she quickly looked away as Millbank's hand on her derrière pushed her forward.

Willie's grip on Aimée's shoulder had temporarily lightened when he saw Millbank's hand on Mignon's buttocks, and in that moment Aimée made her decision.

She wrenched her shoulder from under his hand, spun around, and darted away. She didn't head for the forest as Brandy had done. She knew she would never get that far before one of the men caught her. She raced straight toward the cliffs, as she ran begging heavenly forgiveness for taking her own life.

Poised at the edge of the steepest slope, she gazed down for a moment at the rushing water that churned with chunks of ice and whispered, "Vale, *mon amoureux,* I can't let any of them possess me after you." Then she stepped out into space.

Chapter 23

When a shoe came loose on Benjamin's horse, he had to pause to pry it off; and it was then that he suggested that Vale go ahead. He would follow in a few minutes, though more slowly. Vale's mount was too excited by the touch of spring in the air to wait patiently, then afterwards walk as sedately as Benjamin's would. Vale felt restless too, and he welcomed the brisker pace as his horse trotted lightly along the forest path.

The soft breeze was blowing away from Vale, so he didn't smell the smoke from Marcel's burning cabin. He had no idea anything was wrong until he saw flickering orange lights reflected on the snow ahead. His horse saw it at the same time that the breeze shifted, bringing the alarming odor of smoke. The frightened animal came to an abrupt stop, hurriedly backed away a few steps, and, when Vale's knees urged it on, half reared and tried to turn. Vale gave its sides a sharp nudge, and it went forward in a fast canter.

A moment later Vale, peering through the distance, saw between the thinning trees that the barn was on fire; but he couldn't see the cabin or the men and horses preparing to leave at the other side of the cabin.

Silhouetted against the flames were the figures of a girl and a man running toward the rear of the buildings. The girl ran past the barn, her streaming hair becoming a bright banner in the sun; and Vale recognized Aimée. He wondered why she and Marcel were running toward the river when the water pump was in the cabin. Suddenly he realized that Marcel had auburn hair like Aimée's, and the man following her had straggling brown hair. He was a stranger, and Aimée wasn't merely hurrying. She was fleeing! Aghast, Vale kicked his horse's sides, and it leaped forward into a gallop.

When Aimée came to the edge of the cliff and stood poised for an instant, Vale's heart stopped. When she leaped, his heart began pounding like thunder, and he turned his horse to race recklessly through the forest toward the path he knew led down the steep slope. Praying that Aimée had survived the fall, that she wouldn't be crushed by the grinding ice in the river or slip under one of the floes so he couldn't find her, he threw himself from the saddle before the horse had even stopped.

Leaping over the edge, slipping on ice patches, and dislodging little stones that showered before him, Vale recklessly bounded and slithered down the path. He glanced up before he was halfway to the bottom, saw a place where the river's surface was temporarily clear of ice, and then dove.

The shock of the frigid water made him gasp, stunning his muscles with a sharp pain that almost paralyzed him; but he fought his way back to the surface, shook the water from his eyes, and located Aimée's bright hair floating like a fiery stream between the chunks of ice. If she knew how to swim, she wasn't trying. He knew she was either dead or unconscious from the fall—or she wanted that much to die. His heart constricted with additional fear. She was drifting closer to the flow's center, and there was a swiftly running current at the middle of the river that was treacherous enough even without the jagged ice shards that now filled it. He dipped over on his side to swim with powerful strokes toward her, his legs pumping steadily despite the numbing cold.

A passing ice floe struck Aimée's hip, spinning her around; and Vale caught a glimpse of her eyes turned toward him. Recognizing him, she suddenly began kicking, her arms finally fighting the current that now churned around her. He opened his mouth to call encouragement, but an icy wave hit him, filling his throat with frigid, stinging water, taking away his breath, making his strokes falter while he choked. Feeling as if he were smothering, still coughing, he forced himself to resume swimming toward her.

His fingers reached out, brushed, then grasped Aimée's; and with her pumping legs added to his kicks, she paddling with one arm as determinedly as he, they turned and together struggled against the current, straining every muscle as the waves buffeted them. When Vale's toes could at last brush the bottom, he stood up, dragging Aimée erect beside him, pulling her stumbling and gasping toward the bank.

They crawled on their hands and knees from the water, the cold air hitting their wet clothes like a wall, then fell exhausted and winded on the rocky shore. Still holding hands, staring into each other's eyes, surprised that they'd managed to get to the riverbank, they lay gasping for breath. When Vale's hammering heart finally slowed, he dragged himself up to sit with his arms around Aimée.

"M-m-m-mignon . . . Morehead's g-g-g-got her!" Aimée stuttered, her teeth chattering so hard she could barely speak at all. "G-g-g-giving her t-t-t-to an Iroquois!" She clutched at his shoulders, frantically trying to stand up. "M-m-m-marcel in c-c-c-cabin! B-b-b-burned!" She gasped, then fell limply against his chest.

Just as Vale hadn't been able to see the horsemen at the other side of the cabin, he too had been concealed from their view when he'd ridden along the edge of the forest. Willie Ugland, intent on pursuing Aimée, hadn't even glimpsed Vale, who'd been some distance downriver when he'd leaped off his horse to scramble down the cliff path.

One glance over the edge of the precipice at the icy, rushing water far below made Willie shake his head in disgust and turn away.

When Morehead, already in his saddle, saw Ugland alone come around the corner of the burning building, his face darkened with fresh anger. "You let her get away?" he exploded.

"Jumped off the cliff," Willie said tersely.

Hearing this, Mignon broke free from Millbank's grasp

and ran to Morehead to claw at his leg. "You have to help her! Get a rope and pull her out! Save her!" she cried.

Morehead looked at Ugland and demanded, "Do you think there's a chance she's still alive?"

Willie shook his head. "I saw her hit the water and go under," he said grimly. "When she came back up, she wasn't swimming."

"Non, non, non! You have to help her! You have to try!" Mignon screamed.

Millbank approached Mignon to pull her away from Morehead's horse. "Even if she didn't crush her skull on that ice, the current's too fast for us to save her," he said.

"She's been ground up by the ice slabs by now," Willie added.

"One fancy gentleman and two helpless girls—should be easy to get their money, I'd thought; but no matter what we do, it turns around on us," Millbank said wonderingly. "Burn the business and the brother gets away. Beat the brother and he gets killed so we can never find out where the money is. Take the sisters and one jumps in the river and the other's half crazy." He looked at Morehead. "Be lucky if Stalking Bear will take this one off our hands. Whole family is a jinx."

"I never seen the likes of it," Ugland agreed. "Good thing there aren't more of these Dessalines. Get us hanged yet."

Woolsey, who had been standing a few feet away listening, mounted his horse as he commented, "I say forget the money and save us the trouble of dragging this one back just to roll up in Stalking Bear's blanket. Throw her in the river after the other one and forget the whole thing."

Morehead looked down at Mignon as if he were seriously considering the suggestion for a moment. Finally he said, "You'd best behave yourself, mademoiselle, or I'll let them do whatever they want to with you."

Mignon had been staring up at him, but she was so shocked that no attempt would be made to help Aimée, she never even heard the threat. Thinking of Aimée crushed by the ice, of Marcel probably already consumed

by the fire, she made a little sound, half sob, half sigh, and
collapsed at Millbank's feet.

Morehead pointed at Mignon with his riding crop and
said coldly, "Get her up on your horse, Jake. We'll keep
her in the cellar at Le Mouton Noir until we can learn
where Stalking Bear's camp is now."

"I hope it doesn't take too long to find that renegade,"
Woolsey said as he bent to pick up Mignon. He slung her
over the front of his saddle like a sack of flour, adding,
"Every day we'll have to spend guarding her I'll be wondering what new trouble she's going to cause us."

"Dark Otter is almost always loitering around the inn
hoping someone will buy him a drink. If he doesn't know
now where Stalking Bear and his men are, he can soon
find out," Morehead said.

"Not fast enough for me," Woolsey muttered, swinging
up into his saddle.

As Benjamin led his horse to the clearing, he was too
stunned by the sight of the smoking ruins of Marcel's
cabin and barn to do more than take a few faltering steps
closer.

"Ben! Ben, help me!"

Benjamin whirled around to see Vale struggling over the
lip of the cliff carrying Aimée. He dropped his reins and
ran to them, calling, "What happened, Vale? Where's Mignon and Marcel?" He reached out, offering to take
Aimée; but seeing Vale's condition, he started tearing his
cloak open. "You're both soaked!" he exclaimed. "You'll
freeze!"

"I'm not exactly sure what happened at the cabin.
Aimée couldn't say much after I pulled her out of the
river, except to say Morehead was here," Vale answered
tightly, his eyes moving beyond Benjamin's shoulder to
survey the charred buildings.

Ben hurriedly draped his cloak over Aimée, then took
her from Vale's arms. "There's a blanket behind my saddle.
Wrap it around yourself before you freeze," he directed as
he bundled the cloak more closely around Aimée.

"All I could see when I got here was some man chasing

Aimée, and then she jumped off the cliff . . ." Vale began.

"What about Mignon? Did you see her?" Benjamin asked anxiously as he followed Vale to the horse.

Vale shook his head. "All Aimée managed to say was that Morehead has Mignon—something about giving her to an Iroquois—and that Marcel was in the cabin."

When Benjamin heard that Mignon was in Morehead's hands, something inside him began to vibrate so violently he was amazed that his arms held Aimée steady, without shaking her. Tears welled up in his eyes, and he hastily turned away as Vale took the blanket from behind his saddle. Staring at the cabin through blurred eyes, he whispered, "If Marcel was in there, I don't know how we'll even find his body."

"If Marcel is dead, I'd prefer to go back to our own cabin and take care of Aimée before we look for him," Vale said. He put his hand on Benjamin's shoulder and added gently, "Maybe Aimée was hysterical—maybe if that man was chasing her, she didn't see what happened. Marcel and Mignon might have escaped in the forest."

Benjamin lowered his head and sighed. "Maybe, maybe. Vale, you know none of that is . . ." He stopped, his attention suddenly on the girl he held in his arms. "Aimée? Aimée, don't be afraid . . ."

Vale quickly stepped around Benjamin to see that Aimée's eyes had opened, still dazed and shadowed with fear. "Aimée, you're safe now," he began.

"Marcel! *Sacré Dieu!* I have to find him!" she gasped, and wriggled out of Ben's arms. Once on her feet, she turned and ran toward the cabin, Benjamin's cloak falling behind her unnoticed.

"Aimée, stop!" Vale called. If she could find Marcel's body, Vale didn't want her to see how it would look. She paused in front of the cabin, rose on tiptoe, and looked one way, then the other, as if searching for something. Vale and Benjamin hurried to her side, and Vale gripped her shoulders, turning her to face him. "You can't look for him now," he said firmly. "We'll take you back to our cabin. While you're getting warmer, Ben and I will come back and find his body."

Aimée shook her head. "Marcel's corpse? *Non.* I'm looking for Marcel! There's a chance he's still alive; but if we don't find him quickly, he may smother!" She pushed away Vale's hands and turned to face the ruined cabin again. As her eyes darted over the rubble inside, she said anxiously, "There was a trapdoor under a little rug. He was lying on the rug after they struck him. If only he regained his senses in time, he could have gotten down into the cellar after everyone left the cabin!"

Again Vale's hands on her shoulders turned her gently toward him. "Aimée, most of the floor fell into the cellar. He would have been killed."

"*Non, non, non!*" she cried. "Part of the cellar, one small room like a cave, extended past the cabin wall!"

Vale released her and asked urgently, "Where was the trapdoor?"

Aimée turned to scan the ruin again. "It looks so different now it's difficult for me to be sure," she said anxiously. Finally she lifted her hand and pointed. "There! I think by that wall."

Vale turned to Benjamin. "You'd better stay here with Aimée. What's left of the floor is so weak, if it collapses under me, at least you'll be able to pull me out."

He nodded agreement.

"Please hurry, *mon amant,*" Aimée begged.

Vale stepped cautiously over the threshold, then, feeling along the floor with his foot, took another step. He tried to stay close to where walls had been in the hope that the floor there would be stronger; but the timbers creaked warningly each time he moved. When he was near the place Aimée had indicated, he stooped and began to push away the ashes with his hands, searching for anything resembling a separation in the charred boards.

"Marcel! Marcel, can you hear me?" Vale called.

He paused to listen, but only the wind sighing through the cabin's blackened skeleton answered him. Had Marcel already smothered in the cellar, or had he managed to escape the flames? Was his corpse buried somewhere in the rubble nearby? Vale resumed pushing aside the debris, trying to find the trapdoor.

"Marcel, it's Vale! Aimée's here and Ben! Marcel, answer me if you're there!" Vale called.

"Vale? Vale, I'm here!"

Vale heard a faint voice, a tapping on the boards below. He straightened and turned to wave to Aimée and Benjamin. "He's here! He's alive!"

Carefully testing the floor, he took a step in the direction Marcel's voice had come from, then another before he again stooped to sweep away the tangle of debris that had concealed the trapdoor. After he'd lifted the square of charred wood, he peered into a dark passageway, hazy with smoke and almost completely clogged with rubble.

"Marcel, where are you? I can't see you!" he called.

"That's because I'm covered with soot and blend into everything else down here," Marcel answered. "I didn't move any of this wreckage before, so if the wrong person looked down here, they wouldn't think I'd lived."

The splintered boards blocking the passageway began slowly to move aside, raising a cloud of oily smoke that forced Vale to turn his face away. Finally a smudged face appeared in the shadows below.

"The ladder has fallen to pieces; but if the floor is strong enough there, I can jump up and take hold of it, I think," Marcel said.

"It had better be strong enough. I don't have a rope to throw down to you," Vale answered, and moved back a little to give Marcel room.

Marcel's grimy fingers appeared and clung to the edge of the opening. Vale leaned over to grasp Marcel under the arms. Marcel gasped with pain but determinedly struggled out of the passageway. As he crawled onto the floor, it made an ominous cracking sound; but Marcel's ragged, shallow breaths alarmed Vale more.

"What's wrong with you?" Vale asked as he helped Marcel in his struggle to turn over and sit up.

"*Le gorille,* he broke my rib, I suspect." Marcel panted. He raised his eyes to look appraisingly at the cabin and remarked breathlessly, "I wonder . . . if we will both . . . be able to get out . . . before the floor . . . collapses."

"Can you walk alone?" Vale inquired. "If so, we'll stay well apart, and maybe our weight won't strain one section too much."

Marcel's smile was pained. "I got into that cellar by myself, with the roof falling on my head. Just lead the way and I'll follow." When Vale offered his hands, Marcel shook his head and panted, "Let me get up alone. It will pull . . . the wrong parts . . . if you try to help . . . me."

Vale stood back and watched Marcel get laboriously to his feet. Satisfied that Marcel was able to walk, Vale turned and led the way back outside, cautiously testing the floor before he took a step. As he emerged from the cabin he noted Aimée's readiness to welcome her brother and warned, "Don't embrace him. He has at least one broken rib."

Marcel stepped carefully out of the rubble to grasp Aimée's hands. "What happened to Mignon?" he asked breathlessly. "And you . . . *ma petite soeur* . . . your clothes are freezing . . . on you. What happened to you?"

"Morehead and his men took Mignon away. I don't know where they went," Aimée said anxiously. "They were talking about giving her to some Iroquois named Stalking Bear."

Marcel's eyes narrowed with fury. "*Quels salauds.* This Stalking Bear is a renegade—a very evil Indian banished by his own tribe!"

"They said it themselves," Aimée recalled. "Morehead wanted to give us both to Stalking Bear as a bribe for something he wants Stalking Bear to do. I broke free and jumped into the river."

"Off the cliff?" Marcel exclaimed, grimacing with pain.

"Vale pulled me out," Aimée said, then turned to Vale. "I don't know how we both didn't drown. You're a very powerful swimmer."

"When you spend your childhood with the Abnakis, you learn how to swim about the same time as you learn how to walk," Vale commented. He put his arm around her shoulder. "We'd best get back to the other cabin before we freeze."

"My horse is going to limp; and if Marcel's rib is broken, I don't think he'll be able to endure the jolting. He'd better ride yours, Vale," Benjamin warned.

"Aimée can take your horse and we'll walk," Vale agreed.

"Brandy is somewhere nearby. None of them could manage him, and I made sure he escaped," Aimée advised. "I'm sure he'll hear me and come back." She turned away to walk toward the center of the clearing and call, "Brandy, Brandy! *Mon cheval. Reviens!*"

They heard the hoofbeats, the snap of dead branches being pushed aside, before they saw Brandy moving like a bronze velvet shadow through the forest.

After the horse had bounded through the clearing to Aimée, Benjamin turned to Marcel and said worriedly, "That animal isn't wearing a saddle or bridle. Aimée had better let Vale ride him, and she can share Vale's mount with you."

"Aimée could ride Brandy alone just as he is. I'm more worried about how I'll get up on Vale's horse without puncturing my lung," Marcel said slowly, flinching at every breath he took.

It was finally decided that Aimée and Vale would ride Brandy together; and helped by Vale and Benjamin, Marcel managed to struggle painfully into Vale's saddle.

Beneath the blanket, which now enclosed them both, Vale slid his arms around Aimée, pulling her back against his chest. He bent closer to say encouragingly, "Soon you'll be sitting in front of a fire and will be warm again."

She turned her head to caress his cheek with hers. "I was warmed the moment I saw you swimming toward me."

"Why did you jump into the river? Didn't you know I would come after you?" Vale asked softly.

"If Morehead had given me to that renegade, how would you have found me? I couldn't endure the thought of being possessed by Stalking Bear after the love we've shared."

"I would have found you, Aimée," Vale said quietly, "and I would have killed Stalking Bear."

Immediately after reaching the cabin, Benjamin poked the fire and set a pot of water heating so Vale and Marcel could wash off the soot that coated them. Vale gave Aimée one of his shirts to wear while her clothes dried, and she tied a blanket around her waist to serve as a skirt.

She watched anxiously as Vale tore a sheet into strips, then wrapped Marcel's chest to bind his ribs, noting how her brother's eyes glazed with pain each time Vale pulled the material tight. Looking at the deep purple bruises covering the upper half of Marcel's body, knowing there were just as many others she couldn't see, Aimée thought bitterly that his suffering had only resulted in Mignon's being carried away and more scars being added to his features, if not his spirit; and she had to exert every bit of her will not to weep aloud.

Benjamin applied ointment to the cuts on Marcel's face. "It's a wonder your nose wasn't smashed," he remarked.

"The real wonder of it is that my jaw isn't broken. The gorilla seemed to concentrate mostly on that. I'm surprised I didn't lose any of my teeth, though several seem to have been loosened," Marcel replied, wincing slightly at Benjamin's touch, then adding, "What that lynx didn't do to me, Morehead's man finished. I must be a hideous sight."

Aimée studied Marcel for a long moment, silently acknowledging that the thick shock of dark auburn hair seemed to be all that remained unchanged in him. Even his clear maple-colored eyes, looking unflinchingly out of his swollen, purple-blotched face, had altered, taking on a sharpened, harder gleam than she'd seen in them before.

"The swellings will go down, and the bruises will fade," she said comfortingly. "To me you look like the archangel himself."

At her comment Marcel's eyes softened and the corners of his mouth tilted momentarily, though the brief smile caused the cuts in his lips to resume bleeding. Then his face sobered, and he muttered, "An archangel would have been able to save Mignon."

"There was nothing you could do with the fire blocking your way out of the cabin and the roof coming down," Vale said.

Ben paused in wiping the blood that seeped from the corners of Marcel's mouth, and angrily declared, "We'll find Mignon or I'll die trying. If that renegade Stalking Bear lays a hand on her, I swear I'll draw and quarter him!"

"I doubt Morehead would have been able to take Mignon directly to Stalking Bear," Vale said thoughtfully. "If he is, as you've said, an outcast from his own people as well as a fugitive from white law, he and his men have to keep on the move. They wouldn't be able to stay at one location for more than a couple of days, and I doubt very much that Morehead would know where Stalking Bear is at any given moment. I'm sure Morehead will have to first contact one of Stalking Bear's runners, who will carry the message to his leader. Stalking Bear himself will decide if Morehead's purpose is worth the risk of letting anyone know where he'll be at a specific time."

"Then Morehead will have to hide Mignon somewhere while he waits for Stalking Bear's answer," Benjamin concluded. "If only we knew where that might be . . ."

"That's why I want to return to Lavaltrie as soon as possible—tomorrow if you can undertake so long a ride that soon, Marcel," Vale said.

"I wish I could have Soleil to ride; but if we don't have to travel at a gallop, I'll manage," Marcel quickly replied.

"But they put our horses in the paddock!" Aimée recalled. "Perhaps Soleil ran away with the others out of fear for the fire. Maybe we can find the horses tomorrow."

"I'll look for them first thing in the morning," Vale promised. "They might have wandered back to the cabin looking for someone to feed them."

"What will we do when we get to Lavaltrie?" Aimée asked. "Morehead still is in command there."

"I certainly don't intend to approach Morehead. In fact, I wouldn't want him to see us at all until after we've presented your case to Major Templeton. With such serious charges as you're bringing, Aimée, Marcel—with Ben and me as witnesses—Templeton will have to assume the authority to lock Morehead up, despite his higher rank," Vale reasoned. "Once Morehead is jailed and facing a court-martial, it's possible he might be persuaded to confess where his henchmen are holding Mignon."

"But what if Morehead won't speak? What if Templeton hesitates to take the authority, or has to go through some sort of circuitous procedure first and Morehead escapes in the meantime?" Marcel questioned.

"What if, God forbid, Major Templeton is as guilty as Morehead and simply locks us up?" Aimée exclaimed.

"Those are all possibilities," Vale conceded, "but I don't think the major is either dishonest or particularly timid. I can't say for certain this is true, but I did perceive a certain forthrightness about Templeton as well as an expression in his eyes that told me he's interested in furthering his military career. Bringing his commanding officer to justice for such crimes—hardly an easy task no matter which way you look at it—would certainly advance his rank. Maybe he'd even get Morehead's command of Lavaltrie."

"I suppose we could go directly to General Gage, whose reputation appears to be beyond reproach; but this could give Morehead and his gang the time to contact Stalking Bear and deliver Mignon to him," Ben declared. "If even Morehead's going to have trouble finding Stalking Bear, how would we do it?"

"The Indians consider it a particular disgrace if they can't catch and punish one of their own people," Vale said. "Stalking Bear is an Iroquois though his tribe has declared him an outcast. The Algonquins, I should think, would enjoy seeing shame cast on the Iroquois nation by one of their people having to be captured by white men to face British law. Maybe the Algonquins would help us locate Stalking Bear's camp."

Marcel shook his head doubtfully and explained, "When Montreal was taken by the British, the Algonquins all disappeared into the deeper woods. I doubt they'd be interested in putting out much of an effort to help any white man even if we were able to find one of their villages."

"That may be true of the Algonquin tribes, but the Abnakis are also enemies of the Iroquois," Vale said. "They migrated to this area from the Atlantic coast some six or seven years ago; and if the name Walking-in-Honor is still remembered, the Abnakis should welcome us into their village."

"Who was Walking-in-Honor? What would he have to do with us?" Marcel inquired.

"Walking-in-Honor was a warrior who was held in very high regard not only by his own village but by all the Abnakis," Vale replied. "He was the only father I ever knew; and though I was adopted, I was the only son he ever had."

Marcel stared at Vale a moment as he absorbed this information. "You did mention that you had lived with the Indians but had left the tribe when you were twelve. It was what, sixteen, seventeen years ago?"

"That's a long time, Vale," Benjamin commented.

"Seventeen years is a long time," Vale agreed. "Yet the Abnakis sang songs about Walking-in-Honor even before he was killed, and such songs tend to continue as legends for many generations to repeat. They're really the way the Indians keep their history."

"Were you mentioned in any of those legends?" Marcel inquired.

"There was one song mentioning how Walking-in-Honor found his son Lightning-of-the-Winter-Moon and regarded him as a gift from the gods," Vale recalled. "Let's hope that particular legend still is remembered if we have to approach the Abnakis."

"Why were you thought of as a heavenly gift?" Aimée asked curiously.

"It would take some time to explain, and I think we should make our plans for tomorrow," Vale replied. He turned to Marcel. "When we arrive in Lavaltrie, I'll have to think of how we can approach Major Templeton without Morehead's learning about it. While I'm scouting around to find a way to do that the rest of you will need a place to wait where you won't be discovered. Marcel, you're more familiar with Lavaltrie than Ben and I. Can you think of somewhere suitable?"

Marcel looked thoughtful for a moment, then said, "I hid very successfully in the forest near the *pelleterie* while Morehead's men were searching for me. I was in a crevasse—like a wedge cut out of the side of a hill. The trees and bushes grow in front of the opening and arch over the top so closely no one noticed that it was there. Morehead's men went past it several times while I was sitting inside watching them."

"Is it a big enough place to hold us and our horses?" Banjamin asked.

"*Oui*, but it's narrow, and we'd have to lead the horses in one by one so we don't disturb the bushes that conceal the opening," Marcel replied. "Another advantage about this place is that we won't have to approach too near the city to get there."

"It seems like just what we'll need," Vale approved.

"Now that you've mentioned the *pelleterie* and the night you escaped Morehead, I'm reminded of something I've wondered about ever since," Aimée said. She took Marcel's hand and asked, "*Mon frère*, where did you hide Papa's money? Shouldn't we take it back with us—or will it be possible to find it now that the cabin has been destroyed?"

Marcel struggled to avoid smiling but lost; and again the cuts at the corners of his mouth began to bleed. He dabbed at his lips with a handkerchief as he answered, "It never was in my cabin or the barn, *ma soeur*. It has always been here beneath *this* cabin's floor."

Aimée's mouth fell open in surprise. "But why? This place was deserted until Vale and Ben moved in!"

"Where would be less likely a place to hide the gold than a long-deserted cabin over an hour's walk from mine?" Marcel asked. Then squeezing her fingers, he added apologetically, "I wanted to tell you and Mignon from the moment you arrived; but I thought, what if I did and Morehead learned where we were? It would surely be better for you if I alone knew. I was going to tell you as soon as I got out of the cellar today; but in all the excitement I forgot."

"Let's make sure not to forget it tomorrow before we leave," Vale said.

"Mais non!" Aimée exclaimed. "I certainly won't forget it!"

Chapter 24

Vale knew that the Dessaline house was the one place where Major Templeton was most likely to be; but to approach the military headquarters was to risk being recognized by Morehead or one of his henchmen. He remembered how Jeannette had mistaken him for a trapper, when he'd first walked with Aimée to the Dessaline gate; so he made sure to wear his doeskin shirt and breeches and a pair of elk-skin boots, such as trappers used. An old blanket he'd bought at Tadoussac from a Huron woman went around his shoulders like a cloak. He had loosened his queue and gathered his dark hair into two strands, which he then plaited and fastened with hide thongs Indian fashion. His appearance must have nothing about it to remind anyone of the marquis d'Auvergne.

After Vale had left Benjamin, Aimée, and Marcel in their hiding place near the *pelleterie,* he rode as far as the pub closest to the Dessaline house. Pretending that he was one of the pub's customers, he left his horse there and walked the rest of the way.

The handful of passersby still on the twilit street glanced at the tall, lean figure. A half-blooded trapper, they assumed. Several women gazed speculatively at his smoky gray eyes before their escorts, warily looking over the hunting knife sheathed at his hip, quickly drew their ladies aside lest even the hem of their fur-trimmed capes brush the fringe of his boot tops. Vale was satisfied that his appearance had fooled them. His face remained impassive, like that of a man who hid the disgrace of his mixed blood under his pride.

Vale's steps slowed as he neared the Dessaline house.

He crossed the muddy street to a building opposite the gate. He leaned against a wall watching the entrance to the house through half-closed eyes—a harmless loiterer in the gathering dusk.

When Morehead's scarlet-cloaked figure stepped over the threshold, Vale noted the sentries' salutes and other gestures of respect. The Colonel's gilt epaulets gleamed in the lamplight that flickered through the open doorway; and Vale's anger at Morehead's successful masquerade flashed through him like a flame. He quickly leashed his emotions; and his anger became a hot glow seething in his depths, though not a flicker of interest crossed his features as he watched Morehead mount his horse and begin down the street. He would not follow him, for Morehead wasn't likely to meet with any of his henchmen, much less visit the place where Mignon was being held, while he was in uniform.

At last the uniform of another officer appeared. The light coming from the doorway shone on the man's face as he raised his head. Vale recognized Templeton. The major casually acknowledged the sentries' salutes, then paused to look up the street in the direction that Morehead had taken, as if making a decision. Finally waving away the soldier who offered to get his horse, Templeton started down the street on foot. Vale waited a discreet moment before straightening, then he slipped into the shadows to follow.

Templeton went only as far as the pub where Vale had previously left his horse. Vale remained outside for a few moments, wondering if he dared enter; but when a group of men opened the door to go inside, Vale noticed that the pub, though modest in size, was crowded. He could easily mingle with the other customers and remain unnoticed until he thought of a way to approach Templeton. He slipped off the blanket he'd worn draped around his shoulders, regathered his hair into a queue at the nape of his neck, and opened the door to the pub.

Inside the entrance a serving maid looked over Vale so warily he realized the pub catered to a more genteel customer than he seemed. With particular courtesy he asked for a table in the far corner of the room where he could have dinner, so the girl would know he wasn't merely looking for a place to drink.

The girl had indeed wondered if she should speak to the owner of the pub and have this roughly dressed man turned away; now she puzzled over the elegant French he'd used, as she led him to a table. After Vale was seated, he asked for a glass of wine and ordered his meal, smiling up at the maid with such candid friendliness her last doubts dissipated; and as she went about getting his drink she remembered his soundless walk and the silvery flecks in his eyes. She wondered if she could possibly attract his interests.

After the maid had served his wine, Vale leaned back and scanned the customers. Although the scarlet coats of a few British soldiers dotted the room, Vale noticed the men passing Templeton's table did no more than greet him; and although the major returned their greetings in a friendly manner, he invited no one to join him even for a drink. As he ate, Templeton watched those around him with a detachment suggesting that he had other things on his mind. When the major ordered a glass of brandy, Vale realized he intended to linger, and decided now was the time to approach.

Vale laid down his napkin, asked the serving maid to bring him a glass of brandy at Major Templeton's table, and stood up. The maid went away convinced that Vale was a scout for the British or a high-ranking officer on a secret mission.

"There's a matter of utmost importance I must discuss with you, Major Templeton—if you'll allow me to join you."

At the sound of the crisp English voice Templeton looked up from his brandy expecting to see one of his officers. He stared in surprise at the doeskin-clad man beside him.

"You may recall the marquis d'Auvergne?" Vale prompted. Recognition flooded Templeton's green eyes, and Vale added, "Please call me Valjean or Vale, if you prefer, as I am half British. May I join you, Major?"

"Why, yes, please do," Templeton immediately responded, intrigued by the marquis's appearance.

Vale seated himself. The serving maid approached with Vale's brandy, and Templeton fell silent, eyeing the doeskin shirt. Vale took a sip of his brandy, then began, "I'm dressed this unusual way because I've been watching your headquarters from across the street, waiting for you to come out, and I didn't want to be recognized—particularly by your commanding officer."

"Morehead?" Templeton was thoughtful for a moment before asking, "Are you and the colonel having some sort of difficulty that you fear his recognition?"

"The difficulties between the colonel and myself threaten his well-being far more than mine," Vale replied. "Quite frankly, I'm not even sure I should trust you. I'm very inclined to go to General Gage directly, but I expect that that would take more time than I dare use."

"You have a complaint about Morehead's administration of Lavaltrie?" Templeton couldn't prevent the glimmer of satisfaction that passed through his eyes, and he leaned back in his chair. "I would very much like to hear the details."

"Colonel Morehead has been working with an assortment of criminals and amassing himself quite a fortune, I'd guess, as he has moved from one assignment to another in the colonies. He approached Marcel Dessaline, whose house was subsequently confiscated, as you know, burning the Dessaline business in an effort to force Marcel to admit where the family's savings were secreted. Marcel escaped to a cabin in the forest and until yesterday lived there in real fear for his life. Late last fall I and Benjamin Carleton escorted Aimée and Mignon Dessaline to Marcel's cabin, and we all were trapped there by the blizzards. At the first sign of the thaw Morehead and his henchmen visited Marcel's cabin and beat him severely in an effort to learn where he'd hidden the family money. They burned his cabin and barn and left him for dead; then they abducted Mignon, and they plan to deliver her as a gift to an Iroquois renegade named Stalking Bear. They would have taken Aimée as well, but she broke free and jumped off a nearby cliff into the river. Only Providence prevented her from being crushed by the ice floes, or from drowning before I pulled her out."

"You're charging Colonel Morehead with theft, extortion, assault, attempted murder, and a host of other charges I could think of if I took a moment or two!" Templeton whispered excitedly.

"Indeed I am," Vale solemnly agreed. "Marcel and Aimée are now in a safe place waiting for the opportunity to prefer charges themselves. With them is Mr. Carleton who is eager to act as a witness. However, I will not allow my fiancée to be endangered by Morehead; and I insist he be arrested before they come out of hiding."

"It would take a greater authority than mine to arrest an officer of Morehead's rank," Templeton said slowly. "But you say the Dessalines are willing to prefer charges in person, and you and Mr. Carleton intend to be witnesses?"

"It seems to me this should convince anyone of the necessity to detain Morehead," Vale pointed out.

"I've had suspicions about Morehead's activities for some time, but I could never quite figure out what precisely he was mixed up in, much less gather evidence of any kind," Templeton said slowly. "Blast, I want to get him! But *how* is the question."

"The more delay there is, the better the chance that Mignon Dessaline will be delivered to Stalking Bear, who is a renegade not only from the laws of his own people but from the laws of the British and the previous French government as well. Mignon certainly would be an invaluable witness if she could be located."

"Yes, yes. Certainly she would," Templeton agreed, his mind swiftly running over possible ways he could handle so unusual a situation. Finally he looked up at Vale. "My problem is that Morehead is not only my superior officer but commander of this district as well. Only General Gage could remove him from authority. I've been thinking that, to prevent Morehead's escape, it might be acceptable in this emergency to act as General Gage's agent and assume the authority I need to arrest Morehead."

Templeton paused, trying desperately to think of a way to protect his own career should Morehead somehow later be exonerated. After a long moment he said, "Would you be willing to come with me to headquarters—Morehead isn't likely to return for some hours—so I can write a message explaining the situation to General Gage? I want you to sign the message too. You may chose anyone you please at headquarters to deliver it; and after we've sent it off, I want you to fetch the Dessalines and your friend, Mr. Carleton. It is absolutely essential they be present when I arrest Morehead so there's no question as to his identity or their charges."

Vale was silent, thinking that if Templeton was deceiving him, this would be a perfect opportunity to trap the Dessalines as well as their witnesses.

"I know what you're thinking," the major said softly. "I'm not making a trap for you, I promise."

Vale looked up, analyzing the expression in Templeton's steady eyes. Their green depths seemed to conceal no betrayal. "I warn you, Major, my titles are genuine and carry considerable power. I would be missed in several quarters should I disappear. Madame Dessaline would certainly search for her son and daughters, and the Carletons of Boston would be very diligent in their investigation if their son were harmed. You'd best not be laying a trap."

"I'm doing all I can to convince you I'm not involved in Morehead's illegal activities. Surely you can appreciate my position," Templeton pleaded. "If fifty or even a hundred people were preferring these charges, I'd want all of them here. When an officer of Morehead's rank is to be arrested by a subordinate, nothing but the strongest evidence will prevail. If only you and I are present, he could very well have me put in irons instead."

Vale stood up. "Let us go to your headquarters, Major. I'll write a letter of my own to General Gage while you compose your message. Then, as you've suggested, I'll choose the man to deliver both of them."

*   *   *

Morehead had spent the better part of the night with a girl he'd met in the Lonqueuil district. Dawn would be little more than an hour in coming, he noticed as he dismounted in front of the Dessaline house; and he would be tired for the next day's activities after so little rest.

Dark Otter had promised that he would return with Stalking-Bear's answer by noon. Certain of what the renegade leader's decision would be, Morehead had already instructed Willie Ugland to come to him after lunch so he could take the directions to Stalking Bear's camp back to Woolsey; and they could deliver the Dessaline girl and finally get her off their hands. After the renegade had seen Mignon, Morehead anticipated he would be eager to do whatever favors Morehead needed, especially if he were promised that other such maidens could be procured for him in the future.

Morehead handed his reins to the orderly at the gate, taking no notice of the several horses tethered nearby, or of the light that filtered through the draperies of almost the entire lower floor of the house. Military headquarters were always abuzz with various comings and goings, and he'd grown used to ignoring the sounds of horses' hooves outside, booted feet marching past his door, and lights flashing in the middle of the night. When he opened the door and stepped into the entrance hall, a tight-lipped sergeant informed him that Major Templeton was waiting in his office.

Morehead's smile vanished. "Whatever can Major Templeton want at this hour?" he demanded.

"I'm not at liberty to say, sir," the sergeant replied. "Major Templeton only gave me orders to take you to him. He said it was of extreme importance."

"Everything is of extreme importance to that puppy," Morehead grumbled, then gestured for the sergeant to lead the way. As he left the entrance hall two guards fell smartly into step behind him. Had a real emergency arisen, he wondered, for how else to explain such formality?

When the sergeant opened the door to the Dessaline

study, Morehead could see only that Templeton was seated behind the desk in a small circle of lamplight.

"You'd think General Gage was visi—" Morehead stopped abruptly as he entered the room and saw the group of people standing silently at one side of the study.

Templeton got to his feet and, leaning over the desk to turn up the lamp, said crisply, "Monsieur le Marquis d'Auvergne, Mr. Carleton, Monsieur and Mademoiselle Dessaline, is this the officer against whom you're bringing charges: at whose order the Dessaline business was burned in an attempt to extort money; and at whose order you, Monsieur Dessaline, twice were severely beaten; who invaded your cabin, attempted to abduct you, Mademoiselle Dessaline, and succeeded in abducting your sister Mignon?"

All four confirmed that Morehead was the man.

Templeton took a deep breath and turned again to his commanding officer. "Sir, in view of the serious charges these witnesses have brought against you, I have no choice but to arrest and hold you for court-martial."

"You little whelp, how dare you accuse me on the strength of the word of these French troublemakers so lately our enemies?" Morehead demanded. "By what authority do you deem you can do this?"

"Sir, by authority of General Gage, who has replied to my message sent earlier this evening," Templeton answered firmly, holding up a sheet of paper obviously signed by Gage. "At General Gage's instructions I must advise you to disclose immediately the names of your companions in these crimes as well as tell us where Mignon Dessaline is being held prisoner. I must also advise you that, should you refuse to give me this information and stand convicted of these crimes, your sentence will reflect no mercy."

"My crimes! My conviction! Mercy!" Morehead exploded. "I'll have you know, Major, that you've just thrown away your career. I've been investigating these people, and your cooperation with them will bring disgrace on you and your family. They're spies, who have fabricated this story to get me out of their way—"

"Sir, any explanations for your behavior or theirs will be examined at your court-martial hearing. Meanwhile my orders from General Gage are explicit. I must put you under military guard and confine you to . . ."

Realizing that his objections would not convince Templeton of anything now that he had Gage's orders in hand, and that Templeton intended to lock him up rather than confine him to his quarters, which would make escape impossible, Morehead whirled around only to find himself facing the two guards who had followed him into the room.

From behind him Morehead heard Templeton snap, "Corporals Higgins and Blythe, you will take Colonel Morehead to the area we've arranged. He is to be allowed no visitors except for the legal adviser I appoint as counsel for his hearing." He watched as the disgraced officer was escorted from the room, then turned to Marcel. "I am sorry, Monsieur Dessaline, that your house must be used not only for a military headquarters but for a guardhouse now as well. There are no accommodations for military prisoners nearby, and we can't put him in a civilian jail. The only thing I could think of was to lock him in one of the rooms in your cellar."

"As long as Colonel Morehead has been captured, I don't mind at all if he's restrained in my cellar," Marcel replied. "But, Major Templeton, I must ask, how soon will he be questioned about Mignon?"

"You saw how he was—defiant and angry—not at all inclined at the moment to confess to anything," Templeton said, nodding to an orderly to pour them each a brandy. As the liquor was handed round he said, "I think we all could use something to settle our nerves, don't you?"

"It's been a long night," Benjamin agreed, lifting one of the drapes to note that the sky was beginning to lighten. He let the drape fall back into place, then took a sip of his brandy, looked at Templeton, and asked, "Do you think, Major, that he will confess?"

"Colonel Morehead thought that Monsieur and Mademoiselle Dessaline were dead and that you, Mr. Carleton, and the marquis had deserted the ladies. To have all of you come back and bring charges, to have me arrest him, is rather stunning," Templeton reasoned. "After he's had a chance to consider all this, his legal adviser will tell him I've been authorized to make an agreement with him. If he's convicted, which seems inevitable, the penalty for his crimes would be hanging. But should he disclose the names of his henchmen and, most important, tell us where Mademoiselle Dessaline is being held so that she can be rescued, he'll be cashiered and declared an exile." Templeton paused to sip his brandy. "This would, of course, be the worst sort of scandal; but he's behaved so dishonorably I wonder if public disgrace really would matter so much to him if he can save his own life."

"I only hope no harm comes to Mignon in the meanwhile," Aimée whispered, her eyes filling with tears.

"I think not, mademoiselle," Templeton said soothingly. "If she's to be given to Stalking Bear, her safety will be closely guarded until then."

Noting Aimée's tears finally beginning to flow, Vale put his arm around her waist. "My fiancée has had a very trying day and night. I think we'd all better get some rest."

"I sent one of my men to the Hôtel Dieu to arrange accommodations for you all," Templeton said. He turned to Marcel. "Monsieur, again I apologize for having to continue using your house as our headquarters. We'll make other arrangements as soon as this unfortunate incident has been concluded. In the meanwhile the four of you will stay at the hotel as His Majesty's guests, if that's agreeable."

"Most agreeable, Major," Marcel replied, then asked, "But do you suppose Aimée and I could get a few things we'll need from our rooms before we leave? Everything in the cabin was destroyed by the fire."

"Certainly, monsieur." Templeton looked at the orderly, who had lingered nearby. "Go upstairs with them, please, and help them gather what they wish." He turned again to Marcel. "Take only what you'll need until tonight. You can pack whatever else you'll want in a more leisurely fashion then. I need to have all four of you tell our prosecutor the details of your experiences with the colonel. Perhaps it can be done more pleasantly after dinner."

"Thank you, Major. We shall be here," Aimée said, blinking away her tears before she turned to follow the orderly. As they left the room Marcel took her hand as he used to do when as a little girl she was frightened by something.

It was well past dawn when Vale, Benjamin, and the Dessalines arrived at the hotel; but as Templeton had promised, the staff was expecting them. Their rooms had been prepared, and even the bathwater had already been heated.

As soon as the bevy of maids and bellboys had left Aimée's room, she turned to gaze at the tub they'd filled. After almost drowning in that ice-filled river by the cabin, she was sure she would never again enjoy a hot bath as much as she would this one. Recalling that terrible afternoon—was it only yesterday?—brought memories of Mignon, and fresh pain tore through her as she thought of the fear her sister must be suffering at that very moment.

She stepped into her bath, carefully sat down in the oversized tub, and, leaning back, closed her eyes. She wondered if Morehead would tell Major Templeton where Mignon was being kept prisoner, and what Vale and Ben would do if Morehead was willing to go to the gallows without disclosing Mignon's whereabouts. Morehead couldn't remain silent, she reasoned, not after he'd thought over the price he would pay. Perhaps, as Major Templeton had said, Morehead only needed a little time for the surprise of his arrest to wear off. Maybe, after he'd spoken to his legal counsel and realized how hopeless it was for him to cling to his story of innocence, he'd admit everything and accept the military tribunal's mercy. She hoped fervently that Major Templeton could tell them this was exactly what had happened when they had dinner with him tonight.

She would feel strange eating at the Dessaline table in the Dessaline house and not really being at home, she reflected—sipping sherry after dinner and telling a military prosecutor about what Morehead had done to them. At the end of the evening she wouldn't be able to go upstairs to her own bed but would have to return to the hotel to a room she should at least have been sharing with Mignon.

"Please don't think too much about what we've been through, or worry about Mignon," a quiet voice said nearby.

Aimée's eyes flew open. Vale was sitting on the floor beside her, leaning his arms on the edge of the tub. He bent closer to kiss her forehead.

"A little crease forms between your brows when you worry." His lips moved to the corner of hers. "And I don't like to see your mouth drooping so sadly. Morehead isn't a fool, Aimée. After he calms down and realizes his conviction is inevitable, he'll tell Templeton where Mignon's being held."

"That's what I keep trying to convince myself," Aimée said slowly. Noting the concern in his face, she decided to change the subject. Acutely aware of her position in the tub, she asked, "How did you get into my room? I was sure the hotel people locked the door when they left."

Vale's eyes warmed with his smile. "I told one of the bellboys that my fiancée was very upset and needed comforting. When I added that our engagement, owing to these recent unhappy events, has been overlong, he finally gave me your key. Like the cabin boy on the *Santa Luisa*, he was willing to accept payment for his discretion. He'll personally bring whatever we request, but anyone who inquires will be given the impression we're in our separate rooms, and told we don't want to be disturbed."

"You intend to stay with me?" she asked in surprise.

"I've brought the clothes I'm going to wear for dinner tonight. I told Marcel and Ben I'm planning to sleep all day," Vale replied, then added, "I didn't choose a room separate from theirs without good reason, though I'll spend as little time as possible in it."

"You seem to have thought of everything. It appears as if this stay at the hotel will be much like those days on the *Santa Luisa* when Mignon and my mother were recovering from their fevers." She fell silent, reflecting happily on this prospect for a moment, before looking up at him and remarking, "When you lean your arms on the edge of the tub that way, the fringe on your sleeve is very near to dipping in the water."

Vale's eyes glimmered with a beginning silvery light as he withdrew. "I've already taken off my boots. Do you mind if I share your bath? It was, you know, at my order you were given so large a tub."

"You must have planned this even before we arrived at the hotel," Aimée breathed.

"The idea first occurred to me when Major Templeton mentioned that these accommodations had been made for us," Vale admitted, and stood up to begin pulling off his shirt.

"So a bellboy here, like the cabin boy on the ship, will be considerably enriched by our stay," she concluded, though she looked doubtfully at the tub, wondering how they would arrange themselves in it together. Vale put one foot in the water; and her eyes traveled up the well-muscled length of his leg, over his lean body to his face. "Although this tub is large, I'm not sure where to move to give you room," she said.

"You needn't move at all," Vale replied as he lowered himself to kneel beside her legs. He reached for the soap; and as he rubbed the cake between his hands, his eyes lifted to meet hers. When his hands were covered with suds, he laid the soap aside and reached out to take her arm.

Aimée looked down to watch the fingers that slid up her arm leaving a trail of fragrant foam on her skin. He moved nearer, until his chest almost brushed her, his arms loosely enclosing her while his hands soaped her back, sliding around her sides to circle her breasts with suds, the spirals growing smaller, till he bent to kiss their tips, then moved away.

"Lean back while I wash your legs, Aimée," he said softly.

She obeyed, closing her eyes, enjoying the peculiarly

provocative sensation of his fingers, slippery with soap, caressing her feet, and his hand that held her ankle lifting her leg so he could smooth the lather to her knees.

Then Vale asked quietly, "Will you do the same for me?"

Aimée opened her eyes to gaze into his. Crystal lights were beginning to flicker in their depths. She nodded and turned to exchange places with him. Their desire was a tangibly growing presence between them as their bodies brushed in passing. She knelt beside him and reached for the soap.

Although they'd made love many times and she'd caressed each inch of Vale's body, this prolonged fondling allowed her to acquaint herself with every curve of his muscles in a way she'd never done before. This touching without the immediate prospect of fulfillment seemed an even more intimate sharing of themselves; and after she'd finished soaping his legs, she raised her eyes to his, silently asking what he would have her do next.

"There is one place we've each missed," he said softly, and rose to his knees to face her. Taking the soap, he again lathered his hands; and wearing the smallest hint of a smile, his eyes glinting with silver flecks, he began to stroke her thighs, slowly circling around her hips; his hands moving over her derrière, his fingers smoothing soap between her legs, making of the task so tenderly intimate a caress she was tempted by the need to touch him back. Finally, without a word, he put the soap in her palm. His lips brushed hers with only the lightest of kisses to encourage her, and he withdrew.

Aimée's hands trembled as she rubbed the cake between them; and she lifted her gaze to his dappled eyes, now scintillating with hidden lightning streaks. She reached out to touch him as intimately as he had touched her, exploring with infinite detail each contour of his body as she soaped him. When she had finished, her hands lightly lingering on him began again to tremble; and she was helpless to stop them.

Vale's fingers grasped her shoulders, drawing her to

him, though he didn't kiss her. Against her lips he whispered, "We shall rinse each other, my love, then step out of here before we continue this."

He moved away, bending to take handfuls of water, which he then splashed on her body, kissing each area of her skin after he'd cleansed it of soap; and after he'd finished, though desire was making her heart flutter like a bird trying its wings beneath her ribs, she followed his example, closing her eyes as she kissed him, inhaling the scent of his skin, feeling its texture, savoring its taste.

He took her hand as they stepped from the tub, then unfolded a towel to pat her dry. She offered to take the cloth from him; but he shook his head and, sliding his arm around her waist, led her to the bed.

When she was seated on its edge, he leaned close to take her face between his hands and tilt it up toward his. He brought his mouth to hers, and as he kissed her his chest gently coaxed her to lay back. His body slid moistly over hers.

The desire he'd been building in her surged forward with such intensity she reached around him, her arms tightening against his back, her hips tilting to meet his; but he moved a little away.

"I don't want to wait any longer," she whispered in his ear, feeling him shiver at her breath.

He sensed the tip of her tongue tracing the whorls of his ear and would have turned his head away, but for her hands twined in his hair, holding him to her. Her body again reached up for him, beckoning.

"Then you shall have what you want, Aimée—this time," he said with a quiet urgency that only quickened the need in her to an even sharper compulsion. Their union was so welcome she started to move immediately, so recklessly, he began to feel that the fire she'd awakened in him was rapidly growing beyond his control.

"Aimée, are you certain . . ." he began.

Her answer was a soft, unintelligible sound coming from deep inside her throat like a breathless moan. He opened his eyes. Hers, bright and streaked with amber lights, stared up at him. His desire surged higher, his body growing rigid, on the edge of unleashing the forces racing through him. Aimée writhed so eagerly beneath Vale he could wait no longer. His desire leaped the last of his barriers, rushing beyond his will to fuse with hers; and he exploded in a sheet of flame that consumed them both with ecstasy.

After their hearts had slowed their pounding and their racing breath had quieted, they remained united, whispering drowsily of their love until exhaustion overtook them; and they drifted into slumber.

They slept half the day before hunger awakened them. Vale arose, put on his dressing robe, and called the bellboy to bring their breakfast. After the boy had left, they were only half finished with their food when they looked into each other's eyes, noted the glow rising in them, and returned to bed.

Willie Ugland was the least threatening-looking member of Morehead's gang of thieves, which was why Morehead had long ago chosen him to pretend he was a drunk seeking money for his habit in exchange for information about crimes and the movements of criminals in the district. This ruse had allowed Morehead to have a convenient direct contact with his henchmen; and Willie's bewhiskered lopsided face and ragged figure had become so familiar a sight shuffling up to the servants' entrance of the Dessaline house that most of the sentries no longer questioned his purpose. But on the chance that a new guard or some other soldier recently assigned to Morehead's headquarters should stop him, Willie always came prepared with some tidbit of information about a recent crime that would seem to validate his purpose.

As Morehead had instructed, Willie came to the rear door expecting to get from his leader the directions to Stalking Bear's camp; but the soldier on guard stopped him.

"Corporal Higgins, you know Willie," Ugland whined. "I come to tell Colonel Morehead something."

"You'll have to save your information for tomorrow and tell Major Templeton instead," Higgins said. "The major's our commandant for the time being."

Willie's jaw dropped in shock. "Did something happen to the colonel? Has he been sent somewhere else?" he asked anxiously.

"Sure has, Willie," the corporal sighed. "Seems like he's a worse blackguard than those you've been telling him about. Clapped him in irons last night, they did—not really irons—actually we have no proper guardhouse here, you know. Locked him in the cellar while he's waiting for a court-martial hearing. Can't see anyone but his legal counsel who's supposed to come tonight."

"Gawd" was all the stunned Willie could say.

Higgins patted Ugland's ragged shoulder. "Best be on your way, Willie. Templeton's too busy to see you today. Come back tomorrow."

"Locked in the cellar, you say? There be no mistake about this?" Willie asked slowly.

Higgins shook his head. "Me and Blythe was his escort. Locked him in myself. People who own this house came to Templeton with a shocking story last night. Some French nobleman was with them. Makes a body wonder what things are coming to."

"Aye, does that for sure," Willie agreed. Then, reminding himself to act his part, he whined, "Higgins, could you spare me a shilling? I'll be sorely pressed if the colonel can't give me my bit of coin today."

Higgins looked down at Willie's lopsided face, felt sorry for the seemingly harmless little man, and pressed a coin in his hand. "Come back tomorrow to the major, Willie," he advised. "Templeton's not a bad sort."

"Aye, I'll be back," Willie promised. "Thankee, corporal." He turned and shuffled away.

Higgins watched the shabby figure with pitying eyes until it had turned the corner. Willie was thinking frantically of what he and the other men would do without Morehead's leadership. Morehead would certainly be hanged, and Willie had come close enough to the gallows more than once to feel very sympathetic toward anyone facing that prospect. Could Morehead somehow be rescued? Although every one of Willie's companions had committed murder and had no qualms about cutting throats, to invade the British army's headquarters in Lavaltrie was a different thing from engaging in a waterfront brawl or attacking a toff, too late on the street, for his purse. Yet Morehead, strange bloke as he was, had given them the opportunity of making more loot than any of them had ever dreamed of getting—he'd protected them in his way. It seemed wrong to let him go by the by.

Willie was so at a loss to think of a solution, he turned into a narrow alleyway out of the traffic and sat down, his back propped against a building as he considered this catastrophe. He didn't even notice Dark Otter soundlessly approaching until the Iroquois settled himself beside Willie.

"Could not give white colonel Stalking Bear's answer," Dark Otter said. "Followed Willie from soldier's house. Must tell someone Stalking Bear wants woman colonel promised. Too much for me to go back and say colonel locked up, can't have woman."

Willie stared at the Indian. "What am I supposed to do? We got the girl, but—"

"Give woman to Stalking Bear like you promise," Dark Otter solemnly advised. "I go back to camp with you and woman or I not go back at all. Stalking Bear kill Dark Otter if no woman."

"But Morehead's locked up!" Willie protested. "I don't know what to do!"

"When my chief locked up one time, another warrior and I pretended to be women come to give him food." Dark Otter chuckled evilly at the memory. "We not women, man who guarded Stalking Bear learn too late and die. Stalking Bear free now. You get white colonel out same way maybe." Dark Otter's face sobered, and his black eyes glittered with menace. "Stalking Bear helps friends, kills enemies. You bring woman and you his friend. No woman and you are enemy. Dark Otter will wait near House of Black Sheep. When ready, I will show you the way to Stalking Bear's camp."

As Dark Otter spoke, a plan was beginning to form in Willie's mind. If Woolsey washed himself and scraped off his beard, if he trimmed his hair and tied it back with a bit of black ribbon as Corporal Higgins did . . . They still had the uniforms Morehead had given them to go to the *pelleterie*, and one of them had a captain's insignia. Maybe Woolsey could pretend to be Morehead's legal counsel just as Dark Otter had pretended to be a squaw to rescue Stalking Bear.

Willie looked up at the Indian. "We'll have to know how long the trip to Stalking Bear's camp will take so we can get supplies ready. Which direction will we have to travel?" At Dark Otter's hesitance he added, "Morehead will want to know at least that much when we get him out."

"Take food for five days," Dark Otter said slowly, gesturing with his hand toward the northwest.

Willie nodded and lowered his eyes to stare unfocusedly at the ragged knees of his breeches while he thought about where a four- or five-day trek to the northwest would take them—deep forest with not even an outpost to celebrate in once they'd gotten rid of the girl.

He muttered, "Stalking Bear sure must be nervous if he don't even want us to know . . ." As he spoke he turned to look at Dark Otter; but the Indian had vanished without a sound.

Lieutenant Harrison, who would act as prosecutor in Colonel Morehead's case, looked admiringly at Aimée, who stood gazing up at a painting above the fireplace in the parlor. The dark blue satin gown trimmed with black lace was a perfect foil for her hair, he was thinking, until he realized the picture must be a portrait of her mother with her missing sister and Aimée herself when they were toddlers. Disconcerted by her silent sorrow, he cleared his throat.

"Mademoiselle Dessaline, it has been a pleasure to meet

you, although I wish it had been under happier circumstances," he said.

Aimée turned, her eyes darkened to the color of brandy held in the moonlight. "Are you leaving now, Lieutenant?" she asked, and, when he nodded, extended her hand. "I'm sure we will meet again for a pleasanter occasion after all these problems are in the past," she added as his lips brushed her fingers.

Straightening, Harrison turned to the others, his head nodding to each of the men in turn. "Monsieur Dessaline, Monsieur le Marquis, Mr. Carleton, Major, I'm sure all of this will result in the just punishment of Colonel Morehead; but I also firmly believe he will come to his senses and confess fully so Mademoiselle Mignon can be saved. I shall do my utmost to convince his counselor to so persuade him, adding to my argument that if he's foolish enough to choose the gallows, I shall personally bribe his executioner to tie the knot so he takes an hour to strangle instead of painlessly breaking his neck immediately at his fall."

At Aimée's delicate shudder he turned quickly to her and, taking her hand, begged, "Forgive me, Mademoiselle Dessaline. The memory of what you and your companions have told me tonight so infuriates me I forgot you were within hearing, and spoke too bluntly."

"Sir, the details of such an execution are welcome to my ears, terrible as they are, for I have seen what they did to my brother. And if my sister is given to that renegade, I shall be happy to release with my own hand the trap under Morehead's feet when the moment comes," Aimée said so vehemently she startled him.

"Yes, my dear, I can understand your feelings, of course," Harrison replied nervously, and turned away.

"We too should consider taking our leave," Vale said quickly. "Perhaps, Aimée, Marcel, you'd like to go upstairs and decide what other items you'll need from your wardrobe, while I walk with Lieutenant Harrison to the stable and fetch our carriage. Ben, why don't you just relax and finish your brandy."

Benjamin settled back in the chair he'd been rising from, and Marcel and Aimée turned to follow two privates up the stairs to their former rooms. Lieutenant Harrison said his good nights to Major Templeton, then Vale and the lieutenant put on their cloaks and left.

"I didn't mean to upset your fiancée with what I said." Harrison apologized again as they turned to walk around the house toward the stable.

"That's quite all right, Lieutenant. I'm sure she will think of your remarks later and be reassured by your sympathy for her sister's plight," Vale replied.

"It's just that she—all of you have endured so much at Morehead's hands. I can't bear the thought of that scoundrel sending an innocent girl like Mignon to a renegade out of sheer perversity," Harrison added.

"If Morehead should decide not to speak, Mr. Carleton and I will set out for the wilderness ourselves and find Stalking Bear somehow," Vale said firmly. "If Mignon has been . . ." He stopped, his eyes focused on the darkness before the stable. "What the . . ." he began.

Several men had led horses out of the stable and were hurriedly mounting. One of the two wearing uniforms was struggling in vain to mount a horse Vale suddenly recognized as Brandy.

"Blast, you fool, not that animal!" the second man in uniform hissed. Vale's sharp eyes focused on him and perceived he was wearing a colonel's insignia. There was only one colonel at this headquarters—Morehead!

Throwing off his cloak so its cumbersome folds wouldn't hinder him. Vale started to run toward the men; but Morehead had turned his horse. Seeing that they'd been discovered, and recognizing Vale's tall figure racing toward him, he swore an oath and viciously kicked his mount. The animal squealed once in protest, then plunged directly toward Vale, already running so fast Vale had no choice but to swerve aside or be trampled.

"Good-bye, Monsieur le Marquis!" Morehead shouted, and laughed as he raced by.

"You'll see me again," Vale muttered, and turned to run toward the second uniformed man, still struggling with

Brandy, who kept whirling around rather than obey the man who had finally gained his back.

"Brandy, whoa!" Vale called. The horse immediately paused in his turning, then half reared. Vale's muscles coiled, then lengthened as he launched himself up to grasp the man's shoulders, dragging him off the back of Brandy's haunches.

The man hurriedly tried to rise, but Vale was already on his feet and kicked the side of his head. The man cried out and fell to his hands and knees. Vale reached down to grasp a handful of his hair, then pulled his head up to stare at him.

"The British army has certain rules about how their prisoners are treated, but I don't," Vale snarled. Reaching under his coat for the smaller version of his hunting knife, which he'd impulsively strapped at his waist, he laid the sharp edge of the blade against Woolsey's throat. "If you don't tell me this moment where Mignon Dessaline is being held, I'll slaughter you right now like the swine you are."

"Le Mouton Noir, in the cellar," Woolsey whispered, afraid to speak aloud lest the movement of his throat muscles against the razor-sharp blade cause his end.

Vale withdrew the knife and jerked Woolsey to his feet. "If you're lying . . ." he began.

"You'll never get there in time," Woolsey said hastily. "Ugland will have just left with the girl. He, Dark Otter, and the others are meeting Morehead and Millbank at the edge of the forest."

"They're going straight to Stalking Bear?" Vale concluded, twisting Woolsey's arm around his back and giving it a sharp wrench.

Woosley grunted in pain and was relieved to see several soldiers hurrying in their direction. "Yes, yes—you're right! That's where they're going!" he agreed.

"Then that's where we're going too," Vale said, "because you're going to show us the way."

"But . . ."

"And I promise you this, if you try to mislead us—even after we're on the trail—although you'll be the major's prisoner and his soldiers will be guarding you, you won't have to be afraid of being tried and going to the gallows," Vale said softly near Woolsey's ear, "because I'll kill you myself."

Chapter 25

"Walk," Vale snapped, giving Woolsey's bent arm a sudden jerk upward.

Woolsey gasped in pain. Although he was a bit heavier than Vale and had all of Vale's height, he glanced fearfully over his shoulder and hastily stumbled toward the door.

Pushing Woolsey ahead, Vale reentered the house, his eyes narrowed and angry. "Morehead's escaped," he announced tersely.

He released Woolsey's arm, simultaneously giving him a shove that sent the man slamming against the fireplace. Seeing Woolsey's hand near the poker, Vale said coolly, "Go ahead and try it. I might be able to find Stalking Bear without you."

Ben rushed to Woolsey, wrenching him away from the mantel, spinning him around to face him. "Where's Mignon?" he demanded.

Woolsey looked from Vale to Benjamin to Marcel, whose amber eyes were dark with fury; then he called, "Major, get them away from me! I didn't do nothing to the girl! She was at Le Mouton Noir, but they've left for Stalking Bear's camp by now. All Dark Otter would say is four or five days due northwest. I swear it's all I know! That tall one said he'd kill me. Tried to slit my throat out there!"

"If I'd tried, I would have done it," Vale advised.

Templeton came closer to Woolsey and asked coldly, "What is your name?"

"Woolsey—Jake Woolsey. Didn't want to put on this uniform, didn't want to pretend I was a lawyer. I had to,

Major. Couldn't say no!" Woolsey exclaimed, still giving Vale fearful looks beyond Templeton's shoulder.

"You're a liar, Mr. Woolsey," Templeton said, his green eyes glittering with the warmth of broken glass. "Has anyone harmed Miss Dessaline?"

"No! I swear no one's laid a hand on her!" Woolsey cried, vehemently shaking his head.

"You tried to put quite a lot more than a hand on Mignon when you broke into our room at Le Mouton Noir," Aimée recalled. "You practically tore off her nightgown. If Vale and Ben hadn't come in . . ."

Woolsey remembered how Vale had kicked him and almost broken his jaw with his blow. He'd thought later, after he'd regained his senses, that he'd been made a eunuch. From the corner of his eye he cast Vale a look of hatred, but Vale had turned to listen to Benjamin.

"Four or five days to the northwest?" Benjamin was saying. "I can't believe that's all he knows. Maybe we should put him with Vale in the room in the cellar that Morehead was locked in. What do you think, Major Templeton? Vale spent his boyhood with the Indians." Benjamin turned to regard Woolsey, who was now avidly listening. "Did you know, Woolsey? I'd wager Vale learned all kinds of ways to make you tell him anything he wants to hear."

"The Abnakis don't believe in prolonged torture," Vale said softly, drawing nearer to Woolsey. "They just convince a person they'll kill him if he doesn't tell them what they want to know; and if he still won't speak, they do kill him because he's of no use to them anyway."

Woolsey shuddered and turned to Templeton. "Major, I don't know no more. I swear that's all that renegade Dark Otter told any of us. He was supposed to show us the way to Stalking Bear's camp."

Templeton looked at Woolsey with an expression of distaste. "Corporal Blythe, Sergeant Hunter, take this prisoner down to the room Morehead has so unfortunately vacated. If I decide to let the marquis question him further, we'll have him brought back upstairs."

As the two soldiers took the only partially relieved Woolsey past, Aimée swept aside her skirts as if even his brushing them would contaminate her. She ran to Vale, asking, "What will we do if that really is all he knows?"

Vale put his arm comfortingly around her. "We'll do our best to find Mignon anyway," he said quietly. He lifted his eyes to Templeton. "We'd best prepare for at least a week's trek through the forest, Major."

"*We*, Monsieur le Marquis? This is an army matter and—" Templeton began.

"I love Mignon and plan to marry her. You won't leave me behind," Benjamin declared.

"And I did live with the Abnakis," Vale said. "I speak their language and I know things about the forest you can't, Major Templeton. I could be very valuable to you on such an expedition."

Templeton considered this information a moment, then relented. "All right, Monsieur le Marquis. You can go."

"And I?" Benjamin demanded. "If you won't let me go with your party, Major, I warn you that I'll follow anyway."

Templeton sighed. "I guess you might as well go with us if I'll have to worry about your getting into trouble tagging behind."

"Mignon is my sister, Major Templeton. I want to go too," Marcel said.

"I can ride as well as any of you," Aimée declared. "Mignon's my sister too."

Templeton shook his head emphatically. "I will not have a man with a broken rib trying to keep pace with us. I'll not have a woman slowing us down," he said firmly. "I don't care how well you ride, Mademoiselle Dessaline. It's just too awkward taking a woman, highly irregular—petticoats and all, you know—no privacy," he finished, looking embarrassed.

"When you rescue Mignon, you'll have to take her back. You won't have privacy then," Aimée reasoned.

"That can't be prevented," Templeton said. "It's different."

"Major, in this house are a pair of my brother's old breeches I've worn when I went riding alone. I wouldn't wear petticoats on such a journey—I prefer riding astride anyway," Aimée argued. "I'll braid my hair like an Indian woman's to get it out of the way. The Indians travel through the forest with their women. Why can't I? I'll be no trouble to you. Let my privacy be my own concern. Let it be my responsibility to be discreet."

"Mademoiselle Dessaline, you are not an Indian woman; and when I think of my men's reaction to seeing you in breeches . . ." Templeton was horrified at the idea. He turned to Vale, his expression pleading for help.

"Aimée, I know how you ride and I know how you feel about Mignon. But I agree with the major. You just can't go. It's too dangerous," Vale said firmly. "Marcel obviously can't travel with a broken rib. How would he feel having to stay here worrying about not one but two sisters?"

With Vale taking Templeton's side and Marcel saying nothing more, Aimée fell silent; but when she turned toward Marcel, she noted how his blazing eyes revealed the same emotions she felt. She resolved to argue no longer. She would speak with Marcel about this later, in private.

Satisfied that Aimée finally seemed convinced that her idea should be abandoned, Vale turned to Templeton. "When should Ben and I be ready to leave?" he asked.

"It will take almost half a day to get everything organized. I should say we'll be ready to leave tomorrow after lunch," the major answered.

"Ben and I will be here then," Vale promised.

Later that night at the hotel, when Vale came to Aimée's room, she gladly opened her arms to him. Although neither of them spoke of it, they both were acutely aware that this would be the last time they'd have together before he left with the search party; and his lovemaking held the desperate passion of a man who is aware that he might not return.

Aimée didn't ask Vale again to let her accompany him on the journey; but long after he was sleeping she lay awake shaping her own plans.

*   *   *

When Aimée awoke the next morning, Vale had already left her room. This aroused no worry in her, as she'd known he'd leave discreetly so the maid—a different girl came each morning—wouldn't find him there. She wrote a note to Marcel and asked the maid, who'd brought her hot chocolate and a brioche, to deliver it. Only a few minutes after the maid had left, there was a light tapping on Aimée's door.

She hurriedly got out of bed and put on her dressing gown, then called for her visitor to enter.

Marcel immediately stepped into the room and, quickly closing the door behind him, came to take Aimée's hands in his. "You were thinking the same thing last night as I," he guessed.

"It was Ben who gave me the idea. I've been awake almost all night thinking about it," Aimée confirmed, then asked anxiously, "Do you truly think you could undertake such a journey? Answer me honestly, Marcel. If your rib will pain you too much, we might have to return anyway; and I don't want you to add to your injury by forcing yourself. If you think you can't ride, I'll stay here with you."

"If they don't travel at a gallop all the way, which would be impossible, I'm sure I can ride without endangering myself," Marcel answered. "I doubt if my broken rib can move out of place, for Vale bound me so tightly I can hardly bend even a little. How could I come to harm if I rode Soleil?"

"You must promise me, *mon frère,* if there's any fighting to be done, you'll stay out of it," Aimée warned.

"I would remain at your side if only to protect you," he vowed. "In that case my pistol wouldn't be too much of a strain to fire."

Aimée took a sip of her chocolate. Was it possible that Marcel was minimizing the pain he was suffering? She wondered. Her brother, she reminded herself, was far too practical to set out on a trek he might slow and too proud to chance the likelihood of having to be sent back. There was no questioning the sincerity of his promise not to throw himself into any battle; because when Marcel gave his word, there was no breaking it.

"I couldn't take your old breeches away from the house last night under the major's watchful eyes and I don't want to ride all the way to Stalking Bear's camp dressed in one of my riding habits. Do you have clothes you can wear on the journey?" she asked.

Marcel shook his head. "Even if I did, we couldn't take a bundle of clothes with us to Lavaltrie when we go with Vale and Ben to say good-bye. They'd question us for certain. I was thinking, after Vale and Ben had left with the soldiers, we could ask to go up to our old rooms and get some things. We could change then and decide whatever else we'll need. Afterwards maybe you could buy our supplies while I get a packhorse ready." He squeezed her fingers and asked, "Will you know what provisions we'll need? Shall I make a list?"

"After living all winter in a cabin in the woods, I've learned enough to order supplies for all the major's men, I suspect." Aimée sighed.

"Perhaps you have at that, *ma soeur*. Wouldn't it surprise Maman if she could hear you say this?" he commented.

"Maybe not, Marcel. A great many things have happened to us since we left for France, and we all have changed," Aimée said. "Even Mignon is different—much stronger than before. I know, as frightened as she must be, she has the strength to bear all of this—at least until she's in Stalking Bear's hands." She stopped, wondering what her sister would do at such a moment, if she might try to end her life as Aimée had, rather than surrender herself to a man she didn't love. Or would she fight so hard Stalking Bear would beat her into submission or torture her as punishment? Aimée couldn't prevent herself from shuddering at any of the possibilities.

Knowing Aimée's fears, Marcel released her hands and put his arms around her. "Don't think about things like that," he said. After a moment he withdrew to look solemnly down into her face. "Instead of concentrating on what we're afraid of, let us plan what we'll do to prevent our fears from becoming reality."

Aimée struggled to control the terror that had invaded her being like a thick fog blotting out all other thoughts. Finally she asked, "How long should we wait after the search party has left?"

Relieved that his sister was able to focus on hope rather than fear, he immediately answered, "We must convince them all that we're resigned to remaining behind, so we have to act normally. We won't be able to do anything at all until after Vale and Ben have gone with the soldiers."

"Don't you think this might delay us too long? We could lose the search party's trail and find outselves just wandering around in the forest," Aimée reminded him.

"So large a group of men and horses will disturb the woods enough in their passing that even I will be able to follow, unless they deliberately cover their tracks. There's no reason for Major Templeton to go through that bother, especially during their first day or two out," Marcel replied. "If we follow any closer than a couple of hours behind the search party, I suspect at least Vale will perceive someone's presence, turn back, and find us."

"He moves so quietly through the forest we'd never know he was nearby, and would have no chance to hide ourselves before he discovered us," Aimée agreed.

"Then it's settled that we'll do nothing until after they've left?" Marcel asked.

Aimée nodded. "After we've watched the last of the search party pass through the settlement's gates, we'll hurry to our own tasks."

Because the Dessaline house in Lavaltrie was more than an hour's ride from the Hôtel Dieu in the main section of Montreal, Aimée and Marcel met Vale and Benjamin for an early lunch in the hotel's dining room before setting out for Templeton's headquarters. Aimée wore a russet wool riding habit and insisted that Brandy needed exercise. Marcel brushed aside Benjamin's suggestion that he travel in a carriage, saying coolly that one broken rib wouldn't prevent him from taking an hour's horseback ride. He added a little irritably that his rib was tightly bound and his horse, Soleil, was smooth-gaited and gentle, then gruffly changed the subject.

Although all four tried to behave normally, an air of anxiety hung over the little group during the ride to Lavaltrie. Vale and Benjamin knew only too well the dangers that faced them, and their efforts to put Aimée and Marcel at ease were strained. The Dessalines' tensions were caused more by worry that they wouldn't accomplish their secret plans than by the dangers they all soon would face.

When they arrived, they found a platoon of British soldiers lined in front of the Dessaline house awaiting Major Templeton's appearance. Woolsey stood sullenly between two guards, his hands shackled before him. Vale viewed the soldiers' scarlet coats and spotless white breeches with a critical eye and wished they would have put aside their uniforms to wear dun-colored doeskin or buckskin garments as he and Benjamin had. Their eye-catching uniforms were sure to draw the attention of any scouts Stalking Bear might send to lurk in the forest.

Benjamin too gazed doubtfully at the sight of the brightly dressed soldiers. Under his breath he remarked, "If we need to fight, Morehead's men will certainly know where to aim."

"They're a smart-looking sight, but tracking an enemy through the wilderness is a different task from laying seige to a city whose forces know in advance that you're coming. I'm sure neither Morehead nor Stalking Bear will behave with anything resembling a code of honor, and a set of regulations has yet to be written about fighting in a forest. The only rule there is is to be alive at the end of the battle," Vale agreed, and checked his saddle one last time.

"Do you suppose we could persuade Templeton to order a change of clothes for his men once we're away from Montreal?" Benjamin asked worriedly.

"I certainly intend to try," Vale promised. He saw that Major Templeton had come out of the house and was getting on his horse. "We'd best mount," he advised.

As Marcel approached to grasp Vale's hand Aimée

turned to Benjamin. She could easily understand the tumult of his emotions as he set off to rescue his love; and she impulsively put her arms around him as she wished him well.

She stepped away, reminding herself that she and Marcel would soon follow; and as she turned to Vale, her eyes gleamed with a light that made him wonder about her secret thoughts. But when she put her arms around him, she clung so closely he forgot to ask a question.

Standing on tiptoe, Aimée whispered in Vale's ear, "I know you can manage in the forest better than any of the other men, but I'll worry about you all the same. Please be careful, *mon amoureux*."

Her words stilled his curiosity, and he said softly, "We'll find Mignon and return safely. Don't be afraid." As he stepped away he added, "Instead of worrying, spend your time more pleasantly—plan the wardrobe you'll pack for our trip to France—or perhaps design your wedding gown."

Aimée dared not say aloud what she wanted to answer lest any of the others overhear, but Vale read her eyes and knew she dreamed not so much of a grand wedding as the freedom they'd have afterwards. He bent to brush her cheek with a kiss. Then, too much tempted to linger, he smiled wistfully and turned away. After he'd mounted, he turned to look down at her. Their eyes met and locked, and she reached up to touch his arm. He gathered his reins in one hand, caught her fingers with his, and held them until the order was given for the search party to leave. Only then did he release her and turn away.

She watched Vale and Benjamin, hailed by Templeton, urge their horses past the main group of soldiers to ride at the major's side.

Marcel took Aimée's hand as Vale and Benjamin passed through the settlement's gates. "Are you just about ready to begin our own expedition?" he asked under his breath. When she didn't answer immediately, he whispered, "If you're afraid, you can say you've changed your mind."

Aimée shook her head. "If I can find the courage to face the shocked stares I'll get when I walk into the store to buy the supplies we need, dressed in your breeches and with my hair plaited like an Indian woman's, I'll surely have the courage to face whatever we must in the forest."

As Aimée guided Brandy through the street toward the settlement's open gates, she coolly ignored the surprised glances that grew into admiring stares from the men who watched her pass. Two women, horrified by the sight of Aimée clad in breeches and riding astride like a man, gasped aloud and stepped back against their servants. The men, following with armloads of their mistresses' purchases, had paused to gape at Aimée with open mouths. Their bundles scattered; and an Indian, leaning against a nearby building, chuckled and moved away.

"You're causing such a sensation, I wonder how you can keep your composure," Marcel commented.

"After the commotion Lieutenant Crowell caused when I came downstairs dressed this way, I believe I can endure anything," Aimée replied. She frowned and added, "He actually had the nerve to forbid me to leave the house, and order me to go back upstairs and change."

Marcel turned to look at Aimée in surprise. "He did? Why didn't you call me? How did you get out of the house?"

"By reminding him that he was under the Dessaline roof, not his own; that I was neither his daughter nor wife—certainly not one of his recruits—and he couldn't command me about any matter," she answered calmly. "He was so surprised that a woman would say such a thing to him, he just stared at me as I stepped around him and left. I only heard him say one more word—'impertinent'—before I closed the door behind me, but I'm sure many others followed."

"No doubt," Marcel agreed.

When they reached the gates, they were stopped by the sentries and questioned about their reason for leaving.

"An old trapper, who was a friend of my father's, is ill. We're going to his cabin to care for him," Marcel lied, and noting that the soldier who'd addressed him was staring fixedly at the length of Aimée's snugly clad leg, Marcel added warningly, "My sister is not a lady to be gaped at."

The soldier jerked his eyes up to look red-facedly at Marcel. He knew who the Dessalines were, and he'd seen them associating with Major Templeton, who was now his commanding officer. He said hastily, "I'm sorry, Monsieur Dessaline. Beg pardon, mademoiselle. Have a pleasant ride, but please remember that the gates are closed at sundown."

"I'm aware of that," Marcel replied, and, giving his horse a little squeeze with his leg, passed through the gates.

Aimée raised her eyes to the forest in the distance. "We've successfully passed all the barricades the British army has so far thrown before us. Now let's hope, after we catch up with the search party, Major Templeton won't order us to turn back."

"I think we shouldn't approach them until at least tomorrow evening after they've camped for the night. By then I'll be able to tell him we can't find our way back to Lavaltrie," Marcel said.

"But you never get lost in the forest!" Aimée declared in surprise.

Marcel grinned. "Major Templeton doesn't know that, and I hope Vale won't guess," he said, and turned his horse to trot as precisely northwest as the soldiers had done with the aid of their compass.

Melted snow streamed over the forest floor, gathering in low areas into wide puddles that extended their channels farther into the wilderness like shallow creeks. Sounds carried far in the clear air, and with the shrubbery only beginning to leaf, the movements of animals could be seen for some distance, so Marcel set a leisurely pace. He didn't want anyone in the search party to hear a human voice or catch sight of their horses.

Few ground flowers had opened yet; but if Aimée looked straight down into the puddles Brandy was so daintly stepping through, she could see that the soil was covered with green sprouts. The trees and bushes were

coated with thick clumps of green buds almost ready to
unfurl, and a few crab apple trees had already burst into
bloom. The exhilarating effect of green things stirring in
the spring sun permeated the crisp air, and Aimée wished
she could absorb the spirit of the forest's awakening to
drive away her fears of what lay ahead.

The travelers tried to avoid stopping because neither
cared to step down onto the spongy ground. Aimée could
see, as the afternoon's shadows lengthened into violet
streaks, it wasn't going to be easy to find a dry place to
make their own camp for the night. It was late dusk—so
near to darkness that they had difficulty making out their
route—when Marcel found a stony area elevated enough
so the water didn't seep into it.

"I never thought I'd purposely search for rocks to sleep
on, but it's quite impossible to camp anywhere else." Marcel apologized as he helped Aimée down from her saddle.

"I'd rather sleep on stone than with the water lapping in
my ears," Aimée quipped. She turned slowly, inspecting
the area. "I see a branch or two on that dead tree that we
could use to make a fire."

"Non, ma petite soeur. We can't make a fire tonight.
I'm sorry," Marcel said as he peered at the surrounding
forest. "The breeze is blowing away from us toward the
search party, and they could too easily catch the scent of
our smoke. With the woods as wet as they are, Vale would
know immediately that it was from someone else's campfire, and would surely come to investigate. The flames
would reflect on the water for some distance, and we'd be
easy to find."

Aimée sighed with disappointment. "We'll have to eat a
cold supper without even a warm drink to cheer us, but if
it must be . . ."

"Anticipating a night like this, I went down into the cellar where father kept his wines locked up, and took a
small bottle of brandy," Marcel said. "A few sips of that
should help warm our insides when we're ready to sleep."

"That was a wonderful idea," Aimée agreed. "I just
hope none of Templeton's men saw where you went."

"Don't worry about that," Marcel assured. "All of father's wines and liqueurs had to be brought from France and were far too costly to share with our conquerors. They may have been able to confiscate our house, but they don't know all of its secrets."

Aimée and Marcel ate their unappetizing meal quickly; the forest was now so dark that they could locate each other only by the sound of their lowered voices. It seemed useless to remain awake now; so they decided to unroll their blankets.

Aimée was drifting on the edge of sleep when a voice came out of the darkness startling her.

"One of the most dangerous things you can do when you sleep on the ground in the open like this is not to light a fire."

Had she been dreaming? Aimée wondered, peering into the night, seeing nothing. She reached out to nudge Marcel's shoulder, afraid to speak aloud. As Marcel sat up, the blackness was suddenly lit by the flickering of a small torch.

"Animals come too close to a camp when there's no fire to ward them off," Vale said softly as he stopped beside them.

"How did you guess we were here?" Marcel exclaimed. "I did everything I could think of so that you would not hear us or see us."

"I never did hear or see you," Vale answered. "It was just that back at Lavaltrie when Aimée said good-bye, she had a look in her eyes not exactly suitable for a woman sending her fiancée on a dangerous journey. I have no doubt that Aimée loves me and ordinarily would worry about my welfare, so I had to conclude she'd made some other plan. Earlier, when the search party passed this rocky area, it occurred to me, if you were following, you'd likely have to choose this place to sleep; so I came back."

"But it's dark as pitch! How could you find your way?" Aimée exclaimed in amazement.

"Brandy's ears are much better than yours. When I thought I was nearing this area, I called to him so softly you couldn't hear; but he did and answered," Vale replied.

"I did hear him nicker several times, but I thought he was talking to Soleil," Aimée admitted.

Marcel slowly got to his feet. "I suppose now you're going to tell us to go back to Lavaltrie," he said.

"How does your rib feel after an afternoon of traveling?" Vale asked.

"Riding Soleil didn't bother my rib any more than if I'd walked all the way," Marcel answered. "It was falling asleep on this cold, damp rock that made me stiff."

"Templeton's men are camped in a better place than this—on a hill where it's dry," Vale said. "Come with me and you'll have a more comfortable night."

"Do you think the major will try to send us back to Lavaltrie in the morning?" Aimée asked.

"I suppose his argument that Marcel can't ride with a broken rib won't be valid after you've come all this distance and no harm was done. You and Marcel will probably claim you won't be able to find your way back with all this water covering your tracks."

"I know I certainly couldn't," Aimée declared.

"It would be very difficult," Marcel solemnly agreed.

"I don't believe either of you; and I'm not particularly happy you insisted on doing this, though I understand your reasons," Vale said quietly. He paused a moment, his eyes troubled in the flickering light. Finally he continued, "I suspect you would only pretend to turn back, then circle around and follow us anyway, so it might be better for you to join the search party. I won't be able to keep my mind on what I'm doing if I have to worry about your making an easy target as you trail behind us, should any of Stalking Bear's renegades discover our whereabouts. Whether or not Major Templeton will agree with me is something we'll have to find out."

Chapter 26

After a wearisome trek sloshing through water in the dark wilderness, Aimée and Marcel became aware of a slight incline in the ground. Soon they escaped the soggy forest floor and saw the welcome light of a fire ahead. They entered the British encampment. No one stirred except the sentries and Benjamin who immediately approached.

Benjamin looked up at Aimée and Marcel without surprise, greeted them, then turned his attention to Vale. His voice was softened in the night's hush as he said, "I've been waiting for you. When Templeton noticed you had disappeared, he guessed you suspected Aimée and Marcel were following, and went to fetch them. He wants to talk to you after you've gotten them settled down for the night."

Vale glanced at the one tent that had been set up in the clearing. It was softly lit by a small lantern. Then he put out his arms to Aimée and helped her down from her saddle.

"Maybe I should go with you to speak to Major Templeton," Marcel said as he dismounted.

"I think not," Benjamin replied, an ominous tone in his voice. He looked at the blanket-covered bodies of the soldiers who were sleeping on the ground near the tent, at Woolsey who snored with his back propped against the tree he was shackled to. "You and Aimée make your beds nearer the fire, and I'll take care of your horses while Vale talks to Templeton."

"I'll have to unsaddle Brandy, Ben; but you can do the others, and thanks," Vale said. He took Aimée's hands in his. "We're away from the low area of the forest now, and the gound here is dry, so you should be comfortable by the fire. After I've talked with the major, I'll choose a place near you to sleep; so you won't have to search for me if you have need of anything during the night."

"Are you sure Marcel and I shouldn't go with you to speak with Major Templeton?" Aimée asked anxiously. "After all, you are planning to discuss what will be done with us."

"If he's as annoyed as I suspect, your presence will only make matters worse," Vale answered. "Get yourselves some rest. You've both had a long day."

Marcel approached Vale. "Aimée and I aren't here on a whim. We discussed all the possible difficulties of this expedition before we decided to come."

"I could see you'd planned it well," Vale agreed.

"If it becomes necessary, you should tell Major Templeton that Aimée and I are determined to continue our search for our sister," Marcel said firmly. "If he forbids our traveling in his company, we shall follow on our own. He considers this to be a military operation, but Aimée and I are civilians and need not take orders from him. If he forces us to return to Montreal, he'll have to send a couple of his men with us—and I don't think he can spare them."

Vale sighed in resignation. "If it comes to that, I'll tell him," he promised, and turned away.

Aimée found a level place near the fire where the new grass made a soft, thick carpet, and spread out her blankets. But after she and Marcel exchanged whispered good nights, she didn't close her eyes. She stared through the leaping flames of the fire, her attention focused on the tent at the far side of the clearing, her ears straining to hear even a hint of the discussion being carried on inside. She heard nothing. It seemed to her that hours had passed before she saw Vale's tall silhouette emerge from between the tent's flaps.

She watched intently as he paused to stoop for a moment beside Benjamin's blanket-wrapped form, then Marcel's. Finally he approached her hesitantly.

"I'm still awake," she whispered.

Vale bent to arrange his own blanket a discreet several feet from hers before he said softly, "Templeton's agreed to let you and Marcel remain with his search party."

Aimée let out a breath in relief. "I didn't look forward to our traveling alone all the way," she admitted.

Vale lay down on his side, facing her. "Did you think Ben and I would have let you and Marcel wander around in the forest alone?" he asked quietly. "When I told Templeton that you and Marcel were determined to continue—independently of the soldiers, if necessary—I also explained that Ben and I couldn't allow you to do this. We'd leave him, to travel with you. Of course, Templeton didn't want you to go off anywhere unless you'd agreed to return to Montreal."

"I'm sorry we have to cause you and everyone else so much trouble," Aimée whispered.

"Loving you may sometimes give me problems, but it will never be trouble," Vale murmured. His hand emerged from under his blanket and reached out toward her. She found, if she extended her arm almost as far as she could, it was possible to grasp his fingers.

Neither spoke again. The firelight was reflected in their faces, and both wished propriety didn't force them to endure the distance that separated them. Aimée wanted only to be enclosed in Vale's arms. She knew his strength would banish her persistent nightmarish thoughts about Mignon's situation. Her exhaustion crept up on her, but she struggled to remain awake, wanting to absorb the warmth that shone from his eyes, even if she couldn't share the warmth of his body close to hers. Noting that Aimée was fighting sleep, Vale murmured his good night and shut his eyes, knowing she'd now close hers as well.

Aimée gazed at the strong lines of his face, the dark lashes that lay against his cheek, the softly lingering smile his lips wore, until weariness finally overcame her; and she slipped into slumber.

"Major Templeton, I just saw some caribou tracks down by the river," the corporal said eagerly. "I'd say, from the size of them, they belong to a young buck or a large doe.

If it's a doe, she's an old one, because there's no hoof-prints from a fawn. Either way, it's dragging a hind foot and will make an easy catch for a predator. May I have your permission, sir, to track it down and shoot it?"

Thinking the soldier meant to supplement the provisions because he and Aimée had joined the group, Marcel quickly said, "Aimée and I brought our own supplies, Major Templeton."

Templeton put down his coffee mug and looked at Marcel. "I already know that, Monsieur Dessaline; but none of us can be sure this expedition won't take longer than Woolsey said. It might be wise to save our provisions if fresh meat is available."

Vale, who had been sitting on a log with Aimée while they ate breakfast, got to his feet. "You're right about that, Major Templeton," he agreed. "But the sound of a gun-shot will carry a long way; and if Stalking Bear has any scouts in the area, they'll surely hear it. How about my taking my bow and arrows to hunt it down?"

"Oh, please, Vale, could I come with you?" Aimée asked eagerly.

Templeton hesitated to answer, and Vale understood his reason. Early the previous afternoon the sergeant had dropped the compass, and it had smashed. Afterwards, riding at Templeton's side, Vale had become aware that the major wasn't very skilled at tracking; and he knew Templeton was privately afraid of confusing his directions if Vale left the party.

"We could easily find and rejoin your party, as you'd only be moving upriver for the better part of the day," Vale said tactfully.

Templeton's green eyes revealed his gratitude for Vale's diplomacy before the corporal, although he said dryly, "If you wish to remove Mademoiselle Dessaline's fair form from under the stares of my men for a few hours, I would consider it a favor—providing you're certain she won't be in any particular danger."

"It's perfectly safe for Aimée to accompany me," Vale replied. "I'll give her one of my pistols to carry. You'd be surprised at how well she can shoot."

"Marcel taught me how to fire a gun, Major Templeton," Aimée said proudly. "I shot an Iroquois when we were attacked on our way to Montreal."

"Did you?" Templeton couldn't conceal his surprise. He absorbed that news before turning to Vale. "Well, Monsieur le Marquis, I wish you good hunting," he finally said.

"The night I found you in that inn having your supper I asked you to call me Vale or Valjean. I do prefer to be addressed by either name, rather than by my title," Vale advised him.

Templeton looked nonplussed for a moment before he said, "If I'm to address a marquis so familiarly by his given name, I should extend the same courtesy to you. Please call me Stewart. After all, you aren't one of my men."

Aimée wondered at the brief smile Vale flashed Templeton before he turned away. It appeared they had some other, unspoken agreement between them. She said nothing about it until after she and Vale had ridden down to the riverbank to find the caribou's trail.

Vale had dismounted to study the animal's tracks when she commented, "You and Major Templeton seem to have become friends—using first names and all."

Vale glanced up at her and said somewhat distractedly, "We've become friendly, though I don't know if I could say we're really friends."

"Something went on between you two that I didn't understand. Only people who are good friends can carry on a conversation without the others around understanding it," Aimée persisted.

Vale straightened, still engrossed in his task, and swung up into his saddle. "The caribou is a buck, I'm sure. I wonder how it got separated from the herd."

"Maybe some predator wounded its leg and drove it away from the other caribou," Aimée suggested.

"I was thinking the same thing. If it's true, whatever wounded it still could be tracking it," Vale said. "If it's a wolf or even a pack, they'll present no problem for us because they'll withdraw as soon as they know we're nearby.

It also could be a bear just out of hibernation and hungry—and a bear isn't likely to step aside politely."

"Can you see any other tracks?" Aimée asked, now uneasy about the possibility of a bear's watching them.

"No," Vale replied. "Perhaps I'm wrong and nothing is following the caribou other than ourselves. Don't worry, Aimée. If I begin to suspect a bear is nearby, I'll do everything I can to avoid it," he assured her, and urged his horse forward to follow the caribou's trail.

Encouraged by Vale's attitude, Aimée remembered then to ask about Templeton. "What was it that you and Major Templeton were avoiding saying in front of the rest of us?"

Vale gave her a sideways glance. "You must promise to keep it to yourself—for Major Templeton's sake," he warned. She nodded agreement, and he explained, "I realized yesterday that he has little sense of direction in the forest. He's not used to the wilderness, but he's a good officer and trying to learn, so I never said anything to embarrass him in front of his men. I wouldn't like to ruin his chances of becoming commandant in Morehead's place."

"Marcel can guide him until we get back," Aimée said, foregetting she'd lied even to Vale about Marcel's ability to travel through the forest. Suddenly she realized she'd given herself away. She cast Vale a guilty glance, but he was smiling.

"I told you both last night I didn't believe you'd get lost," he reminded her.

"I feel bad that I lied to you," she confessed.

"If it's so easy for me to see through your deceptions, I'm not particularly alarmed at the possibility of future lies of that sort," he said calmly.

"There will be none," she vowed.

Vale and Aimée followed the trail along the riverbank until the tracks swerved and disappeared into the water. Vale turned his horse to enter the river. Aimée followed without hesitance, knowing Brandy didn't balk at a swim; but she soon discovered it wouldn't be necessary for the horses to swin. This part of the river made a sharp bend, so the current seemed to pause. Deposits of silt and pebbles over the river's lifetime had built long bars that extended under the water from each side of the riverbank, forming a sort of natural walkway. The caribou had wisely chosen a place to cross where the water lapped only as high as the horses' knees. Vale easily picked up the caribou's trail on the opposite shore and followed it along the base of a line of bluffs that edged the water.

Although they had traveled little more than an hour downriver from Templeton's camp, the morning sky had been steadily growing more overcast. They had started making their way into a canyon formed by a split through the center of the bluff when a suspiciously moist wind began to blow. A sudden strong gust flattened the shivering young grasses to the canyon floor and sent spirals of loose pebbles against the face of the rocky walls.

Vale paused and tilted his head to examine the arch of the heavens. The sky no longer was merely gray. Tatters of black were spreading among billows of lavender becoming purple. On the horizon a jagged thread of lightning glowed.

"Sudden spring storms like this usually don't last long, but they can be quite violent," he said, and lowered his eyes to meet Aimée's. "I think we should find shelter."

Again his gaze lifted, but this time he was studying the cliff wall, hoping to find shelter. The horses were growing more nervous every moment; and he knew, when the storm approached closely enough, the thunderclaps were likely to make the animals bolt. The only shelter he could see was a large hollow that once had held a great boulder before it had torn loose and rolled to the canyon floor. A slab of rock jutting out above the hollow formed a kind of roof that extended further protection. He pointed out the place.

"That's the best possibility I can see, Aimée," he said, raising his voice to be heard over another gust of wind. "We'll have to lead our horses very carefully up that little incline, because it's all loose stones. Do you think you can follow me if I go first to choose the best footing?"

A rumble of the still distant thunder sounded, and Aimée felt Brandy's muscles tense beneath her. She patted his neck and murmured softly to soothe him before she looked up at Vale to answer, "I think we have no choice."

They dismounted immediately. Holding Brandy's bridle with one hand, stroking his neck with the other, Aimée followed Vale. The horses soon became less concerned with the approaching storm than with keeping their balance on the treacherously loose stones. Aimée released Brandy's bridle and only held his reins to give him space to move in as she scrambled up the incline at his side. When they finally entered the hollow's shelter, she was breathless.

The lightning's fire split the sky, followed by a crash of thunder that made the rock walls around them seem to vibrate. The horses threw up their heads in alarm, but Vale and Aimée spoke softly to them; and the calm of their master and mistress reassured them enough so they only shivered at the next thunderclap. Bright flares lit the canyon floor, and the rain began. Big, heavy drops accelerated into crystal sheets pouring over the rocks, forming a shimmering veil around the opening of the hollow.

Assuming that the violence of the storm must frighten Aimée, Vale turned to look at her and was surprised that she appeared exhilarated by it. "I think you feel the same way about storms as I do," he commented.

She extended her arm to gather rain on her hand. "Even when I was a child, whenever a summer storm was coming, I'd go outside until it began to rain, despite my mother's warnings that I'd get wet and catch a cold. My mother said in exasperation that I was like a little animal, that it would be a chore to mold me into a proper young lady."

"Your mother managed to accomplish her goals; but beneath all that lace and satin I've seen you wear so comfortably, I did perceive that little animal your mother recognized," Vale said softly. He lifted her hand to his lips and touched his tongue to her wet skin to taste the rain. A streak of lightning lit his eyes to silver. "Or maybe I'd more properly be called the animal and you're the wind blowing through my fur, always enticing me to venture a little farther into the storm you're making for me." Recognizing the meaning behind the amber lights growing brighter in her eyes, he lowered her hand and sighed. "If we didn't have two nervous horses to tend, I think you'd enjoy making love in this storm. I know I would."

Aimée felt as if the forces of the thunderstorm were charging her body with energies that could explode with the same power as the skies. She dragged her gaze from Vale's, staring at the crystal stream of water that poured before her; but she couldn't turn her mind from thoughts of how it would be to combine her body with Vale's and unleash their emotions during a storm such as this, their hearts becoming one with the wind and the lightning's fire.

Vale could see the tension in Aimée's profile, in the lights shimmering in her eyes. She lowered her gaze, the burnished lashes spread against her cheeks now moist with the rain; and he stepped away. "There will be other storms, Aimée," he said softly.

"Didn't you once say the Abnakis thought that each time a moment of love was allowed to pass unused, a bit of love was wasted?" she reminded him, then whispered, "When circumstances force us to let one of these moments slip away, I can't help but feel saddened by its loss."

Vale slid one arm around her waist and said quietly, "The moment hasn't been lost, Aimée. We're loving right now."

She considered this viewpoint; and though she knew in her heart he was right, she couldn't ignore her resentment that they weren't free to love as they would.

"The storm is almost over."

Vale's comment aroused Aimée from her thoughts, and she focused her eyes on the entrance to the hollow. The rain had almost stopped, and she could see the canyon floor again. The sky beyond the overhanging ledge was clearing, and the sun was finding its way through the thinning clouds. She followed Vale and his horse from the hollow, of necessity fixing her attention on safely moving down the slope where the loose pebbles had been made even more slippery by the rain. When they reached the floor of the canyon, her mind returned to her dilemma. How she wished that the waiting were over so that she and

Vale could marry. Impatience again flooded her with resentment.

Vale helped Aimée mount Brandy, then turned away to pace slowly along the canyon floor examining the ground. Finally he turned back and swung up into his saddle. "As I'd expected, the caribou's tracks have been washed away. If we don't see the caribou itself beyond this little canyon, we might as well give up our hunt and rejoin the soldiers."

"Perhaps so," Aimée agreed, knowing her own thoughts had drained her of enthusiasm for the hunt even if the tracks had been visible.

The end of the canyon narrowed so, though they went single file, their stirrups almost scraped the walls.

"Get back!" Vale's warning startled Aimée from her lethargy.

She urged Brandy backwards, but the wind brought him the scent of a bear, of fresh blood beyond the canyon. He scuttled sideways, trying desperately to turn so he could more swiftly flee a creature that was his natural enemy. In the narrow space he couldn't turn; and discovering this, he panicked and reared.

"Back, Brandy, back!" Aimée cried, trying to straighten him.

But in that moment Vale's horse, unable to retreat—the animal had been struck a glancing blow by one of Brandy's hooves—plunged forward, dashing Vale's shoulder against the stone wall, throwing Vale off balance as the horse leaped out of the canyon exit.

Temporarily driven from the caribou carcass by the thunderstorm, the bear had no intention of letting human or horse interfere with his meal now. He bellowed in anger and stood up on his hind legs, waving his huge paws in challenge. Although the bear was several yards away, Vale's horse screamed in fear, then reared, striking out with his hooves; and Vale, already half unseated, his shoulder paralyzed with pain, crashed to the ground. He rolled clear of the horse's flashing hooves but found himself even closer to the bear. He got to his feet quickly as he unsheathed his hunting knife, the only weapon he wore, and hoped, if he stood still enough, the bear wouldn't attack.

Aimée was still struggling with Brandy in the canyon. She sawed the bit from side to side in his mouth, making him aware of a much closer pain; so finally he was manageable, enabling her to fling herself from the saddle.

It was like a nightmare unfolding before her eyes. The bear seemed like a shaggy mountain roaring at Vale, his long pointed fangs gleaming in a slavering mouth, caribou blood smeared over his muzzle. The animal waved razor-sharp claws the length of Aimée's hand as he lumbered another step toward Vale. For a moment she was too stunned by terror to move; and in that short space of time the bear struck, its foreleg moving with such surprising speed that Vale had only the chance to begin to leap back. But even this beginning retreat saved him from suffering the full power of the blow. Instead of crushing Vale's back, the bear's paw swept him aside as if he were no more than the branch of a sapling. Aimée's heart stopped. Vale didn't leap to his feet this time. He lay sprawled on the ground like a rag doll, only a few feet away from the bear.

Suddenly she remembered the pistol Vale had given her. It was in her saddlebag. She turned to Brandy, who still stood in the canyon's opening, too terrified to come out and be even closer to the bear, but loath to abandon his mistress, the one human he truly loved. Aimée ran to him and tore her saddlebag open to pull out the pistol.

"Stay, Brandy" was all she said, and she again edged past his shoulder into the open.

"Dieu! Dieu! Dieu!" she cried in despair, for the bear was again on all fours standing over Vale, sniffing at his head.

At Aimée's scream the bear looked up at her. Surprised to see this fragile human creature running straight at him, he retreated a step. Aimée didn't stop until she reached Vale. The bear snarled and again rose on his hindquarters to tower over Aimée. She lifted the pistol in both hands and, afraid that her shot might be deflected by the animal's great bones, aimed almost straight up at its throat.

The sound of the gun's explosion reverberated off the rock walls. The bear staggered, blood pouring down his chest from the fearful wound, and dropped to his fours. She hadn't killed him. She didn't have another shot.

"Sainte Marie, préservez-nous!" she cried, and threw herself over Vale's body.

Time seemed to stop for Aimée. All her senses seemed numb with terror, and she felt as if she were about to faint. She didn't hear the calls that came from the edge of the forest. She never noticed the arrows that flashed overhead, impaling the bear a dozen times. She wasn't even aware of the moccasined feet that approached, then stopped beside her. The brave gazed down at the fiery-haired woman in surprise. He'd thought from the distance that she was a man, for he'd heard it said often that white women wore elaborate skirts, longer dresses than the women of his tribe. Although this woman's peculiar garments perplexed him, he admired the courage she'd shown by trying to shield the wounded man from the bear with her own body. He reached down to nudge her shoulder.

Finally becoming aware of the hand on her shoulder, assuming it belonged to one of the British soldiers who by a miracle had happened upon them, Aimée turned to look up at the Indian's solemn bronzed face.

"Get to your feet, Flaming Thistle, you are safe." he said.

Not understanding his language, shocked by new fear, she could neither speak or move. It was one of Stalking Bear's renegades, she thought. Visions of nightmares she'd been having about Mignon's plight flashed through her mind, and she fainted.

The brave frowned, his eyes darkening with regret. "It is not us you need fear, Flaming Thistle," he said softly, then turned and gestured to his men.

"We could not catch the horse with hair the color of Flaming Thistle's eyes," Hunting Wolf said. "But when we picked up Flaming Thistle, the horse followed us. He stands outside the lodge now and remains quiet unless someone approaches him too closely."

"He avoids strangers always," Vale commented, trying not to flinch at the sting of the ointment the woman called Singing Pine was applying to the wounds the bear's claws had given him.

Hunting Wolf smiled. "Even our chief, Swooping Eagle, cringes at that remedy—and Singing Pine thinks it's more important to rub it thoroughly into the wounds than to spare a man pain."

"Swooping Eagle?" Vale asked incredulously. The Abnaki warrior nodded gravely. "I think I might know your chief! If I could go to him to see—maybe I would recognize him!" Vale said excitedly, then added more quietly, "Yet, we both were children then . . ."

Hunting Wolf stiffened in surprise. "How did you come to know Swooping Eagle as a child? He never visited the white villages."

"I spent my first twelve winters with an Abnaki tribe and was adopted by an Abnaki man, Walking-in-Honor. This was how I learned to speak your language so well," Vale quickly replied.

"Walking-in-Honor?" Hunting Wolf echoed. "Can it be that you are Lightning-of-the-Winter-Moon?"

Vale nodded and asked wonderingly, "Is it possible, then, that Flaming Thistle and I have been welcomed by the same tribe who took me as a babe and the woman known as my mother from the shore of the Great Waters-Spreading-to-the-Dawn?"

Hunting Wolf's expression was as stunned as if he'd just met a ghost. He leaped to his feet. "I must tell Swooping Eagle that you have come!" he exclaimed, and, not giving Vale a chance to reply, ran from the lodge.

The woman, who had been rubbing ointment into the slashes the bear had torn in Vale's back, stopped now to listen. She edged around to face Vale. "You are Lightning-of-the-Winter-Moon about whom they yet sing songs?" she whispered in awe.

"If they sing about Walking-in-Honor's white son, the songs are about me, I guess," Vale said softly.

Singing Pine was about to ask more when Aimée, lying on a stack of furs that served as a bed at the rear of the

lodge, began to stir. The Indian woman looked at Vale,
then at Aimée, torn between the red-haired woman who
required attention and this man who had behaved like a
man when he'd been only a boy. She wondered, now that
he was grown, what had he become? Finally she said apologetically, "I must tend Flaming Thistle for a moment."

Vale got to his feet. "Let me speak to her, Singing Pine.
The only Indians she's ever known are Iroquois, who
frightened her badly. If she sees me standing with you, she
won't be so afraid."

Singing Pine nodded and moved aside so Vale could
pass.

When Aimée's eyes opened to see Vale's familiar face
looking into hers, she reached up to touch his hand. "I had
another nightmare, I think . . ." she began then, noticing
Singing Pine, stiffened with fear.

"We're safe, Aimée. Singing Pine is an Abnaki. Stalking
Bear's renegades haven't captured us, if that's what you
thought. In fact, I think this is the same tribe I lived with.
Their chief, Swooping Eagle, is coming to see if I'm the
boy he swam and hunted with—his friend of long ago."
Aimée had grown a little calmer, though her eyes were
still fixed suspiciously on the Indian woman who stood
nearby. Vale asked, "Are you all right. Did the bear hurt
you?"

Aimée tore her gaze from Singing Pine to look at Vale.
"The bear never touched me—but you, *mon amant*?" She
looked at the ointment that covered Vale's chest and side.
"What's this?" she gasped.

"I was clawed, but Singing Pine washed the wounds and
is putting something on them—it stings like fire, feels
worse than what the bear did—but she says it will help
me heal. My shoulder is stiff from being dashed against
the wall. My hip and leg are black with bruises from
falling off the horse—but no permanent damage done."

"But you were knocked senseless . . ." Aimée began.
She fell silent when she saw two Indian warriors enter the
lodge. They were dressed in doeskin garments very similar
to those Vale wore. One of the men wore a very finely

beaded belt and more feathers in his headband than the other. She assumed he was the chief Vale had mentioned.

"You won't be able to understand them, so you'll have to wait until I can tell you what was said," Vale warned. He turned to the men with a solemn expression.

Aimée watched carefully as Swooping Eagle peered into Vale's eyes. She knew what he was searching for—the flecks of gray that seemed to float in layers lit from behind by the cool fires that burned within—the eyes that had inspired his Abnaki name. Swooping Eagle's grave expression brightened into one of joy, and he grasped Vale's arms warmly.

After a long moment of happily exchanged greetings Swooping Eagle invited Vale to sit down again. Singing Pine could then finish applying the ointment. The three men sat cross-legged on a blanket spread on the floor. They were obviously exchanging reminiscences, and Aimée had no choice but to remain silent and watch.

She'd always been told that Indians were solemn, passionless people until they went to war; but she could see this was just a notion spread by white people who'd never seen an Indian at ease among friends. Swooping Eagle's and Hunting Wolf's faces were as animated as Vale's, their lips as ready to laugh at something humorous; their black eyes glinted with anger when Vale related some offense committed against him. Aimée speculated on the reasons Indians avoided showing any expression when they were in the presence of whites they didn't know as brothers. Did they merely want to maintain an appearance of dignity, or did they consider their emotions too private to disclose to strangers? Perhaps both, she decided.

During the conversation Singing Pine finished her task of attending Vale's wounds, gathered up her bowls, and, without a word, left the lodge. After a time another Indian woman slipped into the lodge. A slender, very comely girl with eyes as large and as deep a brown as a doe's, she was carrying a basket and a pot of some sort of stew. Although she kept her head modestly lowered, her glances were like dark little birds flying to Vale, Aimée noticed.

Shortly after the girl's entrance Swooping Eagle and

Hunting Wolf concluded the conversation and got to their feet. They glanced at Aimée, spoke briefly to Vale and left the lodge without further delay.

"I could see that man was the friend you'd thought," Aimée remarked as she watched the Indian girl place both basket and pot on the blanket where Vale had reseated himself.

"Come here and sit down with me," he said to her. "I'll tell you while we eat."

When Aimée got up and approached Vale, the Indian girl caught her arm, obviously intending to hold her back. Aimée glanced sharply at her; but the girl's grasp on Aimée didn't loosen until Vale spoke a cool succession of words. Then the girl withdrew a step, her eyes on Aimée sullen and resentful.

"What was that about?" Aimée asked as she lowered herself to sit cross-legged opposite Vale.

"Nothing important," he replied offhandedly. He glanced up at the girl, whose petulant expression instantly vanished under his gaze and was replaced by a hesitant smile. He returned his attention to Aimée. "Running Fawn isn't ordinarily a servant. In fact, her family enjoys an elite place among the Abnakis. To have her attend me shows me honor."

"She behaves so humbly toward you, it would seem she regards this task as a privilege," Aimée commented, not forgetting that once Running Fawn had laid her eyes on Vale, she appeared to consider the occasion an opportunity as well.

Vale seemed to dismiss the subject of Running Fawn as he leaned forward to peer down into the stew. "The Abnaki's don't use tableware, Aimée; so I'll just reach into the pot with my knife and spear something I think you may like," he said, choosing a morsel of venison and offering it to Aimée. "It's hot, so just nibble it off the knife," he warned.

Aimée was aware of Running Fawn's surprise that Vale offered her the first bite; but she didn't have a chance to ask why. Vale spoke again to the Indian girl, who gave him her own knife. Then flashing Aimée an ill-humored glance, she withdrew into the shadows.

"How do you like it?" Vale asked, breaking off a piece of the flat bread the basket contained.

"It's very tasty—also very hot," Aimée replied as she took another careful bite of the savory meat. She accepted the bread and was quiet a moment before asking cautiously, "Does that girl dislike me for some reason?"

"Just help yourself out of the pot," Vale directed as he peered into the vessel for a piece of venison for himself. "Running Fawn has nothing against you personally, I'm sure," he answered tactfully. "She just thinks you should wait until after I've finished eating."

"Is it the custom for the women to wait for the men before they eat?" Aimée inquired cautiously.

"When a man and woman are in the privacy of their own lodge, they do as they wish," Vale replied. "It's just that I'm considered a special guest; and mostly because you're dressed as you are, they're wondering if you're a servant or my slave."

Aimée stared up at Vale in surprise. "A servant or a slave!" she exclaimed. Her eyes narrowed with indignation, and she remarked coolly, "That *would* make my status humble indeed!"

"The Abnakis don't really understand the customs of white people, and they're trying to figure out our relationship," Vale said slowly. "They're too polite to ask directly. The fact that you were hunting with me and are dressed like a man, and that you threw yourself over me, offering your own life to the bear in the hope you'd save me, tells them you might be at least a very devoted servant."

At Aimée's thoughtful silence he reached out to cup her temples with his hands. Running Fawn gasped softly. "You saved my life, Aimée," he said quietly.

"You've saved mine more than once," she murmured.

He shook his head. "I never offered myself as a sacrifice as you did to the bear."

Becoming uneasy at Running Fawn's increasing interest, Aimée moved away and changed the subject. "You said the Abnakis consider you an honored guest. I could easily see that those two men like you personally, but I remember you once said there was some sort of legend about you. What is it, Vale?"

Vale took a bite of vegetable, chewed it thoughtfully, and swallowed before he answered her question. "When Bess and I landed on the Atlantic shore after the ship sank, she was too exhausted to move. The sailor who had rowed us to the beach was too injured to look for help. It was cold and the first snow had begun to fall. It was, I understand, one of those early winter storms, half rain and half snow; and there was lightning. I began to cry as any baby would in such cold and damp, and the Indians heard me. My cries and the flashes of lightning guided them to us. When Walking-in-Honor took me from Bess's arms, I stopped crying; and the storm suddenly stopped too. He considered this to be a sign from heaven. He said that my body had absorbed the spirit of the storm, and he could see it still living in my eyes. As I think I told you before, Walking-in-Honor was highly regarded; and if he said I contained the spirit of the lightning god, the others accepted it too."

"The lightning god?" Aimée whispered. Then studying Vale's eyes, thinking about how quickly he could move, she nodded. "Yes, I can understand how they would believe that."

"When I was ten, Swooping Eagle and I were hunting quail one day and encountered a bear. Swooping Eagle's bow had broken and he was cornered. I shouted for help, shot the bear with a dozen arrows; and he finally fled." Vale smiled at the memory. "It was late in the fall; and the bear was fat and lazy, ready to go to his den to sleep for the winter. All the noise I made must have gotten on his nerves, because the arrows I was using then certainly couldn't have felt like much more than bee stings. Nevertheless there was a great celebration; and it was said that I'd saved Swooping Eagle because I had the power of the lightning god in me."

"But you did save Swooping Eagle's life—and it took a lot of courage for a ten-year-old boy to face a beast like that," Aimée said solemnly.

Vale shrugged and commented, "I'm sure the songs have exaggerated the entire incident, making me seem like the lightning god personified—which obviously I am not." He arose with the smooth, languid motion Aimée had first seen when they'd made love on the ship.

"Now I know where you learned to get up that way," she remarked.

Vale vividly recalled each detail of that night's love making, and his expression was regretful as he said, "I dislike telling you this, Aimée; because I'd prefer to spend the night the same way as you're thinking; but when we're ready to sleep, Running Fawn will remain in the lodge. Both of you will sleep on the floor while that pile of furs will be my bed."

Aimée was aghast at what she considered to be more intrusion than courtesy. "Can't you say you don't need her help? Can't we send her away?"

"That would be insulting to her as well as her father, and it would make me appear less than grateful for all the help they've given me," Vale replied unhappily. "Besides, Aimée, my muscles are stiffening from that fall, and the places where the bear clawed me burn like the devil. I wouldn't be able to make one move without flinching. Tomorrow night we can send her away; tomorrow night I should feel considerably better."

Aimée said nothing. She would have been happy enough just to sleep near Vale; but if they'd wanted to make love, there were a number of ways she could manage with a minimum of movement from him.

"I think I see what's on your mind, and I certainly would like to learn what you'd do—if Running Fawn wasn't going to be here," Vale said softly.

"I'll wager from the looks she's been giving you, she has some ideas how she'd manage that too—if only she could think of a way to get rid of me," Aimée replied tartly.

Aimée found it difficult to fall asleep with Vale so close yet, because of Running Fawn's presence, so impossibly far away. If the wounds from the bear's claws became infected and Vale grew feverish, she would know immediately if she were sleeping with him. If his rest was disturbed by pain, she might comfort him, she thought worriedly. She found herself listening to the sound of Vale's soft breathing; and each time he made even the slightest movement she wondered if he was in pain.

Vale's sleeplessness had little to do with his wounds. He had perceived that enmity between Aimée and Running Fawn didn't concern differences in background or social customs. Each considered the other a rival, though he could see nothing in his behavior that encouraged this. While he didn't want Aimée to become jealous of Running Fawn's attentiveness to him, he also wished to avoid offending the Indian girl, because he planned to ask the Abnakis for help in locating Mignon. Insulting one of their daughters wasn't likely to make them receptive.

He was aware that if he moved around too much, both Aimée and Running Fawn were sure to come hurrying to his side; so despite the discomfort of his injuries, he lay as still as possible, not wanting to create a situation that brought them together in any way they might imagine they must compete.

Vale was lying on his back, eyes closed despite his wakefulness, wondering if he could refuse Running Fawn's further assistance tomorrow in some way that wouldn't offend her. Hearing the almost imperceptible rustle of a blanket being turned back, he opened his eyes to slits and watched as Running Fawn arose from her sleeping place to pad silently toward him. He quickly reclosed his eyes, speculating about what she planned to do as she approached his bed. She stood silently beside him a moment, then slipped under the blanket with him. He was too surprised to react immediately. Her warm skin was like velvet against his side, and he realized that the rustling he'd heard was running Fawn taking off her dress. He lay still, wondering what he could do that wouldn't cause a commotion to awaken Aimée; he felt a small hand beginning to caress his thigh deftly.

Abruptly the hand was snatched away; and the girl's body was jerked off the bed to land with a soft thump on the floor. He sat up with a start, stiffly leaned over the

edge of the bed, and saw Aimée's tousled hair catching
light from the fire's faint glow as she straddled Running
Fawn's hips, struggling to pull the girl's dress over her
head.

"*Coureuse! Habillez-vous!*" Aimée hissed, obviously trying to restrain her voice as she wrestled with the girl.
"Now I dare you to go to your father and say you were
insulted!" she added as she jammed Running Fawn's hand
into a sleeve.

Aimée stood up, pulling Running Fawn to her feet with
her. As she dragged the girl toward the door, she muttered, "A maiden creeping naked into a man's bed means
the same in a house on rue Saint-Sulpice as in an Abnaki
lodge, I'll wager." At the door she grasped Running
Fawn's shoulders and whispered angrily, "You don't understand French or English, but you'll know what this
means!" She thrust the girl out of the lodge.

Vale watched wonderingly as Aimée turned to face him.
She looked at him silently from across the room. In that
instant she could not help wondering if he'd in any way
encouraged Running Fawn. After all she didn't know the
language or the customs of these people. Might any
caresses have been exchanged, for Vale had been drowsy
and could have mistaken Running Fawn for Aimée herself? She pushed aside such thoughts; but as she approached him her suspicions were written in every line of
her body. When she stood beside his bed, he put out his
hand.

"I did nothing, Aimée," he said quietly.

Her anger softened at his words, and she sat on the pile
of furs. She hung her head, regretting the suspicions that
had suddenly flooded her with jealousy, but she couldn't
bring herself to speak of it. Instead she said softly, "Perhaps Running Fawn's father and your Abnaki friends will
be angry with me now."

"It's possible that Running Fawn will say nothing about
the incident, which certainly is embarrassing from her
point of view," Vale replied.

Aimée thought about this possibility and hoped he was
right. She lay down beside Vale and, unable to keep a hint

of sarcasm from her tone, murmured, "If *la provocatrice* returns, she'll have to crawl over me to reach you; so you need have no qualms about going to sleep now."

Vale turned to kiss Aimée's cheek, then settled himself more comfortably on his uninjured side. But when he closed his eyes, sleep didn't come. He found himself thinking of the real reason behind this night's turmoil—they weren't yet married.

He had gradually become aware of Aimée's growing tension over their single state, though she never mentioned it; and he understood the emotions behind the jealousy that had momentarily gripped her. It seemed as if forces beyond their control kept seizing their lives, pulling them back from their goals, throwing up barricades before them. He was sure Aimée must occasionally give a thought to the possibility of becoming *enceinte;* and knowing what it was to be born illegitimate, he recoiled from the prospect of his own child someday questioning how quickly he'd been born after his parents' marriage. There was only one solution to the problem, he reminded himself. They must find Mignon as quickly as possible so he and Aimée would be able to continue with their own plans.

The Abnakis could surely speed their locating Morehead's gang even if they had to follow them all the way to Stalking Bear's camp. He thought of the various ways he might approach Swooping Eagle with his request; and thinking of the rituals Swooping Eagle would have to go through—consulting with his council, recruiting the warriors that would be needed—suddenly Vale thought of another Abnaki ritual.

Neither the Montreal nor the Boston colonial governments would consider a marriage ceremony performed by an Abnaki chief legal, though the Indians had found it suited their purposes for thousands of years. Perhaps it would give Aimée some respite from her worries if she had at least some sort of wedding to think of. He knew he would consider such a ritual as binding as any other. Later, when they were in Montreal or Boston—whichever Aimée preferred, or both if she wished—they could have their marriage legalized by white law and ceremony. He resolved to speak to Swooping Eagle about this tomorrow to learn if the marriage could be arranged so quickly.

Aimée spent the remainder of the night bitterly regretting her impetuous attack on Running Fawn. She felt as angry with herself for doubting Vale even for a moment as she was angry with Running Fawn. Added to this was worry about what Running Fawn would say to her family. Aimée reasoned, the girl could lie about what had happened out of revenge, and it would be her word against Aimée's and Vale's. She wished fervently that she'd thought of a more dignified way to getting rid of the girl. Visions of the tribe's anger buzzed through the darkness to hover threateningly in her thoughts, until she was convinced the Abnakis would not only refuse to help them find Mignon but probably eject them from the village as well.

Dawn had barely begun to lighten the doorway when Aimée, still too restless to sleep, slipped off the pile of furs and left the lodge.

The dew-sparkling village was as silent as if it were the middle of the night, she noted; but she knew it would be all too soon before the Indians would awaken, and Running Fawn would probably lead her father, Swooping Eagle, and who knew how many others to the door of their lodge to complain about Aimée's ejection of the girl during the night.

Thinking that she might walk a little and perhaps at least gain enough strength to face with dignity the ordeal she imagined lay ahead, she turned toward the back of the lodge. As she rounded the corner, she was surprised to discover Running Fawn huddled against the shelter's bark wall. Aimée's anger automatically flared at the sight of the shivering girl; but when her dark eyes jerked up to stare at Aimée, so plaintive with regret, Aimée's temper lowered. She suddenly realized that if Running Fawn had thought her to be a servant or slave, the girl's advances toward Vale might have been acceptable in her eyes.

Suddenly Running Fawn leaped to her feet, but Aimée caught her wrist in a firm grip. Wanting to talk with Running Fawn, intending only to gesture, Aimée raised her free hand. Running Fawn flinched and tried to pull away, as if she thought Aimée meant to strike her. Aimée sighed and shook her head, indicating that they should sit down together. She released the girl's wrist and seated herself cross-legged in the grass as an indication of her good will. Running Fawn took a step backwards, then warily sat down beyond Aimée's reach.

Aimée pointed to the place where Running Fawn had huddled and, trying first one gesture, then another, finally was able to make the girl understand she was asking her how long she had been there. Running Fawn quickly answered that she'd hidden there all night. Sympathy for Running Fawn's plight swept aside all fear that the tribe would censure her for turning Running Fawn out. It was clear the girl was terrified that anyone else should learn of the incident.

Aimée pointed toward the lodge and indicated a tall man—Vale; then she pointed toward herself—her own heart—and said the one word she'd learned: "*Sakia.*"

Wonder flooded Running Fawn's face. This servant or slave girl was in love with Lightning-of-the-Winter-Moon? Running Fawn considered this. Everything the red-haired girl—whom the tribe had come to call Flaming Thistle— had done confirmed that she loved him. Running Fawn nodded in understanding, assuming that Flaming Thistle wasn't able to marry Lightning-of-the-Winter-Moon because her status was too far beneath his in the white man's world, that she was too impoverished to offer a dowry. All Flaming Thistle seemed to possess was her love and the knowledge that Running Fawn had crept into Lightning-of-the-Winter-Moon's bed. The Indian girl frowned at the memory of her madness, knowing she would be in disgrace if anyone ever learned of it.

Noting Running Fawn's changing expressions, Aimée understood none of the girl's thoughts, save one: she was ashamed and frightened. Aimée again made the gestures indicating Vale, this time linking him with Running Fawn sleeping. At the girl's renewed alarm Aimée put her fingers over her mouth, promising she wouldn't speak.

Tears of relief and gratitude filled Running Fawn's eyes. She briefly caught Aimée's fingertips with hers, squeezed them, then suddenly leaped to her feet, whirled, and ran away as silently as a shadow flitting over the grass. Surprised, Aimée quickly stood up to look after her. She didn't realize the girl had fled at Vale's appearance.

When Vale rounded the corner of the lodge, Aimée was standing in a shaft of golden dawn light, poised as if ready to fly after Running Fawn, as unaware of his gaze as a deer upwind. The sun struck a fiery halo in her loose curls, making her seem like a living torch beckoning to him, lighting his way. Sensing his presence, she turned; and as her eyes fell on him, they lit with amber sparks that told him the sweet wild wind he'd called her was the passion in their love that set them both alight.

Vale walked slowly toward Aimée; and stopping but a step away, he was silent for so long a time she wondered at his thoughts.

"I found Running Fawn," Aimée finally said. "She spent the rest of the night hiding here rather than returning to her family. I let her know I wouldn't speak of what happened."

"That was very generous of you, Aimée, a kindness she'll never forget," he said quietly. He took her hand and started walking toward the front of the lodge. "The village is awakening, and Swooping Eagle has sent someone to tell me I should have the morning meal with him. Do you mind eating alone?"

"Are you going to ask him about helping find Mignon?" Aimée quickly inquired. After he had nodded, she added, "If he agrees to help us, how soon do you think we'd leave the village?"

"He has to speak to his council, and they must agree before any arrangements can be made. I would guess we'll have to remain here at least until the day after tomorrow," Vale replied. He was silent a moment, as if thinking something over; then he finally said, "I'll probably spend most of the day with Swooping Eagle. If Singing Pine comes with one or two of her friends, I would like you to do whatever they want you to without arguing."

"What do you mean, Vale? What would they ask me to do?" Aimée was perplexed.

"It won't be anything unpleasant—possibly bathing in the river, perhaps dressing you in some other clothes," Vale answered.

"Bathing in the river! At this time of year it must be like ice!" she exclaimed.

Vale bent to kiss her forehead. "Do it anyway," he said softly, and backing away, he turned and left her utterly mystified as to his purpose.

Later when Running Fawn returned to the lodge bringing their breakfast, Aimée noticed she too wore a secretive smile. As they dipped bits of coarse bread made from corn into a bowl of hot gruel, Aimée considered ways she might possibly ask Running Fawn what pleased her so much, but she finally realized it was impossible to ask such a question with gestures.

After breakfast, when Aimée was trying to comb the snarls out of her curls with her fingers, Singing Pine entered the lodge with another woman, who Aimée surmised from her gestures was named Laughing River. As Vale had warned, they motioned that they wanted Aimée to go with them. She glanced at Running Fawn and realized the girl planned to accompany them. Fortifying herself with the knowledge that Vale would never tell her to do something harmful, Aimée followed the women, as he'd asked, without argument.

As Vale had predicted, the women took Aimée to the riverbank and motioned for her to undress. Feeling self-conscious under their gaze, Aimée slowly began to unbutton the shirt Marcel had given her. Singing Pine sighed with good-natured impatience at Aimée's dawdling, while Laughing River smiled at the white girl's shyness. Running Fawn stepped away, touched her chest by her heart, extended her hand in a graceful motion toward Aimée, and softly said the one English word she'd learned: "Friend."

Then the three women set about efficiently helping Aimée out of her clothes until she stood naked and shivering in the crisp spring air. There was a flurry of conversation in Abnaki as they stood back to look at her with open curiosity. Aimée's face reddened under their gaze while Running Fawn motioned admiringly toward the length of Aimée's legs and the smooth slope of her hips. Singing Pine was obviously impressed by the round curve of her high breasts; and Laughing River measured Aimée's waist with her hands, exclaiming over its smallness.

Finally the women pulled off their own dresses and led Aimée into the river. She decided they truly must be friends if they were willing to endure the bone-numbing water to help her bathe. They rubbed a root on their hands that foamed like soap, and their touch was as soft as moth wings as they washed her from the crown of her fiery hair to her toes. After they'd rinsed her, they led her back to the riverbank; and as Running Fawn and Singing Pine wrapped a blanket around her, Laughing River squeezed the icy water from Aimée's hair, leaving the waist-length curls scintillating with a blaze of lights.

The women bid Aimée to sit on a blanket in the sun; and while her hair dried, Running Fawn and Laughing River sang to her, their voices clear and full. Despite the strangeness of the song's tempo, Aimée's emotions were stirred by its poignant, curiously tender notes. They paused at intervals, and Singing Pine leaned close to Aimée to speak solemnly, as if she were instructing her in some way. Aimée listened attentively, wishing with all her heart that Vale could be present to explain the meaning of it, she of course had no idea that this was a ritual forbidden to men—and to him most of all.

Finally the three Indians took Aimée back to her lodge where they posted a fourth woman outside the entrance as if she were a guard; then they took the blanket from Aimée's shoulders.

Aimée was surprised when several large baskets were opened to reveal a tumble of mayflowers. The women took handfuls of the blossoms and rubbed them on Aimée's body until the spicy-sweet fragrance became part of her skin, more effectively scenting her than any of the carefully blended perfumes of King Louis's court.

They dressed her in a shift made of doeskin as soft and supple as velvet; the sleeves and hem were so deeply fringed that the strands fell over her wrists and ankles; and the neck hole and shoulders were decorated with white quills and little green beads so intricately sewn their design was as delicate as lace. It took all of Singing Pine's and Laughing River's combined skills to coax Aimée's waist-length curls into two fat braids which they twined with mayflowers. Finally Running Fawn tied first a headband, beaded like the dress, around Aimée's brow and then a matching belt to gather the soft doeskin shift close at her waist, indicating proudly that the belt and headband were gifts from her; the dress was from Singing Pine, and the buttery moccasins were Laughing River's. The children of the tribe, she gestured, had gathered the mayflowers. Finally she took Aimée's hand and touched her own heart, then rested her hand on Aimée's and whispered, "Friend—*sakia*—friend."

Tears leaped to Aimée's eyes, and she hugged first Running Fawn, then Singing Pine and Laughing River. She didn't know how to thank them.

When they took her hands, urging her to leave the lodge, she wondered if they meant to bring her to Vale so he could inspect her new appearance. But as she stepped outside, she was surprised to discover the village seemed deserted. She glanced uneasily down the spaces between the lodges they passed, and saw no one. Running Fawn, noting Aimée's perplexity, smiled reassuringly. Mystified by the events of the afternoon, wondering what was to happen next, Aimée found the three women leading her down a path into the forest.

Aimée finally saw what appeared in the distance to be the entire village gathered in a grove of pines. As she and the three women approached, the people silently parted to make a path. The woman, who had acted as the guard outside the lodge, came forward leading a silver-gray horse, whose mane and tail were twined with flowers. She put the reins in Aimée's hand, then stepped away. Aimée looked questioningly at Running Fawn, but the girl gestured for Aimée to continue walking.

Turning, Aimée saw that the last of the people had retreated from the path. Before a small lodge draped with spruce and cedar boughs, Swooping Eagle and another man stood waiting. Both wore heavily beaded robes trimmed lavishly with feathers.

Beyond them Vale stood alone under the pines, clothed in garments as deeply fringed and intricately beaded as hers. His hair too was braided, and he wore a headband with a tall white feather affixed at its back. She had never before seen him dressed in full Indian gear. She paused now to stare at him as avidly as he was looking at her.

Aimée's heart gave a strange little lurch as a mixture of love and desire rushed through her, and she began to understand why they were there. The pines sighed in the wind, their whispers confirming the secret Running Fawn had kept from her: it was her wedding the Abnakis had prepared.

Vale smiled, and Aimée hurried toward him, her heart filling with such joy it seemed it might burst as he took her hand and said softly, "*Sakia*, my sweet wild wind, I love you."

Chapter 27

Vale translated the wedding ceremony for Aimée; and though she was referred to as Flaming Thistle and he as Lightning-of-the-Winter-Moon all through it, they knew, as they gazed into the other's eyes, that both considered the ritual as validly binding to their hearts and lives as any that could be performed in a cathedral.

After the ceremony Aimée learned that Swooping Eagle's tribe celebrated a marriage as enthusiastically as the people of Montreal or Boston. Language presented no barrier to her understanding the congratulations and wishes for happiness that were so warmly given.

When the tribe led the couple back to the village, Aimée was astonished to see that a wedding feast had been prepared; and Vale explained that to surprise her, they had cooked the banquet in a clearing as far as possible from the lodge where Running Fawn and Singing Pine had gotten her ready for the ceremony.

A whole deer had been roasted on a spit along with numerous game birds. Salmon that had come upriver to spawn had been grilled over the coals. There were caldrons of steaming wild rice, pots of yams, turnips, wild celery, baskets of bread, corn, bowls of crab apples, spring strawberries, as well as nuts and seeds gathered from the forest the previous autumn. Spruce beer flowed freely; and after the meal the drums began to throb softly in the night.

Dancers in beaded and feathered costumes, with flowers garlanding their necks, began to circle the fire, their anklets jingling in rhythm with their steps, while a singer told the story of Lightning-of-the-Winter-Moon, adding new verses about how he and his love had returned to the tribe.

Vale told Aimée that although he'd asked Swooping Eagle for the ceremony to be arranged, Running Fawn had supplied the necessary dowry. The gray horse was very valuable to the Indians, but the beaded belt and headband which Running Fawn had given Aimée as part of the dowry to be later presented to Vale were far more than personal ornamentation: they were used like gold among the Indians. Aimée was deeply touched by Running Fawn's generosity and wanted to give the girl something in return, but she had only a locket and felt it was too meager a gift. Running Fawn accepted the locket with an awe that Aimée found puzzling. The girl, Vale explained, regarded it as a talisman and believed Aimée had entrusted her with the safe keeping of part of her spirit because Aimée's miniature was painted within.

Finally Vale reminded Aimée that Swooping Eagle and his people would have many tasks to attend to the next morning; and the polite Indians wouldn't call an end to the celebration until after the newly married couple had left. Although Aimée had enjoyed the festivities, she was eager to be alone with Vale; and she quickly agreed to slip away to the lodge draped with cedar and spruce boughs.

Aimée had moved through the exciting events of the day and evening in a charmed bubble, where none of her previous worries could touch her. She had been so absorbed by the joy of the celebration, entranced by Vale's nearness and the knowledge that he at last was hers, she hadn't noticed how the diamond clarity of the stars had slowly blurred, then become obscured by the gathering clouds.

As Vale, holding her hand, led her down the shadowy forest path, she finally became aware of the damp wind that was beginning to gather strength. She asked him to pause and listen to the sighing of the pines above them. They lifted their heads and saw beyond the trees a thin thread of lightning; they heard the far-off rumble of thunder. The sky threw clouds like torn lace into the wind. Aimée turned to Vale and, watching the paths of lightning reflected in his eyes, began to untwine the plaits of his hair.

"You said, before the bear attacked us, that you would like to make love during a storm," he recalled.

Aimée nodded but didn't reply. A new feeling was taking hold of her, a hesitance she couldn't explain even to herself. Although her desire was as swiftly running as the clouds racing past the moon, she found herself suddenly shy.

As he reached for the thongs that clasped her long braids, she lowered her eyes to stare at the beaded design of his shirt front, wondering at her strange mood; at the same time she was so acutely aware of the nearness of his body that she wanted to throw her arms around him, to possess him here on the path carpeted with pine needles. After her curls were freed to the rising wind, his fingers under her chin tilted her face to his. She saw in his eyes that he was aware of her inner conflict.

She smiled tremulously. "It's strange that after you've shared my bed so many times and after I came so boldly to yours in Boston, now that we're married I feel as awkward as if I were yet a maiden, and at the same time I'm as eager as when you stepped into my bath."

Vale's hands rested lightly on her shoulders as he said softly, "You're thinking like an Abnaki woman, my little *sakia*: our desire tonight will result in more than love making—it will consumate our marriage in the eyes of God. As aroused as I am, I too feel the awe of this." He drew her close to him; adding, "The expression on your face now is the same as it was the day we first met, when you knew I was about to kiss you—shy, yet budding with passion."

She lay her cheek against his chest, listening to the happy beating of his heart, realizing its eagerness belied his outward calm.

He stepped away, and she looked up at him. The wind blew a strand of his hair over her cheek, allowing her a moment to feel the intimacy of his nearness before snatching it away. A raindrop landed on his forehead, exploding like a jewel into a shower of sparkling fragments that coated his lashes with crystal dust. A smaller drop fell on his cheek; and she rose to stand on tiptoe, to learn with the tip of her tongue how the rain tasted when it mingled with his skin. Although he carefully leashed his desire, she could see, in the lightning flashes that streaked his eyes with silver, that the nearing tempest was uniting with his passion, building his tension.

He read the knowledge in her face and said softly, "Other women are afraid of storms, but not my little *sakia*." He took her hand and turned to resume walking toward the lodge.

"The only storm I could truly fear would be the one that might take you from me," she murmured.

He tied back the flap covering the opening to the lodge, thinking about her words and the meaning he knew they held which she didn't want to admit; but he only asked, "Do you mind if we leave our doorway open tonight?"

"Won't someone see us?"

"The wedding lodge is purposely built a discreet distance from the village so the newly married couple can do what they wish in privacy. No one will come near." He turned to look down at her. "The only storm you would fear, then, would be the possibilities Running Fawn's impulsiveness presented last night?"

Aimée was ashamed to answer that she might doubt him in a moment as foolish as that.

"What could another woman offer after I've learned how it is to have you in my arms?" His fingertips coaxed her to look up at him, and he said softly, "If there was more joy to know, more excitement to share—if it was possible to reach even greater heights of pleasure than your love can give—I would have to refuse. I could endure no more. I would fly apart like a shattered crystal goblet, and the wind would spread my dust among the stars in the night skies."

She caught her breath at the beauty of his words; but before she could think of anything to say, he bent to touch his lips to hers. The time that had passed since their first meeting was somehow erased. He kissed her gently, as if she were innocent and he must subdue his own passion while he taught her about love. Despite his restraint she could feel the trembling that rose through the depths of

the hard body pressed to hers; and she was awed anew by
the intensity of his desire. She leaned against him, shivering in response, like the grass now blowing in the wind.

When he moved away, she remembered her jealousy,
and wanting fiercely to kiss him again, needing to make
peace with him for her previous suspicions, all she could
think of to say was "Will you forgive my foolishness?"

He smiled ruefully in understanding and admitted,
"What you call foolishness in yourself is nothing compared
with the commotion I would have caused had I awakened
to see a man creeping into your bed." He lifted her hand
to his lips and added softly, "Why don't you undress, my
sakia, while I take off my own clothes? It will save us
time."

Aimée turned quickly to obey; but while she untied the
belt at her waist, as she slipped out of the doeskin garment, she knew Vale's eyes were intent on her, watching
every move she made. Yet after they both were naked and
she lay on the pile of furs that was to be their marriage
bed, he drew up her knees to sit with his chest against her
legs, his arms folded around them, his chin resting on her
knees—as he had done on the ship.

"I asked Singing Pine and Running Fawn to use mayflowers on your skin instead of the more customary blossoms. I asked for the lodge to be decorated with the pine
boughs because I can never forget the scent of mayflowers
and pine that was on the wind when we shared our first
kiss and I fell in love with you," he said softly. "Tonight is
more a triumph for me than the wedding nights of other
men because my love for you seemed so hopeless then.
That day when I left you by your gate, I knew you would
always be a pain in my heart if I couldn't somehow make
you mine."

"I too loved you from that moment, yet it seemed my
love was impossible. I argued with my feelings all the way
to Paris, but though I was convinced you were a spy, I
couldn't put you out of my heart and dreams," she
confessed. "Yours was my first kiss, but no one else's
could matter to me after that—even if I never would be
able to love you."

Vale moved away to lie beside her and stare at the darkened dome of the lodge's perfumed ceiling. The wind outside whistled through the pines, making them sing just as Aimée's love made his heart sing. The lightning flashed beyond the open doorway as a silvery veil of rain moved over the opening. He turned his head to look at her and whispered, "Kiss me, Aimée. Blow through my heart, sweet wild wind. Fill me with your love."

Slowly she sat up and leaned over him. Her lips were cool and moist, like a flower petal blown by mist, as she kissed him lingeringly. He kept his eyes open to watch the effect he had on her, her face tightening with passion as her lips, barely brushing his, lightly traced the outline of his mouth. Her hands stroking his chest pierced him with fire, and he felt as if his muscles were vibrating with the need her touch was building in him.

He threaded his fingers through her hair to hold her mouth firmly against his in a more compelling kiss. The warmth that had risen in him had increased to a hot glowing at the center of his being, but he didn't pause in his insistent kisses. His blood lit with sparks that raced brightly through his veins, like the lightning that shot through the dark sky beyond the doorway. He knew her love was the only wind that could blow through his soul, ignite him, and fan his passions to wild, sweet flame.

His body moved sinuously under hers, the entire length of him becoming a caress. Waves of exquisite sensations ran through her, heightening her desire to madness, until she made a sound like a suppressed cry, which, if freed, would echo in the forest. The sound shrieked through his soul.

Vale suddenly twisted out from under Aimée, grasped her arms, and pulled her down so she lay at his side. He moved over her, holding her tightly, almost roughly against him, his desire so intense it was rapidly overwhelming his control. A flash of lightning lit his eyes to silver fire, and her hands pressed tightly to his back.

As a nearby clap of thunder sounded she tilted her hips, and his body claimed hers. The thunder rolling through the lodge reverberated inside her as well, and she breathed, "You do have the spirit of the storm god in you."

"Your storm is mine," he murmured as she folded her legs over his. He felt as if his beginning movements took him into her soul. The torment of ecstasy that flooded him was so exquisite he began to whisper, *"Sakia . . ."* then stopped. He had no breath left to speak.

The bud of his passion burst into bloom; and he watched a great purple flower unfold slowly before his closed eyes, revealing a heart of flame.

Chapter 28

Early the next morning Swooping Eagle sent Running Fawn to the wedding lodge to summon Vale. He had no choice but to leave Aimée and accompany Swooping Eagle to the council of elders who were to discuss whether the Abnakis should join the search party for Mignon. He had been right to predict it would take a lot of persuasion to get the elders to agree.

It was one matter to accept Lightning-of-the-Winter-Moon's beloved as one of their own but quite another matter to join a troop of British soldiers and possibly make war on another group of Indians, even if they were Iroquois. The elders remembered it had been the British who had driven the Abnakis from their ancestral homes on the Atlantic coast, the "dawn land" for which they'd been named. They were closely related to the Algonquins, who had fought against the British on the side of the French; and although Swooping Eagle's people hadn't involved themselves in the struggle, it took a complicated adjustment of attitudes for them even to consider standing at the sides of the redcoats.

That the British army was actually asking for their help to locate a high-ranking officer and bring him to white justice was appealing to the Abnakis. The idea of tracking down Stalking Bear, a renegade his own tribe seemed unable to subdue, added weight to Vale's argument. As Vale had hoped, the elders were tempted by the reminder of how proud a moment it would be for the Abnakis if they succeeded where the British and Iroquois—both former enemies with whom they'd made an uneasy peace—had failed.

Finally, after spending all day in the council's lodge,
Vale obtained what he'd sought. The council agreed to let
the warriors who wished to participate in the search leave
the village the next dawn.

Many preparations had to be hurriedly made; and when
Vale at last reentered the wedding lodge, Aimée simply
welcomed him into her arms to sleep for the few remaining hours before dawn.

Vale assumed Major Templeton and his men would
have traveled only during the day that he and Aimée had
set out to track the caribou. Once Templeton had realized
that they weren't returning, that something had happened
to them, Vale was sure the major would have ordered his
soldiers to set up camp on the riverbank, then would have
sent out men to find them. Although he and Aimée had
been away for three nights, the British camp was likely to
be less than one day's journey from the Abnaki village.

Only a dozen of Swooping Eagle's warriors were lucky
enough to possess horses, so the others who wanted to join
the search for Mignon went on foot. Aimée was amazed
that the men could trot beside their mounted companions
for several hours yet seemed as tireless as the horses. The
group paused several times during the course of the day,
the Indians on foot taking the mounts of friends, so no
one would slow their progress even slightly with accumu-
lated weariness.

Although Vale had a great many things to discuss with
Swooping Eagle and Hunting Wolf as they rode, Aimée
knew part of his attention remained on her as unswerv-
ingly as hers was on him. The breeze, trying to tug his
hair from his queue succeeded in loosening one strand that
fell over his forehead; and she imagined its texture as vividly as if it were yet brushing her cheek as when they'd
kissed. Vale's leg tightened against his horse's side, and
Aimée recalled the muscles of that leg tautly pressed
against her thigh as they'd neared the peak of their lovemaking. She gazed at the reins in his hands, the long, tapering fingers holding the spirited gray in firm but gentle
control; and she remembered his passionate caresses.

Vale's lips, now pliantly forming Abnaki words, seemed to move again over her body; and she wondered how she could endure waiting until they finally had the privacy to love again.

At such moments, as if the force of her thoughts had somehow been transmitted to him, his gaze would turn to meet hers. Though he never paused in what he was saying to Swooping Eagle or Hunting Wolf, the flecks of his eyes seemed lit by the fires glowing behind them; and she felt a shock of excitement, as if he'd hurled a lightning bolt at her. Knowing her feelings were so clearly written on her face that anyone would be able to read them, she'd turn her eyes to the forest's greening depths and valiantly try to focus her mind on something other than her body's clamoring. Invariably she found herself reliving the afternoon of the wedding—and the night that had followed.

Only one thing marred Aimée's happiness. Mignon was yet in Morehead's hands; and the terror she must be suffering as she anticipated being given to the renegade Stalking Bear was a bitter contrast to the joy of Aimée's wedding celebration among Swooping Eagle's people. Visions of her sister's misery arose before Aimée's eyes, and her only comfort was Vale's promise that Mignon's rescue approached nearer with every passing hour.

As Vale had calculated, the Abnakis found Templeton's camp near sundown. The soldiers leaped for their firearms at the approach of so many Indians; but Marcel, seeing the flash of his sister's auburn curls in the setting sun, threw aside his weapon and dashed out from behind the rock where he'd concealed himself.

Aimée slid from her saddle into his welcoming arms. "I'm all right, Marcel. These are Abnakis—Vale's friends! They're going to help us find Mignon. *Oui*, they're the tribe Vale lived with," she repeated as she noted Marcel's still wary eyes. She grasped the sides of her brother's face until she saw that his attention was fully on her, then added more quietly, "Marcel, Vale and I were married yesterday."

"Comment!" he breathed in shock. *"Ma soeur,* how can this be? Who married you?"

"The Abnaki chief and their priest, Marcel. Vale translated the ceremony for me. It was really very much like ours. The wedding in the forest was beautiful," she said excitedly. Seeing that the shock on his face hadn't lessened, she quickly reassured, "Don't worry, Marcel. We'll be married again in a church."

"What happened to you?" Benjamin asked as he hurried to their side. "Where have you been all this time?"

"With the Abnakis, it seems." Marcel sighed.

"We were attacked by a bear and the Abnakis—that man over there, Hunting Wolf, rescued us," Aimée declared.

"It's good Maman isn't here to listen to this jumble of explanations. By the time we got it sorted out, I think she would be hysterical." Marcel shook his head and bent to kiss his sister's cheek. "You *are* married?" he asked again, hoping he'd misunderstood her.

"Oui!" she answered firmly.

Marcel saw in his sister's radiant face how happy she was, and he said, "It isn't that I disapprove of Vale, of course. I just would have preferred you'd done this in the church. Ah, well, as long as you'll be married in the church when we return to Montreal." He put his arms around her; and when he withdrew, she saw his eyes were bright with tears. "You know I wish you happiness, Aimée. I just was worried about your being gone so long."

"Vale had to persaude the council of elders to agree to help us," she explained. Then taking Marcel's arm in one hand and Benjamin's arm in the other, she urged, "Come and meet Swooping Eagle and Hunting Wolf. They're really very good friends."

Marcel looked warily at the two Indian warriors who, with Vale as interpreter, were talking with Major Templeton. "By all means, let us meet them," he agreed.

Templeton's provisions had begun to run low, as Vale and the Abnakis had surmised; and it was the game they'd brought down with their silent arrows on the trip to the camp that the British now enjoyed for supper.

While they ate, Vale again acted as interpreter for the Indians; they discussed the strategy they might use for locating Morehead, Stalking Bear, or both. It was finally decided that Swooping Eagle's men would comb the area for any signs of either renegade because the Abnakis could move through the forest more quietly and their presence was far less likely to be discovered. Even if they were seen, it was doubtful Morehead would think they were in league with Templeton's search party. Hunting Wolf divided the men into groups of three, explaining that scouts dispatched at night were almost invisible, whereas the campfires of the unsuspecting renegades were far easier to see.

Templeton watched as the Indians melted into the shadows of the forest, and wondered at their willingness to stay awake and search while the British soldiers would, of necessity, remain in camp. Vale reminded him that Stalking Bear was an Iroquois, by tradition an enemy of the Abnakis; and Swooping Eagle and his men would be very happy to humiliate the Iroquois by helping to capture their renegades. He didn't mention that the Abnakis hoped to humiliate the British by locating Morehead—but Templeton suspected that anyway.

Vale and Aimée were aware that they wouldn't be able to resume their honeymoon while they were in the British camp; and wanting to delay the moment when they each would roll up in their separate blankets to spend a sleepless night thinking about the other, they encouraged Marcel's and Benjamin's questions as they sat before the fire.

After they'd recounted all that had happened to them in the time they'd spent away from the British camp, Marcel looked at Vale and said cautiously, "Aimée said you were planning to remarry in a church."

Vale nodded in understanding for Marcel's concern about his sister's future. "We'll be remarried as soon as we return to Montreal." Then he smiled. "Perhaps again in Boston so your mother can attend and be sure it was properly done."

"Have you decided yet where you will live?" Benjamin inquired.

"We made that decision when we still were in Marcel's cabin in the forest," Aimée quickly answered. At her brother's surprised look she added, "So much happened to keep us occupied, I forgot to tell you later."

"Are you returning to France?" Marcel asked, hoping Vale hadn't made that choice.

"Only long enough to sell my property there," Vale replied, noting Marcel's relief. "When we return, we intend to live in Boston. My plans are to buy ships from the Carletons and establish a shipping line."

"That sounds like a good idea, Vale; but you'll have a lot of competition from the other companies," Benjamin reminded him.

"But my company will have two special qualities to recommend it," Vale said firmly. "My ships will be built to my special order—the fastest cargo vessels that can be designed, carrying as much sail as they'll hold."

"The Carletons will be happy to build whatever kind of ships you want, Vale," Benjamin assured him. He grinned and added, "I can see Father and Paul arguing every night you and Aimée are in France about how to design your ships."

"But what is the second quality you want your company to have that others won't?" Marcel asked curiously.

"Ships have always stood in port waiting until their holds are filled with cargo, which is very inconvenient for someone who needs an order by a specific date," Vale said. "I've been thinking that I'd like to try to fix my sailing dates on a regular schedule whether my ships' holds are filled or not."

"That would involve a risk at the start, but I'm sure you would attract a lot of customers if you could keep a set schedule," Benjamin said thoughtfully.

"I believe that after the sale of the d'Auvergne and the de la Tour estates I'll have enough money backing me up to take that chance," Vale said firmly.

"I think that's a wonderful idea, Vale, one that should be very welcome to businessmen on both sides of the Atlantic," Marcel said eagerly. "I remember that never knowing how long a ship would stand in port was a constant headache to my father."

"I'm glad you agree," Vale replied. He turned to Aimée and took her hands in his. "There's something I meant to ask you as soon as I was sure you'd marry me, and now seems as good a time as any." He paused, wondering what she would think of the plans he'd made. Finally he asked, "Do you remember Sarah and Adam Thornton?"

Aimée nodded, mystified as to his purpose. "We all went to that party in their home the night you gave me the necklace and were so late arriving," she recalled.

"Their house is for sale; and if you like it, it can be ours," Vale said slowly.

Aimée's eyes widened with surprise. "But Sarah said someone had already bid for it; and if he decided in the spring . . ." Her voice trailed off. "It wasn't you who made them the offer, was it?" she breathed.

Vale nodded. "I asked them to wait to sell it until I returned to Boston—if you would marry me and liked the house, I would meet any bid they received while we were gone."

Aimée threw her arms around Vale's neck. "Oh, *mon amoureux*, I never suspected for a moment! I love the house! It's beautiful, beautiful!" She turned to look at Marcel. "*Mon frère*, wait till you see it! Even Maman liked it, and you know how particular she is."

"It would be nice for Mignon to have you living so nearby, that is, if . . ." Benjamin stopped, his voice choked off by his tears.

Aimée released Vale and went to take Benjamin's hands in hers. "You've known Vale far longer than I. Would you say he's a man to make rash promises—to give his word if he can't keep it?" she asked solemnly.

Benjamin took a deep breath and shook his head. "I've never known Vale to break a promise," he whispered.

"Vale has promised me we'll find Mignon—that she'll be safely in our hands when we return to Montreal," Aimée said firmly.

Benjamin and Marcel both looked questioningly at Vale.

He nodded confirmation. "I did promise Aimèe I wouldn't go back until we found Mignon. I have no doubt that, with Swooping Eagle's help, we'll get Mignon back."

Aimée smiled reassuringly at her brother, then returned her attention to Benjamin. "Now you must tell us the plans you made with Mignon. How did you manage to be alone long enough to discuss all this?"

Benjamin stood up and approached Marcel. "I suppose you might at least have one of your sister's fiancés formally ask if you mind his marrying your sister."

Marcel got to his feet and managed to smile, though his maple-colored eyes still were shadowed with worry for Mignon as he replied, "I would be happy to welcome you as a brother, and I'm sure my mother will approve of your marrying my sister." He looked at Vale and added, "*Both* of you."

"After you've seen Boston, you might consider moving there too," Aimée suggested. "You said you wanted to start another kind of business. Why not in Boston? I know Maman was beginning to feel quite at home there, and I'm sure by now she feels even more so."

Marcel ran a hand through his hair as he considered this new possibility for his future. "Maybe you're right, Aimée," he said slowly. "I'll have to think more about this, discuss it with Maman. Montreal is, perhaps, too crowded with ghosts for any of us to be happy there again."

Aimée and Vale, as anticipated, rolled up in their separate blankets, but they defiantly placed them side by side so they could at least hold hands. They gazed longingly into each other's faces and whispered about the plans they'd made, until the sky began to lighten with dawn.

Noting that Swooping Eagle's scouts had begun to return, Vale watched their expressions as they drifted into camp. It wasn't until Hunting Wolf and the two men who'd accompanied him entered the clearing that Vale suddenly threw off his blanket and got to his feet.

Aimée's heart leaped with hope, and she sat up to watch him stride toward the Abnakis. Vale's back was to

Aimée as he spoke with the Indians, so she couldn't see his expression. She could read nothing in the faces of the Abnakis, and she held her breath. When Vale finally turned, she leaped to her feet, her pulses pounding with joy. She knew from his smile that Hunting Wolf had found Mignon.

Chapter 29

Vale hurried to notify Major Templeton while Aimée awakened Marcel and Benjamin with the good news. After Templeton's aide had aroused Lieutenant Scott and Sergeant Hunter, the entire group assembled outside the major's tent to sip steaming cups of tea and gather their still drowsy wits. Vale seated himself cross-legged on the ground between Swooping Eagle and Hunting Wolf so he could translate the discussion.

Hunting Wolf had been eyeing Woolsey suspiciously. The Abnaki spoke briefly and quietly to Vale, who looked calculatingly at Woolsey, whose ankle was shackled to a nearby tree.

"Hunting Wolf suggested that Woolsey not be allowed to hear the plans we're going to make," Vale said.

"I darsay, there's nothing he could do about it with his foot chained to a tree," Templeton remarked.

"If he realizes his friends are about to be captured, he might finally decide to give us some information about them," Lieutenant Scott suggested. "The brigand hasn't said a useful word since we left Lavaltrie."

"Nothing at all?" Benjamin exclaimed.

Templeton's eyes narrowed. "All he's told us was what Vale got out of him initially: that Dark Otter was to guide Morehead and his henchmen to Stalking Bear's camp, that they needed supplies for four or five days and were planning to travel northwest from Montreal. He's not yet told us even the names of the others in league with Morehead."

Woolsey had been watching Vale warily. Although he'd realized from the moment he'd first laid eyes on the major that Templeton would do nothing that did not conform

with army regulations, and so was completely predictable,
Vale was another matter. When Woolsey saw Vale put
down his mug and rise, he hurriedly scrambled to his feet
too. As Vale approached, Woolsey recognized the look in
Vale's eyes; he'd seen it the night Vale had held the knife
to his throat and promised to kill him if he deceived them
in any way.

"Don't let him near me, Major!" Woolsey cried, backing
away as far as the chain on his ankle allowed. "He's no
better than those savages he's sitting with. He already
threatened to kill me! You can't let him do nothing to me.
I'm *your* prisoner. It's against your rules, ain't it?"

"I'm not even going to touch you, Woolsey," Vale said
clearly, then added so softly only Woolsey could hear,
"Not in the daylight with everyone watching." Aloud he
inquired, "Do you realize, though you're a civilian, you'll
be tried in a military court just like Morehead? It's actually the only court available in Montreal at the moment
because the city is under martial law—and you did impersonate an officer to rescue Morehead. Unlike civilian
courts, military courts presume you're guilty unless proven
innocent, and their penalities do tend to be harsher. I'm
sure you realize that any favors you do us now would be
in your best interest later."

"I don't know nothing, but what I already said,"
Woolsey insisted. "Dark Otter didn't tell us nothing else."

"But certainly you know at least how many men Morehead has working with him," Vale prompted.

Woolsey thought of how easily a man's throat could be
slit during the night; how silently he could die, his corpse
going unnoticed until the next morning. Even if he could
stay awake every night, he knew how quietly Vale could
move, how swiftly he could strike. He vividly remembered
the sensation of Vale's blade against his skin. "There ain't
many of us—just Millbank, Ugland, Horton and Melvin,"
he muttered. "Stalking Bear's got about thirty men, far as
I know."

"If you can think of anything else that would be of interest to us, I'm sure you'll see the wisdom of telling us,

won't you?" Vale said in what seemed like a reasonable tone to those who couldn't see the expression on his face.

A chill of fear ran down Woolsey's spine, and he nodded hastily; but after Vale had turned away to rejoin the others, he privately vowed to work that much more industriously at opening the lock on his ankle chain that night. Even if a court would spare him from hanging, his conviction was inevitable; and he didn't intend to be shipped off to some penal colony if he could warn Morehead so they all might escape.

"Swooping Eagle and Hunting Wolf said Morehead and Stalking Bear are now camped together," Vale was saying. "Morehead appears to be trying to make some sort of bargain with Stalking Bear for Mignon."

"*Les méchants* might already have come to an agreement," Marcel said, getting anxiously to his feet.

"Hunting Wolf thought not," Vale said. "Stalking Bear seems to have been under the impression that Mignon was going to be a gift. He's reluctant now to give Morehead anything for her. That he's willing to talk at all is an indication of how much he wants her."

"How long a time do you think we have?" Benjamin asked worriedly.

"None to waste," Vale answered grimly. "We can't know how long they've been negotiating or how near to agreement they are."

"If there's any way at all to do it, I should like to try to get Mademoiselle Dessaline out of their hands before we make any attempt to capture Morehead," Templeton said slowly.

"Swooping Eagle has suggested a plan," Vale said.

"Tell us what it is," Templeton urged. "His men have seen the camp and know its situation firsthand."

Vale spoke to Swooping Eagle at some length, then more briefly to Hunting Wolf, before he again addressed Templeton. "Swooping Eagle agrees we should try to rescue Mignon before we attempt anything else. He thinks a couple of his men could search out and silence Stalking Bear's sentries before the others surround the camp. One or two of us might be able to get into the camp and bring out Mignon without being discovered. Of course, Mignon's rescue should be done while it's dark; but Swooping Eagle prefers to wait until dawn before we attack openly. Hunting Wolf assures me we'll have enough time to reach the camp and get Mignon out, even if we don't leave here until after dusk has fallen; it is best to leave then because we'd be less likely to be seen moving through the forest at night."

"We could launch our attack anytime after we have Mademoiselle Dessaline safely in our hands," Templeton said. "Why does Swooping Eagle want to wait until dawn before we close in on Morehead? Does he have some religious reason for not wanting to fight at night?"

"The Abnakis don't want to fight in the dark because they think in the confusion your men, who are not familiar with them, might mistake them for Iroquois," Vale replied slowly, hoping Templeton wouldn't be offended. He took a deep breath and continued translating Swooping Eagle's words: "They think your men's scarlet coats and white breeches make as good a target during the night as the day, so the darkness won't camouflage you anyway." Noting Templeton's expression, Vale added, "I did suggest when we left Lavaltrie that your men should change out of their uniforms."

"Yes, you did say so," the major admitted. "The problem is, they have nothing else to wear."

Vale turned to Swooping Eagle and spoke rapidly. The Indian nodded agreement, and Vale turned again to Templeton. "Swooping Eagle's men have brought a change of clothes for themselves, and they're willing to give it to your men so they'll be less visible."

Templeton's eyes ran over the garment of the Indians, which closely matched the doeskin skirt and breeches Vale wore. He sighed. "I suppose, if you can dress that way, and if it'll minimize our casualties—I guess we can get out of uniform," he agreed reluctantly.

"There's one thing more I must ask you to do—which Swooping Eagle has suggested," Vale said.

Wondering what other unorthodox ideas Swooping

Eagle had, Templeton gave Vale a dreary look but nodded for him to speak.

"If your men are going to wear buckskins, is it too much to ask them also to wear headbands with an eagle feather to show the Indians they're with Swooping Eagle? The Abnakis will do the same to make sure your men know who they are," Vale said.

Templeton was silent for a long moment as he considered what General Gage would think when he later read in the report of this expedition that British soldiers had laid aside their uniforms for buckskins, moccasins, and feathers in their hair. Finally he said, "I suppose, if it will lessen the confusion, we just will have to look like a bunch of bloody Indians."

"It will save lives," Vale promised, then added, "and I think you'll find yourself very grateful to this particular tribe of 'bloody Indians' before this matter's been resolved."

"I'm sure I will. No offense meant," Templeton said quickly. "It's just that this is so——"

"Untraditional?" Vale suggested.

"I wouldn't care if I had to wear war paint," Benjamin vowed. "I want to be one of the men who go into camp to get Mignon."

Vale shook his head. "I'm sorry, Ben. You're a fine marksman, but this is one time no shots can be fired. Other abilities will be needed to make this a success." Vale saw the expression on Marcel's face and quickly added, "You know you can't possibly sneak around in an Indian camp with that broken rib."

"Mignon will be frightened if she sees only Indians coming for her," Marcel protested.

"She won't be afraid of me even if I am wearing a feather in my hair," Vale said. "Hunting Wolf and I will get her out."

Stalking Bear's lawlessness had caused him and his followers to be ejected from their tribe; and because they had to conceal their location from their own people as well as from whites, they seldom were able to stay in one place long enough to bother setting up shelters of any kind. But the previous autumn, while the whites and Indians alike had been too concerned with their own battles to think very much about Stalking Bear, he had found an area in the forest that was isolated from both white settlements and other tribes. The renegade group had set up a number of small lodges there. Their buildings, which resembled Abnaki dwellings more than they did Iroquois long houses, were hastily covered with skins rather than slabs of bark; but during the winter Stalking Bear had grown fond of the little makeshift village he'd finally established. He guarded its location so jealously he'd been loath to let even Morehead know where it was—but Morehead had lured him with the promise of the white girl.

The women of the Iroquois people had a great deal of influence upon the tribe's government. The descent of families was traced through them; and they were both outspoken and free to choose their mates. Because Stalking Bear was a renegade, his family crest, totems, and all honor had been taken from him; no Iroquois woman would even glance at, much less consider coupling with him; and like the rest of his men, he could only possess the women he occasionally discovered wandering too far from their village. Those women fought him fiercely and had to be beaten half senseless before he could possess them. Their beauty was quickly destroyed, so he just as quickly lost interest in them. The women of the white villages, he'd heard, were more obedient to their men than Iroquois women; so when Morehead had offered Stalking Bear such a woman, the Iroquois was very interested. When he'd seen the girl, her hair golden like the sun, her eyes blue as a lake under the sky, desire had risen so hotly in his blood he'd been willing to consider even the insult of paying for her, though she'd originally been offered as a gift. That the girl stood before him with eyes humbly lowered, spoke not at all, and remained where Morehead placed her until Morehead told her to move again, made her seem to be all that the renegade wanted in a female. But even Stalking Bear, who had seen so much blood and had committed so many cruelties, would have been surprised if he could have read Mignon's secret thoughts.

Morehead hadn't touched Mignon or allowed his men the smallest liberty with her; but he'd taken his pleasure from her in another, even more perverse way by telling her over and over about Stalking Bear, describing in detail his atrocious behavior with the other women he'd possessed. And finally Mignon had become so terrified she could not bear the thought of living. She became obsessed with dying—the only escape she could imagine was yet possible to her. She thought she'd seen her brother burned to death in the cabin, her sister ground to shreds by the ice in the river. All her dreams of loving Ben and plans for her future had been smashed; her very existence had become a mockery. During the several days while Morehead and Stalking Bear haggled about her price, she lay in the lodge to which she'd been escorted, listening to the occasional movements of the guard posted outside the doorway as she planned her own death.

By not fighting Stalking Bear when he came to her, and by submitting herself to him, she could perhaps fool him into assuming she'd accepted her lot as a slave, thereby gaining his trust. He must eventually sleep, she reasoned; and when he did, she would take the knife he wore in a sheath at his waist and kill herself.

Mignon had spent every waking hour anticipating the moment when Stalking Bear having finally struck his bargain with Morehead, would come to her. But now when she heard his voice outside the lodge as he dismissed the guard, she'd gotten so used to waiting that it didn't occur to her that her vigil was over. She sat up on the pile of skins she'd used as a bed, and watched him lift the flap that covered the doorway.

He paused to look at her a moment before he entered the lodge, his eyes glittering like onyx, holding an expression that alarmed her. But no one had told her the agreement had been made, she reminded herself. Morehead would have come to tell her, if only to enjoy the fear he might evoke in her. Stalking Bear must merely be taking another look to judge her worth, she reasoned. She swung her legs off the bed and stood up, expecting him to walk around her as he'd done before, inspecting the length and widths of her.

The bronze skin of his bare chest gleamed in the faint glow from the fire; his muscles rippled as he stepped inside the lodge and let the covering over the doorway fall into place. He reached up to take off his headband, then carefully laid aside the feather his tribe had awarded him in the ceremony initiating him into manhood. Mignon could not help but be reminded of her own plan as he unfastened the sheath that held his knife, and placed it beside his headband.

Why would he remove these things unless he planned to take her now? The sudden thought was like a drop of ice falling into her brain. She took one wary step back.

Mignon's hopes that Stalking Bear was only going to inspect her again were finally shattered when she saw him begin to slide his buckskin breeches down his narrow hips. Whether the bargain had been made or not, she knew he meant to possess her now. She must remember her plan: She must not fight him; she must make him trust her, she must fool him so that she could kill herself. His black hair, now loosened, reminded her of a lion's mane. That's what he looks like, she thought as he moved sleekly toward her, an animal, a magnificently made animal that means to mate with me whether it pleases me or not. Maybe if she closed her eyes, maybe if she thought about something else, she could bear this. Maybe if she . . .

Stalking Bear bent and pulled up the hem of Mignon's skirt. She stiffened with horror at what was about to happen to her. He jerked the cloth, and it shredded. When the tear reached the seam at her waist, he gave it so sharp a pull she almost toppled forward as the dress fell away from her body. Obviously disappointed at the sight of still another layer of clothing, he caught the bodice of her chemise and tore its fragile lace and it too fell away; and she was naked. Her jerked her about.

No, no, she thought. She couldn't bear it, after all.

But his touch was gentle enough, though he wasn't intentionally caressing her, she knew. He was merely exploring the texture of her skin. When he lifted one of her curls to brush it to his cheek, she knew the silk of her hair pleased him. She resolved again to continue to please him, to keep her final goal fixed in her thoughts. She must endure him, no matter how repulsive all this was to her. It would be over soon—she'd escape and he wouldn't be able to drag her back to him then.

When Stalking Bear gestured toward the pile of furs that was her bed, Mignon forced herself to lie down on it obediently. But as she watched him climb in beside her, she shuddered inwardly and closed her eyes. The feel of his skin against hers, his hard muscles, the greasy strands of his hair, the scent of blood and cruelty and violence—she couldn't endure him, after all. She could not bear the thought of his invading her body even if she herself meant to leave it soon. Yet, he was at her portals, momentarily to . . .

Gasping, Mignon squirmed to avoid him, but he only chuckled, thinking her movement meant she was enjoying the sensation of his body on hers. She was helpless to escape him. He was too strong, too heavy. He was going to force himself on her, and she could not stop him.

"*Sacrée Marie, préservez-moi,*" she whispered. "*Mon Dieu, absolvez-moi.*"

She heard Stalking Bear's gasp and thought it was from pleasure, but he stopped moving. Abruptly he seemed heavier than before. She opened her eyes, but his hair and her tears obscured her vision. Suddenly he rolled aside. She was free of his weight. A gentle touch smoothed away her hair and tears, and she looked up into eyes filled with smoky gray flecks.

"Vale!" she sobbed, and threw her arms around his neck. The miracle of his presence momentarily blotted out all else.

"You have to be very quiet, Mignon," he whispered. "We're going to get you out of here."

Mignon's arms were locked around Vale's shoulders; her breasts crushed to his chest. Suddenly remembering her nakedness, she withdrew from him curling her legs up to hide her nudity. She was aghast to see another Indian standing behind Vale.

Noting Mignon's alarm, Vale said softly, "Hunting Wolf is my friend. He came to help us."

She looked cautiously beyond Vale's shoulder and saw that Hunting Wolf was offering her a blanket. She accepted gratefully, and Vale stepped back. He and Hunting Wolf tactfully turned and fixed their attention on Stalking Bear's body which lay sprawled on the floor beside the bed.

"I can see he did not accomplish his purpose with her," Hunting Wolf commented.

"For that we are grateful to you," Vale answered in Abnaki. His foot pushed Stalking Bear's corpse over on its stomach, and he bent to retrieve Hunting Wolf's knife.

Mignon glanced once at Stalking Bear, then turned away. "How did you know I was here?" she whispered.

"Aimée can tell you later. Right now we'd just better get out of here," Vale said hurriedly.

"Aimée?" Mignon breathed. "I thought she was . . ."

Vale smiled. "She's alive and so is Marcel. They're waiting for us now. Ben too."

"Marcel? Ben?" Mignon's eyes filled with wonder. She couldn't absorb all this at one time.

"Walk between Hunting Wolf and me as if you're our prisoner," Vale whispered. "We hope, if anyone sees you with us, they'll assume we're Iroquois taking you to Stalking Bear's lodge."

Mignon glanced at Vale, then the Abnaki. "You do appear to be an Indian dressed as you are, but neither you nor even Hunting Wolf looks like an Iroquois to me."

Hunting Wolf whispered to Vale, obviously asking a question. Vale answered, then told Mignon, "Hunting Wolf wanted to know what you'd said about him. He's very happy you think he doesn't look like one of those renegades. Nevertheless let's all pray we fool them only for a couple of minutes."

Mignon nodded, clutching the blanket around her shoulders; but her heart was pounding with fear they'd be discovered. As she followed Hunting Wolf she lowered her head and dragged her feet exactly as she had whenever she'd been escorted from the lodge before.

The little village seemed deserted. Morehead's men, as well as the Iroquois, had gone to sleep, secure in the knowledge that their sentries protected them. Hunting Wolf, Mignon, and Vale were almost to the edge of the clearing when Woolsey came thundering out of the forest riding the gray horse Running Fawn had given Vale.

"Morehead! Morehead!" Woolsey shouted. "They're all around this camp! Templeton, soldiers!"

Hunting Wolf didn't pause even to glance at the Iroquois renegades who poured out of the nearest lodge. He reached behind to grasp Mignon's hand and started running.

Mignon stumbled and almost fell at the sudden jerk of the hand pulling her; but she caught her balance; and still holding the blanket around her, ignoring the sticks and stones that cut her bare feet, she followed the Abnaki into the forest. Mignon couldn't hear Vale's footsteps behind her, and for a while she wondered if he was following. Then she realized she couldn't hear Hunting Wolf's steps either and hoped Vale was merely being as silent as the Indian. She wished fervently that she herself didn't make so much noise. How could they avoid stepping on the dead twigs that snapped under her feet, and the dry leaves of the previous autumn that now crackled so loudly as she raced over them?

Suddenly she heard shouts behind them, a crashing in the forest. The Iroquois were in open pursuit, and they were coming in the right direction. Mignon's panting was growing louder at each step she took. Her breath felt like a stream of fire pouring into her lungs; but the noise of their pursuers was becoming ominously close. Mignon knew it was she who slowed Hunting Wolf and Vale; and she prayed for the strength to run faster, for the strength merely to stay on her feet.

Vale called to Hunting Wolf in Abnaki; Hunting Wolf said one word in reply. Then a chilling cry came from behind Mignon. Vale had uttered that cry when the Iroquois had attacked them on the way to Montreal, and she knew it meant he was stopping to face their pursuers alone.

"*Non, non!*" she cried, pulling on Hunting Wolf's hand. "He can't stop them by himself!" Her efforts to halt Hunting Wolf affected him so little he never even paused in his steps as he continued dragging her behind him.

Suddenly Hunting Wolf released Mignon, and another hand caught hers. Unable to see who it was in the darkness, she gasped and raised her fists to beat at the shadowy figure.

"Mignon! Mignon, it's Ben!"

"*Mon Dieu, merci, merci, merci, merci,*" she sobbed, and laid her cheek against Benjamin's shoulder.

"I think I'd better find you another blanket, *ma soeur,*" another voice said close by her ear.

Mignon lifted her head to look into Aimée's shadowy face. She let out a little cry and threw her arms around her sister.

Finally Aimée pulled away from Mignon's embrace. "I think I must find something for you to wear before you distract Ben too much from fighting Iroquois," she whispered. "Besides, Marcel is waiting to greet you."

"*Marcel! Mon frère.*" Mignon wept and reached out for his hands.

"Please, Mignon, don't embrace me as you did Aimée. I have a broken rib," Marcel warned, and pulled her into his arms as a burst of gunfire came from the British soldiers stationed in the shrubbery nearby.

Having already killed one Iroquois, who had come through the forest faster than his brothers, Vale ran toward another dark shape bounding along the path Hunting Wolf and Mignon had taken. The renegade had no idea that Vale was coming until Vale catapulted into the path, his shoulder striking the Indian so hard he was bowled over. Vale's momentum carried him with the Iroquois's body; and the renegade felt his back hit the ground at the same moment Vale's knife plunged into his heart.

Vale immediately sprang up from the Indian's body, ready to find another enemy when he heard the gunfire begin. Knowing he was directly in its path, he threw himself to the ground, wriggled his way behind a thick tree, and rose only as high as his knees. He pulled off the bow he'd worn slung over his shoulder, and reached back into his quiver for an arrow. Fitting the feathered shaft to his string, he drew it back and waited; his eyes followed the shadowy form of another renegade, as a lynx would watch the approach of an unwary fawn. The arrow sang into the night, and a scream marked its target. Vale quieted his shivering bowstring. Then he arose to a half crouch and continued on his way toward the Iroquois village and the prey he really sought—Morehead.

As Vale had anticipated, Morehead had not left the village immediately. When Woolsey had called out that soldiers surrounded them, Morehead looked cautiously out of the doorway of his lodge; and seeing Iroquois pouring from their shelters, he waved to Woolsey to come inside. Woolsey ran across the camp, dodging around the Indians that raced by, and stooped to enter the lodge.

"Templeton's out there with soldiers?" Ugland, who had been with Morehead, asked anxiously.

"Not only him," Woolsey panted. "It's that Dessaline we thought was burned twice over, the red-haired girl, both fiancés and a pack of Abnakis too."

"Damn," Morehead said quietly.

"What are we going to do?" Woolsey rasped between breaths.

"What about the blonde and Stalking Bear?" Ugland exclaimed.

"Don't know nothing about Stalking Bear, but I saw the blonde and the redhead's fiancé sneaking away with an Indian," Woolsey panted.

"That devil would have made one fine thief if he'd been on our side," Ugland commented in awe.

"Be quiet," Morehead snapped. "Let me think." He was silent a moment before he said more calmly, "Those renegades can't win. Let's get out of here."

"What about Millbank, Horton, and Melvin?" Ugland asked.

"If they see us, they're welcome to come along, but I'm not going to hunt around for them," Morehead replied.

"Just thought of something," Woolsey said, "All the soldiers changed into Indian clothes. They and the Abnakis are wearing an eagle feather in their hair so they can tell each other from the Iroquois. Wouldn't hurt none if we had feathers too."

"Stalking Bear has a bunch of them on that lance he sticks in front of his lodge," Ugland recalled.

"You get three of them for us," Morehead directed.

"What if Stalking Bear sees me?" Ugland asked.

"You're a purse pincher by trade—you can get them," Morehead snapped as he ducked out the doorway. Spotting the gray horse Woolsey had ridden into the camp, he headed toward it calling over his shoulder, "Woolsey, get a couple more horses."

Woolsey had returned with the mounts and waited with Morehead until Ugland came back clutching a handful of feathers, a headband, a beaded belt, and a couple of leather thongs. "Stalking Bear's dead," he said as he handed the items around. His lopsided face curled with humor as he said, chuckling, "Didn't look like he enjoyed his wedding night much."

"Get on your horse and stop wasting time. Those gunshots are getting closer," Morehead snapped. Then turning his horse, he kicked its sides and it bounded into the forest.

Once they were away from the Iroquois village and under cover of the trees, Morehead slowed the horse to a walk. The silver of a moon barely relieved the darkness; and Morehead hoped that Templeton's men or the Abnakis would mistake them for soldiers who were merely moving to a better position from which to fire at the renegades. After seeing a number of dark shapes running through the shadows, recognizing from the flashes of gunfire that they were soldiers who ignored them, Morehead congratulated himself on the success of his ruse.

He calculated they were almost past Templeton's line of men when he noticed a shadowy figure standing beside a horse not far away. Although the figure wore breeches, he perceived it was feminine; and the outline of the horse's body was unmistakable. He didn't need to see the animal's color to know it was Brandy. Only one person would be able to search through the horse's saddlebag—its owner, Aimée. He nudged Woolsey and pointed her out to him.

Woolsey peered through the darkness and immediately knew what Morehead was thinking. If Templeton or any of his men came in pursuit of them, having Aimée as a hostage would increase their chances of escape. If no one tried to detain them, they would at least have a little amusement from this venture that had failed so dismally.

Intent upon finding something for Mignon to wear, Aimée wasn't alarmed when she heard the snap of a dead twig. Marcel was only a few yards away helping Mignon hold the shredded blanket around her, and they all were behind the lines of fighting. When she heard the leisurely rhythm of a horse walking toward her, she raised her head to peer into the darkness. All she could perceive was the ghostly shape of the gray horse she had given Vale at their wedding and the white tip of the eagle feather its rider wore.

"Vale," she whispered, relieved that he'd safely returned from defending Mignon and Hunting Wolf's retreat. She stepped away from Brandy's side unconsciously extending her arms, anticipating Vale's embrace. She was only mildly surprised that two other riders flanked the gray horse. The gray continued to move toward her.

"Vale?" she asked.

The rider's silhouetted form was the same height as Vale's, with similar proportions. The horse stopped beside Aimée. She peered up at the rider's shadowed face, trying to discern if it was Vale. Suddenly he bent; and his arm snaked under her shoulders, scooping her up to his level. She was stunned when she recognized the face grinning into hers.

"Woolsey!" she exclaimed.

"At your service—Colonel Morehead and Willie too." he chuckled.

Aimée screamed, "Marcel!" But Woolsey kicked the horse, and it leaped forward to bound into the forest.

When Marcel heard Aimée say Vale's name, he began to guide Mignon out of the shadows, where they'd stood; but at her exclamation of Woolsey's name, followed by her scream, Marcel left Mignon behind. He drew his pistol as he ran toward Aimée, but he was too late. She had already been snatched up, and he could only discern three shadowy horses racing away. Knowing he'd never be able to mount Brandy, hoping he could hit one of Aimée's kidnappers and catch his horse, Marcel took careful aim at the third rider and fired. The man plunged to the ground and Marcel hurried forward, but the horse raced on to follow the others.

Cursing the animal and the mare that had bore him, Marcel whirled around and ran back toward Mignon.

"Stay there, *ma soeur!*" he called as he raced past. "I must find a horse."

Marcel ran toward the clearing where he'd last noticed Templeton conferring with Lieutenant Scott. His rib was a fiery sword slicing his words with each breath as he called, "Major! Where's a horse I can use? They're getting away!"

Templeton and the man standing with him turned quickly. "Who's getting away?" Templeton demanded.

Unable to run any farther, Marcel half stumbled, half walked into the clearing as fast as he could. "Woolsey and someone else. Probably Morehead. There was a third. I shot him. Trying to get his horse. But it kept running." He panted. "They got Aimée. Only horse was Brandy. Can't ride Brandy."

"I can," the man standing with Templeton snapped. He stepped closer to Marcel. "Where's Brandy now?"

"Vale! Thank God it's you," Marcel breathed. He turned to point toward the forest. "Brandy's over there— Mignon too. She can tell you . . . the way they went."

Marcel glanced again at Vale, but he had vanished. He already was racing through the shadows in the direction Marcel had indicated.

*   *   *

Aimée was surprised at how securely Woolsey was able
to hold her against his side despite her squirming. She
pounded on his back with one fist and on his chest with
the other, but he endured it stoically. Finally she kicked
the horse's belly; and the animal, thinking he'd gotten the
signal to run, leaped forward.

Woolsey cursed as he fought to control the horse with
one hand; but he didn't loosen his grasp on Aimée, as
she'd anticipated. "Should have known you'd do something
like that," he muttered, and slung her facedown over the
front of the saddle.

She renewed her struggle to slide off the horse, but he
twisted her arm behind her back; and when she tried to
pull away; he gave it a wrench. The pain that tore through
her shoulder made her gasp.

"I can hold you this way as long as I have to," he said.

Aimée dared resist him no further. She knew it would
take little effort on Woolsey's part to dislocate her shoulder.

"It's too bad I have to hold you with one hand and the
reins with the other," he commented. "Sure could think of
better ways to pass the time when a pretty little tail like
yours is bent over my saddle this way."

Aimée stiffened in anger; but with even this slight
movement Woolsey's grip on her arm tightened in warning.

"You don't have to worry about my trying to get
away," she said panting. "I can hardly breathe and I feel
as if my head will explode hanging down this way."

"If you faint, I could let go of your arm," he observed.

Although her fury rose to new heights, she carefully remained limp in his grasp as she said breathlessly, "With
my stomach squeezed against the saddle as it is, I suspect
I'm more likely to retch in your boot."

Woolsey was silent for a long moment, and Aimée
could sense his discomfort over this prospect.

Finally she asked plaintively, "How would you feel if
you were bent in the middle, head dangling, bouncing on
your stomach with every step the horse takes?"

"I'll let you up if you won't cause trouble," he said slowly.

Aimée, in reality fighting for every breath, quickly nodded agreement. Woolsey released her wrist, then with his free hand he helped her turn over and sit up to ride sidesaddle. With his arms so tightly encircling her, she had no choice but to lean against his chest.

"Is she giving you trouble?" Morehead's voice came from the darkness ahead.

"Tried some, but I think it's over now," Woolsey answered.

"If she does again, throw her off the horse," Morehead directed, then added, seemingly as an after thought, "Just make sure she hits a tree."

Woolsey bent to whisper near Aimée's ear. "Hear that? He means it."

"Do you do everything Morehead says?" She spat out the words.

Woolsey nuzzled her hair for a moment as he thought over his answer. "Don't see no reason not to. Morehead's usually right."

He'd been holding his reins in the hand that rested before her waist. He switched them now so that he could control the horse with the arm that curved around Aimée's back. Aimée was suspicious of his intentions and those suspicions were confirmed when his free hand began to unbutton the front of her shirt. Her fingers locked over his.

"Want to be smashed against a tree?" he murmured. When she didn't loosen her grip on his hand, he warned, "Don't think I won't do it."

Knowing he would, she lowered her hand. She felt his fingers slide inside her shirt, fondling her through the thin batiste of her camisole. Face flaming with anger, she said tightly, "Vale is going to kill you, Woolsey."

Undisturbed by her threat, he rubbed her nipple with his fingertip. "Nice you don't have stays on now," he whispered. He dipped his head to her bodice. Holding the edge of her camisole with his fingertips, he caught the flimsy cloth between his teeth and gave it a little jerk to start it tearing.

When Aimée felt his fingers moving over her bare skin, she shuddered. "You know he'll follow us, don't you?"

"Be pretty hard to," Woolsey murmured against her hair. "Wish he would, though. I'd like to have another chance at that fiancé of yours."

Aimée recalled how frightened Woolsey had been whenever Vale had approached him, but she only said coolly, "He isn't merely my fiancé now. He's my husband."

Woolsey raised his head in surprise. "Morehead's going to be disappointed you're not a virgin anymore," he commented, then shrugged. "Me, I don't care."

Aimée sighed, seemingly in resignation; but she was far from resigned to her situation. The horse was moving at an easy pace; and she doubted she'd be seriously injured if she were to slip off. Her mind raced to find a way she might make Woolsey relax his hold on her. She could think of only one.

"I'd assumed you intended to use me as a hostage," she finally commented in a softened tone.

"Only if someone caught up with us," he murmured. "Don't look much like they will now. We're pretty far away from them."

"So you would have waited after Morehead to rape me—or maybe even after Willie too?"

"Willie came last with everything," Woolsey replied. He raised his head to look into her face and remark, "I'm kind of glad he's dead. He was more than a little crazy. I never liked him much. You wouldn't have liked him if he'd lived to get to you. Morehead's kind of odd that way too." He paused, then added slowly, "Maybe you'll even be happy to have me after Morehead. I got no peculiar tastes."

Aimée was revolted by the situation, but she knew Woolsey wasn't aware of how his touch disgusted her. He'd been encouraged by her lack of resistance. She guessed he might even be stupid enough to hope she enjoyed his caresses. She had to make him relax his vigilance, so she forced herself to whisper, "I don't think I have any, as you say, peculiar tastes either, but then I only had my wedding night with my husband."

"That barely gets the hard part over with for a woman—just enough to whet the appetite," he murmured. "Maybe you're getting a little hungry for more, being a new bride and all . . ."

Aimée lowered her eyes as if she agreed but dared not say it.

Woolsey looked at her speculatively. This was a development he hadn't foreseen—that she might be willing. Yet, he'd met women who were aroused by danger and pretended to resist while they'd secretly been excited. If he wasn't too rough with them, they would move as eagerly at the end as if they'd wanted him from the beginning. But he'd never possessed a woman as desirable as Aimée. His eyes raised to the darkness ahead as he suddenly resented the idea of Morehead's having her first. Morehead rode on, having no inkling of the opportunity that seemed to be unfolding. Woolsey returned his attention to Aimée. She was looking up at him again, and a glimmer of moonlight lit her eyes to dark amber.

"Always did like a red-haired woman," he whispered, and brought his lips to hers.

Aimée hadn't been looking at Woolsey as he'd assumed. She had been estimating how long it would take until they were at the middle of the little clearing they were about to enter—a clearing where there were no trees for her to fall against, only nearby shrubbery that might conceal her flight. Though she inwardly cringed with revulsion at Woolsey's touch, she controlled her feelings and pretended to return his kiss with as much passion as he gave it, even while she was counting each step the horse took.

Her fingers seemed to caress his chest; but when his hand slipped from her bodice to rest lightly on her shoulder, she suddenly gave him a sharp push, slid under his arm and off the horse. She felt pain streak through her ankle as she landed, but she ignored it and dove into the bushes.

"Morehead! She got loose!" Woolsey cried.

Aimée bent low and half ran, half limped into the

forest as she heard Morehead's horse turn in a flurry of hoofbeats and shouted imprecations.

"She went that way!" Woolsey called.

"You imbecile!" Morehead exclaimed furiously.

Aimée realized, from the sound of their voices, they were coming in the right direction even if they couldn't immediately see her. She turned off at an angle toward a grove of spruces, relieved that the pain in her ankle seemed to be subsiding. She remembered when Vale had shown her the hollow in the base of a fir tree; and running under the cover of a row of thick bushes that stood directly between her and her pursuers, Aimée chose a fat spruce, dropped to the ground, and wriggled under its low-hanging branches to the center. Curling herself into a ball, she watched the horses approach so close she could have reached out to touch their fetlocks.

Morehead's lowered voice reached Aimée clearly as he dismounted: "She could have crawled under one of these trees. We'd best look into each of them."

Aimée could see the outline of Morehead's boots through the branches; and she prayed he wouldn't inspect her tree first, though it seemed inevitable. She held her breath.

Abruptly there was a rustling sound from the edge of the forest.

"Maybe that's the girl," Morehead whispered.

"Or a deer or a bear," Woolsey suggested. "If I was her, I'd be thinking about bears, lynxes, and such. Maybe we wouldn't seem too bad to her if she'd give them a thought."

"Shut your mouth, Woolsey." Morehead hissed the words. "Let's see if she made that sound."

At Woolsey's mention of predators Aimée thought of the bear that had clawed Vale and of the lynx that had attacked Marcel; and a cold ripple of fear ran down her spine. She remained motionless, watching Morehead's boots turn and walk softly away. She wondered if he meant to mislead her into thinking they'd left so that she'd come out of her hiding place.

Finally she lowered herself to her stomach and crawled

through the fallen needles at the base of the tree, around to its opposite side. She could barely discern the shadowy outline of a clump of hawthorns only a few yards away. Morehead and Woolsey would never believe she would go through those bushes with their treacherous spines. She wriggled out of her jacket and, hoping it would give her some protection from the thorns, hastily muffled her face, allowing only her eyes to show.

A pistol fired, shattering the silence. Then there were the rustlings and flutterings of myriad small animals and birds fleeing.

"It was a lynx, but I got him!" Woolsey's triumphant voice came from the other side of the clearing.

"Damn you!" Morehead exclaimed. "Now she knows where we are!"

"*Merci, diables,*" Aimée breathed as she slithered out from under the fir tree. Rising only to half her height, she darted into the hawthorns.

During the hours that followed, Aimée's heart was thumping wildly in fear, but she deliberately chose the most difficult courses in the hope that Morehead and Woolsey would assume she had neither the courage nor the stamina to climb over sharp rocks, struggle through undergrowth that tore at her clothes and hair, or make her way into dark gullies where predators might lurk. She already had two predators tracking her—Morehead and Woolsey—and lynxes or bears seemed no worse a threat.

Chapter 30

When Marcel had come running out of the shadows to beg for a horse so that he could pursue Aimée's abductors, rage and terror had struck Vale like twin blows to his stomach. The force of his emotions had sent him racing back up the path, catapulted him into Brandy's saddle, and launched the big horse into flight.

But the wind whistling past Vale's ears became Walking-in-Honor's insistent urgings to stop and heed his lessons of the past. Fear for a loved one's safety had often sent warriors into traps or made them rush past signs that could lead them to victory. Anger was a power to be contained so its passion could strengthen the body even as it fired the mind when one faced an enemy. Vale had finally slowed the horse to a walk and, in doing so, found that in his headlong rush he'd lost the trail. He'd had to turn back, carefully study the way he'd come, then, finding the direction Morehead and Woolsey had taken, resume more wisely. The delay had lost him time, but it had driven home the importance of Walking-in-Honor's wisdom.

At many intervals, when Vale had become doubtful of the trail, he had moved slowly enough to study the surroundings carefully, and so he'd glimpsed a sign that confirmed he was going the right way—a hoofprint in the softened mud, the glimmer of the white edge of a freshly broken branch, a shower of spring blossoms fallen too recently from the bush someone had brushed to have yet withered. He suspected Aimée was leaving clues for him whenever she could, because he found first one of the leather thongs that had bound her braids; then another hanging off a bush that projected over the edge of the trail; and a button from the old jacket of Marcel's that she had worn.

The eastern horizon had begun to change from black to deep indigo when Vale entered the little clearing where Aimée had fled Woolsey's embrace. Vale dismounted to try to make sense of the confusion of hoofprints he saw. Noting that the horses had finally made a sharp turn to the right, Vale decided to lead Brandy so he could continue to read the signs, which led him into a grove of spruces where the men had dismounted. Unknowingly, Vale tied Brandy's reins to the tree Aimée had earlier hidden under, then he cautiously followed the boot tracks.

The lynx was sprawled where it had fallen, and Vale paused to lay his hand on the body and judge its receding warmth. It hadn't been dead long, he decided. He raised his eyes to scan the surrounding area. It seemed deserted; but when he arose, he cautiously stepped into the deeper shadows at the edge of the forest.

Why had the horses milled around so much before Morehead and Woolsey had dismounted? Why had they first gone by the spruces, then come in this opposite direction to kill a lynx only to let it lay? He speculated on the possible answers and could think of only one. Hope quickened his pulses. Somehow Aimée had escaped their grasp, and they were on foot hunting for her. They apparently had disturbed the lynx and had shot it. If this all had happened as recently as he thought, Morehead and Woolsey couldn't be very far away—and neither could Aimée.

Morehead and Woolsey's taking a hostage made sense to Vale only if they kept her until they were out of the immediate area of the battle. Afterwards a prisoner they must guard from escaping, who would betray them whenever possible, necessarily slowed their flight and increased their chances of being followed. They had held Aimée through most of the night instead of simply abandoning her long ago, and this aroused Vale's worst suspicions: they'd wanted her as a female and only incidentally as a hostage. That they'd stop to search for her now confirmed his fears. Making a supreme effort to control the emotions this aroused in him, Vale decided Morehead and

Woolsey's coming this way had been a mistake—they'd not caught Aimée here. He decided to retrace his steps to where Brandy was tethered.

He noticed Brandy wasn't grazing on the tender new grass but was nosing the spruce. Although some horses loved the taste of pine above all else, Vale knew Brandy wasn't one of them; and the horse's attention to the tree made Vale curious. He walked around its base slowly and, reaching the opposite side, suddenly dropped to crouch beside it. On one of the low-hanging branches was a long strand of auburn hair. His heart began to pound as he realized Aimée had hidden inside this tree and had crawled out here. The grass her moccasins had flattened had sprung up moments afterwards and so gave him no hint of the direction she'd taken. He turned to study the area, wondering where she would have gone to throw her pursuers off her trail. When he saw the hawthorn bushes, he knew.

Visualizing the fearsome scratches hawthorn spines made, he realized she would have stayed among the bushes not a moment longer than necessary. He straightened to walk around them. In the mud near the bushes he saw one small moccasin print. He started soundlessly in the direction it indicated.

Vale had entered a heavily wooded area thick with shrubbery and greening weed stalks. He heard a noise—had someone kicked a fallen log? He dove behind a chokecherry bush. Glancing up, he noted that the bush was tall enough to hide him and he arose, drawing the bow that he'd carried from his shoulder. Reaching back to pull an arrow from his quiver, he warily peered around the side of the bush.

Woolsey was standing a dozen yards away. In his hand was a tangle of dark green cloth. Vale stared at it, wondering what it was, until Woolsey tossed it aside. In its flight it momentarily spread out; and Vale noted sleeves, the glint of a metal button. It was the jacket Aimée had worn.

Vale could think of only one thing. If Woolsey tossed aside a bit of Aimée's clothing, Aimée herself might lie hidden among the weeds, beaten and used. Vale fit the arrow to his bowstring and raised the weapon.

As Vale released the arrow the bowstring's familiar quiver matched the trembling of his heart, and the low whine of the missile's flight echoed the silent scream of grief that arose from Vale's soul. Woolsey flung out his hands and, without a sound, dropped where he'd stood, the arrow in his chest.

Heedless of danger, Vale ran out from behind the bush to glance at the body of his fallen enemy and confirm his death, then trotted around the area searching for Aimée. He was so intent on his own purpose, he didn't notice Morehead step out of the forest, raise his pistol, and carefully aim.

Despite Vale's preoccupation his ears heard the click of the pistol being cocked; and he stiffened automatically. He whirled around to face Morehead at the same moment the gun went off, and the ball snapped his bow instead of plunging into his heart as Morehead had wished. The smoke from the gun's muzzle hadn't time to dissipate before Vale plunged through it at Morehead.

Vale's temper had flared so high that the fires of his passions scorched his brain, impairing his judgment; and he hit Morehead glancingly, merely striking him aside. But Vale rolled only once when he landed, then sprang to his feet and turned to his enemy.

Morehead, still on one knee, had his back to Vale; but before Morehead had the time to rise fully, Vale clasped his hands to form a double fist and then drove them both into the back of Morehead's shoulders. He pitched forward to sprawl on his face.

Although Morehead was only momentarily stunned, he closed his eyes, sensing that Vale wouldn't hit him again if he feigned unconsciousness.

Seeing his enemy down and unmoving, Vale walked slowly toward him. Morehead used the moment to unsheathe the knife he wore at his waist. When Morehead felt Vale's foot cautiously pushing at his shoulder, he remained limp, knowing his heaviness would convince Vale he was unconscious, as well as put Vale at least a little off balance. As Vale's prodding foot finally began to turn him over, Morehead caught Vale's ankle and twisted it, pitching Vale to the ground. Although it took Vale only an instant to regain his feet, he found himself facing Morehead's blade.

Vale took a wary step backwards as he reached for his own knife. Not taking his eyes from Morehead, he felt for the ends of the thongs that tied his sheath closed. "Where's Aimée?" he asked, his voice more quiet than he felt.

"She ran off in the forest somewhere. I suppose Woolsey wasn't to her taste, but then he is rather crude," Morehead said, and lunged at Vale.

Vale stepped sideways at the same moment his fingers drew out the knife, but Morehead had just as quickly swerved away.

Morehead had seen the fury that had swirled up in Vale's eyes at his mention of Woolsey's advances at Aimée, and he hoped to arouse Vale's anger to a pitch that might make Vale careless.

"My interest in Aimée as a female has been considerably diminished, since I believe Woolsey may have accomplished his goal first," Morehead taunted. "I'm quite certain some animal must have gotten her by now anyway—I mean, in addition to Woolsey, that is." Morehead's thrust at Vale pierced only the air.

Vale had finally contained the fury rising like a volcano in him. It had become a small, hotly burning light in the core of him, revealing itself outwardly only in the crystal lights flickering behind the flecks in his eyes.

Although Morehead held his knife so the blade emerged from the thumbside of his hand, enabling him to use it at almost any angle, he noted Vale held his blade in just the opposite way. He snickered, "Do you plan to stab me as the senators did Caesar? Or do you even know who Caesar was?"

Vale said nothing in reply. He just turned slowly as Morehead circled him searching for an opening. He had been watching Morehead each time he'd moved, measuring his speed, judging his way of fighting.

When Morehead again sprang forward, Vale didn't step

aside. With the speed of a striking snake Vale reached out to catch Morehead's wrist, spun him around so his back was suddenly against Vale's chest, and, reaching past Morehead's shoulder, drew the tip of his own blade neatly across Morehead's throat.

Immediately thrusting Morehead aside so he wouldn't be spattered with blood, Vale bent to plunge his blade in the soil to cleanse it. Then he arose to walk silently away, not giving even one glance to his fallen enemy.

Never for a moment had Vale forgotten Aimée; and as he made his way back to where he'd tied Brandy, despair flooded him. Would he ever find her now?

In the night-darkened forest Aimée hadn't been able even to consider the possibility of finding her way back to Templeton's soldiers and Vale. She'd had no idea which direction to go, and she'd been too intent on eluding Morehead and Woolsey. Despite all the tricks she'd thought of to deceive them, they'd always somehow rediscovered her trail. At the first sign of dawn she had taken off her jacket and arranged it over a log in a clearing, desperately hoping the ruse would lead them to think she'd collapsed in exhaustion. Then she'd dashed back into the forest, finally taking a path among the trees that was clear of underbrush, thornbushes, and slippery rocks. She had run openly at top speed, intending simply to put as much distance as possible between them and her.

Her lungs seemed ready to explode; her heart pounded so furiously she thought it might break; and her legs stumbled clumsily under her. It was then that she turned into the shrubbery to lean against a tree trunk and watch the dawn lighting the sky with gold.

While she struggled to catch her breath she thought of the sunset of the previous evening and closed her eyes to concentrate more fully on the direction Hunting Wolf had taken when he'd led the soldiers to the Iroquois' camp. Mentally placing herself behind the gathering of British troops and Abnakis, where she'd searched through Brandy's saddlebags, she recalled how Woolsey had scooped her up, and retraced the directions he and More-head had taken in the forest.

Finally Aimée opened her eyes and raised her head. She must head east, she decided, and could only pray she'd calculated all her turnings accurately. She stepped away from the tree and began to run at a more leisurely pace than before.

The dawn wind shifted its direction, suddenly bringing a familiar scent that filled Aimée with so deep a longing that tears began to blur her vision. Although she realized she should stay alert for sounds of danger and any suspicious movements in the forest, she was distracted by the spicy-sweet fragrance of mayflowers.

The perfume evoked a vision of the day she'd fallen from Brandy. Upon feeling a strong arm so gently slide beneath her shoulders, she had opened her eyes to look into Vale's. His face had been bronzed by the sun; and his eyes, more startling for it, had been lit by the same silvery fire she had come to know so well. He'd said it had been that moment when he'd fallen in love with her.

Surely Vale must be searching for her now, she reasoned. But the forest was so vast, how could he find her? Thinking of the hopelessness of her circumstances would make her give up, she realized, and decided she must try to cheer herself instead. Think of the future when all this was behind them. Perhaps one evening when they were sitting before their own fire, they would recall this adventure and think of it as no more than an exciting memory. The house in Boston now owned by the Thorntons would then belong to the d'Auvergne family. Children were added to her vision, and her steps faltered, then stopped. She lowered her head as a new flood of tears filled her eyes, blotted out her surroundings.

After a moment she again resolutely reminded herself to concentrate on hope, and not sorrow, not despair. After Vale found her, they would begin to make her vision a reality. Perhaps she already carried his child, she thought in wonder. For the possible child, for Vale and herself, for their love, she must keep walking, however weary she was.

Finally taking a deep, shuddering breath, Aimée wiped her tears away and lifted her head.

She was standing at the edge of a wide meadow. The sun was just beginning to show its fiery rim over the tops of the distant trees on the far side of the field. She must travel east to return to safety—east across the meadow; yet if she entered so large an open area, Morehead or Woolsey might see her. She took several steps forward to peer to the right, then to the left. The meadow stretched so far in either direction it would take her a long time to skirt it; and during such a trek, she realized, she'd also have a good chance of being discovered. The clearing was filled with tall grass, she observed. Did it grow high enough that if she heard or saw anyone, she might stoop down and be concealed? She looked at the rippling grass, speculating on this possibility. The early sun's golden-orange light seemed to beckon to her. Wanting to get across the meadow as quickly as possible, she started walking fast; but she kept swiveling her head warily from side to side, alert for a hint of Morehead or Woolsey.

Aimée had traveled almost to the center of the field when her eyes caught a glimpse of something moving among the trees at the meadow's edge. She dropped down in the grass, her heart pounding in fear. She raised her hands slowly, cautiously gathering her long hair together, hoping its bright flair hadn't already been seen by an alert eye. As she crouched there twisting her hair into a knot, her eyes fell on the little blossoms that covered the ground at the base of the grass stalks. How ironic it would be, she thought bitterly, if Morehead or Woolsey were to find and rape her here on a carpet of mayflowers.

No one was crashing through the meadow and she doubted they would have bothered to creep up on her. Conceding finally that she might have seen the flicker of a deer's tail, the flight of some bird, she took a deep breath, hoping to calm herself, and raised her head slowly. Her heart seemed to freeze between beats. It was no deer or bird she'd seen. It was a horse and rider entering the meadow—Woolsey, she guessed, for even though the long

violet shadows still fell over the edge of the clearing sh
could see that the rider was taller than Morehead.

He must not yet have seen her, she reasoned, and wo
dered, if she stayed where she was if he might not discove
her. Or should she run now and hope to reach the fore
and hide before the horse caught up with her?

As the horse stepped from shadow to light Aimé
caught her breath in disbelief. There was no mistaking i
color—the same shade as her eyes—brandy in the sun. He
heart fluttered and began to beat again. There was onl
one person besides her who could ride Brandy.

Incredulous with joy, Aimée rose from the grass. Sh
stood there a moment, poised like an eagle ready to soa
into the sky, then began to run toward Vale. The wind un
tied the knot she'd made of her hair; and her curl
streamed free, like a fiery banner moving across the rip
pling, golden-green meadow.

Brandy stiffened, and the sudden tightening of Vale'
legs against the horse's sides wasn't necessary to urge hir
forward. Not even Vale's command could have held th
big horse back. But Vale's hands had dropped the reins
giving Brandy his head; and the horse galloped throug
the tall grass toward his mistress. As he approached, h
slowed just enough so the man on his back could lean ove
to reach for his beloved and sweep her up into his arm
Proudly arching his neck at his feat, Brandy felt Vale'
signal to turn; and he gladly obeyed to bound tr
umphantly toward the dawn and home.

Aimée looked up into eyes glowing with points of si
very light and breathed, "I didn't know how you cou
find me."

Vale gathered her close to the heart that beat so joy
ously for her, and said softly, "A sweet wild wind led m
to you."